# *The* WHITE RAVEN

A Novel

Carrie D. Miller

Many hugs, Dam !!

Carrie S. Miller

**FiveFold**Press
www.fivefoldpress.com

Publisher's note: This is a work of fiction. Names, characters, places, and incidents are a product of the author's imagination. Locales and public names are sometimes used for atmospheric purposes. Any resemblance to actual people, living or dead, or to businesses, companies, events, institutions, or locales is completely coincidental.

Cover design by Damonza (www.damonza.com)

**The White Raven / Carrie D. Miller** - 1st edition
ISBN 978-1-947024-01-4

*To Weeda,*
*who relit my dormant creativity so many years ago.*
*I'll never forget that.*

*This book is also dedicated to friendship.*
*Those that have ended, those that are now, and those that are to come.*

# Prologue

They are close. I sense their hatred. Though I am prepared, I must force myself to be calm. I do not fear what comes although I know I will be dead soon. Running from this place now is not something I wish to do, nor do I care to fight anymore. I'm ready to seek out a new land, a new time, and to continue on to the next life I am cursed to begin.

My Pyrenees is at attention by my side, hackles raised. "It is time to go, my girl." She whines and lowers her head, her big brown eyes pools of concern. "You go ahead," I say with a smile. "I'll be along soon."

I hear the gallop of fast-moving horses and the shouts of agitated men as they approach my home. The sound of heavy boots bounding onto the porch makes my skin prickle. Torchlight fills the windows and I steel myself. The front door splinters when one of those heavy boots comes through it.

"I knew there was somethin' not right about you." The man in the lead is Morris Stiles, the town's bully. I'm sure he took quick ownership of the lynching party so he could exercise his insatiable need to inflict pain and suffering without the threat of retribution. Not to mention the chance to snare himself a witch.

His face seethes with hostility. The men who crowd into the room behind him wear the same expression. The grin forming on his face as he looks me over is filled with decaying stubs that once passed for teeth. Many months ago, I offered to ease his pain, but was met with the back of his hand followed by a brown, revolting gob of spit aimed at my face.

Life in Calico has been filled with hardships. Each time I felt a modicum of acceptance, someone like Morris Stiles would speak against me. My goats and chickens were taken one by one, and the sheriff was not the least bit sympathetic or helpful in retrieving them. I am not one to back down so I held on, hoping for the relief of simply being ignored.

Now, yet another angry mob is at my doorstep. I know my lover has not had a direct hand in this. I am certain that due to the effects of much drink, his lips recounted events he should have kept hidden. I confessed to him this very morning that I am, in fact, a witch, and his reaction was what I had expected. I am unable to hide my true self for very long, and I am either revealed by my actions or by my simple confession. I will not deceive my lover with lies and trickery. I have told myself time and time again to stay away from love but the pangs and yearnings cannot be ignored, not even by one such as myself.

There is no fear on my face as I glare at the five men who have invaded my little home. Each one averts his eyes. As I inhale, my lungs fill with the thick, heavy air the men brought with them—full of sweat, dirt, whiskey, and anger.

I glower at the still grinning man. "Morris Stiles, you are a fool." My voice resonates throughout the room. The sound makes the men jump and look around, wide-eyed.

Morris grunts and spits a brown mass onto the floor. "Them's funny words coming from a whore a' Satan!"

I scoff. "Tell me one thing, just *one* thing—any of you—that I have done to remotely reflect the work of the devil?" No one meets my eyes and nothing intelligible passes from their lips. Feeling the mood of his men shift, Morris lurches forward.

"Don't matter! You do things no livin' person should be doin'. Ain't but God himself that can mend a broke back, or make Jenny's fever break even after Doc said nuthin' could be done. You got wrong in you, woman, and we gon' fix that!" He lunges for me. Emboldened by Morris, three other men follow. I do not cry out as they grip my arms and shoulders with rough, dirty hands. Morris binds my hands in front of me. The smell of their breath and body odor stings my nose. I am ushered from my home with shouts and laughter. The night is fresh and crisp after the all-day rain. I welcome the clean air into my lungs.

"Why don't she fight?" someone mutters behind me. "Why don't she scream? Ain't never known a woman not to go screamin'."

"'Nother thing that ain't natural 'bout her. Like them purple eyes!"

I am shoved up onto an old, work-worn mare. A timid voice comes from behind the rest.

"But she made Pa's leg stop hurtin'. He's able to get out in the fields again. Ma said it was a miracle and that God was workin' through her."

"Shut yer mouth, boy!" Morris slaps the young man hard on the back of the head. He grips the boy by his collar. "Yer Pa's lucky she didn't turn that leg into a cloven hoof!" He pushes the boy backward and turns to face me.

3

"We gonna show you what we do to *witches!*" He throws his head back and hoots maniacally. Several men follow suit; some punctuate their exuberance with gunshots into the air.

The horse underneath me snorts and pulls back from the man holding the reins, jerking her head from side to side. He yells obscenities at her and yanks her bridle. I run my hands along her taut neck and make her listen to my words in her mind. She calms to the song I sing to her.

I am paraded down the main street through town towards the cemetery where the gallows stands. Many outlaws have met their end in this manner, and it appears so will I.

The cemetery is unusually bright this evening with torches on every fence post. They cast a harsh yellow glow onto the weathered wood of the gallows. I am aware of the shouts, calls, and other verbal assaults around me, but I hear nothing except the steady beating of my heart. I focus on controlling my movements and breathing. I will not give them the satisfaction of seeing my fear. While I am not afraid of death itself as I have done it eleven times before, it is the act of dying I fear. But I am pleased by the method they have chosen, for it is a fast end if done properly.

I am shoved up the steps and I will my legs to keep up. I am jerked around into position in front of the freshly tied noose of new rope. Morris presents it and me to the crowd—the ringmaster to this circus.

"Lookie what we got here!" He shoves me forward as if they couldn't already see me. "By her own confession to Roy Shackleford, she's a gawd damn *witch!*" The crowd becomes deafening.

I catch the eye of the town preacher at the far end of the massive throng. His face is smug and his eyes dance with spiteful glee. Under my glare, his grin falters and he moves behind a large elderly woman who's covered herself in a quilt and grasps a wooden cross tightly in her meaty fists.

Morris continues to speak random sentences describing my unnatural and ungodly ways, inciting the crowd further. I look upon their hateful faces, devoid of any resemblance to the humans they were earlier in the day. I pity them all for their small, feeble minds. I become aware that Morris is attempting to put the noose around my neck.

"I wish to speak!" I yank myself away from Morris's grip. Much to his dismay, I am stronger than I have led him to believe.

I am booed and hissed at, and the crowd calls for my immediate death. I clench my teeth and hiss back at them. *"Silence!"* The force in my voice, the unearthly sound I make, strikes them dumb. *"You will listen."*

"Almost half of you have benefited from my healing skill." My gaze seeks those I readily find who have been under my care. Their eyes do not meet mine.

"I have caused no harm to any of you, nor your land, nor your property. I have done only good deeds. Refute that, anyone!" People shift their feet and hide their faces behind those in front of them. The people in the front look at the ground. In the silence, I hear the flapping of large wings and see the heavy flames of the torches dance in the air currents. I cannot see the creature but I know it. I have always known it. A sharp, angry cry from the bird peals out above the crowd. There are gasps and cries of fear; some crouch down as they stare into the black sky. I feel strangely calmed by the bird's presence.

Morris steps forward to speak, and my thoughts close his windpipe. He grips his throat, his eyes widening. My eyes warn him not to proceed. *I will be allowed to speak, Morris, but* you *no longer will.*

"As I look at each of your faces, I know none of my words will make the slightest difference. Your minds are small and petty. The only danger here is you. You believe you are ridding the world of some great evil tonight. But all you are doing is worsening your own lives. Ponder that as you lay your heads on your pillows. The evil here is you, for there is none in me."

I release Morris from where he stands still gasping for air. As he tries to recover himself, he waves several men forward to put me back into place. Coughing is all he can manage as he puts the noose over my head and jerks it tight. When he is close to my face, he spits at me. The smell of it would be nauseating if I could feel anything other than rage.

He shoves each man out of the way so he is the one to pull the lever that controls the trap door upon which I stand. He stumbles and is still sputtering to get words out, but he can only cough and spit. As my last act of defiance, I make those the only sounds that will ever come out of his mouth. My petty revenge makes me smile.

The movement of the well-worn mechanism opening the trap door is loud in my ears. It is all I hear though I'm certain the crowd has reached a frenzied state. For the length of a breath, I am suspended in midair. I look above the crowd as I plummet downward, seeing a flash of white wings in my periphery.

I relax my neck and let the noose perform its job without resistance. I want this over quickly, to have my neck snap immediately. The noose tightens as my weight pulls my body down. The pain is but a quick jolt and then the world is black and silent to me.

# Chapter 1

I wake with a start, gasping. I'm shivering but that's not what woke me. I stay in my cocoon of blankets, eyes wide, searching the room with my Sight. There is nothing abnormal about. The morning sun is trying to fill the room, but the heavy gray clouds are making it challenging. There is a tightness all over my body and pain at my neck.

It is another few breaths before the realization comes that I've had a nightmare. It was one that I've not had in quite some time. The memory of my death in my last life, of being hanged in front of a massive throng of fear and ignorance. Heat surges through me. I am no longer cold; I am livid and I want to scream out the largest clap of thunder ever heard in Salem. For a split second, the stench of Morris Stiles's breath fills my nostrils. My stomach rolls and I fight the urge to vomit.

I close my eyes and visualize a soft, white light enveloping me. It is warm and soothing. It absorbs the negativity that grips my body. It pulls out the anger and pain and holds them fast. The soft light begins to dissolve and then fades away completely. I take a deep breath now without fear of that stench. I imagine warm sunlight on my face, the sound of waves lapping against the shore, the smell of pine trees. After a moment, I am back to myself.

I sense eyes upon me and there is pressure on the blanket behind me. It's a slow movement, creeping quietly towards me. Whatever it is doesn't want to be detected. It moves stealthily, pausing for a few seconds in between movements. I grin at the thought of her assuming she could ever sneak up on me. A warm, soft paw is placed on my cheek, followed by another, then a chin.

Arial gives me a quiet mew. Having sensed the disturbance, she wants to soothe me. She's snuggled her body against the back of my head, purring. She sniffs around my face with her cold nose; it tickles and makes me giggle. The upset has also brought my Great Pyrenees, Maggie, to attention at the side of the bed. She stares down at me with large brown eyes.

"It's all right, baby bear." Seeing my smile, she tilts her head. "Just a nightmare."

I reach to scratch Arial on the cheek. "Thank you both. Your comfort makes all the difference." She meows softly again and moves away as I motion that I want to get up. Maggie moves with me and both follow me to the bathroom.

Closing the bathroom door is pointless. In this old house not many things are plumb anymore. While I've had a good bit restored, the catch on the bathroom door wasn't high on my list. Besides, if I closed it, they would just sit there and snort, woof, meow, and paw at the door. Might as well let them in.

Arial hops onto the pedestal sink for her morning drink. I turn the faucet on out of habit as I walk by. Sitting down on the toilet prompts the Pyrenees to pad over and lie at my feet.

Arial still sits on the sink; she's turned the water off herself. Good cat. I grab her face and kiss her forehead. She disapproves. A stretch comes over me and Arial joins in. While I think she will fall off the sink during her enormous stretch, the graceful cat does not falter.

The aroma of coffee hits my nostrils. I love that smell. "Coffee time," I sing aloud to no one in particular and head down the hall. The coffee is waiting for me. No magick needed—a programmable coffee pot works just as well.

Steaming mug in hand, I sit at the kitchen table and gaze out at the gray morning. Having come to this time seventeen years ago, I couldn't be happier with it. An age that is accepting of witches! Well, more tolerant anyway, more so than I have ever experienced. At least I don't go to sleep each night in fear of an angry mob breaking down my door. Not only does this town accept witches, it celebrates them and makes millions every year in tourist revenue. This was an astounding revelation, to say the least, especially given the town's history.

I traveled a great deal before hearing of a place with the nickname 'Witch City.' Salem turned out to be perfect for me. I searched the tourist shopping areas looking for something that could be both my home and a shop. Despite its dilapidated state, I fell in love with this house the moment I saw it. Built in 1870, the Queen Anne–style home is three stories, dominated on one side by a conical tower complete with a large bay window on the first floor, and a covered porch spanning the rest of the front. It is set back from the street enough to have a decent-sized front yard, which I enclosed with a picket fence.

It had been renovated heavily over the years until it was abandoned a decade ago. My renovations were extensive—not only to accommodate my vision, but also to undo the many poor modifications made by the previous occupants. While the city has strict rules on the matter, I received the necessary permits and approvals very quickly and without incident, thanks to a little magickal persuasion.

It took a great deal of planning, designing, and construction to return this neglected building to something resembling the regal and picturesque home it was originally. The neighbors were not happy with the many months-long mess and construction. I did, however, make it up to them by visiting each one with a basket of homemade treats and coupons for free merchandise as soon as the shop was ready.

I opened the doors to Dovenelle's at the beginning of August. I'm very pleased with the modest but steady traffic the shop has gotten in just these few weeks, even before the official grand opening that I have planned for Samhain, better known nowadays as Halloween. This age and this country celebrate it so differently, so *commercially*, which makes it the perfect day to have the grand opening of a witch shop even though it's over two months away. I'm not concerned with making money at this point; I need to learn the business better as I've never had anything of this scale before. This shop is a far cry from the little stalls at village markets and fairs that I am used to. The customers right now consist mostly of curious locals and the friends of other shop owners who are sent to check out the place.

Since the rumors first snaked along the grapevine that a new witch store was opening, I have been scorned by many of the shop owners in the area. Competition is not welcomed by the various charlatans and tricksters who call themselves witches or mediums or psychics.

All but one turned their backs. Jo Riddle opened her arms to me the instant we met. She is a strong woman with true gifts—

one of the very few genuine witches I've discovered in this town. I am fortunate and honored to call her friend.

The shop was the first thing to get set up. I am being lazy with everything else. I had few possessions when I moved in, so I have been buying items piecemeal. My living area has only the bare essentials of furniture at the moment. I shop when I force myself to make the time for it, but my evenings are full of spell work. All the candles, potions, charms, and some of the jewelry I make myself. Each item is imbued with true magick. Some of the personal hygiene products, like lotions and bath salts, I make also. The rest come from trusted suppliers around the world. I have traveled to each one to ensure the people making them are genuine and have good intentions.

My reminiscing has moved me through several cups of coffee. Heading back to the bedroom, I coax my unruly hair into a ponytail. The only change to my appearance I've made in this life was to cut my waist-long hair. How freeing it felt! I've discovered that this age has colored contacts I could use to hide the natural amethyst of my eyes but no, I will not hide myself to be accepted by others.

As I get ready for the day, all of my movements supervised by the animals, I can't help but smile. This is the happiest I've ever been. I have been through so much pain and suffering in my previous lives, but here I feel like I've finally found a place where I belong and can thrive. When the recurring dread and despair that this life will end too soon creep into my mind, I pack them back down tightly. I've set aside all thoughts of my curse for now. I will make this a good life.

# Chapter 2

From my bedroom, I hear the front door chimes announce the arrival of customers. After less than a minute, a wave of negativity pulses through me. There is something about them that has made my skin prickle. It has nothing to do with intentions of stealing; it's something darker.

Looking over the balcony from the living room, with Maggie on full alert at my side, I see four teenage girls, laughing and talking loudly. Greeting them cheerfully is Sylvia, Jo's daughter, whom I hired to help in the shop. My eyes are drawn to the brunette of the bunch. I know immediately that she is a descendant of Morris Stiles. My nails dig into the railing to quell the sudden desire to scream. Hot anger flares across my body. While her nose and chin are slightly similar to Morris's, almost nothing else about her appearance is—but there is Stiles blood in her veins, I have no doubt. So it seems the dream last night was prophetic. To what degree it will ultimately be, I cannot imagine. The thought makes me shiver.

I watch her walk through the shop. Sylvia is eyeing the group carefully while still being hospitable. Experience has taught her that teenagers love to shoplift.

The girl is picking through the incense cabinet, smelling every stick and cone, making faces at items she deems smell 'gross' or 'like shit.' At that comment, I clear my throat loudly. All heads snap up in my direction. I raise an eyebrow at the girl, and she sheepishly looks away, quickly putting back the offending incense.

She knows I am watching her so she's politely meandering, not touching or smelling anything now. Out of curiosity, and a certain level of self-preservation, I look deeper into the girl. I sense nothing preternatural about her; she is a typical teenager for the most part. Her home life isn't the best. She has had a hard, masculine-dominated road since her mother died when she was very young. She is thinking seriously of joining the military. She likes to shoot—hunt actually—and she wants to prove to her father that she's tough. Military life will not serve her well. It will turn her into an apathetic person, and she will become hard and cruel—very much like Morris. She already has great prejudices but mostly towards those of a different color, thanks to her father. This girl is smart, though. She does well in school, which is not something her father cares much about. Yet another reason she would choose the military life: a smart girl wouldn't make daddy proud. A girl who is killing people, now that is something daddy could brag about. Despite myself, I pity her.

I will myself calm and start quietly down the stairs. Maggie is in front of me, surveying everything around her. Her heavy paws make no sound on the polished wood steps. I am sure the girl will bolt if she sees me coming, so I wait to approach when her back is turned. She's bent over looking at the charms inside a glass case.

"Good morning, Melissa."

"Oh!" She snaps up and turns quickly, stumbling on her own feet. "Shit, you scared me!"

She glares hard at me for an instant then looks away. She swallows and adjusts her shoulder bag across her body, clutching the strap tightly. All eyes are upon us now; her friends are huddled together, whispering that she must be in trouble. Sylvia stifles a grin.

Smiling, I extend my hand. "Welcome to Dovenelle's. I'm Aven Dovenelle."

She takes my hand warily. As my fingers wrap around her hand, I invoke a sense of calm in her. She relaxes and her squared shoulders soften. I release her hand.

"I'd like to do a reading for you, Melissa. On the house, of course, no catch."

She's not noticed that I've closed the distance between us. I am beside her now with a hand on her shoulder. She looks up at me and blinks away her confusion.

"How do you know my name?"

"Because I'm a witch," I say with a wink.

Her eyes widen as though she's just deemed me a crazy person, and she starts to pull away. I laugh lightly and take her hand.

I turn back to her friends. "Girls, while you wait, Sylvia can make you some lovely apple cinnamon tea if you'd like." They decline my offer with giggles. I look down at the apprehensive girl who has stiffened under the laughing eyes of her friends. "Ready?"

"Um, I guess," she says. "This isn't going to cost me, right?"

"Not a penny. You remind me of someone." I look at her kindly. "You don't have to if you don't want to."

"Nah, it's cool," she says, lifting her chin. She looks back at her friends before turning the corner, thinking that I don't see the eye roll she gives them.

The short hallway to my reading room is lined with tapestries and lit by a single Tiffany-style sconce lamp. The door at the end is painted a glossy poppy red with a hand-painted wooden sign within a large wreath made of dried herbs and flowers that reads "Dare to enter?" I flip the sign over to the side reading "Silence! Witch at work." I give Melissa another wink. Her answering smile is more mollifying than genuine.

The door opens without my touch.

"Nice trick," she says. I extend my hand to invite her forward.

She stops momentarily to survey the room. A lengthy 'wow' passes from her lips, which makes me smile. That is exactly the reaction I want from visitors to this room. I have it adorned with everything that makes me feel warm and comforted. The colors of autumn—dark red, amber gold, and lush green—dominate the color scheme. The bronze chandelier above holds an array of large, cream-colored candles that light with a flick of my hand. It perfectly illuminates my reading area, comprised of a settee covered in jacquard fabric for the guest and a high-back chair for me. These two are separated by a small, round table made from dark mahogany and hand-hewn with a variety of animal figures.

The left side of the small room has the original fireplace, restored to its former grandeur. The mantel is home to an oil reproduction of Waterhouse's "The Magic Circle." I loved that painting the moment I saw it. The woman reminds me so much of myself in my early lives. The painting is flanked by two gargoyle candlesticks, carved from black walnut and polished to a shine, topped with fat pillar candles the color of ripe pumpkin. Amidst the silken greenery draped across the mantel is a large raven statue made of iron and stippled with white paint. The right side of the room is dominated by a massive object on the wall, taller than it is wide, that is draped with thick black velvet.

"What's behind that?" Melissa reaches out to touch the cloth.

"Don't!"

"Okay, okay. Geez!"

I motion for her to take a seat on the settee. She ignores my gesture and continues to tour the room. I purse my lips and clasp my hands in front of me. With flared nostrils, I take in a calming breath.

She eyes each item on the fireplace mantel. I think she is stalling more than interested in the decor. She barely glances at the painting. Her hand reaches for the raven. I clear my throat and her hand drops.

"This is cool," she says, cocking her head to the side. "Looks a lot like the bird I saw out front before we came in."

My mouth falls open, but I snap it closed. The white raven shows himself to everyone but me. I only know that my elusive stalker is, in fact, a white raven from the comments of others. Although I sense the presence of something, some sort of tug at the edge of my mind, I cannot see the source of it. When I look in its direction, I see only the movement of what it disturbed as it flew away and hear the beating of wings or what I perceive as a cry of grievance. On a few rare occasions, only when I am near death it seems, I have seen a glimpse of wing.

I pull myself from this old irritation to deal with the current one.

"Have a seat, Melissa." My tone does not invite any more dawdling.

As I pass by the fireplace, a small fire softly bursts to life. At this time of year, the warmth isn't necessary, but I like the look of it. This room should always have a fire. Melissa, wide-eyed again, quickly hides her surprise behind a sardonic expression.

"Yes, Melissa, I am a real witch." I sit down in my chair and lean back, crossing my legs. "Although I don't match the stereo-type you're used to—pointy black hat, flowing robe, gothic makeup. My cat isn't even black. And yes, this could just be a bunch of tricks. Someone could be controlling everything by watching us on a web cam. But I am certain that in the next few minutes, you won't be thinking these are tricks anymore."

I feel her heart flutter. "There's absolutely no reason to be afraid. I simply want to talk to you."

Melissa scoots back in the settee and seems unsure where to put her hands or feet.

"How can I put you at ease, Melissa?"

"Um," she says, fidgeting with her purse strap again, "how about we just get on with it." She looks away as she realizes how rudely that came out.

"You are Melissa Jane Stiles, seventeen, born and raised in Bakersfield, California, where the majority of your extended family still lives. Your mother died when you were three. You, your father, and two brothers moved to Salem five years ago because your dad met a woman online, but that didn't last. You are smart but you want your friends to think you are a hard-ass who doesn't take shit from anyone. You are a favorite with many of your teachers, but you pass it off to your friends that you are playing them for good grades. We both know that is a lie; you like school and you want to learn. You put a hard exteri-or up because you feel you have to. Your father doesn't want a smart girl—he wants a tough girl." Melissa's expression changes several times during my speech and now it has gone hard. The mouth that had been open in awe snapped shut at the last mention of her father. She glares at me, her lips pursed.

*Be calm*, I say to her in words that she cannot hear but that her body understands. She shudders at the new experience of her mind being invaded but takes a deep breath and turns to the fire.

"You are a bundle of unmanageable emotions, Melissa. With your home life, that is completely understandable. If you will feel better by crying or lashing out at me, please do so."

Her eyes gloss over and the flames reflect upon their surface. She slides her hands under her backside.

"Do you want me to continue?" My voice is calm.

Still looking at the fire, she jerks her chin up.

"You think that joining the military is the only way that your father will accept you." Her head snaps back. I put up a hand to stop her before the cursing begins.

"You need to know that this path will only bring you an unfortunate future. While you may gain the respect of your father, you will lose yourself. You will become someone you end up hating. You will become worse than your father ever was."

Tears stream down her face as she blinks at me. "How can you possibly know all this?"

"It is in your blood. You are a Stiles and, unfortunately, the legacy of your forefathers has been perpetuated through each generation. But it can stop with you."

She is looking at her lap now.

"Melissa, look at me." After a moment, she meets my eyes.

"I knew one of your ancestors—a great-great-grandfather named Morris Stiles. It was 1886 in Calico, California."

Melissa shakes her head. Her face has regained its hard façade. "Okay, with that, you lost me, lady."

She gets up but doesn't go to the door. She moves to the fireplace.

"You had me going," she says, wagging her finger at me, "you really did!" She's shaking her head as she grips the mantel, her shoulders quivering.

While my first instinct is to go to her and wrap my arms around her, I'm certain this is the last thing she would want.

"Morris was not a good man, to say the least. There is much about him I could tell you, but I will save you that. What you do need to know is that he murdered a woman for the simple reason that she was different. She used her talents to heal people, to bring about prosperity and fertile crops. Morris saw only the workings of the devil in her. At the first opportunity that presented itself, he formed a lynching party. He strung her up in front of the whole town and pulled the lever himself." I keep my emotions from my voice.

Both her hands are on the mantel now, and her head is slumped forward. After a few breaths, she straightens herself and turns to me. "So you think I'll become like this Morris guy if I join the Army?"

"Yes."

She nods and turns back to the fire. She presses her forehead against the mantel.

"I know I have a dark side," she says. "It comes out sometimes. A lot, really. I get so angry, I just don't know what to do with it. I feel sometimes that it will eat me alive."

I bite my lip to contain words of comfort and wait for her to continue.

"You are freakishly right on, though," she says after a snort. "While this is all *totally* ridiculous, my gut says different." She looks back at me. "And I believe you about that Morris guy.

Don't ask me why, though. It all sounds fucking crazy." She winces at me after cursing, apologizing with her eyes. I give her a smile.

She comes back to the settee and sits down heavily. "What else?"

The smart Melissa has won against the angry Melissa. I weigh what information she absolutely needs to know.

"What I've told you is enough. You feel all this in your gut, as you said, but it goes deeper than that. You have been struggling inside yourself for quite some time. Personally, I feel that you should exploit your intelligence and get a degree in some sort of biology. You like that icky stuff." She giggles.

"You don't need to prove yourself to anyone. *Anyone.* You are the one who leads this life. Make it your own."

I stand up and she follows. Moving around the small table, I extend my arms in offer of a hug. Without hesitation, she steps forward. I sense that this move surprises her, but she hugs me back firmly. I wonder when she was last hugged.

After almost a full minute, I release her and put my hands on her shoulders. "I have a couple of books I'd like to give you." Her face lights up but falls as her eyes dart to the door.

"Stop worrying so much about what your friends think of you. Be who *you* want to be. If after seeing the real person they are still your friends, then they are keepers." She smiles and hugs me again.

I pull several books from the library shelves, and she quickly stuffs them into her bag. As she and her friends leave the shop, Sylvia leans over the counter and stares at me as I watch them walk away through the bay window. The wide-eyed girls surround Melissa once they reach the sidewalk and seem to be peppering her with questions. Melissa's chin is high as she responds to her friends, and pulls the books from her bag.

"Why are you staring at me, Sylvia?"

"Ugh." She snorts and comes to join me at the window. "I am always dying to know what goes on in that room, but I know you'll never tell. That kills me!" She throws her head back in mock desperation. I snort at her.

"But I totally felt a major difference in her energy when she came down the hallway. Good work, witch lady." She bumps me with her hip. Maggie comes to my side, curious as to what we are looking at.

"When's your mom back?"

"End of the week," she says, reaching down to ruffle Maggie's great mane. The dog jukes away with a light woof, landing in a play stance, tail wagging. Sylvia giggles at the goofy dog.

"You know," she says, scrutinizing Maggie now, hands on hips, "I don't think she's ever let me pet her."

"She's more of a romper than a lover." I give the big dog a wink.

# Chapter 3

The UPS delivery man is bringing in the last of the inventory. The smells coming from the stacks piled in the shop's kitchen are heavenly. A mixture of lemongrass, cinnamon, clove, sweet orange, and so many others. The boxes are filled with soaps, hair care products, and perfumes—all handmade by a small family company in the Northwest.

From across the street, I sense my good friend coming. *My good friend.* My smile is no longer for this delivery but for the fact that I finally have a friend—a true, real friend.

I hear the greeting between the delivery man and Jo as they meet on the porch. Jo offers to help the skinny man with the boxes, implying that there's no way he could possibly lug all of them since his wife is obviously not feeding him. He rolls the loaded hand truck into the kitchen, extolling the merits of his wife's cooking. Jo and I lock eyes, and she pretends to grab his butt when he passes her. I tut at her and shake my head. He's quick to make his escape.

Jo inhales deeply. "Oh, my Goddess, this room smells fantastic!" She picks through the boxes, inspecting each label and sniffing.

"How's your mom? What did the doctor say?" I ask, handing her a box cutter.

Jo's chipper mood vanishes. She sets the box cutter down and falls into the nearest chair with a despondent sigh.

Feeling the depression rolling off her, I sit beside her and take her hand. "Jo, what is it?"

"It's not good." She doesn't meet my eyes. "The doctor said it's a brain tumor. And too late to really do anything about." Tears well in her eyes and she blinks, wiping her cheeks.

"Oh, Jo, I'm so sorry." I take her other hand and hold them both. She inhales deeply, squeezing my hands, her shoulders quivering.

"Well, it is what it is, as they say. Stupid saying." She seems to search for words, and I don't prod her. She and Matilda are so close; I know how much this must hurt Jo.

"Anyway," she exhales, straightening her shoulders and gently pulling her hands from mine, "she's as ornery as ever."

"That's a good thing."

"Tell me. She's not going to go without a fight. Speaking of which, Claudia made a real ass of herself over all this. Goddess, I can't believe they're sisters. She's already made herself high priestess of the coven, saying that Mom is in no condition for such a responsibility anymore." Jo's hands are fists in her lap. My eyes widen.

Jo proceeds to paint a picture of the jealous older sister, always in the shadow of her younger, better-at-everything, and prettier sister. The honor of high priestess was given to Matilda because of her power and knowledge of the Craft. She was loved by most and respected by all. The family did not hold that the eldest receive such a position automatically: it had to be earned, and no one thought Claudia a leader. She was petty and a know-it-all. But in the wake of Matilda's announcement, Claudia preyed on their shock and grief and had the power in her hands before anyone realized what happened.

"I argued with that cow, but since I'm not a member of the coven, I had no say, blood or not." Jo unclenches her fists and rubs her hands on her lap. "The shouting took a real toll on Mom; she couldn't handle it and gave in. It was hard to watch actually." She pinches the bridge of her nose. "Needless to say, Mom insists on staying in her house until it's absolutely necessary she go into some sort of managed care facility. She hates the idea. Goddess, we all do."

She waves a hand in front of her as if to push away the awful thoughts.

Her face suddenly brightens. "So! Anything exciting happen while I was away?"

I search her face, gauging whether I should try to comfort her or go with her change of topic. Her eyes plead with me to move on.

"Well, let's see. The great-great-granddaughter of the man who murdered me in my last life came by a few days ago," I say matter-of-factly.

"Ha!" She slaps her leg and gets up, heading to the cabinet for her favorite mug—the one with the caption 'You think I'm wicked now? You should see me without my coffee'—and pours herself a cup. She blows across the top and takes a sip.

I mentally kick myself. I have never glossed over anything about myself to Jo, or to anyone for that matter, which more often than not has led to disaster. But there is something about the older woman that makes me want to tell her everything. The fact remains that we are completely different witches, and what I can do no other witch can. Some of the things I've shown her and told her defy her experiences and understanding of magick.

She's been open and accepting, although it's overwhelmed her at times. Having such a friend is new to me, and I need to remember to temper what I tell her—ease her into my unusual life slowly. It's difficult, though.

"What did the little bitch want?" she asks blithely, retaking her seat.

She can always make me laugh. I tell her a little of how my last life ended and then of my encounter with Melissa. She sits patiently and makes concerned faces and nods at the appropriate times. I suspect she's humoring me.

"You should write a book! You've got some great stories, that's for sure. Oh! Speaking of books, I brought you one." She pulls out a small, tattered book from her voluminous folds of fabric.

Holding the book, a tingle moves across my skin when I read the author's name, Patricia Jones. The book itself is nothing magickal—a collection of poems about ravens.

I manage a quiet 'thanks' as I rub my fingers across the name.

"What? Something wrong with the book?"

"Nothing's wrong. The author's name, Patricia Jones." I look up at her. "What made you buy this book?"

"I'm not sure, really. I passed a stack of books at a flea market the other day and that one spoke to me. You don't strike me as a reader of poetry, though. Why? Know the author?"

"No." I wave the conversation to an end. "It's nothing, never mind."

"No, no. You know I hate when you do that. What is it?"

"You'll just think I'm back to storytelling again." I wink at her.

"Well, your stories are good." She settles back in the chair, mug in hand. "Spill."

I sigh deeply. It's time to tell her.

"Patricia Jones is the name of the eighteen-year-old whose body I took over when she died."

Jo lets out a snort and almost spills her coffee. "Look, I believe in reincarnation just as much as the next witch, but hearing that you took over a person's body is kinda hard to swallow." She raises her brows at me and purses her lips.

Hurt by her words, I look down at my hands in my lap.

"I'm sorry, that was mean. I could have said that better."

"It's all right. It's just that you are the first *real* friend that I've had, so I burst to tell you everything. It's been so nice not to have to hold back what I say. I sometimes forget how ridiculous it all must sound—even to a fellow witch."

She frowns and apologizes again.

I lean forward. "Jo, I can prove what I say is true. If you'll let me."

She is eyeballing me now, leaning away. "And just how would you prove it?"

"Give me your hand."

She hesitates, her eyes narrow at me. "What are you gonna do?"

"Trust me," I say in my most convincing tone.

Warily, she sets her mug on the table and puts her hands in mine. I have to do this gently or she will cease to be my friend.

# Chapter 4

As we sit at the table, the kitchen around us shimmers. Jo tenses and I squeeze her hands a little tighter for reassurance. Slowly, the room dissolves into a soft, gray mist. Jo looks around with an appraising eye.

The shifting mist begins to form solid objects, and she squints to make out what they are. The blurry shapes quickly sharpen into the buildings of an urban neighborhood. The heat from the pavement radiates upward while the bright morning sun overhead glares down on us. We are standing near a crosswalk amidst throngs of people bustling in all directions. The sounds of countless automobile engines, horns, shouts of profanity, and the smell of exhaust assault our senses. Jo recoils at the violent change in surroundings.

"Oh, my Goddess," Jo exhales, covering her gaping mouth with her hands as she whirls about, taking it all in.

She whips back at me with still wide eyes. "*Are you freaking kidding me?*" My response is a simple, knowing smile.

At that moment, a sweaty, overweight man in a crumpled suit rushes right through Jo, his hand gripping his weathered briefcase. Jo shrieks obscenities to the Goddess, and her whole body shudders. She's frantically brushing herself off as if she's just walked through a tangle of cobwebs.

"That was *not* pleasant!" Jo says, dancing out of everyone's way, making sure no one violates her again. I can't help laughing.

"I bet you are loving this." She glares at me, and I only laugh harder. "Laugh it up, sister, but payback's a bitch."

"And just *how* would you pay me back for *this*?" I flourish my hands at the scene around us.

"Oh, shut up," she says, wrinkling her nose at me.

I grab Jo's hand and pull her towards me. I turn her around and stand behind her with my hands on her shoulders. "Watch."

At the street corner opposite us, Jo's attention is taken by something above where I wish her to look. I nudge her and point to a short, pudgy teenage girl hoofing as quickly as she can to the intersection, her head hanging as low as her loaded backpack. The T-shirt she wears used to be white, and her shorts are the same orange color as her frizzy, unkempt hair. Her shoes are ill-fitting, most likely meant for a boy but handed down to her. She trudges along with eyes on the pavement, hands clutching her backpack straps.

"Patricia," I whisper in Jo's ear. She tenses and her hands flutter to her chest.

Patricia seems desperate to get to wherever she's going; she's most likely late for school. Her father will whip her again if she gets another tardy notice. Actually, he really needs no excuse to beat her ass.

As she zigzags around people blocking the intersection, she takes no notice of the shout from the old man she's almost knocked over and barrels forward. She doesn't see the oncoming bus, and no one reaches out to pull her back.

Jo shrieks and turns away, but she can't block out the sounds of screeching tires and a surprised scream that peals out and is quickly cut short by a sickening thud. The next few seconds show a dozen people paralyzed, staring at the young girl on the ground in front of the bus. The driver is on his feet, staring down over the steering wheel at something he can't quite believe. The sounds of the accident haven't affected the vast majority of the surrounding people. Their days are much too important to be interrupted.

Jo's motherly instinct propels her through the busy intersection. She pays no notice to the cars and cyclists passing through her. "Somebody help her!" she screams repeatedly.

I follow slowly. Jo is on her knees by the girl, trying to touch her but unable to and offering words of comfort Patricia cannot hear.

"Why isn't anybody helping her?" She's glaring at the gaping and useless people standing around the fallen girl. I have no explanation for the apathy of this big city. Patricia's blood is slowly seeping onto the pavement from beneath her head.

"She's not in any pain, Jo, I promise." I place a hand on her shoulder and realize she's softly crying.

I ask her to step back and tell her that my Spirit is coming. I have to pull her up. She looks at me with confusion, her heavy black mascara making trails down her cheeks. I give her a reassuring squeeze around her shoulders.

The noisy, congested surroundings grow still and quiet in the instant of a breath. Everything around the body of Patricia blurs and loses all color. Jo catches something out of the corner of her eye and gasps. It's me but not quite.

My Spirit is the very likeness that she knows me in now except that it is emitting soft, silvery light and has the ethereal beauty that only a spiritual entity can have. She quickly turns to me to make sure I'm still behind her. I motion for her to keep

watching. My Spirit drifts swiftly along the pavement, legs unmoving, with a gentle smile and soft eyes fixed on Patricia.

Patricia's chest heaves in a final gasp as her life leaves her.
Casting a bright glow in all directions, Patricia's Spirit lifts from
her body. She slowly turns to see my Spirit and smiles. Her face
is peaceful and unmarked. She looks down at her body and the
smile quickly fades. After a slow shake of her head, Patricia's
Spirit turns away. Behind her, wisps of black and silver vapor
have appeared, swirling outward and growing. A portal is forming as Jo watches in awe.

"The Veil," I whisper. Jo takes a sharp breath.

The Veil's dark beauty ripples and intensifies to coalesce into
a large, oval expanse. Feelings of warmth and comfort fall over
us; the Veil brings with it a sense of peace, erasing all fear and
doubt. Without hesitation, Patricia's Spirit drifts into it, the black
mist billowing around her, engulfing her, welcoming her. The
Veil churns momentarily as it fades from black to dark gray, to
silver and then into nothing.

I sense Jo's tense body relax. I can't see her face but I know
she is smiling.

My Spirit approaches the lifeless body of Patricia and seems
to study it for a moment. In the distance, we hear the approaching sirens breaking into the serenity of the moment. My Spirit
kneels beside Patricia's body and strokes her brow. The nasty
gash on her temple closes, and the blood on the ground draws
back into her body. My Spirit's form softens and becomes a
shimmering mantle of light. It envelops Patricia's body and is
slowly absorbed by it like water into a sponge.

The world comes crashing back around us, making Jo jump.
The next few minutes are filled with shouts for help and rushing

EMTs pushing people out of the way. I take Jo by the arm and the scene melts away.

In fast-forward, what shows before us is the emergency room, Patricia's body surrounded by haggard nurses and an impatient doctor who's making it obvious that his time is being wasted. The patient is fine; he has more urgent cases to attend to. The background noise includes the sounds of a man yelling about not having any goddamn insurance and not knowing how they will pay for Patricia's stupidity again. They need to let his daughter go now if she ain't dying because he can't afford this shit.

Patricia is sleeping behind the privacy curtains, or so everyone thinks. As soon as she is alone, she gets up, puts on her ruined clothes and quickly makes her way out of the hospital, skirting by everyone in the busy lobby, including her father and mother, with a smirk.

Jo turns. "That's you, right? You're in there?"

I nod.

"Wow," is Jo's eloquent response. "But you don't look like her now. I don't get it."

"Later."

Now we are in a small bedroom where Patricia is surveying the scant furnishings.

Along one wall is a twin bed with a faded purple comforter and stained, flat pillow. The opposite wall has a makeshift bookshelf filled with books of all sizes and the best knickknacks that the thrift shop has to offer. Scattered on the walls are a few posters of unicorns and various boy bands. The room has no windows and is lit by only a single, harsh bulb overhead.

Jo gazes around the room, wringing her hands. We hear the pounding of footsteps from the stairwell. There is determination in those steps. A mirthless grin curls Patricia's lips as she turns towards the sound. Jo lifts a quizzical eyebrow at me. I motion for her to wait and watch.

Patricia doesn't answer her father's calls. The father is pounding his booted feet down the hallway towards Patricia's room. The bookshelf quakes with the weight of his gait. For the former Patricia, this was a dreaded sound she'd heard too many times.

He bursts through the door, filling the entire doorway with his bulk. A short, round woman stops abruptly behind him. Patricia is pretending to go through the book collection on the shelf.

"What the fuck, girl?" His face is red with rage. "You sure as hell got a lotta explaining to do."

She tosses a book on the bed and turns to face him, standing tall and strong. By the reaction of both the father and mother, she can tell they no longer see their daughter's watery blue eyes.

"Explain what?" She has a confidence and strength he has never witnessed in his daughter before, causing him to pause.

He puffs his chest and crosses his arms to make himself more intimidating. "How the hell did you get out of the hospital?"

"Oh, that." She loses interest in the conversation and turns back to the books. She picks another one up and flips through the pages. "I walked out."

With two long strides, he reaches Patricia and grabs her upper arm, jerking her around to face him. She is faster than he is and blocks the fist he'd planned to bring across her face. Jo lunges forward, but I stop her.

"Oh, no," Patricia says with eyes as narrowed slits. His superior expression falters with the revelation that his daughter is not only defying him but also stronger than he is. "You won't be doing *that* ever again." She digs her fingernails into his wrist and brings his arm down to his side. He is putting all his strength into not allowing this but to no avail. His mouth hangs open as he releases his grip on her other arm.

Patricia's mother, true to form, is standing idly by, watching the display as if it were one of her soap operas. She sees something new that she cannot process: Patricia standing up to the man, something she never dreamed of doing herself.

Patricia takes a step back from the sweating, red-faced man. "I'm moving out."

"The hell you are."

She graces him with a look of sheer contempt. "You are not able to stop me. This body is eighteen, and it can do whatever it wants." The words she uses confuse both parents. She is challenging him on purpose. The desire to punish him for the evils he has done to Patricia burns deep in her chest.

The mother has found her voice. "How dare you speak to your father like that, missy! What has gotten into you?" Her face is full of shock.

"I was hit by a bus, *mother*. Don't you remember?" She uses Patricia's teenage voice as she rolls her eyes.

Patricia glares at both of them. "You two should be ashamed of your behavior and your treatment of your children. You are despicable, vile creatures, and you do not deserve the right to bear children. People like you make me sick. You have children only so you can control them, to make yourselves feel important and powerful, when the fact is that you are cowards and villains—bullies of the worst kind. Patricia never had the courage to stand up for herself, but she does now."

The father and mother are dumbstruck. They exchange glances as if to gauge what to do. They see the figure of their daughter, but the voice, the words, and the eyes are those of a stranger. Patricia knows that the father wishes to inflict pain upon her—that has always been his way of managing his children. The mother would stand by and allow it simply so that she would not be the recipient of his anger instead.

She addresses the mother. "Leave now."

The woman doesn't move, confusion rampant on her face. Patricia's face is steel. "*Get out.*" The woman looks to her husband. He jerks his head for her to go.

He has found his voice again. "I don't know what the hell is going on here or what the fuck happened to you, but you're stepping real close to the edge, little girl." He takes a step towards her.

"Don't even try to threaten me, you pig," she spits at him.

He curls his misshapen upper lip at her.

Patricia closes the distance between them, and he takes an involuntary step back, eyes widening. "I have come to the conclusion over the many years I've lived that men like you will *never* change unless something drastic happens to them. You are a nasty person, Harold Jones, and you have been all your life. I will change that tonight." She straightens as tall as she can get. His jaw falls open.

Jo's body is rigid and radiating heated anger. I place my hand on her shoulder, and she relaxes only slightly.

"You have doled out much pain in your thirty-eight years, haven't you? I mean for you to know what that feels like. You will know what you have done because I am going to make you *feel* it. All of it."

Flames rise from her clenched fists; his muscles jerk to run, but he is not fast enough by any means. She grips him by his upper arms and locks him in place. The flames from her hands travel to his chest, forming a mass. She draws out all of the memories of his past deeds—all the pain, terror, shame, and torment experienced by his victims, including his own children and wife. He is quaking beneath her hands, and she is smiling, knowing that the worst is yet to come. The hateful energy is forming a swirling, pulsing orb of fire across his chest. His eyes gape at the sight of his own evil. It is beginning to burn him. He tries to scream, but no sounds rise from his throat.

"You will be a changed man, Harold Jones, if you survive this," she says, a vengeful smile full on her face.

He shakes his head, begging 'no no' with his lips. With a push of her own energy, the burning mass plunges into his chest. His body convulses under her grip. She holds him in place as the scalding crimson flame encompasses his body, alive with a mind of its own, coiling around him like a hungry snake. She releases him now, for he is held in place by his own evil. He writhes under the unimaginable agony he has doled out since the age of three. The poor animals he tortured, the little sister he molested, the young boy in school he accused of sodomy in public only to try it on him in private just to see what it was all about, and so much more.

His body slowly absorbs the heat and flame. Once it can no longer be seen, he collapses. He lies on his side, twitching and whimpering. The energy has not dissipated; it has condensed itself so that it can inflict its torment from within until spent. In his eyes swirl the blazing red flames.

She kneels down and puts her face to his, unsure if he can see or hear her. "*If* you survive this," she repeats, a flash of my face appearing over hers. Patricia Jones leaves without looking back.

# Chapter 5

Jo is hunched over, gripping my hands. She's gasping for breath. I tell her she's fine, that we are back in the kitchen now and she should slow her breathing.

She leans back and places her hands on her chest. Her face is ashen, and there are tiny droplets of sweat on her upper lip.

"I'm so sorry, Jo! I've never shared a memory with anyone before." I never considered how overpowering it all must be—plunged into the life of someone else, especially a moment filled with such emotion. She is adept at vision walking but reliving someone's memory, being in the midst of all of it, is much different. I didn't think of how much it would affect her. I feel terrible now. "Let me get you something."

She leans her head back in the chair, eyes clamped shut.

Before us on the table appears Jo's favorite brand of whiskey and a rock crystal glass with a single, round ice cube. I pour three fingers and hand it to her. It's still early in the morning, but I know of Jo's fondness for such a thing and she looks like she could use a bracer. She's peeked out of one eye to witness the sudden appearance of the bottle and glass. She shakes her head and reaches for the glass, muttering that it's five o'clock somewhere.

Half of the amber liquid disappears quickly between Jo's lips. She leans back again and exhales a long breath. With a little shiver, she finishes the rest in one gulp.

She puts the glass down onto the table with a thud. She grips it tightly, her other hand trembling.

Having composed herself to her satisfaction, she looks at me. "Was that real?"

I nod.

As she leans forward to put her face in both hands, she mumbles a few colorful expletives followed by a call to the Goddess. I hide my smile with a hand over my mouth. I shouldn't be finding this amusing but I can't help it.

"I've never—" she starts, "I mean, that's just...wow. So much more...*intense* than my vision walks. Seriously. I can't—" She stops trying to make coherent sentences and looks up. She huffs out a big breath and falls back in her chair. "Remind me never to piss you off."

I laugh out loud and then quickly stop myself, thinking that she might be serious. "When I take over a body, I am inundated with all their memories, their emotions. Patricia's past overwhelmed me. I couldn't let him get away with what he'd done. He was a horrible man."

She waves a hand at me dismissively and pours herself another drink.

Drink in one hand and bottle in the other, she stands. "I need some air."

"Let's go to the roof. You've not seen the finished product!"

We head upstairs to my living quarters and then ascend the narrow staircase off the kitchen. The steep incline of the stairs forces Jo to grip the handrail as she pulls herself along, grumbling with each step that her old knees are not liking this.

I pull open the door and push out the screen door, ducking through onto the roof.

Jo's mouth falls open at the sight before her. The terrace encompasses a good portion of the roof, dominated by a pergola made from reclaimed wood that covers a small sitting area. Trumpet creeper vines filled with deep orange blooms snake up the columns of the pergola to form nearly a second ceiling atop it, so thick it blocks out the summer sun. On the right, abutting the steep pitch of the roof, is a long, raised flowerbed made of mortar and river rocks filled with herbs of all varieties, each battling for space.

The slight breeze wafts the scents of lavender and jasmine in our direction, and Jo closes her eyes to inhale the soothing fragrance. Movement catches my eye amidst the herbs, and I spy the flickering tail of a cat, half buried in the catnip. Dotted around the terrace are many colorful, mismatched pots and tall vases overflowing with a variety of trailing plants and fragrant flowers. A little magickal encouragement has made everything grow in nicely. The harlequin butterfly bush is doing its job perfectly; a dozen butterflies dance around its copious reddish-purple flower spikes—all of whom are being closely monitored by a semi-intoxicated tabby.

Taking Jo's hand, I pull her to the sitting area. I plop down on the double chaise. She places the whiskey bottle on the stone coffee table too harshly and winces at the sound.

"Now, I want answers to all of my questions, understand?" Jo wags her finger at me with the look of a stern mother. "No more messing around—I want the truth!"

"Yes, ma'am!" I'm taken aback by her attitude but I go with it. I have no experience with how someone would react to such a revelation.

She settles her large frame into the lounge chair across from me. She smooths her flouncy skirt over her legs. Although it's late August and the sun has shown itself harshly in the last few weeks, Jo is wearing her typical black, long-sleeved dress. She often jokes that black is slimming so she wears no other color. Today's ensemble is of lightweight rayon with a lovely embroidered white band around the V-neck, cuffs, and hem. Her long auburn hair, streaked with fetching silver wisps, falls like a curtain down her back.

As I watch her fuss with the folds of fabric, I smile fondly at the woman who has become my best friend. Of all the people, the witches, I've met since moving to Salem, she is one of the few with true power. Most who call themselves witches—or worse, *warlocks*—are charlatans and outright crooks. Tourists flock to them regardless, caught up in the fervor induced by visits to the famous cemetery or the various museums that recount the horrific acts of the Witch Trials.

But Jo is different; she has the vision and a genuine connection to the energy flows. There is true magick in this woman, but I don't think she realizes just how much.

She seems lost in thought, looking at something behind me. I sit patiently across from her. Now I wish I had a drink. A highball glass filled with gin and tonic appears beside me on the end table. Jo takes no notice.

"That is such a gorgeous bird," she says. Surprised, I turn and don't see anything, of course. I knew I wouldn't, but I do hear the flutter of wings.

"He never lets me see him."

Taking note of the forlorn tone of my voice, she focuses on me.

"Really?"

I nod, turning back. I take a long sip of my drink. She notices the glass but says nothing.

"Interesting. I see him all the time."

I frown. Why this bird shies away from me I've never understood. But it's always been that way.

"Anyhoo, I have no flipping idea where to start! *So* many questions." She leans back and stares at me, obviously wanting me to offer something up.

"Okay, well…now where do *I* start?" Perhaps the gin will guide me. I take a few more sips.

"As they say, start at the beginning."

"Oh my," I say, shaking my head, "that's a long way back."

"All right, there's a good place. How old are you?"

"Pushing a thousand, I think."

Jo chokes on the sip she's just taken. "Are you freaking kidding me?"

I purse my lips and shake my head.

"Holy crap."

"Yeah."

"Um, well, you look great, by the way."

That makes me laugh. She raises her glass. "To hot older babes. Cheers!" We clink our glasses together.

"Okay, so how come you aren't short, red-haired, and freckled like Patricia?"

I hadn't a clue where to begin about my lives, so this topic is as good as any. "Long story short, I change the body. It's quite a painful process, but I like this look. I change the bone structure, skin texture, hair color, and so on. It takes several days."

Jo's mouth could collect flies. She looks me up and down like she's seeing me for the first time. I extend my arms out and whip my head side to side, exaggerating the flowing of my shoulder-length hair. She chuckles briefly.

"Why not just use a glamour spell?"

"Because that would be a spell I would have to constantly put energy into maintaining. I might slip for any number of reasons."

She nods in agreement, not having realized this aspect of using glamour.

"How did you die?"

"When? Can you be more specific?"

"Huh? That's a pretty straightforward question."

"Well, I've died many times." I shift in my seat.

"Are you serious?"

I nod.

"Okay, well, um…you're going to have to explain all that."

"Let's see. This is my thirteenth life, so I've died twelve times so far."

Stunned into silence, Jo displays only an incredulous look.

After blinking several times, she takes another sip. "How does *that* happen?"

"How does what happen? The dying part? Pretty simply actually. Burned at the stake, beheaded, hanged, crushed, and so on. All the typical ways people think a witch can be disposed of." I am more flippant in my response than I mean to be.

Jo's expression is grim. "Aven, come on, you have got to be kidding me with all of this."

"I wish I was, Jo, I really do."

"I'm just…I can't think of what to ask next. My brain is just overloaded." She sips the last drop from her glass. "I mean *really*."

I'm not making this easy for her but I'm at a loss for what else to say. This is a conversation I've never had before, and it's not going very well.

"Sorry, I can do better at this." I straighten my shoulders and take a deep breath, as if preparing a lecture. "So, I'm about a thousand years old, but the years aren't consecutive. I've lived twelve times before, and you have witnessed how I entered my thirteenth. Each of my faces starts out differently, each voice, each pair of eyes. I use magick to alter the body I choose into the likeness that I remember most fondly. Seeing my reflection in the mirror gives me a sort of peace, comfort, at these familiar features. I've been in this age for about seventeen years. When I enter a new life, I travel around a lot until I find a place to settle. I've learned to adapt quickly to new places and times; that's a necessity, really—how to talk, how to act, all that. But this age was the most shocking; the technology advances alone are incredible. You can't imagine my excitement when I learned about indoor plumbing and air conditioning!"

My little speech gives her a moment to collect her thoughts.

"You come back each time like that—I mean, the same way?"

"Picking out a new body? Yes. I select only those that I sense are about to die."

"So you reincarnate."

This doesn't seem to be a question, but I nod anyway.

"And you can select whomever you want to come back as?"

"Yes...but I would never *take* a body. The person has to be on the verge of death."

"And you remember all your former lives? All of it, everything?"

"Yes. Well, mostly yes."

She is pondering all of this for a few moments, then her face brightens. "That is *bad ass!*"

My mouth falls open. "It is most certainly the *opposite* of bad ass."

She sees the cloud fall over my face. "What? What is it you haven't told me?"

There is so much I haven't told her. I fall back into the chaise with a sigh.

"Let's continue this another day." I realize I'm not ready for this conversation. "I need to get down to the shop."

"Oh, no, you don't." She jiggles her empty glass at me, the diminished ice cube tinkling around in the glass like a large diamond. "I still have a little ice left, so keep talking, sister."

I love this woman. She makes me grin in spite of myself. She's added a couple of splashes of whiskey to her glass.

I stare at her for a long moment. Her gaze never falters, only softens as she senses my distress.

I'm just going to come right out and say it. "I am cursed."

Her eyebrows go up, but she says nothing. She patiently waits for me to continue.

"I live a regular life. My body can be killed or die of natural causes. When that happens, I enter the Veil. For some inexplicable reason, I cannot move on to the next plane. I can stay in the Veil for years, decades, although time has no meaning there. I stay as long as I'm allowed. Eventually I am pushed out—back into this world."

Her brow furrows with an unspoken question.

"There are so many 'whys' I have too. Why was I cursed? Why can't I move on? Why must I come back time after time? And then there are the two big 'hows.' How was I cursed, and how do I break it? I don't know the answers to either of those."

I let the silence hang between us. Jo's brows are knitted together as she studies my face. Emotion is building in my gut. The bitterness and self-pity I bury down deep and try to forget about is a kettle always on simmer, threatening to boil over at any moment. My words spew forth before I can stop myself.

"I am doubly cursed, you see. Not only must I continue living over and over, but I remember it all, everything. There are so many things I wish I could not remember. So much pain, so much torment. When one has lived for the length that I have and as what I am, hate is no longer simply a feeling thrown at you, but a menacing and tangible force that beats you down until you are dust. I have traveled the world seeking a spell to rid me of my curse. Each time I ascend into the Veil, I spend as much time as I am able searching the ethereal realm for signs or hints of what curse this is, why it was visited upon me, and by whom. I am met with only silence and blank stares."

In the distance, a mournful call repeats several times. My elusive shadow is not far away and I suspect has been listening. I lean back and close my eyes, trying once again to reach out to the white raven. And again, there is nothing, like it is not even there, despite the faintest tug I feel against my energy.

Finally, Jo sets her glass down and leans forward to touch my ankles. "I am so sorry," she whispers, her face reflecting the gravity of my words. I reach for her hands and give them a squeeze.

"You mentioned being burned, hanged, and other awful things that I won't think about. And you remember all of that! I can't imagine what you went through so many times or how you get through all those memories."

47

I bury it all down deep, but I can't say this since my throat has gone tight. I can't feel this anymore. I shake off the welling anxiety and make another drink appear. I take a long draught.

The raven sounds again and gets Jo's attention this time.

"He's always around you, you know," she says absently, looking off behind me again.

"I know." I don't turn around; he won't be there. "But he never shows himself. This has been going on for several lifetimes. I think almost all of them." I can't remember a time when the bird wasn't there.

"Hmm." She sits back in the lounger, glass in hand once more, three-fingers filled—but she's out of ice now.

"Ice?" I ask.

"Please."

I look at her glass and a rocky orb quickly forms amidst the amber liquid.

She whistles. "I wish I could do that. Would save me a lot of trips to the freezer." She lifts her glass to examine the glittering rock. "I've seen you do some pretty incredible things, but this ice business is *slick*." She looks at me then with raised eyebrows. "Is that something you can teach me? To manifest objects?"

"I wish it was, Jo. I have tried to teach others in the past but to no avail. You have to be born with this magick already in you. Don't look so down—you have gifts I don't have. You see auras and energies much better than I, and I've never been very good at incantations or rituals."

She scoffs and continues her questioning. "Were you born like this? I mean, did you always have this kind of power?"

"Yes and no. I don't remember much of my first life, so I can't say for sure if I was born with it, but I believe I was. And I've had a great many years to develop it. As I go from life to life, I get stronger with practice. I've learned many, many things on my own by experimenting. Some were harsh lessons." I turn away, not wanting to remember. "There have been a few occasions where I had a little guidance. A shaman or healer who wasn't too envious or fearful of me has imparted their wisdom, although none could help me with my curse."

"You don't remember your first life? That's odd since you remember all the others."

"I remember bits and pieces. Flashes of smiling faces with blonde hair, a green landscape, but that's about it. It's probably because it was simply uneventful and boring. I've never tried to remember or look back."

Another *hmm* leaves her lips, and she's staring off behind me again.

"I saw the white raven in your memory."

My eyes widen. "Really? I don't recall his presence there at all."

"Yeah, he was there. Up to the right on a window ledge, above the pharmacy sign, when Patricia was at the intersection. It was hard to see him with the sun glare, but it was definitely him."

It's my turn to *hmm*. "Why do you think he doesn't show himself to me? I've asked myself this question for lifetimes."

"I dunno, it's weird." She's fiddling with the talisman on one of her many necklaces. The dark crimson stone is the size of a walnut, with naturally terminated edges of black, affixed to a long black cord with pure silver wire that is now blackened with age. As she rubs the stone with her fingers, it smolders deep within. She calls this pendant Black Fire, for in the dark the stone looks predominately black but its heart glows red when light shines upon it. She uses the stone to help her focus when in trance. Her face is passive, the lines on her forehead are smoother, relaxed, and her eyes fixed on nothing in particular.

"Ravens themselves are messengers from the other side. It's said that white ravens carry secret knowledge. When a white raven shows himself to a witch, it means that the secret knowledge is of dire importance."

Jo is quiet for several minutes. My palms are sweating, but I feel a sudden chill pass over me. I want to prod her to continue but bite my lip instead.

"He is always with you," she finally continues, talisman clutched in her fist. "You two have a connection. Something deep and long-standing."

"Why doesn't he show himself to me?" I can't help myself. My heart pounds in my chest.

She shakes her head slowly. He is behind me now, his call fills the air. I whirl around. "Come to me!" I jump up from the chaise and rush to the edge of the roof. But it's no use. All I hear is the flapping of large wings in retreat. I smack my palms on the coping and the sting shoots up my arms.

This gets Jo's attention and she releases her grip on the talisman, blinking rapidly and inhaling deeply.

"Is he the reason for my curse? Is he my *jailer*?" I've often thought this: that this bird is my guard, keeping a watchful eye on my sentence from afar. Cowardly and cruel.

She comes to me and puts her arm around my waist. "I'm sorry, sweetie. I don't know." She feels my anxiety, the heat coming off my body, and gives me a squeeze.

I wrap my arm around her shoulders and lean my head on top of hers.

"I chased him once for what seemed like *miles*," I say, remembering a life when I was twelve, running through the forest under the bright moonlight in nothing but my nightdress. My determination to catch up to him was thwarted by the many gnarled and twisted branches that snatched at my dress, making me feel like the forest itself was trying to stop me.

She pulls me back to the shade of the pergola. We resume our places on the lounges. Neither one of us speaks for a long time. Jo is fiddling with her talisman again, staring down at the coffee table where she's placed her glass. The edges of the crystal capture the sunlight within its geometric cuts and reflect cheerfully on the stone.

"What do you know about your curse?" The abrupt break in the silence startles me.

"Not really much more than I've already said. I live, I die, I come back, I remember."

"Even after all this time? I mean, isn't there a Spirit or ghost or some other entity in the Veil that knows anything that would help?"

I snort. "You'd be surprised just how unhelpful ghosts and Spirits are. I have tried conversing with the entities within the Veil. They speak only when they wish and no amount of screaming and begging will help. I think they regard me as an outsider who has somehow managed to infiltrate the Veil."

"Huh." Jo's brain is working. "That's a clue in itself, I think."

"I never thought about it that way." My conversations with those who travel in the Veil have led only to frustration. However, looking back now with different eyes, I see that they did indeed skirt around me and keep their distance.

"What's it like in there?" Jo almost whispers.

"Lonely," I blurt out. Floating aimlessly through an endless sea of grays and blacks, left alone to wander and wonder, is a lonely existence indeed.

"I'm sorry." Jo's face turns sad. I know she wants to ask me more about it but doesn't.

"At first, I didn't know what it was or what was happening," I say without thinking, remembering my first experience entering the Veil. "It was dark and there was no sound or smell, nothing. Beings of white Spirit were moving around me so fast. They would slow to gawk at me and then veer away quickly. I was terrified." I shudder at the memory. "I didn't know what to do or where to go, or what here even was. I was certain I was dead but I didn't remember dying. I called for my mother and father, I cried, I ran—or flew rather—and I begged for help as the Spirits shied around me. It was quite terrible."

Jo's eyes have gone big, and I realize I've scared her in speaking so badly about the afterlife.

"Oh, no!" I scoot down to the end of the chaise. "It won't be like that for you, I promise! Really. I've watched Spirits enter and be greeted by guides or be surrounded by the Spirits of loved ones long passed." I squeeze her knee and her face relaxes a bit. "Which makes me think you are right about them shying away from me being a clue. I never saw that happen to any other Spirit. It's like I don't belong there."

Jo nods and pats my hand. "I wonder if my Nana will be there," she says, sighing.

"Spirits typically don't retain the emotional baggage from their lives. There are exceptions, obviously, but I don't see why she wouldn't come unless she's moved on to a different plane."

Jo considers this a moment, then murmurs an agreement. She leans forward and puts her hands on either side of my face. "What you've gone through, what you have experienced, breaks my heart." Her eyes fill with tears, and I put my hands atop hers. "I am so sorry." Her tears fall freely.

I put my arms around her and hug her tight. The embrace of a friend such as she, such as I've never known, brings a lump to my throat, and I find myself misty-eyed as well.

"It has taken me a long time not to dwell on what has happened to me and even longer not to be made bitter by it." This is a partial lie because I am bitter, but I try not to think about it. "And to be completely honest," I pull away so that she can see the sincerity in my face, "this life—moving to Salem, deciding to open a shop, *you*, and Sylvia—has made me the happiest I've ever been. I could never have imagined I would have this life, this happiness. And you are a big part of that."

Jo bursts into fresh tears and pulls me tight. Her sobs turn into soft laughter as she rocks us side to side.

The sharp cry of a raven pulls us out of our comforting embrace. Jo seems a little embarrassed.

"Let's go see what my daughter is up to downstairs. I'll bet she's got all the new ritual candles burning at once, the little pyro."

# Chapter 6

The shipment that arrived last week has been unpacked and set out on display. I am going through the inventory list again to make sure I've not forgotten anything. I'm too focused on checking the candle varieties to hear someone coming onto the porch. The bells jingle as the door opens, and I turn to greet my first customers of the day with a welcoming smile. It falls at the sight that greets me.

Being shoved through the door by his upper arm is an angry teenaged boy guided by an even angrier man. A *handsome* angry man. I'm glad I put a little effort into my appearance today. However, a great deal of hostility is radiating off them both. Jo and Sylvia have stopped their respective puttering and are also admiring the man. Sylvia's eyes widen as she recognizes the boy, but she says nothing.

The man quickly scans the store and locks eyes with me. A flash of surprise takes over his face, and he seems to have lost the words he had ready to use. He swallows and takes another step forward. "Excuse me, ma'am, are you the manager?"

"I am the owner, yes." I clasp my hands in front of me.

Tightening his grip on the boy's arm, the man thrusts him towards me. "My nephew has something he wants to return."

"Oh?" The young man has my full attention.

The boy doesn't meet my gaze; the floor seems to hold greater interest. Instead, his hand shoots out and in his open palm is an Eye of Horus pendant. With a sharp inhale, I snatch it from his fingers. He's not purchased it. I know exactly what is sold in my shop each day.

I glare down at the boy and take a few steps towards him. "Why, you little son of a—"

"*Easy*," interrupts Jo from across the room. She's giving me her reproachful eye, punctuated by hands on hips. The man's hard eyes are on me also, but I ignore him.

I turn the valuable and delicate pendant over in my hands to check for damage. I march over to the case where I placed it only last week. The blue velvet cushion that the pendant should be on is bare except for the indentation where it had lain.

"Sylvia, did this young man purchase this pendant?" My question is pointless, but I want to make him squirm.

"Nope." Sylvia holds her chin high. "I remember him and his buddy, though. They came in a few days ago. I think you were over at Mom's."

The man stands with his arms folded tightly across his chest, glaring at his nephew. "I'm sorry about this, ma'am." He jabs the boy with his elbow. "You need to say something, Will."

Will buries his hands deep in the front pockets of his jeans. His 'sorry' is barely audible.

"You sound *really* sorry." His attitude infuriates me further. Hands on hips, I take another step towards the boy. "So, William Jacobs, you and Kyle Crandall decided that stealing from a witch was a good idea?" At hearing his name and that of his friend, his head snaps up at me, eyes wide.

The man, taken aback, unfolds his arms and addresses me. "You know my nephew?"

"I do not." I place the pendant carefully on the counter. "But I do know that it was his idea to come to my shop and Kyle's idea to distract Sylvia here with a little bit of flirting while your nephew lifted something."

Sylvia's jaw drops, and she stares at the boy who's now gone red in the face.

"So that was a trick?" She doesn't hide the hurt on her face. "Kyle doesn't really want to go out with me?"

Will lets out a derisive snort. "Kyle doesn't do fat asses." That remark earns a snarl from me and a smack on the back of his head from the man. Will stumbles forward, glowering at his uncle.

Sylvia's face falls. Her eyes well up and heat fills her cheeks. Sylvia may be big-boned with a round face, but 'fat' does not apply. Children today are as cruel as ever.

"Now that's enough out of you! You apologize *right now.*" He grabs Will's arm again, a vein pulsing at his temple.

"Not likely." Will jerks away from his uncle and stomps out the front door. The man stares in disbelief, jaw clenched and neck muscles constricted, as his nephew marches down the steps.

I am too livid to speak.

*Get back here.*

The boy lurches to a halt in mid step. Confusion twisting his face, Will turns around and comes back through the front door. His uncle takes a step towards him, but I touch his arm. Standing so close, I feel the man's body heat and smell the faint aroma of bergamot and sandalwood. Will slams the door, irate and shocked by whatever has propelled him back into my shop.

"You are a nasty little prick, William Jacobs." I sense the uncle's eyes on me again, but he says nothing. "Come here," I point to the floor before me. Jo moves towards us.

*I'm fine, Jo. I won't hurt him.*

Her eyebrows go up and she stops, hovering just behind him.

I find his feeble attempt to fight against my will humorous. His defiant face glistens with sweat, and he is breathing rapidly through his nose, with fists clenched at his sides.

He frowns but cannot help turning his head to Sylvia. "I am sorry for what I said, Sylvia." His jaw is working hard against the words. His uncle's mouth drops open. Sylvia straightens but remains silent. Knowing her, if she spoke now it would be nothing but colorful expletives involving sexual acts he could perform upon himself.

"Give me your hand." His hand shoots out, palm up. I take it, and he watches helplessly as I make slow circles on his palm with my thumb.

"The next time you wish to steal something, William Jacobs, you will think better of it." A small flame sparks into his palm and he yelps, jerking his hand back instinctively. I allow it. The uncle stares, uncertain of what he's seen. Sylvia doesn't conceal her smirk.

*This will last for as long as you hold that anger, boy.* Will's mouth falls open at hearing words in his head. His face hardens, and he glares up at me. My lip curls, enjoying the turmoil raging behind his eyes.

"Unless there is something else your uncle wants from you, you may leave." I drop my control over him.

Will shudders at the release and stumbles slightly. His blustering is now gone, replaced by fear. He bolts for the door and hits the yard in a dead run.

"You have got to tell me how you did that," the man says, staring open-mouthed at his fleeing nephew. "*My* kid would never..." He doesn't finish and shakes his head.

I turn on my heel. My attempts to withhold my temper are failing. I need to get away before I say something I'll regret. I know everyone's eyes are following me as I stalk up the stairs. Maggie is at my heels, tail up and ears perked.

As I round the top of the stairs out of sight, I have to stop and take several calming breaths. Why am I so angry over this? Maggie moves beside me and sits. Her head tilted, she lets out a concerned whine.

I wipe the tiny beads of sweat from my forehead and lean against the wall. Suddenly exhausted, I slide to the floor. Maggie whines again and lays her head beside me. I smile at her loving eyes. Her tail swishes gently back and forth.

Hearing movement downstairs, I close my eyes, taking in the scene with my Sight.

"Well, uh...okay." The man looks around awkwardly and rubs his hands together. "I guess I'm done here. Have a good day, ladies." He nods to Jo and Sylvia and heads for the door.

"Don't mind Aven," Jo says, stepping forward. "She's very protective of her shop."

"That's understandable. Nobody likes their stuff stolen." He glances around the store with an appraising eye. "Especially by a prick teenager," he says under his breath then looks at Sylvia. "I am really sorry for what he said to you. He's been a real handful since his dad went to Afghanistan, but that's no excuse, I know. He will definitely be grounded for this." He clicks his tongue.

"If I had done any of this when I was his age, my ass would have been red for a week."

Sylvia gives him a weak smile and then busies herself behind the counter.

Jo laughs in agreement. "Same here. It's totally different nowadays."

"Yeah, and not really for the better, if you ask me." He extends his hand to Jo. "I'm Calvin, by the way. Cal. Cal Jacobs."

"Josephine Riddle, Jo for short. I live right over there. And this is my daughter, Sylvia." He nods to Sylvia and says hello. "I've got a little business myself but nothing like this. I mostly do readings and spirit communication."

Cal laughs then stops himself at Jo's expression.

"I'm sorry, I shouldn't have laughed. I just don't believe in any of that."

"Quite all right." Jo waves away his comment. "Some people simply have a lack of vision." She smirks at Cal who chuckles and continues towards the door.

"Well, it was nice meeting you two even though it was like this." He looks up at the stairs and opens his mouth. He swallows his words and turns away.

Both women watch him walk down the cobblestone pathway to the gate.

"Nice butt," Jo mutters to herself, smiling fondly.

"Mother!"

"What? I ain't dead." She throws her daughter a look and starts up the stairs.

She gets to the top and notices me on the floor with Maggie. She pulls over a chair from the kitchen table and sits beside me.

She's staring down at me with mock censure.

"Well, well, well," she says, exhaling loudly, arms crossed over her chest. "Seems you aren't *all* powerful then."

"I never said I was." I turn away with my nose in the air. Maggie is looking back and forth between me and Jo, her head still on the floor.

"Hell," she snorts.

"What are you snorting at?" I slide myself up the wall. "Want a sandwich?"

"No, thanks." She gets up and returns the chair to the table. "I'm going to ask that guy out to lunch."

"Seriously?" I turn around and receive the raised eyebrow. "I mean, good for you!" I quickly turn back around and busy myself with sandwich making. "You could do with a little cougaring."

"I was actually thinking the same about you." She gives me an exaggerated series of winks when I look back at her.

"It wouldn't be cougaring if he's older than me," I say matter-of-factly.

"Honey, you are *definitely* older than he is."

I stare at her confused for a moment and then realize what she means. I wrinkle my nose at her.

"He was pretty handsome." Then my face sours. "But that little bastard of a nephew…"

"Speaking of, how did *that* happen? How did you not know something had been taken? You are worse than a junkyard dog!"

"I think that's what made me so angry. I missed it! I can't believe that little punk got the better of me." I sit in the chair next to her, arms tight across my chest. "I wasn't in the shop at the time, but *still*. I should have felt something was missing."

"Well, you really are overwhelmed right now. I mean with getting the shop ready, all the delayed shipments, planning the grand opening bash, that tiff you had with little Miss Perfect Pants last week, and now the business with that Stiles girl. Goddess knows what you had to do to get that rooftop terrace set up. And, truth be told, I think the bottle you keep everything stuffed into leaks from time to time. Oh, yeah, and the fact you haven't been laid in how long?"

My cheeks bloom red. "Shut up!"

I'd forgotten about Miss Perfect Pants, as we fondly refer to the "new age" store owner a few blocks away. Mandy has disliked me from the instant I introduced myself a few months ago. Jealousy is never so ugly as when it's worn like a second skin. She bills herself as a "medium" and specializes in channeling departed loved ones. She does a wonderful display of carefully placed lights, a bit of manufactured smoke, some strategic aromatherapy, and a performance worthy of an Oscar. After she snidely insulted me on our second encounter, I told her as much in front of a store full of people. She actually lunged at me and attempted to claw my face with her stiletto nails. I grabbed her wrist in mid swing. Mandy's display was overly dramatic which I'm sure was orchestrated to show how unjust my comments were. I left her store with her spewing obscenities at me.

That night, she had a terrible case of itching scalp. I do love my petty revenges. It's taken me many lifetimes to embrace the fact that I can, and should, defend myself or retaliate when it's called for. Though I seem to be pettier in this life than ever before. Then again, this age is full of deserving assholes.

# Chapter 7

"No, don't put the big one in the front. Somebody is bound to knock it off with an elbow or something," Jo directs Sylvia as they rearrange the crystal ball collection.

Even though Jo has her own business, which is by appointment only, she spends a great deal of time helping me. I don't mind in the slightest. In fact, I love having her around and can't imagine her not being a part of this. I've come to consider her a sister and, sometimes, a mother. Her easy way and positive attitude make her company a joy.

Sylvia huffs. "But it's so cool looking. You can't see it behind the others." Her hands tremble under her mother's scrutiny. The large quartz sphere slips from her fingers as she places it on the stand. Both ladies shriek and grab for it before it hits the floor.

"See! Clumsy girl," Jo snaps, reaching to take the ball from Sylvia who tucks it into her belly.

"It's not me! *You* are making me nervous. Go away!"

Jo gives her daughter a snide look. "You break it, you bought it." She turns away, nose in the air, not seeing Sylvia's tongue jutting out at her.

I shake my head at them and go back to the shop's kitchen. It's funny to watch Jo and Sylvia, who is ridiculously like her mother, spar during the smallest of tasks.

The front door bells peal through the shop. With my Sight, I see Cal, much to my surprise. I dart to the microwave to check my reflection and run my hands through my hair, tucking the wayward sides behind my ears. Good enough.

"Hello again, ladies!" Cal's booming voice is much more amiable than before. Wondering why he's back, a twinge of irritation flares up at the thought that his nephew took something else and he's come back to return it. I push that aside; I've checked everything twice and all is accounted for.

Sylvia has moved into the library and pretends to be busy arranging books, ignoring Cal's entrance. I sense that she's still embarrassed, but she's a strong girl and the events of yesterday will be forgotten in a few days' time. I feel a twinge of envy at Sylvia's ability to forget and move on.

Jo and Cal are laughing at something funny Cal has said, and she playfully smacks his arm. He locks eyes with me as I come around the corner and his cheeks flush slightly pink; he stammers and takes a step back from Jo. Jo tries not to snicker and turns towards a display cabinet, covering her smile with her hand. His reaction to seeing me again makes my stomach flutter in the most pleasant way.

"Welcome back, Mr. Jacobs." I smile sweetly. "I hope your return doesn't mean that something else was pilfered." I eye him with playful suspicion.

His eyes widen. "Oh! No, no," he says with his hands up in surrender. "Nothing like that at all. I was on my way to a job and thought I'd swing by real quick to apologize again."

"That's very kind of you, Mr. Jacobs." I'm trying to be formal, yet Jo is distracting me with her infectious smirks.

"Please," he says, taking a few steps forward, "call me Cal." Only the counter separates us now. The intensity of his gaze makes my cheeks warm.

"All right, Cal." I have to look away.

*Ask him if he wants a tour of the shop,* Jo thinks at me.

"Excellent idea," I blurt out. Jo snorts laughter and Cal looks at me confused.

"Sorry." I wave my comment away, laughing at myself. "Would you care for a tour of the shop? Do you have time?"

He looks at his wrist to check the time on his nonexistent watch. "I'm pretty sure I do."

"Great! Well, let's start back here." I gesture for him to follow me down the hall to my reading room. I mostly want to get away from the many faces of Josephine Riddle.

I sense Cal's eyes watching me as I walk. My body tingles under his gaze. I remember I'm wearing old yoga pants that have seen better days. My top is an even older plain T-shirt that used to be dark red but is now a sickly pink. Cal, however, is nicely dressed in pressed khakis and a deep purple button-down shirt, which fits nicely across his chest. Purple looks very good on him.

*Oh hell, did I put deodorant on this morning?*

Jo bursts into laughter in the front room.

*Get out of my head, lady!* I snap back at her.

*Well, then, shut your damn mind off and I will!* She is still laughing.

Okay, so that was my fault. I was still "broadcasting" as Jo likes to call it.

The door opens at my approach, and I invite him to enter first. He smells of bergamot and sandalwood again—the aroma is much stronger than before, though not overpoweringly so. I inhale deeply after he's walked past.

Once in the room, I begin to close the door out of habit, then I stop myself. I am feeling very awkward right now. Damn that Jo. If she hadn't been giving me her damn smirks or reminded me how long it's been since I've had sex, I'd be much less self-conscious right now. *And* if I wasn't dressed like I'm prepping for a garage sale.

"Well, this is my reading room," I say, fanning my hands out.

Cal looks around. "Reading room? I don't see any books."

Is he playing with me? I can't tell. I laugh anyway. "No, not *book* reading. I read people. I tell them about their lives, their future, or their loved ones, or answer whatever they ask really."

"So, you're a fortune teller?" He looks dubious.

"I don't care for that phrase, but I suppose what I do could be construed as telling someone's fortune." Feeling naked in front of him, I cross my arms over my chest then let them fall back to my sides. I clasp my hands in front of me, trying to stop fidgeting under his scrutiny.

He nods and puts his hands in his front pockets. Walking slowly around the room, he peers at the various curios and wall hangings. He seems to be stalling, or maybe he's as nervous as I am. I find him difficult to read and resist the temptation to peek into his mind.

He gazes up at the painting above the fireplace and then looks back at me.

"That lady looks a little like you."

"Yeah, a little. My hair used to be that long." I self-consciously reach for my hair and secure an errant tress back behind my ear.

He nods again as he surveys the rest of the room. His eyes fall upon the large black drape on the wall across from the fireplace.

"What's that?" He takes a few steps towards it. No one is immune from the appeal of its mystery.

"A portal to the Spirit world," I say with a deadpan face.

His laugh fills the small room. "Right!"

"Okay, so, next room." I exit quickly and wait for him in the hallway.

Back in the front part of the shop, Jo and Sylvia are thankfully out of sight. I don't look to see where they've gone.

Spanning my hands out, I introduce the room he's already been in.

"This is the main section of the shop. After I bought the house, I had the walls removed from the entryway, parlor, and living room to make this area. Knocked out the wall up there so I could have a balcony." He is nodding approvingly as he looks around the cavernous space.

I tour him through the different displays and shelves. "This section is candles and incense, then here are the personal care products. Crystal balls and other divination items are there. Over here is jewelry—some I've made myself." He is standing by the case that holds the pendant his nephew nicked and points to it with an impressed expression. "No, not the Eye of Horus pendant. I found that in Egypt years ago." I continue, pointing at the different sections and describing each. He is nodding and peering as we walk past, obviously unfamiliar with the majority of what I'm pointing to, but making a good effort to show interest. Then I make my way to the room to the left of the front door.

"And here's the library." I love this room. Shelves of dark hand-hewn wood line each wall except for the one with the bay window, which holds a wide window seat, complete with cushions and a cat sleeping in the sunlight.

"That's Arial. Great mouser and napper extraordinaire. She's for sale, too. *Cheap*."

"Ha!" Cal laughs at the sudden sales pitch. "I don't think I need any cats today, but thanks." Arial pays us no attention, not even an ear twitch when she hears me offer to sell her to a perfect stranger.

Cal turns to inspect the bookshelves and jumps at the sight of a big, white dog. "Oh, wow! Pretty dog. Didn't see her there before. Is she friendly?" He steps towards her and she saunters away, going behind the couch.

"Oh, yes, Maggie's friendly but a bit aloof sometimes."

"Gorgeous."

Maggie turns back to him and fans her tail, clearly appreciating his compliment.

The bay window provides an unobstructed view of the waterfall fountain in the front yard. I have sat there many hours, mesmerized by the movement of the rippling water. I've caught Sylvia doing the same but usually with lazy Arial asleep in her lap. The middle of the room holds an antique couch upholstered in dark red velvet and a red and gold high-backed chair where customers can sit and read if they wish. From the shop's kitchen, I'll provide tea, coffee, and pastries for those lingering shoppers. I offer him something.

"Thank you, no. I can't do caffeine after noon. Keeps me awake." He's pretending to be interested in the books, picking a few up and reading the backs.

"I do have decaf." Talking about my shop has relaxed me somewhat, but I can tell he's humoring me.

"I'm good, thanks." He turns and walks towards the doorway. I move aside quickly to get out of his way. He fumbles past me, careful not to come into contact with me.

"So, when did you open?" he asks, standing by the front door, looking antsy.

"Not officially until October 31st. We're having a big Halloween party as the grand opening—more of a promotional thing, really. Unofficially, we opened earlier this month for just a couple of days a week. I won't start advertising until after the grand opening. I want to get used to all of this before the masses come. I hope come, anyway. We get the occasional tourist, but more locals than anyone else." I could keep gushing but stop myself. He's looking pretty disinterested.

I put a big fake smile on my face. "So, um, thanks for coming by. Apology accepted on the nephew thing. It's all good." Speaking fast, I open the front door, wanting to usher him out quickly to relieve his agony.

"Oh, uh, okay." He seems surprised at my sudden change in attitude. "Sorry to keep you," he mumbles as he walks out the door.

"You weren't keeping me," I say quickly, not wanting him to leave. "You just seemed really eager to go."

"I did?" He looks embarrassed now. "I didn't mean to. I just don't get any of this stuff."

I smile at his awkwardness. "There's nothing you need to 'get.' Not everyone believes in magick or divination, and that's okay. To each his own, as they say."

"Right." He's standing on the porch looking around, hands back in his front pockets.

I come out and wave my hands around grandly. "This is the porch."

He lets out a hearty laugh. Several bistro tables dot the long porch. Customers are welcome to sit and enjoy the front garden and the occasional fairy that comes by.

I didn't realize how much I'd been sweating until a breeze wafts through my thin clothing and chills me. I pray he doesn't see how cold I've gotten. The bra I have on does nothing for coverage. Oh gosh, he's noticed. I catch him looking down at my chest, and he grins as he turns away to survey the front yard.

"So, uh, you live here too?" He doesn't face me when he speaks. Movement at the end of the porch has caught his eye. He may have spotted something flying around the New England aster bush. The fairies do love their purple blooms. More than once I've caught them plucking the flowers and donning them as hats and skirts. Fairies can be quite hilarious when they're drunk. Just don't laugh at them—you'll regret it. Sylvia knows this firsthand.

"Yes. Upstairs." I cross my arms over my chest.

"Cool."

*Quick! Ask him out before he leaves!* Jo's thick Boston accent assaults me out of the blue. Where the hell is she? I don't look around.

"Listen," I say, looking at his feet. "I've found a cute little local bar not far if you want to grab a drink…with me." I'm lying. I have no idea where the nearest bar is. "You know, just like, whenever." I sound like a teenager—I feel like one too.

"Yeah, sure, that'd be cool." Teenager number two joins the conversation. He starts down the steps. He's almost to the gate when he turns. "I'll give you a call."

"Sure," is all I can get out of my mouth, and I extend my hand in a thumbs up. I mentally smack myself in the forehead for doing such a stupid gesture.

I watch him walk casually down the sidewalk—he's trying to make it appear casual, anyway—with his hands behind his back, checking out the surroundings.

Childish titters come from the aster. I stop myself from telling them to shut up. You don't tell fairies to shut up. I eyeball the bush a moment and lower my head in shame. A fresh round of tittering follows me into the store.

"Well, that was just *sad.*" Jo is standing behind the counter, shaking her head.

"Shut. Up." I drag my bruised ego into the shop's kitchen for something alcoholic.

"Oh my *gawd*, that was *so* painful." Jo follows me into the kitchen.

"Didn't you hear me tell you to shut up?" I rummage around in the freezer for ice. Damn it, I forgot to turn the ice maker back on after it overflowed. Magick ice it is.

"Well, if it helps, he was just as uncomfortable as you were."

"I sure hope so." I slump into a chair, drink in hand.

We both hear heavy footfalls coming up the steps and give each other questioning looks.

"Aven?" Cal's voice carries into the kitchen as he opens the front door. Jo's eyes go big. She grabs the drink from my hand and shoos me out of the chair.

Wide-eyed, I step out of the kitchen. "Hello. Forget something?"

"Yeah, I did." He laughs at himself and pushes his hands into his pockets again. "I don't have your number, so I can't call you—so I'm back."

I don't hide my grin.

"How about Saturday? Drink at Phil's around eight?"

"Sure. Sounds good." *Where the hell is Phil's?*

"Is that Phil Spicker's place on Webb?" Jo pops out from the kitchen. Cal nods. "I know Phil. He and I go way back. He makes some killer fries." She pats her ample belly and returns to the kitchen.

"See you then." He nods at me and is out the door in less than a heartbeat. I can just see his hands come up to cover his face. My grin gets bigger.

I turn to Jo and gape at her. I'd already written him off as yet another guy scared away by the barest hint of magick—or perhaps by the Garage Sale Queen look.

Jo takes a sip of my gin and tonic. Her face puckers. "How can you drink this nasty stuff?"

# Chapter 8

Josephine Riddle sits on the floor in her cozy parlor amidst a scattering of colorful and bejeweled pillows. This is her sacred space—the place she uses when casting spells, for meditations and vision walking, or anything else that requires quiet and focus. Living in a small house with a teenaged daughter is often a challenge in the quiet department, but when Jo is in her sacred space, quiet is the law. That is one of the few house rules Sylvia actually obeys.

In the comfortable surroundings, Jo sways side to side with the steady beat she taps out on her well-worn medicine drum. Long wisps of incense smoke spiral slowly through the air, surrounding her with the heady scents of Nag Champa and sage. A dozen candles of all shapes and sizes cast the room in a warm golden glow.

On the floor before her is the Black Fire talisman cradled in the talons of a dragon perched on his back legs. With the stone raised high above his head, his expression makes one feel that he will protect the little treasure with all his might. The statue is one of her prized possessions—a gift from Jo's late husband on her thirtieth birthday.

The rare proustite stone reflects bits of light in an almost rhythmic pattern as if to follow Jo's drum beat. In the muted light, the deep crimson of the stone smolders against its black edges. Jo often uses the talisman to focus her Sight, especially when she needs to delve deeply into something specific. She reflects on the spectacular and horrific memory Aven had revealed to her. She can still smell the exhaust from the congested traffic and vividly recalls the bright red blood that slowly seeped from beneath the young girl's head.

The memories make Jo shudder. Being an empath, she feels emotions and energies keenly—so intensely at times that she wears protective charms of obsidian and schorl polished to a high gloss in order to reflect the negativity. However, right now her protective stones hang on the door handle, leaving her open to whatever may come in her vision walk, relying on the watchful eye of the Goddess to keep her from true harm.

Jo is from a long line of heritage witches. Her family tree has roots in the magickal ways that run hundreds of years deep. When she was younger, she veered from the tradition of her family so that she could practice and experience other forms of the Craft. Not following her family's own tradition had not sat well with Jo's mother, but Matilda understood her daughter's need to learn and experiment with other ways.

However, Jo's grandmother wasn't so understanding. For her, you followed the old ways, the ways of your family, without question. Not even on her deathbed did Jo's grandmother forgive her. While Jo has few regrets in her life, this is one. Nana was a powerful and commanding witch and Jo could have learned so much, but in hindsight, Jo realized the old woman's ways simply didn't fit into her lifestyle or how she connected to the Goddess. In rearing her daughter, Jo is letting Sylvia choose her own path, providing guidance when needed or requested. While Sylvia has only a little innate magickal talent, she's become deft at creating medicinal teas and tinctures. Having a child so late in life was a struggle early on, especially after Marty died, but Jo's grown very proud of her sometimes wild and mischievous daughter. Sylvia is definitely from Jo's apple tree.

A light scraping above gets Jo's attention. She feels the presence of the white raven and knows that he is on the roof. He has been coming to her home more frequently lately. He simply watches her. She feels no threat from the striking bird. He often looks quizzical and anxious. The flutter of wings draws her attention to the window where he's landed and is peering through the glass, one eye fixed on Jo. The bird's feathers are unusually bright white for a white raven, which normally have feathers that are more of a cream color. She assesses the creature staring in at her, its wings twitching nervously. His eyes are also unusual for a white raven; his are a brilliant violet, much like those of her good friend, Aven. At the thought of Aven, the white raven lets out an odd cooing sound—almost mournful, Jo thinks. His head is bowed low, and Jo can feel the sadness coming from him.

Jo takes several deep breaths to clear her mind. As she continues to lightly beat the medicine drum, the glow from the flickering candles begins to blend with the coils of incense smoke. Electricity travels the length of Jo's spine. It is beginning.

Jo visualizes her friend, Aven Dovenelle, with the waves of her jet-black hair, the piercing dark amethyst color of her eyes, the angular cut of her cheekbones, the little cleft in her chin, and her very long legs. The image of Aven appears in Jo's mind as clearly as if she were standing before her. Jo then transforms this image from the everyday look of Aven into that of her Spirit, draped in gossamer and surrounded by soft white light. Her Spirit's hands and feet are bound with black cord. Emerging from the ground is a skeletal hand, and it grips the cord tightly. The imagery in Jo's mind is of Aven's curse.

Slowly, the room blurs and begins falling away. Around her, the wisps of smoke twist and shimmy, coalescing into the shape of a large bird. As it circles Jo, the form solidifies into a white raven. While this was not the intended focal point of her meditation, she does not question it. When shapes or sounds, smells or feelings come to her during a vision walk, she lets them enter freely, without fear or hesitation. Everything has a meaning, her grandmother always said. There are no such things as coincidences—the Universe isn't that lazy.

She no longer sits on the floor in her cozy little room. Around her now is a vast, dark forest illuminated by the light of an overly large full moon. The welcoming smells of moss and wet leaves fill Jo's nostrils. She inhales deeply. The night air is cool, and a soft breeze caresses her cheeks and ruffles her long hair.

The moon's glow reflects off the bird's feathers as it angles around her once more to alight on a branch of a dead and gnarled tree, which looks nearly as ancient as the moon itself. The tree stands out not only by virtue of its wicked bends and hooked fingers, but also because it is the only barren thing around her. The forest is lush with all the greens of summer and frequent rain. As the bird lands, the splintering sound of its talons digging into the dead wood makes Jo shiver.

She is not alone in the forest; voices are in the distance, getting closer quickly. They are running in her direction. It's a cacophony of angry shouts, raging cries, and howls, but she can't discern what they are saying. She sees bold lights now through the thick trees; they are torches, she guesses. The lights appear to dance around each other in the darkness, bobbing up and down, to and fro. But this dance is not something Jo wishes to be a part of. Her first instinct is to run but, to her great surprise, she cannot move. She looks down to find her arms and legs bound to the ground with rusty shackles. She finds that she is wet, and the ground beneath her is drenched.

The white raven rises up to an impressive height and stares down at Jo. He seems to not notice the oncoming mob. In that moment, fear grips Jo's chest. Not from the bloodthirsty throng, nor from being chained, but from the bird's hateful glare. It lowers its head and paces on the branch, its fiery eyes never leaving Jo's. She starts to feel lightheaded from the dreadful energy in this vision. She takes a deep breath and visualizes herself surrounded with white, protective light. Seeing the glow emanate from Jo, the raven screams angrily and his wings flare out. His screeching becomes deafening and overpowers Jo's bared senses. She shrieks in pain and flings her arms above her; they are no longer shackled.

The vision is gone. She is back in her cozy little room, which has gone dark now that the candles are extinguished. The smell of burnt feathers turns Jo's stomach.

On the window ledge, the white raven is bowed low, panting heavily. He stares at Jo with a worried eye for a long moment before jumping off into the night sky.

Shaken and gasping, Jo needs a drink. She half expects a glass to appear with whiskey and a single ice cube but no, Aven isn't here.

The malevolence of the vision lingers and leaves the taste of moldy water in Jo's mouth. She calls out to the Goddess asking for the calming of her heart and mind, the purge of the negative forces that grip her. In the quiet, she visualizes the warm embrace of the Goddess. Her heartbeat slows, and she can swallow without fear of that wretched taste. After a few minutes, she uses a nearby stool to push herself up. She quickly pulls the protective stone necklaces from the door handle and places them around her neck. Once under their influence, she feels more herself again, although she knows that sleep will not come to her tonight.

# Chapter 9

As the claw-foot tub fills with hot water, I add a few drops of frankincense and lemongrass essential oils to calm my nerves. The luscious aroma quickly fills the small room. I've been anxious all day about my date with Cal tonight. A relaxing bath will calm me. The bathroom door creaks open, pushed by a cat who has a dog on her heels. I'm not allowed to be in the bathroom alone. It's nice to have their company. When I talk to myself, it feels less awkward. With an exaggerated sigh that only a Pyrenees can make, Maggie sprawls herself along the wall opposite the tub. Arial hunkers down on the toilet lid and settles, wrapping her tail around her body. I'll have an audience while I bathe.

The many candles around the bathroom are lit with a single thought, and the lights over the sink wink out. I pull off my clothes and ease into the water. Lying back with a contented sigh, I close my eyes.

I lose all track of time when I'm in the bathtub. Water is my element. Whether it's watching a flowing river or listening to a bubbling creek or even hearing the trickling laps of a fountain, water fills me with a peace that little else can. While I have plenty of time before meeting Cal, I've set the alarm on my cell phone just in case. It's too quiet, so another thought prompts Gregorian chant from the CD player in my bedroom.

Something pricks the edge of my tranquility. It's very faint, so I pay it no mind. It's probably just the neighbors arguing again. I tune it out and focus on the undulating plainsong of the Gregorian monks.

It's not long after that a sharp stab of negativity hits me. Arial's hiss and the deep growl from Maggie combined with my own feeling puts me on full alert. I open my senses to discover what is there. Something is speeding towards me. It's filled with a dark eagerness that makes me nervous.

The pressure against my energy is getting stronger and closer. Both animals are up, hackles raised. I'm very curious as to what or *who* this is, so I let it come. I close my eyes and lie back again. Outwardly, I'm the picture of relaxation.

An acrid stench attacks my nostrils, and I can't help but grimace. I open my eyes to see the bathroom filled with a faint red glow that's growing stronger. Arial darts from the bathroom with an angry hiss, and Maggie stands in front of the tub, her attention fixed to the corner of the ceiling across from me.

Inky black tendrils form within the darkness of the corner. They swirl and twist, trying to form a more solid mass but seeming to lack the ability to do so. Short tendrils lash out in my direction. The stench grows stronger, choking the room. The pungent odor is familiar, but I can't place it.

I stay within the confines of the tub, feeling a small measure of protection from the water over my naked body. Despite the heat in the room, the water has gone cold.

"Who are you and what do you want?" There is no fear in my voice.

The answer comes in the form of a sickly coughing sound and a stench blown in my face. I gag.

"Morris Stiles!" I am appalled. The swirling collection of tendrils emits a rough, gurgling sound. Is that laughter?

How has his Spirit come to be here? An unwelcome Spirit from my past returning—this has not happened before. His anger and hatred pushes at me.

I glare through narrowed slits at the shape shifting grotesquely on my ceiling.

"You seem very pleased with yourself to have found me." The response is more harsh cackling.

"I'm not sure why you are so pleased. Here I am, a full-fledged *witch*—just as you suspected—happy, healthy, and successful in a future world you can have no part in." I sneer at the loathsome mass.

The tendrils splay out in all directions accompanied by an enraged howl. I laugh, which enrages him more. The core of the blackened mess grows slightly, and the red glow that fills the room deepens.

The face of Morris Stiles is burned into my memory. The ruddy, pock-marked skin dotted with pustules and few teeth gracing his mouth. His constantly sunburned head protected only by a few wisps of greasy gray hair and gnarled hands with crooked fingers, misshapen from years of cattle work and fighting. His hatred for himself was exacted from all those around him. The more innocent the better. His Spirit has retained the same self-loathing and hostility. It appears he's sought the one person who bested him.

It doesn't take me long to realize how this happened. I shake my head at myself and cover my face with my hands.

"I caused this. This is my doing."

As if to agree, Morris's shapeless form lets out a shriek that rattles the window panes and mirror. Maggie lunges upward, barking and snapping. The mass of tendrils jerks back from the dog and recoils into the corner.

"Not what's happened to you, you evil bastard! You *deserved* what I did to you!" I slam my fist on the side of the tub. "And don't you dare for one second think you did not!" I push my energy at him, pushing his tendrils back into the mass. The red glow in the room dims.

"I caused your *return*. I made Melissa Stiles aware of you. She didn't know a single thing about you, her loathsome great-great-grandfather, until I told her of you." She must have started looking into her genealogy. Her energy has given him form, but to this extent? My thoughts change gears. "What have you been doing to her? There's no way just her thinking about you would have given you enough strength for *this*."

The mass only cackles, the core pulsing with each wicked sound.

Rage washes over me. "You son of a *bitch*!" That poor girl!

I rise from the water, compelled upward by my wrath. As I square my body to face him, the water is morphing into blue and white fire, rising around me. The bathtub is now a cauldron of white fire, and the droplets coming off me are bits of blue flame. The red gloom that dominated the room is now eclipsed by cold blue light. The flames lick up around me and climb the wall behind me.

My voice sounds of gravel as I address him, hands raised at my sides.

"Morris Jasper Stiles, you are a vile and deplorable Spirit. You are not welcome here. I command you to leave my home and to never return!"

The blue and white flames burst towards him. They cut into the shrieking mass. The form writhes, screaming in pain. I send another wave of fire and the blackness bursts like broken glass. Deafening screams fill my ears but are quickly extinguished.

In the moment he is gone, the fire pulls back to me. The blue light fades, and the bathroom is once again filled with the golden glow of candles. Maggie relaxes and goes to the corner, sniffing the air.

I look at her with sad eyes and sigh. "This is what happens when you meddle."

# Chapter 10

I am dizzy from the surge of energy so I leave the tub slowly and sit on its edge. I feel violated by Morris's visit and, despite the bath, dirty. It takes several deep breaths before my pulse quiets and the ringing in my ears subsides. I shake my head at myself for what I've done. I will check on Melissa in the morning.

I consider cancelling with Cal but then remember I don't have his number. Resigned, I push myself up. There's more than an hour before meeting him, but I *need* to get out of the house. After towel drying my hair, I run my fingers through it, pulling it up in a twist and securing it with a silver hair chopstick. I dress quickly, opting for comfort rather than to impress.

In my favorite pair of stretchy jean capris and a peasant blouse of dark red, which Jo says is my color, I feel a little better. Around my neck is my favorite pendant, shaped from a flawed piece of round, black jadeite. The inclusion is spectacular. In the right light, you can see a circle of slightly iridescent gray and dark green—the perfect new moon.

The evening is warm, but there is a pleasant breeze with a faint scent of the ocean wafting in at times. I wander around my neighborhood, delighting in petting the dogs that are being walked and chatting idly with their owners. The walk helps clear my mind and rid me of the unpleasant thought of Morris Stiles seeing my naked body. My selfish thoughts then return to Melissa, and a wave of guilt makes me flush.

My limited experience with local bars led me to expect Phil's to be the typical dive, but it surprises me. While still a bit divey, it has been well cared for and looks very clean. There is the barest hint of cigarette smoke from years ago when smoking was allowed. The light fixtures are yellowed but not from age or grime. Seeing how they all match and are clean, my guess is that they were deliberately selected to keep the mood low-key and cozy. It worked.

The decor consists of memorabilia from local sports teams and the occasional framed picture of dogs playing poker or pool. A fairly large bulldog statue sits in the middle of the backbar, facing the front door so as to greet each customer. It's the first thing one notices upon entering; you don't often see a statue of a dog wearing a black satin top hat and smoking a pipe.

Cal is already there when I arrive. He raises his arm to get my attention. He's at the far back table, opposite the fairly new jukebox and tiny patch of dance floor checkered in black and what-used-to-be-white linoleum. At this hour on a Saturday night, Phil's has but a handful of customers—all local by the looks of them. At the obligatory pool table, a man seems to be teaching his attentive young son the finer points of the game. Two older gentlemen are seated at the bar watching the news on the small TV up in the corner. A tall man with a shiny pate, presumably Phil, is behind the bar in lively conversation with a young man in gym clothes who has what appears to be a glass of milk in his hand. As Phil hears the screen door bang closed, he locks eyes on me and belts out a warm greeting. I smile and wave in return. I like him already.

Cal gets up from his chair at my approach.

"Hey there." He pulls out the chair across from his. "Have a seat."

A tall glass beer mug rests on the table, empty. Cal seems a good deal more relaxed than before. His wide smile accentuates the tiny laugh lines around his bright blue eyes. I take the proffered seat and lean forward, my elbows on the table.

"You started without me." I nod at the glass.

"Ha, yeah," he says. "I was done earlier than I expected so I decided to just come here and hang out."

"You come here a lot?"

"Depends on how you define *a lot*." He laughs lightly and waves Phil over.

"I love seeing new faces," Phil says as he approaches, wiping his hands on a towel and then tossing it over his shoulder. His thin face stretches tight with a genuine smile, full of strong, healthy teeth.

"Phil Spicker," he says, extending a still damp hand. I acknowledge his greeting with a firm grip of my own. "Welcome to my dog's place."

At my confused expression, he nods over his left shoulder, still gripping my hand. In the darkened corner just behind us is a large dog bed filled with an even larger bulldog on his back, all four legs up in the air. This elicits an involuntary 'aww' from me.

"Yeah, he's a mess," Phil says, gazing with loving eyes at the old dog. "His name is Phil, too."

"I'm Aven," I say as he turns back to me, finally releasing my hand.

"She owns that new witch shop on Derby," Cal says.

"Ohhh." Phil's eyebrows rise in recognition. "So *you're* the one." He eyes me with mock disdain.

"Oh, my." I put my hands over my heart, feigning surprise. "Does my reputation precede me?"

Cal's expression tells me that he doesn't know what Phil's referring to, and I don't elaborate.

"It does indeed." He crosses his arms over his chest. "You've caused quite a little storm there, haven't ya?" By his expression, I know he is having fun with me.

"I don't know what you mean, good sir." I put on my best innocent face.

Phil guffaws. "I'm sure ya don't!" His boisterous laugh startles Phil the dog. He gives his owner a snort then lets his head fall back and hang over the lip of the dog bed.

"What can I get ya?"

I ask him what brands of gin he carries and, thankfully, there's an acceptable one. I order a gin and tonic, healthy. He clicks his cheek in acknowledgment and heads for the bar. I ask Cal where the ladies room is and excuse myself.

"What was all that about?" Cal asks, rising at my return. He reaches for his beer glass, forgetting it was empty.

"Well," I say, putting my innocent face on again, "apparently, I've pissed off a few shop owners for a couple of reasons."

Phil returns with a highball glass in one hand and a beer in the other.

"Only a couple?" He winks at me and I grin back. He doesn't linger. I'm sure he thinks Cal and I are on our first date. Can you call this a date? An experienced barman like Phil knows when to hang around and when to make himself scarce.

"Phil knows everything that happens in this neighborhood, if you couldn't tell." Cal takes a long draught of his dark beer.

"I can see that." I take a sip of my drink. The gin has a nice bite.

"Anyway, after I closed on the house, I got all the permits and everything I needed for the renovations in record time—without any hassles or delays. I guess that didn't sit well with a lot of people. There are rumors floating around that I bribed some people to make it happen so quickly. Which is bullshit, by the way." I take another sip of the nicely prepared gin and tonic. I notice Phil staring at me, and I raise my glass to him approvingly. He winks and turns away. "I can be quite charming when I need to be."

"I'll bet you can," Cal says with a lascivious twinkle in his eye. He immediately regrets his words and his cheeks flush. I'm also a little embarrassed but give him a chuckle to ease his discomfort.

"Nobody likes competition," Cal says, "especially if they think you'll outdo them."

He stares at his beer then finally makes full eye contact. "It's a nice place. Looks good. I've only been in a couple other stores like that, doing plumbing jobs, and they've all been, well, either too creepy goth—is goth the right word?—or too hippy for me." I nod to his goth question.

"I know what you mean. I refuse to be a contributor to the witch or pagan stereotype. My shop has only those things imbued with real magick."

He makes a face at my last few words, but I ignore it for now.

"If that cuts into my bottom line, then, oh well. It won't send me to the poorhouse." I have accrued a great deal of wealth over the centuries, hidden away deep in a dormant volcano on a deserted island. It is mostly gold and jewels as paper money either deteriorates or becomes obsolete over time.

"You mentioned plumbing jobs. I guess you're a plumber?"

"Yes and no. My family has a plumbing business, and I help run it. When I was younger, I did a lot of the work, but I'm older now and hire younger backs for that kind of work." His beer mug is already empty.

I ask him more about the business and what it's like to work with family. He beams as he talks about them. The business was started by his father, who passed a few years ago. Cal runs it in partnership with his sister, who is a few years older than he is; he confesses she's the smarter of the two. His younger brother had no interest in plumbing and opted for a life in the military. While he is in Afghanistan, Cal is taking care of his son. Will's mother ran off when he was a baby. At the mention of Will's name, a frown takes over my mouth. Cal notices and quickly changes topics. I watch him talk. His full lips make me think he is a good kisser, and I like the way his eyes light up each time he mentions the business or his sister.

His body relaxes as he talks. It's helping me relax also. Or, perhaps, the strong drink deserves the credit. He launches into talking about his 'younger days' when he was part of the Boston College Men's Crew. He loved rowing but had to give it up when he tore his shoulder. As he talks, he accentuates important words with hand gestures. His hands are rough, and it's obvious that he chews his nails, but they look strong from years of hard work and rowing. He's kept his athletic build. The golden lighting brings out the blond in his hair, and reveals hints of silver threaded throughout the slight waves. When I first saw him, full of fury and stress, I still thought him quite handsome. Now that we are inches from each other and his mood has warmed with pleasure rather than anger, he's a great deal more handsome to me.

At the end of what Cal has apologized for as an unrequested, long-winded tale of his life, Phil comes over unsolicited with two more drinks. We both give him a smile and he's away again, this time sporting a grin.

"Don't let me do all the talking," Cal says, turning the glass's handle towards him.

"It's not like I'm going to tell you to shut up and let me say something." We both laugh. *Besides, you have a really sexy voice.*

I settle back into the chair. "Well, you know I run a 'witchy' shop and live there also, and I bribed a few people to get my permits." He acknowledges my sarcasm with a nod and a grin. "I share the house with a lazy cat, Arial, whom you declined to purchase, and a Great Pyrenees, Magdalyn, or Maggie, for short. Never married, no kids, no living family remaining. My hobbies include reading, gardening, making things like candles and soap, drinking piña coladas, and getting caught in the rain."

He laughs aloud. Our knees make a connection as he relaxes in his chair. Neither one of us remarks on this or moves our knees. My attempt to put myself at ease with jokes and sarcasm has been thwarted by physical contact. A warming sensation fills my belly.

Staring at my glass, I continue.

"But seriously, my life's dream has been to be accepted for who I am, and in moving to Salem, I've finally found that place. Money is not the reason for my shop. It's more of a vindication; I can finally live as I am, be who I am—for the most part any-way—and having this shop fills me with that sense of acceptance." Surprised by my unexpected openness with this stranger, I now feel exposed and embarrassed. I search for words to inject a bit of sarcasm to alleviate my discomfort but find none.

His eyes study my red face. "So you really believe in this witchcraft stuff? It's not just for show?"

I meet his gaze. "I do."

He purses his lips and nods absently, like a bobble-headed doll.

"I take it that you don't believe in magick?"

"I do not." He is looking at his beer. He opens his mouth to continue but seems to think better of it.

I don't hide my grin. If this goes anywhere, I can't wait to see the look on his face when I prove him wrong.

"It's okay, go ahead and say what you were going to. You won't offend me, truly. I've heard it all."

"I don't want to run you off already," he says. "I'm told I can be a real ass, so I'll keep my comments to myself for now."

My heart skips a beat at hearing that he's worried he'll run *me* off.

"Okay, fair enough. But I look forward to continuing this particular conversation." I raise my glass, and he clinks his with mine. He doesn't shy away from my gaze. Hooray for liquid courage.

After ordering some of Phil's killer fries, which we end up sharing with Phil the dog, our conversations go back and forth from his life to mine. Most of mine I have to lie about, like my parents and childhood, but I'm quite practiced at doing so.

The pressure of our knees touching has gotten increasingly firmer. Neither one of us has acknowledged this contact. I think Phil has turned down the air conditioning because it's too warm now. I'm hoping my deodorant is holding up. Cal has rolled up his long sleeves.

Phil comes over to the table, claps his hands loudly to ensure he has our full attention, and rubs them together. "Sorry, kids, but it's getting to be closing time."

"You're kidding?" I'm surprised he's closing so early.

"It's almost midnight. This isn't Boston, toots. I don't make enough money to keep this place open until two a.m. in the off-season."

I can't believe how quickly the time has gone by, or that I've just been called 'toots'. I don't want to say goodnight to Cal so soon.

"Time flies." Cal scoots back his chair.

Phil flips down a slip of paper in Cal's direction and turns away. I ask him what my portion is and he waves me off. "I got it," he says, digging for the wallet in his back pocket.

"No way. I must have had, what, six drinks? What's the damage?"

Cal looks at the check. "You only had four, *slacker.*"

I can't help but stick my tongue out at him. I may be a little tipsy. He looks for a moment and resists making a comment. Now I'm embarrassed and don't press for him to say what he was about to.

As Phil takes Cal's money and the empty glasses, I want to block the awkwardness creeping back in. "So, did you walk here?"

"Yeah, I'm not far. You?"

"Yep. Was a great chance to see the neighborhood." I sit back in my chair, rubbing the sweat from my palms onto my pants.

"Cold?"

"Just the opposite," I laugh. He grunts an agreement.

Not sure of what to do next, I get up. Cal quickly follows suit, and we head for the door. We say our goodbyes to Phil the human, and Phil the dog pads over to see us out. I have a new best friend. I scratch his chin and rub his sleepy head.

The wind is surprisingly cool, or I was just that warm, and a delightful shiver passes over me. I hadn't realized how stifling it had gotten in the bar. Cal assumes I am cold and laments not bringing a jacket because he would be offering it to me now. I thank him for his gesture with words and a squeeze on his upper arm. His muscle flexes involuntarily under my palm, making my fingers tingle. My hand lingers there a few seconds longer than it should. A pleasant warmth travels through my body when I realize I'm standing only inches from him. I finally drop my hand, knowing he's looking at my face but not able to bring myself to look up at him. What a silly girl I feel like right now. Jo is hearing about none of this.

I clear my throat. "Well, I'm this way," I say, gesturing with my thumb behind me.

"I'm just the opposite." He looks behind him and then at me again. "But I could still walk you home, I guess."

"Thank you, that's very sweet, but I'm good." The prospect of him returning home with me is an extremely tempting one, not that anything would happen, but the visit from Morris has knocked me down more than I want to admit.

"You sure? It may not be the safest walk at night." He looks a bit disappointed.

I can't help but laugh. "I'll be totally fine, I promise."

"Okay, then." He takes a step back, hands going into his front pockets. "Have a good night. Be safe."

"You too." I can't find anything else to say, so I turn.

I hear his feet scraping and turn to see him stepping towards me.

"Sorry." He stops short of running into me. "I forgot to say that this was a great way to offset the crappy way we met." We hadn't talked about the incident with his nephew.

"I couldn't agree more."

In the glow of the streetlight, he fidgets, then pushes his hands back into his pockets.

This is stupid. I put my arms around his neck for a hug. A hug is a perfect way to hide your face when you're nervous and also helps make you less nervous. He hesitates only for a second before putting his arms lightly around my waist.

His body is solid and so very warm. His arms squeeze a little tighter around my back, and I sense him sniff my hair. I just want to close my eyes and relax my entire body into his embrace. But I must let go and walk away before my legs turn into complete jelly.

I pull away slowly and step back. I am really hoping he doesn't try to kiss me. Not yet anyway.

He clears his throat. "Can I call you tomorrow?"

I grin at him. "You still don't have my number."

"Ah, shit." He hangs his head and unclips his phone from its case at his belt. After a few taps on the screen, he hands it to me. "Type in your number, I'll finish the rest. Please."

I enter my number and hand the phone back. While he's occupied, I make my escape.

"Goodnight again, Cal. Talk to you soon." I walk backward a few steps before turning around. He calls back goodnight and continues to watch me as I round the corner.

Once he is out of sight, I jump into the air like a little kid— the biggest grin plastered on my face. I am too elated and the night is too perfect to walk home, so I fly.

# Chapter 11

*I*watch my woman raise her arms into the air and bend her knees. She leaps upward. Rather than coming back to the ground like every other human, she propels upward at a great speed. Not like bird flying, for she has neither wings nor feathers. And yet, she flies.

The man she had been in that building with for many hours peers around the corner. At not seeing her, he calls her name and begins walking in the direction she should be going. After a few paces and no response, he looks around and pulls an object from his waist. It glows brightly. He replaces the item after a moment, shaking his head, and turns back.

I like this man. He has a kind spirit although his displeasure with the boy was very strong. I watched him pull the boy down the sidewalk. His face was tight and hard, and the boy fought against him with every step. Their words were angry. The boy had done wrong, and the man was going to make it right.

I think about following him but only watch him for another moment as he disappears around the other corner. I want to follow my woman as she has not flown since she moved to this loud and crowded place.

She is not far from me. She flies slowly, enjoying the feeling of it. The shimmer of magick is around her, like the ripples of silver water, which keeps her hidden from human eyes. But I can always see her. I can always find her.

*She makes wide banks left and right, savoring the night air. She rolls leisurely with each curve and even from this distance, I can see her wide smile and the happiness in her eyes. She loves to fly; flying always makes her smile. But tonight her smile is from something else.*

*I can get a few inches closer but no more. I try, I have tried, countless times to be near her but I cannot. Her energy is so very strong, and I cannot approach without pain in my head and my heart. Long ago, I thought that it was she doing this to me, hurting me on purpose, pushing me away, not wanting my company. After a time, I discovered this was false. She longs to see me, to be near me, to talk to me—as much, it seems, as I do her. On the many occasions when she has pursued me, I have had to flee. The pain is too much to bear. It feels as if all of my feathers are being plucked out at once. She has called to me, cried to me, so many times, but I cannot come. It weighs heavy on my heart.*

*I do not remember a time without my woman. I have followed her throughout her many lives. Sometimes it takes a long while to find her, but I always do. Her energy calls to me, leaves its trail for me to follow. But then, the pull becomes a push and I must stay back.*

*The other woman, my woman's friend, is quite pleasing to be near. She is happy and smiles and laughs a great deal. She chats with herself in her garden when she thinks no one is looking. My woman trusts her as she has none other in the past. I feel that this woman has strong power. I will speak to her. Perhaps she can help me be near my woman.*

*My woman is home now, alighting quietly on the roof. I perch on an eave several houses down. She has heard movement behind her and turns. Her eyes pass over me and they burn me. I sink my talons into the wood to bear it and hold my breath. I endure it as it is not as bad as if I were closer. The pain passes quickly. She turns away and disappears into the house.*

# Chapter 12

It's a glorious morning. My sleep was untroubled by nightmares or even dreams for that matter. I'm refreshed even though it seems like I put my head on the pillow only a few hours ago.

As I lie under the covers looking at the hint of sunrise through the sheer curtains, my thoughts go immediately to Cal. I can't help but smile. Aside from the palpable awkwardness at more times than I care to admit, last night was wonderful. Remembering the pressure of his knee pushing back on mine makes me flush.

I reach for my phone on the nightstand to check my texts, upsetting a cat's deep slumber as I roll over. Only one from Jo in the wee hours asking if he'll be making me breakfast followed by several winking emoticons. My ears heat with embarrassment. I'm going to ignore her for as long as I can.

A stab of guilt hits me. *Melissa*. I knew what Morris Stiles was capable of as a despicable human, so what he's now capable of as a boundless Spirit fills me with dread. At my quick change in mood, Maggie comes to the bed to check on me. I assure her all is well. Arial is unconcerned and still sleeps in a coil, partially turned on her back, with her paws stretched out behind her head. I rub her exposed chest, which earns me a low mew of disapproval.

As I pour myself a cup of coffee, I force my thoughts away from Melissa to plans for the grand opening. I recruited Sylvia to create the invitation and she should have designs for me today. Jo's been tasked with finding a caterer. These mundane duties are boring and vexing, so when both Jo and Sylvia eagerly offered to help, I was more than happy to delegate.

I putter around in the flowerbed on the roof until the sun peeks above the cityscape. I sense movement in the shop below and hear the coffee grinder's tinny roar cutting into the peaceful morning. A few moments later, the screen door to the roof slams loudly as Sylvia comes through, dressed in bright colors as always, her short hair bobbing with each step. She has a binder tucked under her arm and a mug in her hand.

"Good morning," she says in a sing-song voice, her energy radiating pure excitement.

I stare at her in mock disappointment. "You didn't bring *me* any coffee?"

She stops and her face falls. "Oh, my Goddess, I'm *so* sorry! I'll be right back!" She's at the screen door before I open my mouth.

"I'm just kidding!" I chuckle. "This is my sixth cup."

She turns back relieved. "You got me! Besides, that crazy complicated coffee maker you bought only grinds and brews one tiny cup at a time."

"Because it's an *espresso* machine, not a coffee maker." I shake my head at her, looking as disappointed as I can.

"Yeah, yeah." She waves me off with a laugh. She sets her mug on the edge of the wide-brimmed planter and pulls out the binder, waving it. "I got some stuff for you!" she sings again.

"Great! I can't wait to see them. *But*, and please forgive me, I have a very important errand I have to take care of this morning."

She gives me her best pout, which instantly makes me feel bad. "Don't worry! I won't be gone very long. Promise."

"Totally okay. No worries." She picks up her mug and turns away, then turns back with a leer. "Does this have anything to do with *Cal?*" She draws out his name, waggling an eyebrow.

"Good grief! You are just like your mother. And *no*, it doesn't."

"Bummer," she says as she flips the screen door open with her free hand and slips through it before it hits her. "Mom's dying to hear how it went," she calls back as she trots down the steps.

"I bet she is," I say under my breath.

In my reading room, I draw the heavy velvet drape from the imposing object hanging on the wall to reveal a large baroque mirror.

The black scrying mirror stands as tall as I and twice as wide and is mounted a foot from the floor. The crown and skirt of the mirror flare out slightly from the narrower middle with gentle curves rather than hard corners. Thick, elaborate scrollwork frames the glossy, black surface while a delicate inner frame serves to soften the mirror's intimidating appearance. Unlike any other mirror, even those meant solely for scrying, neither my image nor that of the room is reflected on its surface. What shows is pure blackness, smooth and cold, as the mirror silently waits for its purpose to be invoked.

I stand before it with my arms raised slightly from my sides, palms out. I take several deep breaths to clear my mind and ground my energy. Once at peace, I inwardly call to the Veil. After a moment, the glossy surface quivers and begins to splinter, spider cracks wrecking its pristine face. The sound of thick glass cracking fills the room, but no shards fall to the floor. Within the large area of the inner frame, the broken pieces separate, then swirl and change, forming a whirling ether of dark gray and silver. The meager light in the room is snuffed out by the darkness seeping from behind the mirror, enveloping everything in the space around it.

The familiar tug of the Veil's energy dances across the edges of my own. I shiver at its touch and chill bumps rise across my body. This feeling never ceases to thrill me. I stand for a few moments savoring the tingling sensations of its surging and seductive power. I must stay vigilant, though, as the pull of the Veil is very strong. It is the conveyor of Spirits, the ferry to those that have passed, a transitional medium from one plane to another. Once called, it expects to be presented with a Spirit to consume. But there is great power in the Veil beyond its intended purpose, and I learned long ago how to exploit a small portion of it.

I release the smallest amount of my Spirit to the Veil to search for Melissa Stiles. It shimmers with the presence of my energy and pulls at me. I harden my body, clench my hands into fists. It does not know or remember that if I enter fully, it will only spit me out.

I use the flow within the Veil to seek out the young, troubled girl. I picture her face and give a sample of the flavor of her energy to the Veil. It quivers once more as it devours her taste and the swirling ether moves more quickly. I travel with it, or rather, the part of my Spirit does, as it seeks out its target. Should I slip and release too much of my Spirit into the Veil, it would grab hold and not let go. I'd be powerless to resist its pull. My body would be dead and my Spirit would have to start anew in a different one.

Melissa is not home, which was the first place the Veil took me. It does not falter as it continues on, following her trail with more determination than any hound dog.

The color of someone's aura breaks into the darkness of the Veil. The blurry form is a muddy red color, far in the distance. As I get closer, the blur takes the shape of a girl sitting on the floor in a small room. Her muddy red silhouette is encased in dirty browns and grays. Taking note of where she is, I pull back lightly so as to not alarm the Veil with a sudden retreat. My prompting makes it draw backward, returning smoothly to the mirror's portal.

As I recoil the portion of my Spirit into the whole, I must pull firmly and without hesitation. Once I am freed from its grip, the Veil quakes softly in a silent protest.

Deep breaths return me to myself, whole once again, and the surface of the mirror solidifies to shiny black glass.

The minor trek through the Veil has not weakened me but has made me extremely thirsty. I down two large glasses of water from the kitchen sink. The colors of Melissa's aura worry me even more. She is angry and afraid. I hurry to finish dressing and pull my hair into a ponytail. Maggie trots behind me as I take the stairs by twos.

The taxi driver gruffly asks 'where to' and I tell him tersely, matching his annoyance. I am restless in the back seat, but the driver is making good time as we approach Congress, heading to the south end of The Point. My nails pull at the tattered vinyl of the armrest, and I don't focus on anything as I stare out the window.

As we turn off Congress, the driver whips onto a nameless street and after a few hundred yards, we come to a sudden stop. He throws the car into reverse and turns onto a street we just passed. We come to another abrupt stop a few doors down on a dirty, quiet street. I thank him, wish him a better day, and toss several bills through the little window in the partition.

When I open the car door, the dense, muggy heat smacks me in the face. The air is thick and unmoving, blocked by wide homes, divided into apartments, and visibly neglected.

I go directly to a massive brick box of a building, featureless except for the many small, dingy windows lined up evenly on each floor. As I enter the dimly lit lobby, the smell of old cooking oil and cat pee assaults my nose. I think for a moment about how to approach Melissa. If I knock, she could ignore it or refuse to see me, and all sorts of drama might ensue. I decide that surprise is the best option. After ensuring that no one is looking, I close my eyes and picture the inside of the room where I saw Melissa through the Veil.

I can project myself only a short distance. The farthest I've been able to accomplish is about a hundred feet and that drained me to the point where I lost consciousness. The distance to the room is not far, only two floors up. In the moment my body fades into nothingness, the vulgar smells vanish. There is no light, no sound, no sensory stimuli at all. I have to focus intently on where I want to appear. If I fall short, or I am wrong, I could

104

end up materializing inside of a brick wall, or half of my body could be inside a mattress and box springs.

I am on target, however, and the small bedroom comes into focus. I hear faint sounds of talking and see images forming. The air around me shimmers, and I stand in front of two young girls, seated on the floor beside a bed.

"Jesus *fuck!*" Melissa exclaims at my sudden appearance and drops the bong poised at her mouth. A similar exclamation peals from her friend, and she scrambles atop the bed, grabbing a pillow and hugging it tight as if it provides all the protection in the world. The room is thick with the smells of rotgut whiskey and weed, and a thin cloud of smoke hangs low in the air.

I stand rigid, with my hands behind my back, staring down at the incredulous teenagers.

"What the *fuck*, lady?" The friend has gained courage with the protection of the pillow.

I glare at her. "*Sleep.*" She falls back onto the bed.

Melissa has recovered the bong and is holding it tight to her chest. The dark circles under her eyes are accentuated by the red-rimmed whites and sagging face. She stares, mouth agape, trying to determine if I'm real or a product of some hallucination brought about by cheap whiskey and bad weed.

"You disappoint me, Melissa."

"Fuck you." She curls her lip at me. She seems to have decided that I am real.

"Are you capable of any other words?"

"Yeah, I got a couple more for ya." She tries to stand but only succeeds in sitting on the bed. She now notices her friend and panics. "You bitch! You killed her!"

I roll my eyes. "She's only asleep."

Melissa looks back at her friend and her face turns wistful. "I wish I could sleep."

I calm at her words. "You've had a visitor, haven't you?"

She whips her head around and glares at me.

"Yeah, and it's *your* fault!" She flings the bong at me, and I lean my hips to the side so it sails past.

Another attempt to stand fails, and she lands hard on the floor. In frustration, she bangs her feet and hands on the floor. She sways a bit then leans back against the bed. "I wish I'd never come into your store."

I relax my body and sigh through my nose. I sit on the floor, facing her.

"I am so sorry, Melissa. But in truth, this is not solely my doing."

She only snorts at this and leans her head back onto the bed. She closes her drooping eyes.

After a few minutes, she finally speaks, eyes still closed. "I just wanted to know more about him. Everybody looks up their ancestors, right? How many of them end up being haunted by a psycho bastard?" Assuming these are rhetorical questions, I remain silent.

Another few minutes pass. It appears Melissa has dozed off, or passed out rather. I smack her foot.

She jerks forward, eyes wide open, searching the room. She seems startled to see me sitting in front of her.

"Oh, so that was real. *Great.*" She rolls her eyes. "What do you want?"

"I want to make Morris Stiles go away," I say. She flinches at the sound of her ancestor's name. "Tell me what you've been doing."

With a deep sigh, she raises her hands to her face and rubs vigorously. She pushes her greasy hair from her forehead, and then slouches back against the bed as if these little movements have drained her completely.

"A couple of days after, you know, the *reading*," she says with no small amount of sarcasm, "I went to a couple of those websites, you know, where you look up your relatives. It really didn't take very long before I found our family tree." She snorts. "I guess they keep prison records really good 'cuz I found a whole lot of Stileses. Makes me *so* proud." She shakes her head.

"Anyway, after a little bit, I found records from California, and that led me to Morr...*him*." She chokes on his name. "There really wasn't much to read, just stuff like where he was born, where he lived, what he had been in jail for, but there weren't any records of his death." She sits up straighter, seeming to sober up some. "So then I kept thinking about him and was really curious about why there was nothing about his death. Well, that night, I'm lying in bed, thinking—and my mind can really spin when it wants to—and I pictured all sorts of nasty ways a bad man could die in the wild West. I play out these movie scenes in my head, you know. So, anyway, I fall asleep. I had the *worst* nightmare." She pulls her knees up to her chest and hugs them tight.

"So, get this now." She releases her legs and leans forward eagerly. "In my dream, this old guy, no teeth, well, *stubs* I guess, gross skin, nasty hair, is wandering around in the desert. He's coughing and hacking, grabbing at his neck like he can't breathe. He looks totally miserable. He's walking around what looks like a grave almost. It's a long pile of rocks, and he's kicking them, trying to yell at the pile, but he can't make words."

I can vividly picture Morris stalking around my unmarked grave and cursing me with every ragged breath.

"I've always had pretty realistic dreams." She turns suddenly serious. "But *this* was nuts. I could feel his pain, his agony. He could barely breathe, he was choking. Each breath turned into a cough and after coughing, he spits this nasty junk. Ugh. It was totally gross. And I *felt* it!" She shivers at the memory. "Anyway, it just kinda went on like that for what seemed like forever. He circled and circled the grave, yelling and hacking. He even took a piss on it." I snarl at this. "But then, as he's peeing, he falls to his knees. He's banging on his chest, like, trying to breathe. Then he just falls over. He lays there for a bit, twitching." She shivers violently. "It was awful." She stares at the floor for a long moment then looks up at me, eyes filled with tears.

"I felt all of it," she says in a whisper. She blinks a few times then wipes her face. "I woke up sweating, crying. I ran to the bathroom and puked in the sink."

*That bastard.* I seethe at the thought of Morris entering this poor girl's dream and making her relive his pitiful death. He deserved his suffering. She did not. She's staring at me expectantly, waiting for me to make this all better.

"Then what happened?" I ask.

"I dreamed of him every time I fell asleep." Her head falls back against the bed. "But then shit got *real* last week. I was in my room, at home, and all of a sudden everything got red. The room glowed *red.*" She stares at me with big eyes. "Then this black smoke stuff started to form in the corner. It sorta formed a face and I knew instantly it was him. I screamed and he told me to shut up and sit down, that he wanted to tell me a few things about my friend, Aven Dovenelle."

I prickle when she says my name.

"He said I didn't need to be messing around with any witches. I was his kin after all and that shit wasn't allowed. He said if I went around to you again, he'd make me regret it." She shudders again and turns pale.

"He's not going to bother you anymore, Melissa, I promise you that," I say, trying to keep my voice calm.

She nods absently, not believing me.

"He told me that you cursed him, that you made him sick. He couldn't eat, couldn't sleep, could barely breathe because he was coughing all the time."

"Good," I can't help saying. "He was a terrible man and he deserved his end."

"He definitely disagrees with that." Her face sobers.

"I'm sure he does. Look, Melissa, I'm here to help you, to get rid of him." I don't need to hear any more of the shit he fed her. "When you looked into who he was, you unwittingly gave him the energy he needed to come back onto this plane." She wrinkles her brow in confusion. I explain. "When you put effort into something, when you believe in something, you give it power. He felt your energy and drew upon that. The more you thought of him, the more frightening and violent the thoughts were, the more he fed off of you. As he made you more afraid, it fueled him, making him stronger and stronger every day."

She makes an anguished noise and covers her face. I reach out and touch her foot. "Getting stoned and hammered will not keep him away." She pulls her legs away from me and hugs her knees to her chest again.

"Then what will?" In those three words, the raw, broken Melissa shows; the frightened little girl pretending to be tough is gone.

"If his source of power goes away, so does he," I say matter-of-factly.

Her eyes widen with realization. "You have to kill me, don't you?"

I can't help laughing. "No, no, no. I didn't mean it like that! You are giving him energy; your negative emotions, thoughts, and fears are feeding him. If all that goes away, he no longer has what he needs so he will dissipate into nothing."

"But how do I stop thinking about him?" She almost yells this. She throws her hands up in exasperation. "I've tried *everything!*"

"What I'm going to propose will seem pretty extreme, but it will not hurt. I promise."

"What?" She eyes me suspiciously.

"I take your memories away."

"Yeah, right." She starts to get up and succeeds this time. "Whatever, lady."

She stands, hands on hips, wobbling a little. "You can get out now." Tough Melissa is back.

I stand as well. "I am completely serious."

"You need to go." The tremor in her voice belies the harshness of her face.

"It won't hurt. You have to trust me."

"Trust you? *Trust you?*" The fog in her mind is clearing. "This is your fucking fault in the first place!"

Not this again. "Look, you want him gone, right? So do I. If you don't remember he even existed, problem solved." I raise my voice this time; my temper is on the rise as is the temperature in this room.

She can see that I am not kidding and not going to leave. She straightens her shoulders. "I'm not afraid of you."

That deflates me. "I don't want you to be afraid of me." I take a deep breath. "Let me help you."

"I don't need your help. I don't need anyone's help. I was doing just fine before you got here. Now, wake my friend up and leave."

My jaw clenches. "*Melissa.*"

"Go!" She reaches out to push me. I grab each arm and hold her fast. She's screaming at me to let her go and whipping her body around.

"Look at me!" I say. She stops struggling at once and is captive to my gaze. Her lips move to make words but only a whimper comes out.

"I am not going to hurt you," I tell her, shaking her a bit to make my point. Another whimper. Her face is twisted with fear.

I reach gently into her mind and travel through her memories of the past few weeks. It's difficult not to see the fights with her father, or feel the pain of the slaps to her face, or suffer the terror of Morris's visits. I can't help but gag at the nausea that a night of bingeing on stolen liquor brings. Finally, I reach the day she and her friends entered my shop. From that point on, her memories of me, of the reading, her knowledge of her ancestor, and her research will be gone. She won't remember the paralyzing fear of Morris's presence or the short freedom that drugs and booze gave her. I pull those from her mind, taking great care not to remove anything unrelated. As those images fade, her body relaxes and her face softens.

I put my arm around her waist to keep her from falling to the floor. When I am done, she goes limp. Laying her next to her friend on the bed, I gaze at them with a great measure of sadness. "Be good," I murmur to both, brushing a few strands of hair away from Melissa's eyes. I touch each one's cheek and give them a silent blessing.

The smell in the room is revolting. I only hope these two girls rise above their current station in life given the strength I've now imparted to them. I glare at the pot until it smolders within the plastic bag and then disintegrates. I look at the bottle of whiskey, but it's already empty.

With a deep sigh, I close my eyes and fade away.

# Chapter 13

The faint aroma of blueberry muffins greets me as I come into the front yard. Sylvia is baking again. My mouth waters, and I realize that I've not eaten yet today.

The large aster bush that claims a majority of the right rear corner of the yard is unusually quiet. I feel the gaze of dozens of little eyes follow me. I turn mostly from reflex when I hear the flutter of large wings behind me. There is a rustle of branches in the great tree across the street but nothing more.

As I enter, the shop looks abandoned. It is waiting impatiently for people to fill its cozy places with exclamations of delight and questions about what this or that is and does. Looking around, I smile proudly. It looks perfect, exactly the way I wanted it to be.

Voices come from the shop's kitchen—the typical, good-natured bickering between mother and daughter. This argument is about the proper amount of blueberries allowed for mini-muffins.

I lean against the doorframe, watching the exchange with great pleasure. These women came into my life unexpectedly and unannounced, and now I can't picture my life without them.

"It really depends on the size of the blueberries," I contribute to the conversation. They both start and Sylvia nearly drops the muffin tin she's pulled from the oven. Neither must have heard the door chimes.

"Goddess! You scared the life outta me," says Jo, hand on her chest.

"You two are terrible shopkeepers. I could be robbed blind while you both are in here bickering."

"Yeah, yeah," Sylvia says, then turns gravely serious. "Woe to the man who steals from a witch. *Especially* from you."

Remembering Will Jacobs's terrified face when I rubbed his palm with my thumb makes me laugh.

"What did you do to him? I've been meaning to ask." Jo sits down at the table with a fresh cup of coffee and a plate piled high with little muffins.

"Oh, nothing too terrible," I say offhandedly, sliding into a chair and reaching for a warm muffin. "But I am hoping he tries to steal something again from someone, anyone, so he finds out." A devilish grin creeps across my face as I pull the top off the muffin.

Jo shakes her head. "That poor kid."

"Ha!" Sylvia snorts. "He deserves whatever Aven did to him. Little jerk." While she's acting tough, it's obvious his comments still bother her.

"This is the perfect amount of blueberries for these little things." I pick up a second one and toast Sylvia with it before popping it in my mouth.

"Excellent." Her face brightens, and she gives her mother a snide 'told ya' face to which Jo responds with her own snarky expression. Sylvia turns to the stove. "I plan to make these for when we have tea parties." Then she turns and looks at me with some hesitation. "Oh, if you are okay with that. Sorry, I forgot to ask."

"Absolutely!" They sometimes forget that this isn't their own place, and that is perfectly fine with me. "You both have been amazing, and I couldn't be happier with how much you have contributed. I want you to consider this your place too." I feel a little guilty since Jo isn't on the payroll, but offering to pay her earned me a smack on the arm and a snort of disapproval.

Placated, Sylvia smiles widely then turns back to the stove and fills the muffin tin for another batch.

"Where ya been?" asks Jo, biting into another muffin; a blueberry falls into her lap, unnoticed.

I ponder my answer for a long moment. "Righting a wrong, I guess you could say."

This prompts Jo's eyebrows to quirk up, but she doesn't press me for details although the look on her face says she wants to. My statement induces an ominous 'oooooo' from Sylvia, but she keeps to her task.

I ignore them both and debate whether I should eat another muffin. They are mini after all, so I snatch one more. In the quiet of our snacking, the vibration of my phone on the table seems overly loud, and it jolts us from our eating-induced trance. We stare at each other in momentary confusion as the only two other people who text me are in this room. Then I remember that I gave Cal my number.

Excitement churns in my belly, but I shrug at the ladies and casually reach for my phone. It is indeed Cal, and he's asking how my day's been so far. I reply that it's going well. Two pairs of eyes are burning into me, so I give them both a scolding look and leave the kitchen. Sylvia whispers, "That must be Cal."

Luckily, the window seat in the library has not yet been claimed by Arial. I stretch my legs out and arrange the pillows behind my back. Cal and I chat back and forth for a bit, getting all of the pleasantries out of the way.

*Got called out on a job site. One of my guys says he can't finish the job.*
*'Gigantic' spider after him in the crawl space. LOL*
*Called one of my bug guys out here to fog the place.*
*Sending you a pic.*

I laugh at this 'gigantic' spider.

*That is a female hacklemesh weaver. Totally harmless. Promise.*
*I bet she's more scared than your guy is.*

*Serious? It's pretty wicked looking. You know about spiders?*

*I do. Don't kill her! Tell that wuss to get back to work. Haha.*

After many minutes of silence, I assume we are done with our conversation, and I'm disappointed that he didn't ask to meet again. These thoughts no sooner cross my mind when my phone vibrates.

*Okay, he doesn't believe you. Sorry. Wants the bug guy to come.*
*Are you free Friday?*

I'm about to reply to him when another message comes through from Jo, asking when Cal and I will see each other again. I ignore her.

*I am. What did you have in mind?*

*Dinner. Like Italian? And something fun.*

*Love Italian. "Something" fun? Like?*

*Not telling. Want to surprise you. Hopefully you won't think it's lame.*

*Well, I do like surprises. If it's lame, I'll tell you. Haha.*

*Gotta go. Bug guy just pulled up. Jerry is jumping around him like a little girl. LMAO.*
*Call you later.*

My face aches from smiling as I stare out the window, looking at nothing in particular. I marvel at my current situation.
Beautiful house, my own business selling magickal wares to a
somewhat accepting society, two wonderful women friends, and
perhaps, a relationship. What a time I have come back to! I've
thought many times that I'm not allowed much happiness and
perhaps that is part of my curse. Part of me dreads the horrors
that *must* be coming.

I push these creeping thoughts aside in favor of staying positive and hopeful. I'm due for a little happiness, dammit—I have
to be.

I rejoin the ladies in the kitchen. They are still sitting at the
table and most of the muffins from the first batch are gone.
They pepper me with questions, and Jo throws in a lewd comment for good measure.

I huff and fold my arms across my chest. "Don't we have
some grand opening planning to do?" At this, Sylvia yelps with
glee and jumps from her chair. She rushes past me to the front
counter and returns with her precious binder. Jo stares at me
expectantly, but I stare back with my best stubborn face.

Sylvia proudly displays each design option for the invitation and explains the different elements of each one, as a car salesman would with the many cars on his lot. Although I already decided on one particular design the instant I saw it, she's put a great deal of time into each design so I let her continue, nodding and smiling. She needs to pursue a career in marketing.

After she's finished her spiel, I point to the one I like, and she squeals. That was her favorite too, while her mom preferred the darker, more gothic one. Having settled on the design, we discuss who should be invited. Jo suggests inviting all of the other shop owners in the area. Even Miss Perfect Pants, whom no one in this room can stand.

"She'll eat herself alive with jealousy," Jo says with relish. I chuckle in agreement.

"You two are being mean." Sylvia eyeballs both of us.

"We *are* being mean," Jo tells her, "but she doesn't *have* to come." Jo and I both know she will and will more than likely spend a thousand dollars on her costume to ensure she has the best one.

The shop area isn't that big, so we'll be utilizing my living room and kitchen area upstairs, as well as the rooftop terrace, but not my reading room. That door will be locked. I will also have to make the faire folk residing in the aster promise to behave or offer to relocate them elsewhere for the evening—which they will refuse as they absolutely love parties. It's possible they will have a party of their own and ignore us completely. Wishful thinking on my part, anyway. While sometimes they are a nuisance and I could *make* them move, I do enjoy their presence—as long as they keep their mischief-making to a minimum. It would be best if I gave them a job to do during the party to keep them occupied.

We have the list of invitees whittled down to seventy, including many folks from the Chamber of Commerce and City Council plus a few local reporters and bloggers. Jo is inviting several clients and friends, and Sylvia has a guy in mind that she's been eyeing for a while.

"Going to invite Cal?" Jo asks, ogling me.

"Probably not—it's two months away. I'll wait and see where this goes." A lot can happen in two months. "Oh, Sylvia, make sure Phil Spicker is on the list." I return Jo's inquisitive look with a lewd wink. She blushes, much to my surprise.

As the ladies discuss outfits—Jo simply can't wear just anything now that she knows *men* will be in attendance—my mind drifts to the special effects I want for the evening. I entertain the idea of inviting a few of the local ghosts to make an appearance. I might be biting off more than I can chew, though. Earthbound ghosts, even benevolent ones, can sometimes act up and take things too far when they forget how fragile and stupid humans can be.

I am lost in thought, and Jo has to put a hand on my arm to get my attention. She nods her head upward and leaves the room. I follow, leaving Sylvia to her new task of finding a printing company.

Jo's energy has changed; she's anxious. I follow her up to the rooftop. Without speaking, she sets herself in the lounger, and I take my customary position on the double chaise facing her.

Her expression is serious, which changes the soft features of her face, making her look older. "Why do you think the white raven has anything to do with your curse?"

This out-of-the-blue question takes me by surprise. "I don't know," I say too quickly, and Jo's look intensifies. "I mean, well…he has *always* been there. In every life. In the early lives, I didn't know what stalked me. I knew it was a bird of some sort because I heard fluttering and flapping. I can only assume he's involved. It's too much of a coincidence that he just *hangs* around all the time. Why do you ask? What is it?"

She exhales heavily through her nose. "I called up a vision that turned out to be quite disturbing. A white raven was there, and he was full of malevolence and hate. He was massive, as big as Maggie I'd say, and he glared at me with burning fire in his eyes." Jo shudders. As if on cue, the cry of a raven cuts through the silence. Jo's eyes flit towards the sound, and she takes another deep breath.

"Also, I was shackled."

My mouth falls open. She recounts her vision. The mob with torches, filled with unbelievable anger and hatred, coming for her. The white raven glaring at her, *condemning* her. Her panic at being chained, the feeling of the wet ground, the bitter taste of moldy water after the vision had ended. I feel terrible that Jo has experienced so much negativity on my behalf.

"What do you suppose that all means?"

Jo holds her Black Fire pendant in her fingertips, rolling it gently and staring at the ground. "I have some ideas, but I'm not really sure yet." She looks up at me. "Why do you think you were cursed?"

"I honestly don't know."

"Did you do something bad?"

I shift in my seat. "I've done a lot of bad things, Jo."

"Can you give me some examples?"

I huff at this. The things I could tell her would end our friendship forever. What do I say to this question? I've killed innocent people, not on purpose, though. I've murdered deserving bastards, I've stolen, I've changed the course of events to benefit me. What do I tell my best friend so that she stays my friend?

I am silent for a long time.

"I'll take that as a 'no'," Jo finally says.

"Suffice it to say that I don't believe I've done anything that would earn me such a punishment." I say this more harshly than I meant to.

Jo nods, still caressing the stone. Staring at the floor, or more likely into another plane, she says to me, "You don't seem too upset about this curse if you ask me."

An involuntary hiss escapes my lips. "I abhor this thing!"

My exclamation pulls her from her reverie. "You seem pretty happy to me. At least in the—what, a year now almost—that I've known you."

I take a deep breath through my nose. "Yes, I *am* happy. Right now. In the seventeen years since I took Patricia's body, I've put much more thought and effort into making this life work for me than pondering my curse. I have been reveling in this new life and this particular time. Because, honestly, this has been the best life I've stepped into. I am enjoying it. I've wasted so much time being bitter and angry, pursuing an answer I'm certain I will never find."

I clench my fists, then release the tension.

"When I look back on my lives, I'm amazed at how much time I spent on trying to fix this. It's not that I've given up, I've simply run out of things to try, or to ask, or to look for." I sit back in the chaise with a sigh. "So I've stopped worrying about the next life—stopped pitying myself, for the most part anyway. I want to make the best of this life."

"I can appreciate that." Jo's face softens then her brows knit together. "But you still want the curse to end, right?"

Anger flares in my chest, and I jump up. "Of course, I want this damnable curse to end! What kind of stupid question is that?" I can no longer hold the pent-up rage within its confines, and I no longer care to try. The once clear sky is rolling now with dark clouds colliding with one another. There is a deep grumble within that booms across the sky. Jo is transfixed at the sight of the maelstrom and shrinks back in her seat, her eyes wide. She cowers, but I cannot stop myself.

"You only see what I want you to see. I live in constant worry that any moment could be the end, and that I will have to do this *again*. It is an absolute nightmare. And this time, it feels *worse* because everything is going my way! Something terrible will happen and it will all be over. I will be thrust back into the Veil and pushed out. To start over, *again*." Feeling suffocated by my anger, I turn my attention away from my frightened friend up to the sky, which is now a foaming vortex of darkness.

"I don't deserve this!" I release my agony and frustration in a scream that takes Jo to her knees on the ground, hands over ears. Thunder mirrors my pain, and I scream until there is no more air in my lungs. Thunder carries along the last of my cry, echoing across the tempest.

Depleted, squeezed out like a sponge, I collapse onto the chaise, gasping for breath. Sorrow fills the void created by the release of my anger and self-pity.

"I don't think about it so I can get through the day," I say in a small voice, letting the tears fall. Jo has recovered herself and is staring at me with guarded hesitation. Broken and ashamed, I put my face in my hands and give in to the sobs that are fighting to be freed.

The maelstrom has dwindled to a mass of sad nimbus clouds that weep along with me. Jo moves to sit beside me, perhaps to comfort me or simply to get out of the rain. She puts her arm around my shoulders. I lay my head on her shoulder and release the last vestiges of my pride, surrendering to the solid embrace of someone who loves me.

# Chapter 14

"Drink?" Jo asks me as we enter the living room.

"Actually, I'd like one of Sylvia's teas." I need something to help clear my head, not make me numb.

Jo nods and heads downstairs.

That's the only word she's spoken to me since I shouted at her. I don't know what I'm more ashamed of—yelling at her or letting my self-pity get the better of me. Did I call her stupid? I fall onto the sofa. I lean back and close my eyes. Maggie is instantly there, sitting in front of me with a concerned face and wagging tail. I smile at her, and she lies down at my feet. Outside the window in the kitchen, I hear the scraping of talons on wood.

I relax in the quiet. I needed that release—it's been a long time coming—but I should have done that better and *not* in front of Jo.

After several minutes, Jo comes up the steps slowly. My cheeks redden at the idea of facing her, so I lean forward, putting my face in my hands. Maggie sniffs me.

Jo's steps in the living room are amplified by the old wood floor and cavernous space of the loft. The tray rattles slightly as she sets it on the coffee table. She sits in the chair across from me.

"I am so sorry," I say through my hands.

"I know you are," she breathes.

I tear my face away from my hands to look at her. "I feel terrible. I shouldn't have yelled at you. Please forgive me."

A motherly smile fills her face, and she leans forward to squeeze my knee. "Of course, dear! Of course." She gives my knee a shake. "There is so much shit going on inside you, I can't even begin to understand. But, if you ask me, you needed that. You know, since you haven't gotten laid in a long time and all."

That makes me chuckle. I pour us a cup of Sylvia's latest concoction of herbs and spices. It smells divine, of cinnamon and chamomile mostly, and I am already feeling better. I stir in a few drops of honey for Jo and hand her the cup. She takes it with trembling hands.

"Don't mind me," she says with a strained smile. I'm at a loss for what to say. Another wave of shame floods over me.

Jo is looking down at Maggie. "She's such a sweet dog." She leans over to ruffle her fur. Maggie scrambles up but doesn't pull away in time. I inhale sharply as Jo's hand passes right into Maggie's thick neck with no fur or body to stop it. She gasps and jerks her hand back.

"What the Goddess!" Jo says, mouth hanging open. Maggie, standing up now, looks at me apologetically then back at Jo.

This was bound to happen sooner or later. "Well," I say, gazing at my furry companion, who returns my look with a soundless tail wag. "For all intents and purposes, Maggie is a ghost."

Jo continues to stare at me, astonished.

"I had Maggie in my eighth life. That ended badly for both her and me, and she's stayed with me ever since." My voice is full of love for this animal. "I often forget she's a ghost, really. But I do miss being able to pet her and snuggle her." Her tail continues to wag soundlessly against the sofa.

Jo looks at Maggie then back at me several times. "I...I just can't...This is too much." She sets her cup on the tray with a clatter and pushes herself up from the chair, shaking her head. "I'm sorry." I watch her leave, her hand on her chest.

Despite my best efforts, save for the last hour, I might have just lost my best friend.

After the fiasco with Jo, I dive headlong into the shop's day-to-day activities, which are minimal. And as it's already late in the day, there's not much for me to do.

I am wiping off the slight layer of dust on the tables and chairs on the porch. I rearrange them as best I can in the limited space. I'll clean the windows next. Keeping busy is the only thing I can do to keep from worrying about what a mess I've made.

The screen door opens and I turn. Sylvia has been quiet since her mother left, saying nothing to her. She steps halfway out, "Mom's got a headache. Asked if I'd run some tea over to her real quick."

"Sure, go ahead." I turn back to my arrangement concerns. I want to tell Sylvia to give Jo a hug for me and wish her better soon but the words are stuck in my throat. She hesitates. I sense her looking at me and I turn back. "Why don't you call it a day?"

"You sure?"

"I am. Enjoy the rest of the day." I force a smile for her.

"Cool, thanks." She returns my smile with a half-hearted one of her own. She looks inside then back to me. "I could stay, you know—come back after I take her the tea."

"I appreciate it, but it's quiet. I doubt a bus full of tourists is going to show up."

She nods in agreement and thanks me again. A few minutes later, she's bounding out the door with her binder in one hand and a paper sack in the other. "See you tomorrow!" she says as she springs through the yard.

The next day comes slowly after a night of tossing and turning. I picked up my phone many times during the night to check if Jo had sent me a message or to send a message to Jo. I put the phone down with a stab of guilt and embarrassment each time. The poor woman has learned so much about my life, my power, in recent weeks that of course she's overwhelmed; it's a great deal to take in. And I should have told her about Maggie.

I took a blanket up to the rooftop intending to sleep under the stars but to no avail. Eventually, I gave in and resorted to taking a potion from the shop's inventory.

I am up before sunrise with my coffee in hand, sitting on the lounger on the rooftop, looking up at the colors of the predawn sky. The sounds are rampant even at this hour—a disorganized song of cooing, chirping, buzzing, and whirring. And the endless sound of cars, but I don't hear them much anymore. My feathered watcher is on a rooftop a few houses behind me; I can't see him, but I sense his eyes upon me.

How lonely I am without Jo's company. It's funny, all those many years I spent alone and never thought a thing of it, never thought I was missing anything. During one life, I spent several decades living in a cave high in the mountains, seeing people only a few times a year when I needed certain supplies. You never realize what you are missing until you have it and then it's gone. My throat goes tight. Before I can talk myself out of it for the dozenth time, I grab my phone and press 'Call' on the image of Jo's face. The phone rings and rings but there's no answer until I get voicemail. She's awake at this hour, she always is. I hang up without leaving a message.

I am suddenly tired and want nothing more than to go back to bed. But instead, I putter around in the flowerbeds and pots until the sun is fully up. I can easily lose myself in the therapeutic rhythm of gardening. When the warmth of the sun on the back of my neck reminds me that morning is here, I pull myself away from the soil. I am anxious to keep moving so I head down to the shop.

I flip the Closed sign on the door to Open and set a similar sign affixed to a wrought iron pedestal out front on the sidewalk. The day is bright and sunny with a fresh breeze. When Sylvia arrives, chipper as ever, I ask her to make more muffins, hoping the smell will help invite people in—and brighten my mood.

While Sylvia is busy making the batter, I lean in the doorway of the kitchen. "So, how's your mom feeling?" Sylvia's movements slow. She replies without turning.

"She didn't have a very good night." She turns to me, then away again. "And by the looks of those bags under your eyes, you didn't either."

I involuntarily touch the skin under my eyes, frowning.

"She's got a few clients this morning but I'm sure she'll come by after." I can tell she's lying about coming by. Her shoulders are tight and her back too straight.

The day passes quickly with a steady stream of customers. I've not advertised yet, nor do I plan to until after the grand opening. Right now, I'm content with curious locals and the random wanderings of those tourists on the street taking in the sights.

There are grumblings from a few people at not having any hookah pipes or tobacco products. I roll my eyes at these comments. Not to their faces, of course. I politely explain that this shop contains only those things related to magick, to healing, and to improving a person's overall well-being. I am delighted to get questions on what to use for healing a pesky rash and making one's husband more attentive. I have salves and potions for both. An older lady has the audacity to disturb Arial's slumber on the window seat in the library. This earns her an annoyed mew, but then Arial quickly changes her mind and delights in the woman's attention.

Sylvia's muffins and tea are big hits, and various groups of customers hang out on the porch over the course of the day. Most of these people end up buying something, so the muffin ploy works out nicely. I ask Sylvia to craft new muffin recipes. She's thrilled. On the topic of tasks, she informs me that she's narrowed the printing companies to two and has prices to go over with me.

As the day stretches out, I grow increasingly more distressed about Jo's abandonment. Sylvia senses my mood but does not offer up any details other than to say her mom's probably just really busy. We both know that's not true.

When I bring in the Open sign from the sidewalk, Sylvia is hunched over her phone, typing feverishly with her thumbs. After reading a reply, she huffs in exasperation and shoves it into her back pocket.

"Okay, here's the thing. I don't know what happened between you and Mom, but I'm sick of being in the middle of it."

I frown at her. "How have I involved you?"

"Ugh, not you. Her!" She pulls out her phone and shakes it at me. "She's killing me! Blowing up my phone with questions about what's going on over here." She exhales in her very teenage way. "I finally just told her to get her big butt over here."

I smile, overjoyed at knowing that Jo hasn't truly abandoned me. "Well, she'll come by when she's ready."

"Ha!" Sylvia rolls her eyes. "Mom is *stubborn*." She gathers her things and heads for the door. "Anyway, I'll see you tomorrow." She stops halfway out the door and turns back. "Listen, she knows you called. And between you and me, I think she's embarrassed by the way she acted, although she won't admit it."

I open my mouth to say something, and Sylvia raises her hand to silence me.

"I don't know any details and I don't want to know. All I know is that she's not been this happy or chipper since before dad got sick. You brought her out of her funk, and she knows that." She seems to chew on more to say but then thinks better of it. She bobs her head at me as if to punctuate her last statement and leaves.

I am relieved to hear that Jo hasn't given up on me, and I'm surprised that *she* is embarrassed. This makes me want to march right over to her house to set things straight and put this behind us, but I don't. I can't face her yet.

As the sun hangs closer to the horizon, Maggie and I go for a walk along the waterfront and down to the lighthouse. The plot of green by the Salem Maritime National Historic Site is peppered with people playing fetch with their dogs, and families enjoying the nice evening. Maggie picks up a game of chase with a goofy chocolate Lab, juking expertly away whenever he gets too close, and I chat casually with his owners, who live nearby.

After Maggie has exhausted the poor Lab, we continue to stroll along Derby. The smells of ice cream, pastries, and fresh candy get the better of me, and I give in once we reach the candy store. Maggie waits patiently outside. I glance out in time to see her move away playfully from a boy who tries to pet her.

Once home, I sit on the porch swing, which gives me a great view of the yard. It's all growing in nicely, and I can't help but be proud of this place. Maggie explores the yard, nose down, tail up. The aster bush is atwitter at her presence and she trots over to it, as if called. The tiny fae fly out to greet her. A good-natured game of 'pick on the baby polar bear' begins. Maggie jumps and weaves, mouthing the air as the fairies dive bomb her and swoop away.

Before long, night has settled in and the aster is aglow with a hundred tiny lights within. Arial has joined me, sitting casually on the railing, watching the tantalizing fairies. She avoids them, however, having learned a valuable lesson from her first encounter with them. I had to quickly intervene before an all-out war was declared on the cat and brokered an uneasy treaty between them. Arial now knows without a doubt that fairies are *not* cat toys.

# Chapter 15

Excited that Friday has finally come, I close up the shop early and usher Sylvia out the door. She's baiting me, trying to get me to tell her all about Cal, or the Angry Hot Uncle, as she likes to refer to him. I smack her on the butt, pushing her out the door.

Staring at a hundred articles of clothing in my closet, not a single one appeals. Since he wouldn't say what 'fun thing' we are doing, I've no idea what to wear. I opt for beige capris and a white silk tunic with roll-tab sleeves, forgoing a necklace in favor of clear quartz dangle earrings. I made this pair and a few for the shop. The quartz dewdrop briolettes are clustered in a cascading string, like a waterfall, and secured with silver wire.

The restaurant where we are meeting is only a few blocks away, so I walk. I'm not surprised to find Cal already there. He's waiting by the hostess stand chatting with the young girl behind it as she wipes down the menus. "There she is," he says with a big smile as I enter, and I'm quickly scrutinized by the young woman.

It seems perfectly natural for me to hug him as we meet. He returns my hug with a firm squeeze. He leaves his hand on the small of my back when we separate.

As she leads us to our table in the already crowded restaurant, Cal tells me that the hostess, Suzie, is the daughter of a client. Our table is in the back with a view of the long, wide room. Suzie wishes us a good evening and flits her eyes over me once more before she walks off.

Cal tells me about his day and then asks how I've been. I recap the last couple of days, skipping my rant at Jo and the subsequent storm I brewed up.

After I decline the offer of a glass of wine in favor of an Italian beer, Cal approves of my choice and changes his bar order to a beer also. I had a bad experience in France a few lifetimes ago and now have an unreasonable and irrational dislike of any kind of wine, regardless of country of origin. I don't say this, of course.

We order our meal family style, but I'm not hungry anymore. My stomach is otherwise filled with knots and butterflies, battling for territorial control.

Unlike on our first date, Cal is much more at ease. I'm a little disappointed with our seating arrangement. There's no possibility of body parts touching; we sit too far apart, facing each other. This doesn't turn out to be too bad, however, as I get to admire how his muscles move under his crisp, rather closely fitted button-down shirt. The light blue color accentuates the brilliant blue of his eyes. I wonder if he selected the shirt on purpose.

As our drinks are set before us, Cal brings up the subject of the grand opening.

"So, how's all that coming along? When is it again?" He takes a sip of the beer and smacks his lips approvingly.

"It's going great. I can't wait!" I say, and he smiles at my enthusiasm. "It's on October 31st, Samhain. Sorry, *Halloween.*"

"What did you call it? Sowen?"

"*Samhain* is the real name for Halloween. Well, the name used in the pagan world, anyway."

He nods with pursed lips. I laugh at his starched reaction. "This is the perfect segue into the conversation we put on hold last time." I eye him expectantly as I take a sip of the dark beer.

"Yeah, I guess so," he says, snickering. After a long pull on his beer, he puts it down with authority. "Okay, look, at the risk of you telling me to fuck off, here's what I think." My eyebrows go up in surprise at his candor, and he stops, embarrassed. He apologizes for his language.

"Oh, please, don't apologize," I say, waving him off with a grin. "I'm glad you feel so comfortable around me so soon." A faint blush rises high on his cheeks.

He takes a deep breath. "I think this whole magic business—the fortune telling, casting spells, psychic stuff, ghost hunting, etcetera—is really just bullshit to get people's money. I know people who have been robbed blind by *mediums* claiming to be able to talk to their dead relatives." He says 'mediums' with an eye roll punctuated by a snort. "It infuriates me that people are so gullible and that these *frauds* can pull this crap with a clear conscience."

I sit passively and listen to him with no change in expression. I fight the urge to stand up and jokingly tell him to fuck off, but he seems too earnest for a joke right now.

"Let me first say that I agree with a majority of your statement." His shoulders relax, and a hint of relief passes over his face. "I understand where you are coming from. There are, unfortunately, a *lot* of people who are complete liars, and a great many more people who fall for it."

"So you're one of these liars?" he asks without hesitation. I give him a derisive eye. He seems to realize what he's said and looks apologetic. "Sorry. This is the part where we revisit my comment about me being an ass."

"That's okay. Like I said, I understand. And no, I am not one of those liars."

"How can you agree with me and then say that?"

"I said I agree with the *majority* of what you said. What *I* do is real."

He opens his mouth to say something, then closes it, shaking his head and reaching for his beer.

"Look," I say. "You can either choose to believe me now and give this," I wave my hand back and forth between us, "a chance, or you can call me a liar one more time and leave." He stiffens. "If you give this a chance, I will *prove* to you what I say." I lean back in my chair and cross my arms over my chest. I resist the strong urge to read his thoughts.

He stares at me for a long moment. His jaw finally relaxes, and he takes a deep breath.

"I'd like to give this a chance," he says, lacking the bravado of before. He presents his glass to me. I nod in agreement, heart pounding so loudly in my ears that it drowns out the sounds of the restaurant, and clink it with my own.

Our meals arrive, interrupting the sweetness of the moment. The massive dishes of chicken parmigiana and baked sausage and penne pasta are placed between us, and we stare at each other in dismay. He tells the waiter that we will definitely need to-go boxes. The waiter laughs and says that most people can eat more than they think.

At the sight of the food, I'm instantly ravenous. "It's a good thing I've only had three mini-muffins today!"

"I can't believe you wore *white* to an Italian restaurant," Cal chides with a laugh in his eye.

I hadn't considered that when picking out blouses. Shrugging, I dig the big spoon into the penne.

"So, what are we doing after dinner?" I eye him, carefully piling the pasta onto my plate so as not to splatter red sauce on my white blouse.

"You'll just have to wait and see. I can't have you running off if you don't like what I tell you."

I laugh, but he does seem a little nervous.

From somewhere to my right, I feel a stab of negativity. I don't turn but use my Sight instead. Miss Perfect Pants is a few tables from us, volleying daggers at me. Her outfit is more elaborate than usual, based on the few times I've seen her anyway, and I wouldn't have thought that possible. Every finger boasts numerous glittering rings that catch the light as she lifts her wine glass to her lips, glowering at me over the rim. The plethora of bangles on her wrist tumble down her arm with such a clamor that I imagine the tables around her will get very annoyed very quickly. It wouldn't be hard to pick her out in this crowded restaurant; her hot-pink, skin-tight dress stands out and shouts for everyone to take notice, as does her bottle-blonde hair stacked high on her head. But Cal hasn't noticed her and that pleases me.

As the waiter packages our leftovers, Cal asks if I want to have another beer or to begin the fun part of our date. I tingle when he uses the word 'date,' and I'm sure I'm grinning like a fool. I opt for starting the fun. As we leave, Cal hands the bag of food to the hostess, asking her if she could put it in her refrigerator at home as he will pick it up tomorrow. Suzie brightens at the news that he's coming to her house until she clarifies that he is stopping by to give her father a bid for his new project. Her face falls, but she's already agreed to take the food.

Once on the sidewalk, I turn to him. "She's got a crush on you, you know."

His mouth falls open. "No, she doesn't! She's, what? Seventeen?"

"And you don't think seventeen-year-old girls ever get crushes on hot older guys?" I ask with an inquisitive eyebrow raise.

He is visibly embarrassed. "Serious?"

I nod aggressively, grinning. He shakes his head, astounded.

As we walk towards the parking lot, he stops abruptly. "So you think I'm hot?" His face is full of mischief.

Now it's my turn to be embarrassed, and I pucker my face at him. "Come on." I wave him forward. "I'm ready for this fun to commence."

He leads the way to his truck, which proudly displays his company name, Jacobs Family Plumbing, on the door. I compliment him on the truck but hold my tongue on voicing the commonly held belief that a man with a big truck is compensating for something. Too early for those kind of jokes, I think. He opens the door for me, and I have to climb up to get in.

Our general direction seems to be southwest, but I've not explored the city enough to know if there's anything 'fun' in this direction. I tell him if this thing isn't extraordinarily fun, then I'm going to be very disappointed. There's a hint of worry on his face.

As I stare out my window, his little finger touches my hand, which is resting on the console between us. He closes his hand over mine. I respond with my own little squeeze. The butterflies in my belly have won the battle over the knots, and I realize I'm blushing. How old am I? I inwardly shake my head at myself.

We haven't been driving for long when Cal slows. I am staring around in all directions, trying to identify this 'fun' thing. He snickers. Ahead, the mast of what appears to be a pirate ship peeks through the trees. As we round the corner, a waterfall multiple stories high and filled with hideously fake blue water cascades down an equally fake mountain. There is a young girl running down the path of the fake mountain, tiny putter in hand, yelling something about being the first to make it to Blackbeard's ship.

"We are going mini golfing?" I ask, not hiding my amusement.

"The eighteenth hole is a pirate ship," he says with a grin.

I narrow my eyes at him in scrutiny. "How old are you again?"

"Shut up," he says laughingly. He parks the truck and hops out.

I notice he is coming around the truck so I wait. He opens the door and extends his hand. As I exit the truck, the enormous ship fills my view. I instantly pick out the flaws as my mind compares it to a true pirate ship. I have to remind myself of *when* and where I am. It's impressive for what it is, and the kids, of all ages apparently, seem to love it.

Cal takes hold of my hand again. I am pleased with his boldness.

"Well?" he asks tentatively.

I take in the entirety of it. It's a small amusement complex complete with go-carts, batting cages, arcade, and two courses of mini golf elaborately dressed up with the pirate theme. The face I give him crushes his eager smile.

"I'm kidding! This does looks like fun. I've never done any of this." I wave my hand at the expanse.

"Serious?" He pulls me towards the ticket booth. "Then I'll try to go easy on you."

At that moment, I decide that I'm going to cheat.

"Let's start with the Blackbeard's Treasure Hunt course," he says, handing me a putter. "It's really meant for little kids but it's a good place to start since you've never done this before."

Oh yes, I'm definitely cheating.

I thoroughly enjoy myself. We laugh from hole to hole, mostly because of my terrible putting executions—miraculously, the ball still goes in. He's never seen anything like it. Guilt gets the better of me, so I stop cheating after the sixth hole. By the end of the course, my score is almost double his. He finds great humor in this, and I resist the urge to muck with his last putt on eighteen.

I get slightly better on the second course after some close-quarter tutelage that I string out on purpose. He doesn't seem to mind when I ask him to show me the proper stance and arm position multiple times.

It is closing time for the park when he finishes showing me the finer points of swinging a bat. I think he is showing off now and I don't mind in the slightest. Watching him position himself over home plate and line up for the swing allows me unfettered time to admire his physique.

"I can't remember having so much fun!" I gush as we make our way back to his truck. "I've never driven a go-cart or played a video game or swung a bat."

He stops and looks at me, stunned. "Serious? What cave have you been living in your whole life?"

"Oh, shut up," I scoff, grabbing his arm and tugging him forward.

Once back in my neighborhood, he has to park a few blocks from my house. Someone must be having a party as there are no parking spaces open. We stroll along, chatting aimlessly and sharing trivial tidbits about our lives. We share a favorite color, purple, but differ greatly on the topic of ice cream since I don't care for it and he professes that he could eat his weight in it on a daily basis.

"I eat ice cream so I jog. I jog so I can eat ice cream," he says with a laugh.

Somehow the conversation turns to child-rearing, and his mood changes quickly.

"It will be another year before my brother is back from Afghanistan. He'll be retiring actually, and I know Will is happy about that although you wouldn't know it by hearing him talk." Cal sighs heavily, shaking his head. "Bill and I have very different ideas of what discipline is, and I feel obligated to do what he'd do, which bugs me. It *doesn't* work, at least not anymore. Will just seems to get more defiant every day. We used to be pals; I was 'Cool Uncle Cal,' but now…"

I am quiet for too long and he glances at me. "I'm sure the last thing you want to hear about is Will."

"Oh, no, no. I'm sorry. I just have nothing to contribute to the conversation. Children are beyond me." I stop myself before what's in my head comes out of my mouth. I always found children to be cruel and unrelenting in my experiences with them. Partial blame can be placed on the parents, who teach them hate and intolerance, but in the underdeveloped mind of a child, those values morph into something more diabolical. I shudder at the memory of my head being pinned down in a stream, rocks cutting into my cheek, by a large, brutish boy who was intent on drowning me for my witchery. He and I were both ten.

As if sensing my distress, Cal gently wraps his hand around mine. His hand is warm and strong; the pleasant sensation pushes away the dark memory. We walk in silence until we reach my gate.

He sees the aster bush alight and remarks how amazing it looks in the dark. I am thankful that the fairies have quieted at our approach. I'm sure that his compliment has earned him a few more points with them. They had remarked to me how pleased with him they were when they witnessed his handling of the wayward nephew. They had not liked the boy.

He opens the gate for me. Something scampers across the pathway in front of us, and he starts. I am always followed by magickal creatures, and many of them have come to live in my yard. They feel safe around me, knowing instinctively that I will protect them when needed, and I welcome their company.

"I think you have rats," he says, looking in the direction the creature went.

"I'll get Arial right on that."

Once on the porch, I push my nerves aside. "Would you like to come up to the rooftop terrace?"

"You have a rooftop terrace?" He looks at me, surprised. "How? Didn't think that was possible on these types of houses."

"Magick," I say with a wink, and he rolls his eyes. I discreetly pass my hand over the lock; I forgot the key. With a click, the deadbolt retracts.

As we enter, muted lighting flicks on in various parts of the shop and illuminates the way up the stairs.

"That's a great idea. Motion-sensing lighting."

*Oops.* I do that so automatically that I forget I do it at all. I am relieved he thinks it's something else entirely. I need to be more careful. It's not time yet to reveal myself.

He follows me quietly up the stairs and does not notice that Maggie is trailing him. We pass through the kitchen and to the door on the left side that opens to reveal a narrow staircase, each step illuminated by a small candle.

"You leave your candles burning? That's not very safe."

I transform the candles into LED versions between the flickers of the flame that obscure his vision just enough. "They're not real candles."

He peers closer. "Oh. Sorry."

Feeling his eyes on my backside as we trek up the stairs, I blush at the thought of him assessing my butt. The stairs are steeply pitched, and we must use the railings on each side.

I push out the screen door and move aside for him to go first. He gasps and exhales an exaggerated 'wow' as he looks around.

The moon's bright light gives the illusion of being concentrated around the pergola, accentuating it as the focal point. At this time of the year, the trumpet vine's flowers are in full bloom. The plants' massive growth over the top of the pergola looks disproportional to the smallish containers they are planted in at each post. In the moonlight, the dark orange blooms appear blood red.

Two small creatures fly up from the flowerbed on the right and then dive, disappearing below the roof peak. Thankfully, Cal is looking in the opposite direction.

Behind me, the distant croak and call of my feathered stalker rings out, and I wonder if he's followed us the whole way. I don't turn to look for him.

"Would you care for a drink?" I ask, still standing by the door.

"How did you do this?" He is still gaping around him.

"As I said, *magick*."

"Oh, come on, be serious." He turns to me now, a little annoyed.

"Answer my question first."

"Oh, yeah. What do you have?"

I rattle off the contents of my small bar. He doesn't favor any of those and says he'll just have what I'm having.

"Okay, I'll be back in a minute. Feel free to look around."

I make our drinks the old fashioned way, with my hands. As I finish, it dawns on me that he's the first mundane who has been up there, and I mount the stairs as fast as I can. There's no telling what might jump out at him if I'm not in attendance.

I don't immediately see him when I come through the door and I panic slightly, looking around. But he's in plain sight, sitting on the double chaise under the pergola. I exhale in relief.

"What did you make us?" he asks as I hand him a highball.

"Taste it and you tell me." I sit beside him, my knee bent underneath me so I'm somewhat facing him.

He takes a healthy sip and puckers. "Ah, gin. My mom used to drink this." He takes another sip. "I never really cared for it, but this isn't bad." He sits back, studying my face.

"Are those contacts?" he asks.

"No."

"Very cool," he says, taking another sip. "So, how did you do *this*?" He waves his free hand around.

Part of me wants to levitate the river rock coffee table or cause the ring of candles to flame up. If I wanted to run him off, that would probably do it.

"This portion of the roof was used in the past to hang clothes to dry. I hired an architect and told him what I wanted to do with the space. So this area was reinforced and then it was just a matter of hauling all this up here. Lots of stronger backs than mine." The part about hiring an architect was true. After he told me what I wanted was impossible, I thanked him for his time and showed him the door.

He nods approvingly. "Well done. I'm really impressed." He reaches for my hand and squeezes it. Pleasant tingles race up my arm. "I have to say," he starts after clearing his throat, "you aren't like any woman I've ever met before."

*You have no idea.* I only smile and can't help blushing—not from what he's said but from the gentle rubbing his thumb is doing on the back of my hand.

I pull my leg from underneath me and make a move to sit against the back of the chaise. He lifts his arm to invite me to lean back against him. I take his offer, snuggling against his side.

His body is warm, and he smells of bergamot and sandalwood again. The heady scent suits him well. His hand rests on my upper arm, his thumb lightly rubbing the silky fabric of my shirt. We sit like that for some time, and I hear only the sounds of his breathing and my heartbeat. When he speaks, he whispers so as to not cut into the serenity of the moment.

"This is really nice up here."

"It really is. I spend a lot of time here."

"You can barely hear any cars."

I 'mmm' in agreement. I could fall asleep like this.

"You're not falling asleep on me, are you?" He moves his body slightly to see my face.

"Hardly," I chuckle. "This is just so comfortable."

"Agreed," he says, leaning back again.

At some point, each of us has set our empty glasses down and our arms get wrapped around each other. My legs have made their way across one of his, and my head is nestled against his neck. His breathing has become as rapid as my own. Warmth has taken over my entire body, and I struggle to keep my arousal in check. He is rubbing, rather firmly, the outside of my leg and his cheek is pressed against the top of my head. I lift my head and our mouths meet instantly.

My hand moves to his cheek, caressing it as we kiss gently, tentatively. Both my breathing and his have become more ragged, and I move my hand to the nape of his neck, lightly pulling my fingers through his hair. He groans at this and tightens his grip on my hip. I push my lips more firmly against his, and a shockwave travels down my spine when his tongue flicks lightly into my mouth.

He is kissing me hard, and I respond in kind. His hand leaves my waist and travels into my hair, holding my head firmly as if to keep me from pulling away from his lips, which I have no intention of doing.

The hand on my hip moves slowly under my blouse to my waist, resting for a moment, as he gauges my response. Receiving no indication that he shouldn't proceed, he moves his hand upward. His fingers strum fire along my bare skin. I want his hands all over me, and I try to wriggle closer into him which isn't possible. I hear nothing but the blood pounding in my ears and our uneven breaths. I moan softly as his fingertips travel lightly below my bra.

The screen door explodes open, and Jo bursts through screaming my name.

# Chapter 16

The sound shatters the intensity of our embrace and I jump up, straightening my clothes. Jo is still screaming my name, running towards me. She stops just short of colliding with me and bends over, hands on her knees, puffing painfully. She must have run from her house. I have never seen her in such a state.

"Jo!" I put my hands on her back. "What is it?" I try to maneuver her to the nearest chair, but she only waves me off as she straightens. Cal is on the other side of her, hands in position to catch her if she collapses. She raises her hand to him also, shaking her head.

"Aven, please, you have to help my mother." Jo's words come between her gasps for breath. Her eyes are locked with mine, full of panic. She looks incredibly old and frail.

"What? Tell me. Sit, calm down."

"Dammit, I don't want to sit! Listen to me!" Jo grabs my upper arms, her nails digging into my skin. "There's a tornado coming. Her house is right in its path. I see her die!" She lets me go and covers her face with her hands. Wobbling slightly, Cal puts his arms on her shoulders to steady her. She doesn't push him away.

Jo takes a deep breath and drops her hands. Her face is grave.

"Aven, please help her. Stop the tornado. Please save her." Her face becomes as fragile as a china doll. Tears fill her eyes, threatening to spill over at any moment.

The words stop my breath. I close my eyes. There's an older, red brick home, set back from a gravel road and flanked by corn fields. The sky is black; the wind howls viciously and bits of debris fly across my vision. A normal person cannot see the tornado in the blackness, but I can. Its funnel is wide at the top, pulling energy from the rolling sky, and it's growing, moving fast. The narrow tip snakes wickedly across the ground, wrenching free everything it touches, no matter how big. It is heading directly towards Matilda's home through the fields.

I open my eyes to see Jo's face has not changed.

"You see it, don't you?" she asks, the question sounding more like an accusation.

The answer is stuck in my throat.

"Save her. *Please.*" Jo takes my hands.

"Jo." I take a deep breath. "I cannot." She drops my hands.

Her face changes quickly from great sadness to unreasonable anger. "The hell you can't! I've seen what you can do! You brewed up an effing storm the other day! You can damn well *stop* a storm!"

"You have to understand, I can't *interfere* with Nature's plan."

She stands straighter, glaring at me.

I continue. "Your mother is meant to die tonight." She flinches. "Many people are meant to die tonight. It's their time. I can't stop that."

She narrows her eyes, her face red. "Can't or *won't?*"

My answer will condemn me. Nothing I say will convince her that it's time for her mother's life to end.

She shrugs off Cal's hands; he is motionless, standing silent and wide-eyed. She turns away from me, shaking her head. "I can't believe you," she mutters.

She whirls back. "You bitch! You have all this power, power you probably don't deserve, and you won't even use it to prevent an old woman from dying a horrible death!"

Her words cut me. Cal puts his hands up, trying to calm her. "Come on, Jo, calm down."

She turns on him. "You shut your mouth. You don't know *anything*." She steps back, surprised at her own anger. Her fury melts away immediately, and she rushes to me, once more taking my hands. My heart bleeds for my friend, and I grip them tight.

"Please," she whispers, looking at our hands. "Do this for me, Aven, please. Don't let her die like this." She collapses to the ground in sobs. I go to the ground with her, wrapping my arms around her convulsing shoulders. Cal steps forward but stops, unsure of what to do.

I feel her pain, deep in my soul, for her mother. It grips my heart, and my chest tightens; I cannot breathe. I push this away, shield myself from her radiating energy. I don't want to lose my friend and I know if I don't do this, she will never forgive me.

Never, *never*, have I manipulated Nature to bend it to my will. Helping crops grow is one thing, but keeping a Spirit from continuing its journey is completely different. What will happen if I change this? That question I cannot answer, but I do know that I will lose my best friend if I do nothing.

"All right, Jo, all right." Dread creeps over my body as I choke out these words.

She pulls away to look at me. Her eyes and cheeks are wet and swollen; I feel her blood coursing through her body, the rapid pounding in her chest.

"Really?" Her voice is small.

I nod and she collapses once again in relief.

I grab her and pull her up. "We must hurry."

Cal stares at both of us, back and forth as if watching a tennis match.

"Uh, would someone tell me what's going on?"

"No time to explain, Cal. You should go." He furrows his brow. Jo is at the door already, looking back me, jumping with fear and anticipation.

"What's going on?" he repeats as if not hearing me.

I sigh. "Come on then and you'll see." I don't wait for an answer. I join Jo at the door and turn back to him. He is standing forlornly, like a lone man lost in a desert. We duck through the door. When we reach the kitchen, I hear his steps coming down the stairs.

I lead us to my reading room where the object hangs that I will use. Against my better judgment, I am doing this. However, I am excited at the prospect in spite of myself. My body tingles with the unknown that lies ahead.

As I enter the room, I flick my left hand, causing every candle in the room to flame up brightly. Cal is the last to enter and does not see this. I walk quickly to the mirror and whip my right arm upward at it. The thick, heavy velvet flies from it and sails across the room, pouring itself onto the floor beside the fireplace. Cal sees this and his eyes widen momentarily before his brow pinches together, scrutinizing the mirror.

At the sight of the massive scrying mirror, Jo grabs her chest and gasps—her face a mixture of awe and fear. She takes several steps back from it.

I stand in front of the mirror and motion for them to move away from me, over by the fireplace. I get on my knees. As I open my arms wide at my sides, I turn my head to them. "Whatever happens, do not touch me. This is not a request."

I take several deep breaths, anchoring my energy to the Earth below me. I gaze at the mirror and the glossy blackness begins to move, the sharp sounds of cracking glass fill the room. Jo gasps. My body trembles but not in fear. I will have to use the full extent of my power to achieve this and I am not certain of success. Nature is vastly more powerful than I. My heart flutters at this challenge, and every cell within me accepts it. I cannot stop the grin forming on my lips.

As the Veil breaks the surface of the mirror, and my breath grows deeper, the pressure in the room becomes palpable. I sense Jo's fear; it is thick and makes her body tremble. Cal is struggling; within him wages a battle between belief and doubt. I must block these energies from disturbing me.

I release a sliver of my Spirit. As my physical body dims slightly, sounds from both Jo and Cal break into my concentration. I cannot speak in this state, so my voice rings through their minds.

*Quiet.*

Cal jerks at the sudden intrusion into his mind but remains silent, his eyes glued to the spectacle before him.

Tethered to my physical body, my Spirit enters the Veil. The dark gray and silver ether takes me greedily and responds to my call for traveling without question.

The mirror's surface reflects the rapid movement of smoky white and gray, my Spirit not visible within. Its movement slows after a moment, and shapes appear ahead in the mist. Little by little, these shapes resolve into a small bedroom. The sounds of crying are faint but increase as the vision sharpens. A frail, white-haired old woman, dressed in a long, brightly colored housecoat, cowers on the floor between her bed and a dresser. The windows of her room have blown out, and she is surrounded by shards of glass and splinters of wood. Her thin, bony feet are bare.

I can no longer hear what is behind my physical body. All I hear are the sounds of Jo's mother and the tumult of an oncoming tornado. But in my Sight, I see Jo cry out at the vision of her mother in the mirror and lunge forward. Cal grabs her and his face is stern, saying words that I cannot make out. By their expressions, I know they hear what I hear; the room is filled with the sounds of Nature's fury.

My opaque form bends over Matilda. Her fearful eyes see me and she reaches out to me, thanking the Goddess for her rescue. Her arms pass through me. I tell her to be calm, that she will be fine, that her daughter has sent me. She says my name with a relieved sob and tries to grip me again.

The room erupts with a burst of violent wind. The tornado is almost upon us. Matilda screams and puts her hands over her head, tightening her little body into a ball. I lay a hand on her head and she falls silent and still, relaxing onto the floor. She is asleep now.

I cover her body with my own as part of the roof is ripped from above us. I plunge my fist into the wall to grasp a water pipe within, needing to secure myself in place. I make my Spirit heavy, as solid as I can, to shield her from the deadly debris. The wind pulls at me, desperately wanting to suck me into its funnel. The bed and dresser are yanked upward and something knocks me hard on the back. My physical body grunts from the force of the hit and causes me to falter. Cal instinctively moves towards me, but Jo grips his arm tight, stopping him.

The wind is determined to have me and brings down upon my body the contents of all it finds in the small room. My body is beaten about, and I struggle not to crush the old woman. I frantically look around, seeking some object to shield us. The lightning comes faster now and brings much-needed light, but from my disadvantaged viewpoint, I see nothing to help.

I wrap white light around us, encasing us in a small measure of protection. It's not strong enough to withstand the onslaught of the storm, and I fear what comes next. The roar of the tornado is deafening. Driving rain is now beating down on us, stinging me with every bead. My grip on the pipe is slipping. My body is yanked upward. I clench my eyes and ball my left hand, demanding to be heavier, forcing my body back to the ground.

I am weakening. I look around once more through squinted eyes and sheets of hard rain. Nothing. I cry out in frustration. Something hits my side, knocking me partially off Matilda. I scramble back over her. She has a gash on her forehead, but her face is calm in blissful slumber. I will the white light to be harder, stronger, thicker. But it will not hold; the storm is seething around us. I have failed. I cannot save her. What a fool I was to give Jo hope.

I gaze down at the peaceful woman. *Forgive me.*

Jo screams for her mother.

I brace myself once more for the tornado is here.

An unearthly screech cuts through the onslaught. Shocked by the sound, I whip my head around. Something catches my eye across the remains of the hallway. The white raven! I see him there clearly, his feathers glowing with white light. He beats his wings frantically, screeching and cawing, and stabs with his beak what he is perched on.

A flash of lightning reveals a gun safe still standing like a sentinel guarding a ruined stronghold. Yes!

As my right hand still grasps the exposed pipe, my left hand reaches out for the safe. With a pump of my fist, the door to the safe is wrenched off, squealing madly in protest. Papers and boxes fly out in a flurry and are immediately sucked up by the wind. I whip my arm back and the safe flies towards me. My hand throttles its speed and maneuvers it to cover us just as the remaining roof and brick wall explode around us. The tornado freight-trains through the little home, sucking up the skeletal remains of the building and its contents. White light holds the safe in place over us.

Jo's cry for her mother cuts through the Veil.

My physical body is gasping and as tense as a bowstring. I have fallen forward; my hands are fists on the floor, and I'm braced should the safe be crushed down around us. Jo and Cal cling to each other, both wanting to help me and stop the other at the same time. The room is hot, the air is thick, and I struggle to breathe. The pressure in the room has extinguished the candles and fills the room with the acrid stench of burnt wick. The only light is the fast coming lightning through the mirror.

In Matilda's bedroom, held within the protective confines of the safe, I wait. After what seems an eternity, there is silence. The quiet is eerie and tingles with the lingering energy of the tornado. The room where my physical body still tenses is also quiet. Jo is sobbing; both Cal's arms are wrapped around her shoulders. He gapes at me and the scene in the mirror.

My body straightens, taking deep breaths through my nose. In the mirror, the safe rises slowly from us and I set it down on its side. From the direction of the road come frantic shouts calling out for Matilda. I softly tap the mind of one of the rescuers and hear his heavy footfalls coming towards us.

The surface of the mirror ripples, and the images within begin to blur. I pull back within the Veil. Relief fills me as my Spirit sliver merges back into me. The mirror's surface hardens and turns glossy black once more.

Jo rushes at me, falling to her knees at my side. She reaches for me then stops herself.

"Is she all right?" she pants.

All I can do is nod.

"Oh, my Goddess." Her face falls into her hands and she weeps, repeatedly thanking me.

Blood is pounding in my head, and the thrill of energy dances on my skin. I hide my smile. By all rights, I should be exhausted, but I am not. My blood is on fire.

Cal turns on the nearest lamp and joins Jo, putting his hand on her back. He looks at me with a mixture of relief and fear.

"You all right?"

I nod again. The electric rush is fading quickly. I am crashing, the exhaustion settling in.

I put a hand on Jo and she looks up at me.

"Aven, I don't know what to say." Tears are falling freely down her cheeks.

I have to clear my throat to speak. "Say nothing to me. Go to her, Jo. Now. She is living on stolen time. She will still die and there will be no stopping it." Nature will not be thwarted.

Jo's face falls. "When?"

I shake my head and shrug; my shoulders are painfully heavy. "In two minutes, two days, two months." I put my hands to my face. My body is beginning to ache. My back throbs and pain pricks my left side with each breath. When I pull my hands away from my face, there's blood in them.

"You're bleeding!" Cal exclaims, reaching for me. He turns me to face him. I feel the warm trickle of blood from my nose and taste its iron on my lips. I have no strength to aid him as he tries to pull me up. My vision narrows and the meager light in the room dims around me. There is ringing in my head now. Cal puts one arm around my back and another one under my legs. He lifts me effortlessly, asking Jo where the nearest bed is.

Jo leads him to my bedroom, and he lays me gently on the bed. I hear talk of taking me to the hospital and calling an ambulance.

"No, no." I wave my hand at them. It is so very heavy. "I will be fine. I just need to rest." My vision is blurry; their shapes are black masses within the gray darkness. The brightness of Maggie's coat shines at the end of the bed.

"Oh, my Goddess, Aven!" Jo gapes at the exposed skin of my arms and legs. Deep purple bruises are blooming across my skin and cuts are opening up, trickling blood.

"*Jesus.* I'm calling an ambulance." Cal unclips his phone. With a great deal of effort, I flick my fingers and the phone flies from his hand. He stares as the phone slides across the floor.

"Listen, *please*. I will be fine. You have to trust me."

Cal marches over to his phone only to be blocked by Maggie. He reaches down to move the big dog only to have his hand pass through her.

He jumps back. "What the hell!"

"Look, Cal," Jo forgets her grief for a moment, "Aven is a witch and Maggie is a ghost, okay? What you saw was real, and Aven is suffering the effects of it." She sits on the bed beside me, and I grimace with the movement that shakes my body painfully. She apologizes and makes a motion to touch me but does not.

"Water," I whisper. Jo looks at Cal who stares back at her, jaw unhinged.

"The glasses are in the cabinet, top left from the sink." Jo stares at Cal flatly. "You're not in Kansas anymore." He purses his lips as he turns to the kitchen.

"Jo," I whisper, my throat burning as if I've screamed for hours. "Go, now, seriously. Go to your mother. I'll be fine."

She is torn; the struggle in her heart is worn on her face.

"It's okay, really. *Go.*"

Cal returns with the glass of water and sets it down hard on the nightstand. Water splashes out of it. Jo takes it and puts it to my lips. I drink greedily.

"I don't know what the hell all that was, but I'm not buying it." He turns and is at the door in a few strides. He whips back around and glares at me. "I was starting to really like you. Then you have to go and pull this shit." He snatches his phone from the floor and stalks out, his steps pounding down the stairs.

Taking a deep breath, I grimace. "Well, I knew that was going to happen."

Jo pats my leg gently. "He's just scared. Men don't know how to handle fear. He likes you too much to just leave it like that."

I want to believe her, but I've seen that look too many times.

Jo finally agrees to leave, comforted by the fact that Sylvia will take her place. I just need to rest and be alone. Sylvia will be much easier to persuade.

I let the comforting warmth of sleep take me into its embrace as soon as Jo is gone.

# Chapter 17

*I* see the man clearly in the dark. He stomps down the path and flings the gate open. He turns to the house and glares, shaking his head. He pulls a hand through his hair. He wears a mask of anger, but the smell of fear on him is great.

*He is leaving!*

*I launch myself from the ledge of my woman's bedroom window where I have observed her hurt and bleeding. She saved the old woman and she pays the price now.*

*I soar down to the fence and yell at him as I do so. He jumps back as I land on the railing. His mind is not open to me, so I must use words.*

"You do not leave her! Not leave her!"

*I say this in his language, but it has been so long since I have spoken that it comes out scratched and hard. He wrinkles his brow at me. I clear my throat, which seems to scare him, and he takes a step away from me. I say it again. I think it is better. His head tilts at me, mouth open. I say it again and beat my wings. Much better this time, yes. He knows what I have said. His eyes widen and he backs away more steps. I yell and jump up and down on the railing.*

"No leave, you no leave her!"

*His denial and fear make him back further away. He is shaking his head at me, saying harsh words that humans use in times of stress. He looks up at the house one more time before he turns in the direction of his big machine.*

*I sigh and bow my head as I watch him go. He will come back, I know this.*

*His big machine disappears around the corner as my woman's friend comes out. She is wringing her hands and her face is full of worry. My woman has told her that she must go see her mother. The old woman should not be alive, I know, it was her time. I am not certain that my woman should have done this. But her friend was screaming and crying—it hurt to watch her in so much pain. Humans die; that is the way of things. Nonetheless, humans do not like this.*

*She sees me and stops, hand on her chest. She speaks a welcome and approaches me slowly. She tilts her head down at me. Her eyes are swollen and her cheeks are red but her heart is not as heavy as it was before.*

*She is close now and reaches out with tentative fingers. I lean forward and touch my beak to them. She gasps and smiles. Her smile changes her face; she is young again.*

*She thanks me and then apologizes; she must go, go fast. I nod my head and she smiles at my understanding.*

*I watch her run home which is not far. She plods heavily and huffs, her many necklaces jingling loudly in the quiet night.*

*I fly back to the ledge of my woman's bedroom. She lies peacefully, asleep. My skin tingles with excitement under my feathers at being so close to my woman. I can look upon her this close and not feel my feathers being pulled from my body or my head splitting open. Her energy is greatly diminished by what she has done. And now, I will keep watch until I am pushed away once more.*

# Chapter 18

It appears that I have fractured a rib or two. The cuts and bruises are superficial albeit wicked looking. Sylvia has been fretting over me, and I find it more annoying than helpful. I insist that all I need is sleep and that if she mentions calling for an ambulance one more time, I am going turn her into a squirrel. Which turns out not to be a deterrent—she thinks being a squirrel would be awesome.

Sylvia has made herself at home on the sofa bed and is tending to my every need, but no longer rushing to my bedside whenever she hears a grunt or yelp. It turns out that I am not a very good patient. I am the one who gives the advice and does the caregiving. I'm not good at being on the receiving end of these things.

Sylvia gives me periodic updates on Jo's visit with her mother. Jo is beside herself with happiness at being able to spend time with Matilda before death takes her. Both women know the truth, and their time together is bittersweet. But they are making the most of every moment, even if Matilda is confined to a hospital bed on doctor's orders.

My sleep is fitful; stabs of pain wake me each time I move. I dream the white raven is at my window watching over me. Surprisingly, it gives me a little peace.

The next time I wake, Sylvia informs me I've been asleep for almost a full day. I tell her about my dream, and she points to the window. Perched there looking in is the white raven.

My heart leaps into my throat, and my eyes instantly well with tears. I try to sit up, but that brings pricks of light in my vision, a stab of pain in my side, and pounding in my head. Sylvia pushes me back down gently, so I lie on my good side, staring at him. He jumps slightly but does not fly away. I've wanted to see this creature for so many lifetimes. He has shown me only the barest glimpse of him so many times, but for reasons I cannot fathom he shows himself to me now. A pleasant rush of goosebumps travel across my skin, and I realize I'm holding my breath.

His eyes sparkle at me, his body quivering with excitement, seeming to be as thrilled with seeing me as I am him. He is magnificent—so much larger than a regular raven, and much brighter white than the ravens with leucism. His eyes are the same color as mine! How strange.

"Hello," I say.

He hunches down and puts his forehead against the window, making a soft warbling sound deep in his throat. I don't notice that tears are flowing until Sylvia rushes to my side asking me what is wrong. I can't explain what I feel but I am not in pain. She pats my shoulder and goes downstairs.

I blink away the tears and smile at the vision in my window.

*I am so—*

He screeches and jerks his head back, launching himself from the ledge.

I jump up, or try to, only to be stopped by shooting pains. "I'm so sorry! Please come back!"

It is almost an hour before he returns, and I beg his forgiveness.

We are both silent, simply staring at each other. My face aches from smiling. I recall the moment in Matilda's home when I saw him, his stark white feathers glowing like a beacon in a storm. Which is exactly what he was. He showed me the safe, knowing it would protect us. I assume he traveled through the Veil, as all ravens can, to come to my aid. I have been wrong to suspect him, to think he was a party to my curse. In his presence, seeing him fully for the first time, I feel only love from this bird.

I long to speak to him; I have so many questions. For almost all of my many lives, I've wanted this: his presence, his company. I don't know what motivated him to show himself finally but I hope this is a sign that he'll stay.

Sylvia comes in with a tray, announcing that it is dinner time. She glances at the window and stops, seeing the white raven. "Wow! He's still here. Very cool."

He is watching everything; each step and movement from Sylvia is closely monitored. She arranges the pillows behind my back, and I wince while repositioning. He squawks angrily and flashes his wings.

"Oh, don't get your wings in a bunch, I didn't hurt her," she says, pursing her lips at him, and he settles down, still eyeing her intently.

With the white raven near, I am so happy. It is as if there has been a piece missing in my life that is now back. I feel whole, complete. Looking at his soft face, the constant battle I wage with the emotional tides that run through me have subsided; I am at peace with myself. He leans his forehead against the glass; the sweet gesture makes my heart swell.

By the third day of my convalescence, he seems antsy. He fidgets a great deal and paces back and forth on the ledge. Late afternoon comes, and he is shaking his head, stabbing his beak into the old wood. I ask him what is wrong because he looks to be in pain, and he answers with only mournful sounds. I dare not try anything magickal on him; simply speaking into his mind caused him to flee. I watch helplessly as he writhes against the glass.

When twilight approaches, he leaps from the sill with a pained croak.

I cry out when he leaves. Somehow, I know that he will not return. My sobs come hard and from deep within as if a close friend has just died. Sylvia comes to console me, but I have no words for what I feel in my very soul. I want to scream at the unfairness of it but I'm not certain what exactly is unfair. She goes outside to look for him. When she comes back, she tells me he's settled in the large tree in the backyard of the house across the street, panting hard, with his head hanging low.

I ask her to let me be alone. As my sobs subside with a final deep inhale, I realize my ribs no longer hurt. Easing myself from the bed and removing my sleep shirt, I look at my naked self in the full-length mirror. The bruises are fading, now a sick yellow and purple color, in great blobs around my arms, sides, back, and legs. The cuts are only lines of dry scabs that itch. I am healing faster than usual and I wonder if the white raven has anything to do with that. I glance to the window in the reflection, hoping he is there, but of course he is not.

Sitting back down on the bed, I wave my hand in the direction of the bathroom. The faucet in the tub turns on, and the stopper lodges itself into the drain. Maggie decides her vigil is over now and she heads silently down the stairs. Night is settling in, and that means playtime with the fairies. She's missed the last several days having been at my side.

I lie in bed the whole next day, not out of pain but out of depression. The appearance of my long-elusive companion had me dancing on clouds. With his resumed absence, I am hollow, empty.

Sylvia comes up the stairs slowly. She enters my bedroom, phone in both hands, texting intently. She raises her face to me, tears streaming down.

"Grandma's gone," she says, inhaling a sob. "In her sleep."

Her shoulders shudder as she lets the flood of tears come. I put my arms around her and hold her tight. I hadn't felt the woman's death nor the despair Jo must be feeling. I have been so mired in self-pity that I missed the anguish of my friend. Guiding Sylvia to the bed, I sit down with her and pull her head into my neck, stroking her hair. No words to comfort her come to me, so I rock her lightly. Arial comes to sit on Sylvia's lap and pushes her head into her breast. Sylvia cries harder.

After the worst of her crying subsides, she tells me that Jo will head back after the coven picks up the body of her mother. Matilda is to have a proper witch's burial, as is their family tradition. This is done in secret, deep in the woods, far away from any eyes that wouldn't understand and the law that wouldn't allow it.

"Go help your mother, sweetie. I'll buy your plane ticket," I say, my cheek lying atop her head.

She wipes the tears from her face. "No, no, that's too much. I couldn't let you."

"Shush. She needs you. I'll not let you refuse."

After a tight hug, she stiffens and then jumps up, realization spreading across her face.

"Oh, my Goddess, the grand opening invitations will be delivered tomorrow. They need to go out ASAP! It's, like, less than two months away. There are so many Halloween parties, people need to be invited sooner rather than later." Sylvia stares at me with urgent eyes.

"I'm perfectly capable of addressing envelopes and putting them in the mail, believe it or not." I usher her out the door.

With a long hug, she leaves, escorted by Arial. While the cat most often acts aloof and uncaring, it's a big show. Arial leads Sylvia all the way home as if the girl didn't know where she was going.

It's been over a week since the tornado. I have put my feelings regarding the white raven aside and have written Cal off completely. I lament what could have been—something that I have a hard time not doing—then get irritated at myself for doing it.

Jo and Sylvia will be back soon and they will have my full attention. I've closed the shop and cleaned Jo's house. She'll be furious with me but that's just tough. When I opened Sylvia's bedroom door, the chaos that assaulted my eyes made me back away and close the door.

When they arrive late in the night, Maggie, Arial, and I are waiting on Jo's front porch. Jo starts to cry the moment she sees me. We hug long and hard in the driveway. Between sobs, she apologizes for the way she reacted, and I am crying also, begging her forgiveness for yelling at her. Sylvia wraps her arms around us and joins in.

True to form, Jo is livid that I not only cleaned her house but did laundry and made dinner. Her exhaustion quickly wins out over her anger as does the smell of lasagna and garlic bread. Sylvia is disappointed her room wasn't cleaned.

Between mouthfuls, Jo recounts the wonderful time she had with her mother—the card games she let her win, the long talks, the peaceful meditations. She chokes up on occasion then stuffs more garlic bread in her mouth, washing it down with a slug of red wine. She says the coven came to transport Matilda's body. They will call Jo when they reach Massachusetts.

"May I come to the farewell ritual?" I ask.

Jo snarls and takes another gulp of wine. "*No*. I am so pissed about that. I told them you were the one that saved her and should make an exception, but that bitch—" Jo bites her tongue and takes a breath. "The new high priestess Claudia won't allow it," she spits out. "Family and coven only."

"It's okay, really. I've had dealings with covens in the past, and I know how much they value their secrecy."

Jo lets out a derisive snort and stabs a lump of lasagna with her fork.

I am secretly relieved. Although I would go to support my friend, I don't relish the idea of seeing another burning body on a pyre or choking on the stench of burning flesh. Just the memory of that smell turns my stomach.

Jo gets the call the next afternoon. They're still packed and need nothing more than a few changes of clothes and their ritual robes. I wave at the back of their car as they head for some mysterious and secluded part of western Massachusetts.

# Chapter 19

*I* have watched night and day, waiting and waiting, for my woman's friend and her daughter to return.

*I am sleeping on the porch railing when I hear her small machine. The bright lights of the machine blind me as she turns into the drive. They both see me. They are pointing.*

*I hop and open my wings.* Speak to you! Speak with you!

*The woman's eyes go wide and her mouth falls open. The woman and the girl get out of the machine and walk to me carefully as if they might scare me away.*

*I bow my head at the woman, looking at her eyes.* We speak?

*The woman only nods and asks her daughter to go into the house. I hop to the end of the railing by the swing. She walks still more carefully onto the porch. The boards creak loud. I watch her come. She sits slowly onto the swing. It creaks more.*

*I bob my head at her.* You not scare me. Do not be scared of me too.

*She nods again, mouth still open.*

Can you help me? Need help from you.

*The woman takes a deep breath with her eyes closed. I see the calm come over her. Her energy is softening, she is relaxing.*

Hello? *Her eyes open at me, questioning.*

Hello.

*She smiles wide.* I can't tell you how happy I am to be talking to you!

*I bob again. Humans are silly.*

You say you need help from me?

If you can. Can you? *I tilt my head at her.*

I will try my best!

*Her excitement is loud in my head.*

When my woman was injured— *Her brows pinch and she looks confused.*

Your friend. She is my woman.

*She nods in understanding but her look is still confused.*

When she was injured, I could come near her. *My heart beats faster at the memory.* I have never done that. This was the first time. I was so happy. Happy, happy! *I hop around the railing; the memory is so wonderful.* Cannot now. I am no longer able now. I have tried but it hurts just like it always has. You are a strong witch, good witch. Can you help me be near her again?

*Her lips pinch together.* I need to understand better. May I ask you some questions?

Yes, yes.

Okay, are you the same white raven that has been in all of her lives?

*I nod. Her eyebrows go up on her forehead.*

Are you the same bird I saw in the vision of Aven taking Patricia's body? And when she helped my mother, you were there?

*I nod again, hopping.* Yes! I helped! Yes!

Yes, you did! Thank you so very much! Having those stolen moments with her is something I'll never be able to thank you enough for. *Her eyes became glossy and water spills from them. She wipes her cheeks and takes a few deep breaths.*

Okay. *She breathes in again heavily.* Are you a spirit? A ghost?

170

I have form. I bleed.

Interesting. Hmm, so, it sounds like you are immortal and can also travel through the Veil. But you aren't able to get near her? Ever?

*I shake my head.* Never, never. Until she was hurt.

What happens when you try to go near her?

Pain, pain. Everywhere. Like my feathers are being pulled out, like my heart is squeezed tight, like my head will split. *I hang my head and shake my body. The memories of the pains will never go away.*

*Her face turns sad and her mouth frowns. She thinks for a moment.* How long were you able to be near her when she was injured?

*I think of how many sunrises and sunsets it was.* Three days almost.

What did it feel like? What happened?

*I shiver.* It came on slowly, I could feel it coming. But then the push came, along with the pain. I had to fly!

The push?

Yes. It feels like she is pushing at me, pushing me away.

*The woman makes the 'hmm' noise again and her hand goes to the black red rock around her neck. She is thinking.*

Do you follow her through all her lives?

Yes. Mostly, yes. Sometimes, when she returns, I cannot find her. I travel, I fly, I live. Then, always, I feel her energy and find her.

Do you have a message for her? *The woman's fingers spin the black red stone.*

*I tilt my head, not understanding.*

Is there something you need to say to her? Is that why you follow her?

I follow because I must. I must.

I see. *She is nodding again but her eyes seem far away. The stone glows within like an ember.*

*I hop to make her look at me.* Your questions answered? You help me now?

*She is quiet for many heartbeats, not looking at me. I am anxious now, pacing on the railing. Finally, I scream at her and flash my wings. She jumps and the stone drops from her fingers. The ember dies.*

I'm so sorry. *She raises her palms to me.* I may be able to help if what I assume is right. Aven has very strong energy. Very. I see it, I feel it too. It might be too much for you. I think that when she was hurt in the tornado, her energy weakened enough for you to be able to come near.

*I bob my head many times. This makes sense to me.*

*She puts her hand to her forehead and sighs.* Let me think on it. I am so tired. I will see what I can do. *Then she looks at me with drooping eyes.* I promise.

*I bow my head and nod. She needs rest I see. Her energy is dull and flat, and dark shadows lie below her eyes. I nod again and leap into the air.*

*The night is cool and my heart feels light in my chest. I wish to fly, fly high. I have some hope now, of being close again to my woman, and my heart is happy.*

# Chapter 20

Our raucous laughter travels down from the rooftop terrace in the clear, quiet evening air. Dusk is turning into charcoal-colored darkness, and the night birds and insects are serenading us. It is good to have Jo and Sylvia back.

We are enjoying the mild evening with a few drinks and much-needed laughter. In the days that they have been back, they've sequestered themselves in the solitude of their quiet home. Jo slept and meditated and slept some more. Sylvia just wanted peace and quiet, a huge change from the days prior.

"Ugh. I can't believe that bitch is my mother's sister," Jo says again and lets her head fall back against the lounge chair. "Those two women couldn't be more different."

"I know, right?" Sylvia says, throwing her hands up into the air. She's quite tipsy.

"I bet that bitch was *happy* Mom got sick. She swooped in and took over the coven like *that*." Jo snaps her fingers.

I give her a doubtful look.

"No, seriously, Aven, I told you. The minute Mom announced to the coven that she had a brain tumor, Claudia took over. Ushered Mom out under the pretense that the sooner she rested, the better." Jo glares at the ring of candles on the coffee table as if it held the image of Claudia's face.

With her eyes never leaving the dancing flames, Jo tells of what should have been a lovely and loving ceremony to honor Matilda's life and return her body to the Earth. The ceremony turned out to be 'The Claudia Show.' She did nothing but bark orders and parade around, and even went so far as to ignore the family traditions in favor of a farewell ritual of her own devising.

Despite all of the nastiness and yelling, the serenity that filled the night as Matilda's body burned on the pyre gave solace to those who loved her dearly. Even Claudia had a tear traveling down her withered and wrinkled cheek. The black night was silent—even the birds made no sound—as the fire consumed its own. The sounds of the crackling and snapping of the dry wood were accentuated in the stillness and made the little ones cower, only to have the arms of a parent wrap tighter around them.

By the end of the tale, both Jo and Sylvia are crying and I am teary-eyed. My mind wanders backwards to some misadventures in my seventh life and my face puckers.

"What?" Jo peers at me over her glass.

"I joined a coven only once, long ago. Once was all it took for me to be put off by the whole concept. Meaningless hierarchy, *jealousy*, ridiculous rules about how you are to practice magick—all wrapped tightly within a web of secrecy and lies. And don't get me started on the humiliating initiation rites! Hog-tied naked on an altar so that everyone can lay their hands on you. I will stay a solitary witch, thank you very much." I follow no one's rules but my own and I adhere to the laws of Nature as I know them—and I know much more than most.

Sylvia looks at Jo in disgust. "Did your mom's coven do that naked thing? That's awful!"

"Of course not! That's just stupid." Jo has taken great offense and leans away from her daughter.

On the stone table between us lies a tray made from a single, thick slab of polished olive wood holding a collection of the finest liquors I know. Jo's glass is never empty and both women call for 'magickal ice' when needed, insisting it tastes much better than what comes from the freezer. I laugh each time the call is made and I am happy to oblige. I'm a little tipsy as well.

My phone buzzes at my side and I pick it up without thinking. Since the invitations to the Halloween grand opening went out, I have been getting emails, texts, and calls at all times of the day and night from folks eager to RSVP. I'm very pleased with the positive reception my little party is getting.

I squint at the bright screen and click my tongue at what I see. Both ladies tilt their heads at me.

"It's Cal." I never thought I'd hear another word from him.

"Well, son of a bitch." Jo leans forward, a little wobbly. "What's he say?"

"Yay, Cal!" Sylvia chirps. Then her brow furrows as she reflects. "Oh, wait, no. Fuck him."

"That's the idea, I think," chortles Jo, winking at her daughter, whose expression has turned to disgust.

"Mother!"

"Will you two shut up!" I'm staring at them as if they were children. Drunk children, as if I have any right to talk. There is a portion of my face I no longer feel. Sylvia has harbored resentment towards Cal since she found out he left me there on the bed, bleeding and bruised, and cursed at me. Before that moment, he could have done no wrong. However, I harbor no ill will towards him; I understand that reaction better than anyone as I have seen it countless times. Part of me does think less of him, though, for leaving a lady in distress while accusing her of some sort of trickery. Fear makes people say and do things they wouldn't have imagined they could.

I place the phone face down.

"You're not going to reply?" Jo asks, making herself another drink. She taps on her glass with a long fingernail and eyeballs me. She needs ice.

"Nope."

"Good girl." Jo inclines her head at me. "Make him sweat."

Maggie comes up behind the ladies and flops down against the side planter, tongue lolling. If I didn't know better, I would have thought her tired.

"Good play time with the fairies?" I ask. Her tail beats the ground.

"I just can't believe she's a ghost," Sylvia almost whispers.

"Why are you whispering?" Jo whispers loudly.

Sylvia ignores her mother and sits back, frowning. "Can *you* touch her?" she asks with a raised eyebrow.

I shake my head. "Only a Spirit can touch a Spirit." Sylvia's frown deepens.

"What's wrong?" I ask.

"Well, it's like, I *swear* I've heard her nails clicking as she follows me or goes up and down the stairs..." She is staring at Maggie. "But now that I watch her, she doesn't make a sound. Nothing. I don't hear her pant or her tail swish, or anything."

"Your mind expects to hear these things when a dog is around. The mind is a powerful thing."

Jo bobbles her head back and forth, her eyes dazed. She's trashed. Sylvia glares at her mother. "What are you nodding for? You were freaked out too!"

"I wasn't freaked out." Jo perks up. She diverts the direction of this conversation. "So, what's the story with you and her?"

Maggie's tail stops wagging and she puts her head on the ground.

"It's a sad one to be sure." The hint of an old accent slips out. I gaze at Maggie's big loving eyes in the dim candlelight, and my heart aches.

Undaunted by the change in mood, Jo leans forward. "Can you show us?" Her eyes sparkle in anticipation of another vision walk with me. Sylvia is looking confused.

"That is not something I wish to live through again." My tone is serious. "Flashbacks to my past are painful. I feel it all, just as if it were happening to me again." I inhale deeply through my nose and look at Jo. "But you should know how brave and wonderful this dog is, and why she stays with me."

Maggie rolls on her side and closes her eyes.

I settle back in the chaise and pull my knees up to one side. I hug a pillow across my chest.

"It was 1560, in France—a small town in the Morgon area of the Beaujolais region. Prime wine country. Vineyards stayed in the family for generations, and *vinetiers* were highly respected. If you could make a good wine consistently, you were treated like a king." My gaze drifts to the cluster of candles.

"It was towards the end of summer. I lived in a little cottage a mile or so from town. I wasn't welcome in town, although people traveled to see me all the time. I was a good healer, you see, and never asked for payment. But payment was always brought because no one ever wanted to be indebted to a witch. Even the town's Catholic priest visited me three times." I snort at the memory of his old, pinched face, which always wore an expression of scorn when I was at the market but changed to one of pleading and reverence when he was at my door.

"On many occasions, I traveled to the largest vineyard in the area. The elderly patriarch, Montaine, was a sickly man who had given up on the local doctor long ago. He had cancer, now that we know what cancer is, and while that is something I could not cure, I could ease his pain and restore his sense of well-being for short amounts of time. We actually became good friends. He walked me around his beloved vineyard and showed me *everything*. It was so beautiful. The soil and grapes he loved more than his own kin, for they were greedy, careless, and lazy. They wanted his money, his land, and his reputation but never wanted to do any work for it. Sometimes, I think he asked me to visit just for the company. Such a wonderful man, so full of life, so generous." I am sad when I remember Montaine. Emotions are rising from my belly, and I have to take a moment to collect myself. The ladies are quiet and don't press me.

"Each time I visited, this goofy, gigantic white fluff ball came loping up to me, tongue always hanging out and tail fanned in the air. Her name was Magdalyn, and she bounded everywhere she went, always happy to be wherever she was." I rest a loving gaze on Maggie, who is ignoring me. "She'd walk me home most of the time, and sometimes even came to greet me when I was halfway to the vineyard. I don't know how she knew I was coming.

"Anyway, Montaine summoned me one day with the greatest urgency. I found him in his bed, Maggie whimpering by his side. He was surely dying and there wasn't a thing I could do to stop it. I sat with him, because his family had not the stomach to watch over him, and I eased his pain. Montaine faded in and out of consciousness, rambling on about the vineyard and his feckless family. He became very agitated at one point and would not let me soothe him. He snapped his fingers at Maggie and pointed to the first drawer in his dresser. Maggie trotted over and pulled on its handle with her teeth. He motioned for me to go look, and I found a thick, crisp scroll secured with his seal in wax. He was giving me his vineyard; that was his will and it was all said and done. He refused to listen to my protests. Montaine passed quietly and in no pain with his hands in mine. The family came and then, well, let's just say all hell broke loose when they saw his will."

A spark of anger flicks in my heart. I will skip this part.

"Sorry for this long-winded story, but it sets the stage for what happened to me. To us." Jo and Sylvia mutter words of encouragement, fully immersed in the tale.

"So, fast-forward a few months. I loved working the vineyard. No hands stayed on, so I did everything on my own except for occasional assistance from a local boy who would sneak away from his house in the late afternoons to help me with the animals. Everything was going smoothly, and I assumed that the turmoil with the family was over—that they'd accepted their father's wishes. But this was absolutely not the case. When I was coming back from the market one exceptionally hot day, I saw smoke coming up over the hill. I knew instantly that it was the vineyard. I pushed the horses to go as fast as they could, but with the heavy cart it was not fast enough, so I sprang out of the carriage and flew. At that point, I didn't care who saw me."

I close my eyes and images of the burning house and blood flash sharply. I snap them open, not willing to see that again.

"When I got there, it was a sight I had never seen and hope to never see again. The family had come back, all the men, and several villagers they'd recruited. They had slaughtered all the animals and set fire to the house and barn. I rushed to each animal that was still alive, suffering, and took away their pain. I saw a man with an ax chasing Maggie. In an instant, two men were on me and a garrote was around my neck." My palms are sweating and my body's heat is rising. "Luckily, I had taken to wearing a wide metal choker hidden by a scarf—for reasons that are yet another story—so I was able to fight them off. They didn't expect me to be as strong as I was. I killed each one with his own blade. When more men came running towards me, I blasted pain into their hearts and they burst where they stood. As Maggie was running at me, barking to warn me, a blade caught me in the back and went through my stomach. The man who did that burned alive from the inside. When I fell, Maggie was there beside me, but she was bleeding from so many places I couldn't even tell where." I take a shaky breath.

"She lay with me as our blood mingled together on the dusty ground. I made sure she was in no pain. Her eyes went dark and her chest went still. From her body arose her Spirit and she stood over me, guarding me, until the last breath had left my body." Tears are blurring my vision, and they quietly spill over.

Sylvia seems to have been crying for a while, and her hands cover her mouth, her shoulders trembling. Jo clutches her chest with her hands, fighting the tears that are building.

I look over to Maggie, who is still feigning sleep. "And she's been with me ever since."

# Chapter 21

It's after midnight when the ladies leave, too sad and depressed to continue with our jovial banter. I feel guilty for bringing them down. When I look back, I must fight the anger, the self-pity, and the shame I feel over the suffering of those around me. Many lives were spent letting bitterness rule over everything I did. That is one of my biggest regrets. Thankfully, when I mastered flying, I found the perfect way to expel a great deal of these negative thoughts and feelings in the form of thunder and lightning—neither of which strike anyone as odd on a cloudy day. Plus, no one can hear you scream when you are that high up.

As I recline on the chaise, staring up at the lush trumpet vines, my thoughts turn to Cal. His text was short, only saying hello and identifying who it was in case I had deleted his number, which I had. It took me a few lifetimes, but I've learned not to pine. At least, not too much.

As if on cue, my phone buzzes. I'm certain it's Cal as both Jo and Sylvia were so drunk and depressed that I'm sure they hit their beds as soon as they got home. It is Cal, asking me if I'm awake. I sigh and lay the phone on my chest. A delightful shiver passes over my body when I remember sitting with him here under the stars. I recall the taste of him, the strength of his hands, the almost overpowering heat of his body. It has been so very long since anyone has touched me like that. Without another thought, I reply. *I'm awake.*

*Can I come over? Is it too late?*

*I'm really not interested in a booty call.* I'm smiling, wondering if he'll take that as a joke or an admonishment. After several minutes, his response comes through as several messages. I sit up to read them.

*I hope you're joking. I think you are but I dunno.*
*I just wanted to apologize in person not in text for the way I acted.*
*There's so much I want to say. I guess they are more like questions really. I've been thinking about you a lot.*
*Every time I'd pick the phone up I'd put it back down.*
*The way I acted was just plain shitty. I have no excuse for that.*
*I'm sorry. I hope you can forgive me.*

I read the pride in him crumbling as he taps out these words. My cheeks are aching from the huge smile on my face. He's been thinking about me! the schoolgirl voice in my head yells. I cross my legs under me and hunch over the bright screen.

*Apology accepted. I understand more than you know.*
*You can come over. I'm on the roof.*
*The door to the shop will open for you.*

I wonder if he's taken aback by my last comment. I am a witch, mister, get used to it. I want to put this in a text and add a smiley face but decide against it.

His reply is a simple *ok. OMW.* With that, I throw myself from the chaise and race downstairs to brush my teeth and re-apply some deodorant.

The house alerts me to Cal's entrance; it exhales a long-held breath as the front door opens.

I wipe my sweaty palms on my pants and reposition myself again on the chaise. (I've been doing that for the last five minutes.) When he comes through the door, I jump up—my careful plans of being aloof and casual fly out the window.

"Hi," he says, holding the screen door so it doesn't bang against the frame.

"Hi." I can't think of what to do with my hands, so I clasp them in front of me. He seems just as nervous, and his hands are in his pockets as he approaches.

"Thanks for letting me come over. Sorry it's so late." He looks around, avoiding eye contact.

"It's okay. It's not that late." I motion for him to sit across from me.

He falls into the lounger and leans forward, planting his elbows on his knees and putting his face in his hands. He makes an exasperated sound. After a long moment, he sits up, raking a hand through his unkempt hair.

"Aven, I am *so* sorry. I panicked. That really freaked me out. I didn't know what the hell all that was." He finally looks at me and winces. "I keep picturing you on the bed, bleeding with bruises everywhere...and then I *yelled* at you!" He rubs his face briskly with both hands. "I wanted to apologize the next day, but I was too embarrassed. Then the more time went by, the harder it was. I am so ashamed of how I reacted."

"Well, I admit that I'm glad to see that you seem upset by your behavior." This comes out more harshly than I meant.

His tired face holds a pair of questioning eyes.

"I'd hate to think you were really that much of a dick."

This gets a grin from him, and he leans back in the lounger.

"Can you blame me, though? That's a helluva introduction to witchcraft!" He snorts a laugh.

I grin at him. "So, you believe me then?"

He groans. "I don't know what I believe."

"I hadn't meant to reveal myself to you like that. What a way to run a guy off! But, what's done is done. The question that remains is whether you can accept it. Accept *me*." There is no point in stringing this out. If he can't, he needs to go.

"You sure like your ultimatums." He is frowning at me. His words make me pause.

"It's not meant as an ultimatum, Cal. But the fact remains that *I am a witch*." With that, I pass my left hand over the tray on the coffee table. The nearly empty whiskey bottle rises and tilts over as a rocks glass slides smoothly underneath it. A short pour of the amber liquid fills the glass as a glittering ball of ice forms within it. Cal's eyes are wide, and he scoots back in the seat as the glass levitates towards him.

"I think you need this." I eye him with no small amount of amusement.

His mouth falls open, and he looks ready to bolt at any minute.

"Don't panic. Just take a deep breath." My words are calm and quiet. "There is magick all around us, Cal. While only a few can truly tap into it, no one can do what I can do with it." The glass glides to the table and settles with a clink against the stone. "I will not hide it or hide who I truly am, so I've been alone for a very long time. You have no idea how long," I choke on these last words then swallow. "I like you, Cal, very much. And I know you like me too." I had a hundred more things I wanted to say to him but they have all vanished now.

His eyes close and he leans back again. I take this moment to study him; his eyes sport dark crescents underneath, and there's a distinct five o'clock shadow across his jaw. The muscles in his neck are tight, and both his shirt and shorts look as if they were piled up on the floor for some time. I can't fathom where his imagination has led him since the night of the tornado, and it doesn't look as if the journey has been particularly pleasant.

In an instant, he is out of the lounger and stepping around the table. I start at his sudden movements. He bends over me and grabs my face between his palms. His lips crash onto mine. His mouth is hard, desperate. My body comes up to meet his and one of his arms goes around my waist, holding me tight. My arms are around his neck, my hands in his hair.

He puts a knee on the chaise and leans me back, laying me down without letting go or allowing his lips to leave mine. The space between us is warm and filled with electricity. I am suddenly nervous; it has been so very long. The butterflies in my stomach threaten to ruin this moment. I focus on his warm palm against my cheek, the natural smell of his skin, the darting of his tongue—all of it sending pleasant shivers across my skin. His hardness presses against my thigh, and I lift my hip slightly to push into it. He groans and his lips move down to my neck. His teeth graze my skin and I grip his head. His mouth gets more aggressive and I open my leg outward for him to maneuver on top of me, which he doesn't hesitate to do.

My body is moving much faster than my brain, so I turn my brain off. My body is hungry, starved for this, and I won't let it stop the pleasure for supposed logical or rational reasons. If this is a one-night stand, so be it.

I release all of my pent up lust onto him and he does not shy away—quite the opposite. He responds with his own deep desire, and we hold on to each other for fear that if one lets go, the other will be gone. Our bodies are in perfect rhythm, like the tidal flows and the moon. Few words are exchanged, none needing to be said. The tidal waves crash against the rocks time after time until they are spent and dawn peeks over the horizon.

We lie on the double chaise, our naked bodies entwined, and watch the sky turn from dark blue to the pastel colors of morning. We whisper to each other and giggle on occasion, with him acting like a kid given a treasured secret to hold. He is giddy and so am I, having been released from both the tension and the nervousness. His laughter is infectious and he teases me, marveling at his ability to make me moan. I smack him playfully and straddle his hips, challenging his perceived abilities. He accepts the challenge with a mischievous grin.

I awake with the sun full on my face and a cat staring at me from the foot of the chaise. She is sniffing his toes as they twitch in his sleep. Her stance is threatening to attack the dangerous digits when I give her a warning hiss. She lets out a disgruntled mew and jumps down.

I wake him with a lingering kiss. His hands travel up and down my back, his short nails leaving chills in their tracks.

"I really hate to do this, but don't you have to get to work?"

He makes a noise in his throat, squeezing me tight. "Nope. I run the place. I go in when I want."

I lay my head on his chest, savoring the feeling of his hands on me. After a few minutes, he sighs and emits an expletive. "I do need to go. I forgot that Trish is taking today off."

"Reality calls," I say with much regret and untangle myself from him.

# Chapter 22

After taking a long shower and donning bright, flowing clothes to reflect my mood, I trot down the stairs, humming a made-up tune. Halfway down, I realize how sore my hips and back are, and a wide grin curves my lips. I flush at the memory of last night's exploits.

"What's that shit-eating grin all about?" Sylvia eyes me suspiciously.

"You're starting to talk like your mother," I say, ignoring her question.

Sylvia makes a repulsed face and harrumphs, turning back to lean over her thick binder on the counter.

"I figured you'd be too hung over to be here today." I lean against the opposite side of the counter, peering at her papers.

"Oh, my Goddess," Sylvia expels dramatically. "I probably would be if I hadn't made myself puke when I got home."

It's my turn to make the repulsed face.

"What? It really helps. Gets rid of all—well, most—of the booze before it gets into your bloodstream," she states with a great deal of confidence.

"Whatever you say, dear." I shake my head.

"Now *you* are starting to talk like my mother."

I push myself back from the counter and cast my gaze around the shop. "Speaking of, where is she? Does she do your little trick too?"

"Nah. I think she's still in her sacred space. Been there all night. I heard some crazy shit coming from that room early this morning." Sylvia is no fool; she knows never to bother her mother at any time when she's in her space, regardless of what she may hear.

I decide not to text her if she is indeed in there. "I'll set out the open sign."

Maggie's in the yard, lying in the sun by the aster bush. She raises her big head when she hears me, then lets it fall back to the ground. I give her a 'good morning' and she ignores me. She's still upset by my telling of our shared story last night. She doesn't like to remember that horrible day.

Before I can heave the wrought iron sign into place, my phone vibrates in my pocket. It's Cal wishing me a good morning and confirming our plans for tonight. My grin is refreshed and my heart flutters in my chest.

I have only just pushed my phone back into my pocket when it quivers again. I open the gate and set the sign on the sidewalk before reaching for it. It's Jo. Her message is unusually short and full of abbreviations. The woman refuses to use 'text lingo' as she calls it, preferring to type out full words and phrases. She's asking me to come over as soon as possible; she's emphatic.

I send a silent message to Sylvia, telling her that I'm going over to see her mom, and I jog the short block to her house. My legs are wobbly this morning. More thoughts of last night give me pleasant shivers. A flash of Cal's naked body passes across my eyes. My steps falter, and I laugh at myself.

Jo's garden is a mess, unkempt and wild. She likes it that way, saying she'd prefer Nature take it over rather than forcing it to bend to her will with constant grooming. If you ask me, she just doesn't want to get all hot and sweaty. The focal point is a three-tiered pink granite waterfall with a pair of entwined doves as its crown. This once-grand piece of artwork has no pump and is peppered with chips and scratches along its scalloped edges. But it serves nicely as a luxurious bird bath, and you won't hear any of the avian residents complaining about its looks.

I don't bother to knock; she'll be alerted to my entrance by the painful creaking of the screen door. If somehow she manages to not hear the door, my footfalls on the ancient wood floor are impossible to miss. I hesitate at the door to her sacred room. She's not called out a greeting or acknowledged me yet. A lick of panic travels up my back.

"Jo?" There's a few seconds of shuffling and something falls before the door flies open.

"About damn time!" Jo's eyes flit to me as she turns back to the disarray of the room. I am choked by the heavy incense haze hanging in the small space. I cough and wave my hand around to get some air circulation going. She looks as disheveled as her surroundings. Her hair is a high, tangled mass, as if she'd been ruffling it with her fingers over and over. Her makeup is obviously from yesterday, and the black mascara has melted below her eyes. She is pale—looking older than I've ever seen her. The floor is a riot of pillows strewn everywhere; opened books, both large and small; weathered astrological charts with their corners held down by crystals of varying types and colors; and tall, fat black pillar candles standing as watchtowers at the four cardinal points.

"What is going on?" I stare around. "Have you even slept?"

She doesn't respond; she's rummaging around on all fours, looking for something. With an exasperated sigh, Jo pulls herself onto a footstool and looks at me. When she does, her haggard look answers my question.

"I know why you are cursed," she says matter-of-factly, as if she were a bank teller giving me my account balance.

Those are words I never expected to hear from her...or anyone. I can only gape at her. We hear clawing across the roof as I stand before her, struck dumb. Her eyes flutter to the ceiling then back to me.

I am holding my breath, simply blinking at her. It takes me a minute to find my voice. "I'm sorry. Can you please repeat that?"

With hands on her knees, she pushes herself up with some effort. "Come on. I need to get out of here." She passes without looking at me. I am frozen in place, and my hands are numb; I still can't believe what she's said. The back screen door slams, jolting me from my paralysis.

I nearly run to catch up. She's under the great white ash tree, her face turned up to it, basking in the shade and clearing her lungs of incense. I stand on the concrete steps by the back door, and I am afraid. My hands are trembling. Her energy is different—it crackles with electricity, something I've not seen in her before. She's rigid as a bowstring, and there's a pall of dread surrounding her.

She tries to rake her fingers through her hair, but they get caught within the tangles. So she ruffles it more, making an aggravated sound. The resulting look she gives me is like that of a crazed hermit who has finally seen a person after years of solitude.

I can't decide what I am actually afraid of—her at this moment or what she has to tell me.

Her eyes flit to the roof above me. I know the white raven is there. I take a few steps towards her, wringing my hands.

"Yeah, I know." She shifts her weight, looking at the ground.

"You have something awful to tell me. I can tell. It's pulsing from you with every heartbeat." My heart beats in my ears, and my palms are sweating.

She only nods, still looking at the ground, moving her foot back and forth across the grass.

I don't press her. I don't want to. Standing in the middle of the yard, I feel naked and raw.

"I've been meditating, vision walking."

I nod. She's told me of that last one.

"And I've spoken to the white raven." With that she looks up at me, her eyes red and very tired.

"You've *spoken* to him?" I'm shocked...and jealous.

"It's a *she*, actually." She looks up again at the roof, and I turn involuntarily. There is nothing there.

My mouth opens to throw questions at her, but her hands go up, motioning for patience. I snap my mouth closed.

"Let me see if I can make this short." She grips her hands in front of her, rubbing her fingers, and wanders around in the shade of the ash.

"I don't want the short version!" I say, louder than I meant.

"I told you about the first vision—when I was chained to the ground with a torch-carrying mob after me and a gigantic white raven about to claw my eyes out. Well, I needed more information, more details, so I've done two more walks. One real doozy last night, or this morning, I don't know." Her hand wipes her forehead, and she closes her eyes. "The night we got back from Mom's ritual, the white raven was waiting for me. She wanted to talk. She asked me to help her to be able to get near you, if I could."

I step forward, mouth open, but she stops me again with a hand. "We'll talk about that one later. I'm sorry, I'm all over the place. This is tough."

My patience is raw and bleeding, but I make myself wait and try to slow my breathing.

"She told me some things as we talked, and those got me thinking. So I did another walk. There were more shackles, but this time I was in water and cloaked figures were all around me. I couldn't see their faces, but I felt like they were judging me. A smaller white raven was there, but this time, it simply watched everything. Then blood started coming from its eyes." Her whole body shivers. "So many conflicting images in all these visions. It's hard to make out what they are trying to tell me." She closes her eyes again and shakes her head.

"But I think I have," she mutters, barely audible. She inhales through her nose and then looks at me fiercely. Her face is stern but that hardness is slipping. Her chin quivers, and her eyes glisten with the onset of tears.

"Jo, please." I rush to her, gripping her forearms. She gasps and clings to me as if to keep herself from falling.

"Aven, Aven." Her battle with what to say is plain, and she pales. "You have taken so many lives. So many." She squeezes her eyes closed and the tears spill. "You will have to live for each life you have taken."

Her words are a punch in the chest. I let go and stagger backward.

"*What?*" My hands are fists and clouds are building above us.

She raises her hands to beg for calm and for me to listen. "You are special, unique, rare. You have powers no one else has, or should have. Those lives weren't meant to be taken by you. Oh, Aven. You went against Nature."

"I have protected myself! I have exacted justice!" The sky churns with dark clouds and a rumble of thunder comes from deep within.

"The white raven is always with you. She is the usher of spirits, ravens are. She stays with you, waiting for the next soul who needs guidance."

With that, I scream. Jo cringes against the tree. The ground quakes below our feet and flames leap from my hands. I whirl around, looking for that fucking bird. I want to kill it. How dare it follow me, stalk me, waiting for my next *victim*. I shriek again at the thought of this.

"Aven, I am so, *so* sorry." Jo recoils from me, sliding roughly down the tree to the ground.

"What are you saying?" I whip back around, staring at her in disbelief. "Are you telling me that for every life I've taken, justly or not, I must live one? Are you telling me I'm *fucked?*" Do I even know how many lives this is? Two hundred and twenty-six. The number comes to me unbidden. No, no! My mind is swimming with my past deeds. I teeter on my feet and squeeze my eyes shut, gripping my head as I shake it, pushing these thoughts away.

Jo buries her face in her hands, her shoulders shaking with sobs.

I straighten. "But that can't be. I don't accept it." As I say those words, my heart tells me differently. I've taken so many lives—I did go against Nature—and there are always consequences. Despite my feelings of justification for those killings, taking another's life has a price. Unwanted images flash across my mind: the old inquisitor's face twisted in pain as my mind squeezes his pounding heart, a screaming man's bloody manhood after he'd raped one of my mothers, a column of fire with agonized screams from within. I fight back the urge to vomit.

Jo is rising, using the tree to help her up, when I leap towards the sky. I have to get away. I burst upward, the force pummeling the great tree and knocking over the granite water fountain. It crashes against the paver stones and breaks apart.

It's not fair, it's not right! The wind stings my face as I propel myself skyward as fast as I can. The stinging is a welcome sensation; it is something else to feel besides this.

I never allowed myself to think that what I had done was wrong. What *they* had done was wrong, surely! I do know that a few innocents were caught within the realm of my revenge, and I am truly sorry for those. But haven't I relived those few lives who were innocent? There weren't many, there couldn't have been.

*Two hundred and twenty-six.* I will have to live two hundred and thirteen more times—die two hundred and fourteen more times.

As I punch through the dark, churning clouds, I release my rage. The scream that comes does not arise from my throat but from deep within my Spirit. It explodes across the sky, taking the clouds with it. Lightning crackles from me with each anguished cry, and thunder quakes with every breath. When my energy is spent, when I can't scream anymore, I let myself fall.

I want this body to shatter, to splatter across the ground in a thousand unrecognizable pieces. I want to feel the pain of it—I deserve it. And maybe, just maybe, the force from the distance I'm falling will make my Spirit shatter also and then it will be done, over, finished. But no matter how much I hope, it won't make it true.

There is screaming in the distance. Is that Jo? No, it can't be—I am far too high to hear anything other than the roaring rush in my ears. But it *is* Jo screaming, screaming into my mind. She is begging, pleading for something that I'm not listening to. Jo. I see her round, happy face, eyes squinted in a perpetual smile, her crow's-feet and laugh lines almost touching. Sylvia's face flashes by; she is laughing and hugging her mother. Cal's sharp blue eyes fill my vision—I remember the way he looks at me, and my heart swells. These images bring a lump in my throat, and I shake my head to rid myself of them. I don't deserve their love, any of them. I have killed, *murdered*, and I am doomed because of it. My curse will last for an eternity.

There is another's scream lofting up, impossibly high, but I don't turn my head to see. I know it is the white raven. The love I felt for the bird when finally seeing her up close comes rushing back and catches in my throat.

I let myself continue to fall, not caring what happens. I close my eyes and let the blackness take me.

The peace does not last, and I am suddenly aware of the piercing cold. There is a harsh, stinging pain on my exposed skin, and the cold burns my lungs when I gasp. Fear rushes at me when I realize what I am doing. I try to turn my body, but the momentum is too great and my muscles are rigid from the freezing air. I am plummeting to the earth, and now I'm deathly afraid of what I wanted so dearly only seconds ago. I am trapped by the power of my descent, clutched in its grip like a vice. Reaching out with my mind, I pull in light around me, warmth and heat, to calm me. I must focus to project myself such a long distance. I picture the rooftop terrace where Jo now stands with eyes locked on the sky, and the roaring sound fades—as do I.

The sudden change in velocity make my legs buckle, and I collapse to the floor of the terrace. I am vaguely aware of Jo rushing to me, wrapping her arms around me, as my vision narrows and the world around me goes black.

# Chapter 23

I hear faint voices, faraway whispers. A man's deep voice sounds strange amidst the softness of the two women's voices. I can't make out what they are saying. Someone says my name and comes towards me. I can open my eyes only a little; everything is blurry and washed out. Then the blanket of darkness falls over me again.

My dreams, nightmares rather, are filled with my tumultuous past. I hear pained howls and angry shouting, see faces caught in silent screams, their skin peeling and melting. I smell the burning of flesh, my own, but I am cold and rigid. Someone is drowning—is that me? I see thin, bony hands come up out of churning water, desperately clawing at the hands that hold her down. The scent of fetid blood replaces that of burning flesh and I gag, I can't breathe from the stench of it. Icy winds blow at my face and the cold cuts into my skin. More screams fill my ears; I can't shut them out. The screech of a bird overtakes the screams, and I am chasing it. The white bird trails blood as she flies. It splatters my face.

I jolt awake, the taste of blood in my mouth. I have bitten my lip.

"Aven!" Jo rushes to me from the doorway. "Are you okay?"

Cal is behind her and Sylvia is peering around him. They share the same expression, that of unease and worry.

I cover my mouth and Jo hands me a tissue. Embarrassment keeps me from meeting Cal's eyes.

"I called him. I couldn't lift you." Jo's eyes plead for forgiveness.

"She won't tell me what happened to you." Cal steps forward. His hands are in his front pockets, and he is looking uncomfortable despite the concern on his face.

I find my voice. "How long have I been out? What time is it?" My throat is like sandpaper. I take several gulps of water from the glass on the nightstand.

"Practically all day. It's almost midnight." Jo takes the empty glass from my hand.

"Can I talk to Cal alone, please?"

Jo closes the door behind her, and Cal sits on the end of the bed. "Jesus, Aven. Are you all right?" He moves to take my hand but stops himself.

I shake my head in frustration. "You have had the *worst* introduction into my life, I have to say." My attempt at levity fails, for he isn't smiling. "I can't imagine what you must be thinking." I sigh and cover my face with my hands.

He sits quietly for a moment, then puts a hand on my leg and gives it a gentle squeeze. I sit up, gazing at him with eyes that beg for understanding. He scoots forward and wraps his arms around me. This tender and loving gesture, the kindness in his eyes, opens a well I've kept capped for many years. My tears flood out in sobs and gasps, shudders and coughs, and he says nothing. He holds me gently, sometimes giving a firm squeeze, and rocks me from side to side.

When the flow ebbs, I take several shaky breaths. He is stroking my hair.

"Everything in my brain is telling me to run away from you," he whispers in my ear, his head lying gently against mine. I tense at his words; his arms go tighter around me. "But my heart just won't let me. You've probably put a spell on me." He chuckles as he says this.

"I would *never* do that," I choke out. He kisses my hair in response.

I push back enough so I can see his eyes. They look darker blue in this light, flecked with bits of gold and black, and contain nothing but sincerity.

He brushes a few strands of hair away from my wet cheeks. "When I first saw you that day I brought Will, I thought 'Wooow, this chick is *hot*.'" He puts a palm on my blushing cheek. I lean into his hand. "Then when we had that talk about magic in the restaurant, I was like 'okay, *crazy* but still hot.' I didn't want to believe what I'd seen with my own eyes, and *felt*, during that mirror-tornado business. God, that was some crazy shit." He shakes his head, still holding on to some disbelief. "And I tried to stay away from you. I tried hard. I thought getting mad at you would help, and it did, but not for very long. I can't stay away from you." He wipes a tear away with his thumb. "If you have bewitched me, Aven Dovenelle, I think I'm okay with that." His lips are soft on mine. My head is spinning; I must still be dreaming. Never, never would I have imagined a man would be this strong, this *gentle*, and say those words to me.

"Are you real?" I ask, tightening my arms around him and burying my head in his neck. He holds me tight and we are quiet for some time.

I regretfully pull away. "I have to pee."

He guffaws and lets me go. "Don't let me stop you."

I close the bathroom door and catch a glimpse of myself in the mirror. I am a fright. My eyes are red and swollen, my cheeks are splotchy, and my hair could have a family of birds living in it and I wouldn't know. I call out to Cal that I'm going to take a shower. He is silent for a moment, probably weighing whether he should ask to join me or not, and finally says that he'll leave me to it but to shout if I need anything.

The hot water stings my raw skin. I must have raked off several layers descending as fast as I did. The water swirling around the drain is pink, so I inspect myself. My knees are scraped up nicely and bruises mark the center of each like a bullseye. It seems I hit the floor pretty hard. Sitting under the shower, I let the water rain on me. My hair is a dark curtain around my face, hiding me within. I watch the water flow down the drain, taking with it my hope for a reprieve from this curse.

Jo's voice startles me. "Aven? You all right? You've been in there a while."

"I'll be out in a minute," I say, my throat raw.

Every muscle aches as I dress. Not the pleasant ache that a night of good sex brings, but the ache from piano-wire tension and stressed muscles. I pull on my comfiest yoga pants and a plain white T-shirt. I brush out my damp hair and tuck it behind my ears.

The three are sitting in what serves as my living room, the open loft area between the kitchen and the railing overlooking the shop, talking in whispers. They stop at once and stare at me, and it feels like I've just walked out on stage.

Under normal circumstances, Jo would greet me with a quip about my clothing, or not having any makeup on, or how lazy I am with my hair. But now, she sits quietly, looking small…and older.

I don't know what to say, and I stare at them as they stare at me. I hope someone says something soon; this is very uncomfortable. Sylvia looks at her mom, then at Cal, and decides to be the brave one.

"So, the falling to earth thing. Not cool." Sylvia crosses her arms over her chest, looking more concerned than her words let on. Jo's head snaps up at her and Cal turns, confused.

"I didn't tell Cal any of that," Jo says to her daughter through clenched teeth. Sylvia's square shoulders slump, and she sheepishly slides down into the high-back chair.

I look at Cal. "I had some pretty bad news this morning, and I did not take it well."

The confusion morphs into trepidation. "I'm afraid to ask."

I shrug and pad over to the sofa to sit beside Jo. She scoots sideways so I can face Cal, who's perched on the edge of the coffee table.

"I meant to tell you in there, but all I could do was cry." Jo puts a shaky hand on my knee and squeezes. I put my hand over hers and look at her. "I'm sorry for yelling at you. Seems I do that a lot to you lately."

"Well," she snorts, shaking her head, "can't blame you. Either time. You have every right to yell." She squeezes my knee again. "And I'm sorry, too."

"You have nothing to apologize for. I should thank you. Without you, I would still be hoping. Now, I can put that behind me." Her eyes gloss with new tears.

"Okay, *what* is going on?" Cal is staring back and forth between me and Jo.

I inhale deeply and let it out as if I'm readying for a grand speech.

"I am cursed."

His forehead wrinkles but he says nothing.

"I am cursed with reincarnation. When the body dies, my Spirit is forced to come back into a new one and I remember everything. I never knew why I was cursed until Jo discovered the reason. I will continue this cycle—living, dying, repeat, remember—until I've lived a life for each one that I have taken. *That* is the bad news I got this morning."

I take a deep breath. "I never thought this would be an endless thing; I didn't allow myself to give up hope that one day I'd find a way to break this curse. I just needed more knowledge, more information, more time, and then maybe I'd figure it out."

Jo stiffens, and I give her a reassuring smile.

A dubious expression distorts his face. "Oh, come on. Even that's a little much for me to swallow, despite what I've seen."

"I really need you to believe me." My eyes beseech him.

"It's true." Jo's voice is small and distant.

Cal huffs and rakes a hand through his hair. "You can't expect me to believe this."

"I don't expect anything from you. This doesn't affect you, any of you, so we can drop the subject altogether. Let's just forget today happened." I want to very much.

Jo seems hurt, and Sylvia looks at the floor.

"Oh no, huh-uh. I didn't rush over here, scoop you off the floor for the *second* time and wait *patiently*," he side glares at Jo, "to be told what is going on and then have it swept under the rug like that."

I study his face. His jaw is set, and he doesn't flinch at my scrutinizing gaze.

"All right. How much can you take?"

Cal moves to the other chair and sits straight, crossing his arms over his chest. "Do your worst," he says with a slight smirk.

Jo snorts at his arrogance and lets go of my hands, pushing herself back into the sofa. Sylvia pulls her knees to her chest.

I resist the urge to pummel him with visions of my lives, reminding myself how new and crazy this is to him. He doesn't realize what he's saying—but he soon will.

I ponder for a long moment where to start.

"When a body dies, the Spirit leaves it and travels to the Veil, the transition point to the other realms. Most Spirits have a choice: move on to another plane, or reincarnate, losing most if not all memory of their previous life and their time in the Veil. They come back with a clean slate. Some Spirits—those that are misguided, evil, or simply too afraid—will drift in and out of the Veil aimlessly. The more malevolent ones wreak havoc and play nasty games. My Spirit does not have these choices. While I can drift around in the Veil for a good amount of time—although time means nothing there—I am inexorably *pushed* out, for lack of a better term. I remember everything about my previous lives and the time spent in the Veil. When I died in 1886, it seemed as if only a few days had gone by before I was made to leave."

Cal's mouth opens, and I raise my hand. "Just listen, okay?" He nods grudgingly.

"In the first memory I have of the Veil, I was scared out of my wits. It was very dark and there was not a single sound. No smells, no tactile sensations at all. The wave of Spirits ebbed and flowed, and I begged for help from each of them. Not a single Spirit offered any help or guidance. After a time, I felt a tug, like I was treading water in the ocean and something pulled at my leg. Then it became a push, from the Veil itself. It closed around me, as if becoming a solid wall, and I couldn't get back through it. The first time was terrifying. I clawed and scraped at the solid dark curtain, screaming and begging to be let back in. While I had been afraid of the Veil when inside it, I was more terrified by what was behind me—a new world, a new place, a new time. I had no clue where I was or when.

"Without another option, I wandered around, my Spirit drifting with the wind. The land was deep green with low rolling hills. I came across a small hamlet. I heard crying from one of the cottages, a woman sobbing in between screams of pain. She was giving birth, but she knew her baby was dying, or already dead. The husband and midwife were there, giving words of encouragement and prayers to God. I was drawn to the baby for she was indeed dying. When she came out, she struggled for breath. The woman begged to hold her baby before she died, but the midwife was trying to save her. The husband was praying, crying out to God for mercy. When I saw the baby's Spirit rise from her, some part of me instinctively knew that I could now occupy the body. So I did."

I look at Cal, Jo, and Sylvia. Their faces show a mixture of revulsion and awe. I ignore them.

"Anyway, that's how I re-enter this world—through the body of someone who has just died. I've come back as a new-born—which I will never do again—a toddler, a teenager, and an adult. I've experimented with what works best and coming back as a young child is not ideal. I picked a male body once. That is also something else I will never do again." I pucker my face at the memory of being inside a man's body. I instantly feel dirty. Cal shifts uncomfortably in the chair.

"As it turned out, my second life was in Scotland around the turn of the twelfth century." A soft grunt emanates from Cal's direction.

I sigh and close my eyes. "Okay, I can see I'll have to take more drastic measures."

"Oh, hell, now you've done it," Jo quips to Cal. He purses his lips at her.

"I have an idea." Scooting forward, I extend my hands to Cal. "I will show you. Here, take my hands." I motion to the ladies also.

"Another vision walk?" Jo's eyes glint with excitement.

"Not quite—I couldn't take you all through such a journey, but I can show you some parts of my lives. You will see it, feel it, through my eyes—you will be me." I raise my brows at Cal, the only one who's not taken one of my hands. He is studying my face with trepidation.

"Come on, Mr. Do Your Worst," Jo tells him, returning his earlier smirk. Cal harrumphs and scoots forward, laying a hand atop mine.

The lights in the room dim slowly. "Close your eyes." My voice resonates around the four of us. "Open your minds. Do not fight what you see." Chill bumps rise on my skin as mist fills my vision, silvery white and swirling, replacing the darkness behind my closed eyes.

Cal gasps and I feel a lick of fear from Sylvia. "There is nothing to fear. You will come to no harm." I wait for her to calm before I continue. The white mist slowly dissipates, revealing a cloudless, sunny day.

*Rolling green hills spread out before me. The breeze is warm and soft on my face; the sky is clear and bright blue. I hear the lilt of childish laughter and a little girl with fiery red hair springs up from within a cluster of wild heather, sending out a burst of woodsy floral scent. Iona. Her face lights up when she sees my feigned surprise. My heart fills with joy at the sight of my little sister.*

*"You won't catch me, dragon!" She grabs her skirts and runs from me, shrieking merrily as she leaps over mounds of heather.*

*With a burst of laughter of my own and then a long growl, I give chase, for I am a fierce dragon and she a helpless maid—a game we played a great deal, one she insisted on playing whenever I looked glum. My little legs are only slightly longer than hers, but I have to run fast to catch up with her. When I am close I slow down, delighting in her giggling shrieks at the prospect of being caught by the dragon. I let her get ahead of me again and then rush at her. With an immense roar, I leap forward and we tumble, rolling and laughing down the grassy hillside.*

*"Girls!" The wind carries our mother's weary voice. "Lilias! Iona! There is still work to be done. Your silly games can wait."*

*I let out a groan and rise, pulling Iona up with me. Her face is splotched red from excitement, and strands of hair stick to her sweaty cheeks. Her gap-toothed smile makes me laugh.*

*"Come on, then," I say, pulling bits of heather and grass from her wild hair. She takes my hand and skips up the hill, tugging me along.*

The green and purple of the landscape is whisked away by the silvery white mist, quickly revealing a vast ocean.

*I marvel at the water from my perch high above. Innumerable shades of blue stretch all around me, filled with low, dancing waves sometimes tipped with white froth. The expanse stretches to the horizon, which is yet another wondrous shade of blue. The warm, salty air leaves its taste on my lips. I laugh aloud, throwing my arms out into the headwinds. The sound of thick sails flapping is accompanied by the crashing of the massive ship as it cuts through the water at great speed.*

*I look down from the crow's nest to the busy crew, each looking like an ant scurrying to perform the tasks shouted out by the large man standing at the base of the mizzen mast. His coat tails flap in the wind as does the red plume in his cocked hat.*

*He looks up at me then. "Witch! Come! You are needed."*

*I glare down at the arrogant man. He snarls at me and huffs, turning away haughtily, knowing I will obey him. Yes, I will obey but on my terms only. I lift my arms and my body rises. Those who see me cry out to God or cross themselves, turning their backs to the devil in their sight. I hide my grin.*

*I drift down slowly, alighting in front of the man to whom I promised allegiance, Captain Boe. He stands before the great wheel now, arms crossed over his chest, his dark beard nearly touching his arms, looking not a bit impressed by his flying witch.*

The image snaps back to the darkness behind my eyes. My head is throbbing, and I am faint. Dropping my hands, I grip my head, pushing at my temples.

"I'm sorry," I pant, "I can't do any more."

"Here, drink this." Jo's voice is full of concern, her hand on my back.

I peek through my eyes and take the glass of water. After I chug the whole of it, the pounding in my ears starts to subside.

"Are you all right?" Cal has moved back to the coffee table, his hands on my knees. I nod and hand the glass to Sylvia, who's reached for it to go refill it in the kitchen.

I settle into the sofa and take deep breaths through my nose.

"Oh, my Goddess, you were a *pirate?*" Sylvia exclaims too loudly for my pained head as she returns with the glass. Her mom shushes her.

"No, no." I wave her question away. "I only sailed with pirates. I wanted to see the world. So I agreed to help them in exchange for safe passage and to be otherwise left alone."

"That was incredible," Jo breathes out, a hand on her chest.

"I'd love to show you more, but I am so drained." Cal's hands are rubbing my upper arms and I relax into the soothing motions of it.

Cal squeezes my shoulders. "Don't worry about that. You need to rest."

"You believe me now?" I ask through a small smile.

He grunts a laugh. "Yeah, you win."

Jo pats my leg. "Which lives were those?"

"Pirates was number ten. Iona was in two."

"What did the captain want?" Sylvia's eyes glimmer with anticipation.

"Ha!" shoots from my lips. "Well…" I stretch out the word to give me some time to decide how to answer. "The ship we were on was a stolen man-of-war. As you can imagine, the English were not happy with that. And it seemed there were three ships in pursuit." Sylvia is bouncing in her seat, staring at me with wide eyes. "No, I didn't help them steal it. But I did help them get away. I brewed up a little storm behind us, allowing Captain Boe to get a great distance from them."

Cal shakes his head at me and Jo gives me a playful tsk.

"That's awesome," Sylvia says, beaming. "You rock." That makes me laugh aloud.

"Pizza anyone?" Jo asks. "I'm starving."

"There's one in the freezer," I say, and Sylvia is up in an instant, heading for the kitchen.

"I need a drink," Jo says, pushing herself up from the sofa, and goes for the sideboard where I keep her favorite spirit.

"Amen to that," Cal says.

Cal takes my hands and pulls me up into his arms. "It's going to take me a while to process what…the things you said, what you, uh…showed me. I can't wrap my brain around all of this right now, I'm sorry. But I do believe you."

I take his face in my hands and brush my lips against his. His arms move to my waist, his kisses tentative and light. I press my forehead to his chin. "You don't have to apologize. The fact that you are still standing here means more to me than you'll ever know."

One arm tightens around my waist, while the other hand moves up and down my back.

"Can I stay tonight?" he asks. I nod, snuggling into his neck.

Despite the pleasant memories I showed them, dinner is subdued. We sit at the small, round kitchen table, hunched over our plates of pizza. Cal eats heartily while Jo picks, muttering about how much she despises mushrooms. My slice gets cold before I can finish it. Few words are spoken and little eye contact is made. The eight-hundred-pound gorilla attending dinner eats no food and drinks nothing, but consumes the light and laughter from everyone instead.

My skin itches under the uncomfortable tension that grips our little group. After a few sips of water, I put my glass down on the table with a thud, getting everyone's attention.

"You can't let this get inside you." It is difficult to look at anyone; the pity in their eyes is like a slap in the face. "Don't pity me. I can't take it. I do well enough to manage my own."

Taking a deep breath, I push out more words. "Look, this is my lot and that's that. We have to get back to the way we were; I can't have you all reminding me of it every time you look at me. I have to accept this and do what I do best—put it in the back of my mind and forget about it." But I don't believe these words. I will never accept this *curse* and will never put it aside. Every moment of every day will remind me that I am doomed to repeat this cycle for an unimaginable amount of time. I remember everyone I've killed, be it purposefully or accidentally; their faces are etched in my memory. There is no light at the end of my tunnel—it's walled up with two hundred and twenty-six bricks.

In the middle of an agreeable nod, Jo stops short and looks at me. "But you don't have to carry this all on your own, you know."

"That's right," Sylvia chimes in, "you have us."

The swelling of my heart threatens to choke me. I inhale deeply to stave off the sobs that well up. "Thank you for that." I reach out on both sides of me and grasp their outstretched hands. I squeeze my eyes closed. "But you can't help me."

"That may be true," Jo says, "but you can take our love and support and not shut us out. I can see you doing that and I'm not going to allow it." She gives my hand a little shake. "We witches have to stick together."

I can't meet her loving gaze. I squeeze their hands and nod. The negative part of me feels that I don't deserve their friendship after all I've done. The positive part rails against this thinking. I absolutely deserve their friendship, this life, and the happiness I have right now. I will never accept that what I've done was wrong.

The moment of uncomfortable silence is thankfully broken when the cat leaps onto the table, walking directly across to the tiny pile of mushroom pieces on Jo's plate. I silently thank Arial for the welcome interruption, and she flicks her tail as she digs into the mushrooms. Cal eyes the cat questioningly.

"She's real," Sylvia says, mouth full of pizza.

"Phew," Cal looks relieved and reaches up to stroke Arial's back.

That night, he makes love to me, slowly and gently. Not an inch of my skin is left untouched or un-kissed. As I shudder underneath his lips, tears well up and overflow. I cover my face, embarrassed for crying yet again but unable to quell the tide. My body is racked with sobs from deep within, and Cal holds me tight. He doesn't speak; he caresses my hair and back until I am quiet.

Suddenly, fear stabs into my heart like a cold penknife. I'm afraid this will end, that something awful will happen and I will die, ending this wonderful life. I'd once again be without friends and without love, having to start over again in a strange place in a strange time. The closet where I stash this kind of thinking is too full to contain any more. This fear makes me gasp, and I cling to Cal once more, using him to distract me from myself. I don't think he minds too much.

# Chapter 24

For several days, Cal stays at my home, forcing me to rest and taking care of my every need. It's wonderful to have him here—the perfect distraction from reflecting on my fate. But an urgent call from his sister about a troublesome client forces him to go. We walk to the front gate arm-in-arm. He gives me one last tight squeeze and nibbles my neck with an evil grin, knowing what that does to me. I smack him playfully on the chest and push him away. He turns, grinning smugly, and waves as he rounds the corner.

Turning back to the gate, my phone vibrates in my pocket. Jo is asking to meet me on the rooftop; she has something to show me. The spark of excitement is quickly overshadowed by trepidation. Something inside me prickles at Jo's words.

"What's your mother been up to?" I ask Sylvia as I pass through the shop.

"Nothing like what you've been up to." She leers at me, then waggles an eyebrow.

I throw her a look of feigned shock.

I pace when I reach the rooftop, anxious for Jo to leave the curse alone; there's nothing she can do. The truth is that I don't want to talk about it anymore, don't want to think about it anymore, don't want it to have any power over my life. I wring my clammy hands, getting more anxious as the moments tick by.

Jo's footsteps sound on the stairs and a second pair is in tow close behind her. I pull open the screen door for them.

"Well, don't you look like you're going to come out of your skin." She barely glances at me as she walks past. She's looking around the rooftop. Sylvia follows her gaze.

"Can you blame me? Your last news wasn't that great."

Jo turns with genuine hurt on her face.

"I'm sorry." I go to her, placing my hands on her upper arms. "Too soon to joke about it?"

She pats one of my hands and nods.

I squeeze her arms and let go. "Okay, so what's up? I'm kind of afraid to know."

Jo is still looking around and finds the object of her search behind me. I hear wings and talons on roof shingles but I don't bother turning. My body stiffens, instantly angry at that damn bird. This death stalker that duped me into liking it, watching over me when I was down. For what purpose? She is an unwelcome voyeur of my life, my *lives*.

Jo raises an eyebrow at my response, confused. She studies my face.

"The raven's just doing what she's supposed to do." She looks anxious now, as if she's made a mistake.

I close my eyes and unclench my fists. "I know."

"Hey, look!" Sylvia says behind me. What's the point of me turning around? She will only fly away. Jo motions for me to turn.

"What's that around his neck? Sorry, *her* neck?" Sylvia asks, squinting.

The rustle of feathers is followed by a soft warbling sound. I turn slowly, not sure now of what to expect. What's Jo done?

But there, perched on the tip of the main tower peak is the white raven—my view of her not obstructed by warped window glass or curtains. The heat that had been coursing through my body, the angry flames that licked at my heart, vanish at the sight of her. She seems bigger than when I saw her through the window. Set against the stark white of her silky feathers, her amethyst eyes glisten like small jewels, holding inside them an immeasurable amount of intelligence and wisdom.

I inhale sharply and the bird staggers back, losing her grip. She croaks loudly, clawing back to the top, wings out for balance, and looks down, one eye cocked at me, studying me intently. Her wings twitch as she looks me up and down. Around her neck is a thin black chain. It holds a polished gray stone against her quivering chest. The stone appears to pulse, flashing with bits of iridescent blue and green in the sunlight.

I can only stare at the bird, my weakening knees threatening to send me to the floor. My mouth has gone dry, and I doubt I could speak now if I tried. The bird nervously readjusts her grip on the steep peak and scrutinizes the ledge below her, closer to me, gauging whether she should take the leap or not. My stomach jumps when she does, flutteringly madly with her proximity. She looks at Jo, who gives her nods of encouragement, and then leaps once more down to the edge of a tall vase by the screen door. She is now only a few feet from me. My breathing quickens and blood pounds in my ears. I barely hear Jo ask me if I'm all right.

My anger has vanished, replaced by a sense of fulfillment as if I've just been reunited with a long-lost friend. Tears fill my eyes, and I tell myself not again, I will not cry anymore. But these tears aren't born of sadness but rather of a pure joy that I cannot explain. Still, I refuse to cry anymore.

Without taking my eyes from the white raven, I whisper to Jo, "What did you do? Is that one of your charms?"

She comes to my side. "When we talked, the raven and I, she told me that she could never come near you." I pull my gaze away from the bird and look questioningly at Jo. "Your energy is too strong; it pushes her away. It physically hurts her to be near you." My mouth shapes an "oh" but no sound comes out as I stand there dumb and deeply sad. "So I made something that I thought would shield her from your energy, deflect it, so you two could meet."

Realization blooms through me. "That's why she was able to come near me when I was in bed. I was very weak."

Jo nods.

"But as I got better, my energy returned; hence, she flew away."

Jo nods again and the raven croaks repeatedly as if to agree. "Labradorite seemed to be the best stone to use. I've found it shields energy better than anything I've used before. And I added my special touches, of course." She eyes her creation with pride.

I feel a sudden desire to rush at the bird, scoop her up in my arms, kiss her, and snuggle her, but I'm sure that will only frighten her. I take a small step forward, inclining my head. "Hi," is all I can come up with.

She bows her head. I extend a trembling hand. She pulls back slightly so I withdraw it.

Jo leans into me and whispers, "Why don't you go have a seat? Let her come to you when she's ready."

I nod and turn away, slowly so as to not alarm the bird. Jo motions to Sylvia to go downstairs, and she moves tentatively to the door, skirting around the jumpy creature. She holds the screen door so it doesn't slam.

Jo joins me on the chaise, and we are now in audience with the white raven, still perched on the vase. She bobs her head and ruffles her feathers, gurgling softly. I jump a little when she leaps up. She lands roughly on the back of the lounger, facing us, her balance somewhat off.

"I think we are all a little unhinged." Jo chuckles softly, acknowledging the bird's lack of grace.

I give Jo a passing smile, but my attention is on the raven. Her glossy feathers reflect the bright sunlight, giving her a glow that shimmers when she moves. She blinks at me, the violet of her eyes deep and rich. Being so close, seeing her in such detail, takes my breath away.

"Can I speak to you now?" I ask the raven. I turn to Jo. "Will your charm help with that?" She looks confused. "I tried to speak into her mind when she was at my window but that seemed to hurt her."

"Hmm," Jo says, cocking her head at the bird. "I don't know, honestly."

*You may speak now.*

The sound of the sweet, lilting voice in my head makes me gasp and cover my mouth with my hands. I stare at the white raven, eyes welling with tears once again. That voice! A laugh escapes my lips as do a few tears. Jo brings her hands together on her chest, rejoicing in this new development. She must have heard her also.

*I have wanted to talk to you for so long! Now, I have no idea what to say.* I take several deep breaths to calm myself. My skin tingles with goosebumps, happy goosebumps.

*Me too, me too. I asked your friend to help me. I am happy now.* The bird inclines her head to Jo. Jo bows back, her eyes glistening.

Guilt washes over me. *I know now why you've come and gone; why you'd run when I chased you. I'm so sorry for hurting you. Please know it wasn't intentional.*

*I know, I do know that. At first, I did not, long ago, but after a time, I understood what was happening.* She shakes her body and ruffles her feathers as if to push away painful memories.

I touch Jo's arm. "How long will the charm last?"

"I don't know that either. This is new territory for me. I'm damn proud of myself right now, though." Jo's expression is one of relief and great satisfaction.

"You should be!" I grab her hand and hold it. "I can never repay you for this, my friend."

"Oh, hush." She waves me off and looks at the bird. "You two have a lot of catching up to do." She stands slowly, surveying the bird for signs of fright at her movements. "I'll leave you alone." She gives me a warm, loving smile and bows again to the bird, who returns her gesture.

Jo watches us as she walks away. When she reaches the door, her face has changed. Her mouth is hanging open in surprise and something else, revelation maybe, as she studies us for a long moment. I open my mouth to ask what is wrong, but she shakes her head, waving me off, and ducks through the door.

Jo's strange reaction puzzles me, but I quickly put that out of my mind. I'm talking to the white raven!

*Please, tell me of your life. You have always been with me, but I know nothing about you. What is your name?* This comes out in a rush.

The white raven is quiet for a few moments, and I wonder if she can no longer hear me.

*I do not have a name. No one has given me a name.* She looks almost sad as she says this.

*Would you like a name?*

*What would you call me? What would be my name?*

*Ren,* I blurt out without thinking. Where did that come from? But it fits her. Pure.

*Ren. Ren?* The bird mulls the name over, her head tilting. *Yes. My name is Ren.*

*Well, Ren, tell me of your life.* I like the sound of her name in my head. It feels natural to say it.

*I follow you. When you are gone, I am sad. Alone again. I get mad at what happens to you. Mad, mad! I try to help. Sometimes, I can. I dive, I peck eyes, I claw hair and face. But other times, I cannot. I can only scream and flash my wings. When you are here, I follow, I watch, all the time. When you are gone, I wander.*

Her voice is like a song. Though her words make my heart ache for her, her voice in my head is comforting and fills me with joy.

*I know when you come back so I search for you. No matter where, I find you.*

Of all she has just said, one question comes immediately forward. *Why?*

*I do not know.* Her words are laced with sadness.

*I am so sorry you have suffered for me. I truly am. I wish I knew why. Thank you for helping me. And thank you for being here. Though I never saw you, knowing you were there gave me a certain sense of comfort.* Not until I spoke those words did I realize it. This elusive creature— always there but not, with me always but not—never let me feel alone because I wasn't. I realize that now and my throat tightens. *Thank you.*

She inspects the area below her and, with a little hop, lands on the seat cushion. Walking awkwardly over it, she hops onto the coffee table. She looks at me with one eye, up and down, then continues forward, each step well thought out. She considers my knee and I nod, trembling and smiling.

With another small, more graceful hop, she lands on my knee, instinctively gripping with her talons for balance. I ignore the sharp pain, too excited and elated to worry about such trifles. She puffs her feathers and settles down on my leg. She is light in spite of her size. I feel her little heart fluttering.

My hands are still, folded in my lap. I unclasp them, making my movements slow and deliberate, and move a hand closer to her. She watches it but doesn't shy away. I lift a few fingers and watch her; I feel her trembling more. I put my fingers down and let them rest right beside her. We sit in silence for several minutes, one another's presence enough to fill the void. Her breathing is slowing, as is mine, and the tension in her body eases.

Searching for words but finding none, I allow this peaceful time to speak the volumes that words would only diminish.

# Chapter 25

Curled on my side with Ren snuggled into my stomach, I've spent the night on the chaise. Several times, she awoke with a sharp croak, then settled back down. In the breaking dawn, she stirs; her feathers brush against my skin as she stretches. Opening my eyes, I am greeted by shiny violet jewels looking back at me.

*I dreamt of my last mate,* she says.

I adjust the cushion under my head to get a better view of her. *Oh?*

She looks a little sad at the thought of him. *He was a beautiful male, big, strong. Not white like me, there are not many, but black as a moonless night. We had many chicks together. Together for a long time.*

*I didn't know you had children.*

*Oh yes, many, many.* The smile in her voice is evident and her eyes brighten.

*I'm barren,* I say without remorse.

*I am sorry for you.*

*Don't be. I'm not. That would just be something else to lose.*

With that, her head bows and she turns away.

*I'm sorry, I've upset you.* I gently touch her chest with my fingers. Sometime during the night, we'd both relaxed into each other's presence without even noticing.

*It is sad, yes, to live past your mates and all of your children. Time and again. I have become accustomed to it but it is never easy.* She turns back to me and leans into my fingers, her eyes half closed.

*I have never seen other ravens around you.* My fingers trace the labradorite stone at her neck. The charm nestled within her feathers is cold to the touch.

*You are gone for long times. That is when I live for myself.*

I am amazed how her small words cut into me. I feel myself wanting to apologize for everything she has gone through.

*I am so sorry for all that you have suffered because of me. I wish I knew what draws us together.*

*Do not be sorry for I am not. This is our lot. I cannot ask for better for I know no better.* There is no sadness in her voice.

I close my eyes, running my fingers down her chest and her wing.

*How many lives have you lived? Do you go in and out of the Veil as I do?*

*Not die. Never died.*

My eyes snap open. Hers are closed and her body is soft. Tightness in my throat threatens to choke me. She feels the change in my energy and opens her eyes.

I search her smooth face. *You have lived this entire time? Almost a thousand years?* I can barely say these words.

Ren regards me with a tilt of her head. *Do not be sad for me. I have had many adventures, I have had many loves. I have lived a good life. This is my lot.* The matter-of-fact way she says this pulls me back away from the edge. I want to apologize again but there's no point.

*You have a marvelous attitude.* I smile at her. I will no longer feel sorry for myself. This poor creature has a greater curse than I;

however, she seems to have come to terms with it, so who am I to wreck that? She is much stronger than I.

*It is better now that we are together.* She settles back down and rests her beak over my wrist.

I hope Jo's charm lasts. I need to chat with her about it; maybe we'll make a backup just in case. Several backups.

After a short while, Ren becomes restless and says it's time for her breakfast. With a promise to be back, she hops to the end of the chaise and leaps into the air. I drift back into half-sleep, partially aware of the waking morning, the birds chirping, the cars droning around me. A honk and a shout wake me with a start.

Sylvia is helping a customer when I come down after showering. Sylvia is a natural with people; she has never met a stranger and can talk to anyone about anything. Unlike me, she isn't put off by someone's bad energy or negativity; she powers right over it as if it didn't exist. I think she takes it as a challenge to improve their mood if she can. I am very lucky, immensely lucky, to have her and her mother in my life.

The smile on my face as I watch her is instantly struck down by the lurching fear that plagues me. I'm *too* happy, I have too much, something will take this away. I take a shaky breath and push those thoughts away. Maggie trots to the base of the stairs and looks up at me, tail wagging, tongue lolling. She's not vexed, she shows me, nor should I be. I long to snuggle her fluffy mane.

My phone rings and it's Cal. His trip to Worcester is proving longer than expected. He should be back in a day or two and asks me to dinner. It's hard not to tell him yet about Ren, but it's too momentous a thing for a phone conversation.

Sylvia is walking the customer to the front gate and, to my surprise, gives her a parting hug. She comes back in, bouncing and smiling.

"That woman was *so* nice! Bertie. She's here from Denmark. Apparently, coming to 'Witch City' was on her bucket list." She tells me the woman's life story and all about her travels in the States. I marvel at Sylvia, wishing I had her zest and love of people.

"She fell in love with the shop! She's got two friends traveling with her and says she'll bring them by tomorrow after lunch."

"Remind me to put you on commission."

"You bet I will!" She beams at me and trots off to reorganize the shelves that now have vacant slots, thanks to her salesmanship.

"Your mom working this morning?" I call from the library, putting books back in the right order.

She appears in the doorway of the library, looking a little sheepish. "Well...she was holed up in her space all last night." My eyebrows go up, and I set the pile of books down, giving Sylvia my full attention.

"I know, I know." She raises her palms up in surrender. "I have no idea what she was doing in there. It was relatively quiet, considering some of the sounds I've heard come from that room." She shakes her head. "She packed up this morning, really early, and took off for the mountains. Said she was going to see her *mother*." Sylvia gives me big eyes.

That makes me pause. What would she need to speak to Matilda's Spirit about? I nod at Sylvia absently, lost in thought.

"Okay, so you're nodding. I looked at her like she was crazy. I mean, I've seen a lot of things—nothing should really surprise me anymore, but come on! Am I the only one who remembers that Grandma is dead?" Sylvia's exasperated look returns.

I chuckle lightly. "Sylvia, death is not the end, not by any means. It's possible to communicate with loved ones that have passed. In some cultures, it's customary to set a place at the dinner table each night for them. Some also make daily commutes to their ancestor's burial site to sit and chat."

Sylvia digests this information for a moment then looks at me. "What do you think she wants to talk to Grandma about?"

"I don't know. I hope she's not still bothering about this curse business." I pick up the books and hug them to my chest. "Did anything come up with Claudia or someone from the coven?"

"Not that I can think of. I don't think she's spoken to Claudia at all since the pyre." She stares out the window then turns back to me with a little jump.

"Oh, I know! Do that thing you do, peek into her mind or whatever that is. I'm sure you can find out what she's up to." Sylvia plops down in the nearest chair, eagerly awaiting my acquiescence to her suggestion.

"No, no." I give her a chiding look. "That's an invasion, and I don't do that unless *absolutely* necessary." Sylvia's face falls. "If she wanted us to know what she was doing, she would have said. We need to respect her privacy."

"Oh, poo." She crosses her arms over her chest and feigns pouting, then grins at me. "Had to ask."

I wave at her with motherly admonition to get back to work.

# Chapter 26

Cal comes by the shop to pick me up for our date. The shop is closed, and Sylvia has gone home to an empty house. Jo is still on her travels. I worry about her traipsing around in the woods alone. If I don't hear something from her by the morning, I'll use the Veil to find her.

The moment I see Cal walking up the pathway, I am instantly hungry for him. The door unlocks for him as his hand reaches for the handle, and he snatches it back when it opens without his intervention. I laugh aloud at the look on his face.

He laughs back, shaking his head. "I don't think I'm ever going to get used to that."

He sees me within the shadows cast by the setting sunlight and the mirth melts from his face, replaced with desire. He is upon me in several long strides, enveloping me in his strong arms, covering my mouth with his. I grip his back, feeling the taut muscles underneath his fitted shirt. I dig my nails in for a firmer grip, so he doesn't, *can't,* let me go, and he groans, moving his hands down to my rear, pulling my hips into him. His hardness pushes against me, and I move my hips slightly to taunt him.

He pushes me against the wall by the library and I let him. I wish I had worn a skirt. While my days without him have been full, more than full now with the active presence of the white raven, I need him desperately. I need him inside me; I need the closeness of union that only intimacy brings. I have been starved of this, all of my lives, this passion, this *release*. Seeing him, I am greedy, wanting to devour him whole.

His hands are under my blouse, raking trails of fire across my skin. I fumble at the button on my shorts. He has them open in an instant, his hands pushing them down past my rear as he bites at my neck. He falls to his knees.

We are late for our reservations, but Cal knows the right person to smooth it over. I follow the maître d' with Cal's hand resting on my lower back. Cal pulls out my chair and runs his hand up my back as I sit. I gaze into his glimmering blue eyes, and he brushes my lips with his. My heart is as light as the air around me.

He sits opposite me, looking around the restaurant as he unfolds his napkin. He sees something displeasing over my shoulder and grimaces, looking away. With my Sight, I look behind me and see the unpleasant sight *again*. Miss Perfect Pants is once again at the same restaurant we are. I roll my eyes.

"I am starving," I say, picking up the menu.

"Me too!" He snickers and we both giggle over our shared naughty secret.

"Well," I straighten up, sipping from the glass of water, "tell me about this fun trip you had."

Cal groans and makes an exaggerated exhale. "There was *no* reason for me to be there, none. My sister usually handles the inspection stuff, but that jackass doesn't want to deal with a 'little girl.'" Cal huffs in disgust. "He's such an ass. Trish hates him. Well, she secretly loves to torment him because she knows how much he dislikes working with her."

"I like your sister already."

"Speaking of," he swallows and takes a big gulp of water. "My family is having a get-together next month. I'd like you to come."

The waiter comes back for our drink orders. He is stiff and not particularly pleasant. He leaves quickly with a curt nod after we make our requests.

"You really want me to meet your family?" I ask, wiping my clammy palms on the napkin in my lap.

"Sure, why not?"

"Well, hmm, let's see. Oh yeah, because I'm a witch. Isn't your whole family Catholic?"

"Non-practicing. We should be fine if we steer clear of religion and politics. My brother is the loudmouth when it comes to those two topics, but he's in Afghanistan. And don't worry, Will won't be there. He's going on a camping trip with some of his buddies and their parents. I'm not real happy about that. He gets more distant every day. He needs to be around his family but he doesn't seem to give a damn anymore."

I'm glad to hear Will won't be there. I wonder if he's tried to pilfer anything since I hexed his hand.

When the waiter returns, he hands the wrong drinks to each of us. We switch our glasses, and he mumbles an apology as he walks away.

"Sure, I'll come. But I will be sweating the whole time." I'm nervous just thinking about it, and I take a long sip of my gin and tonic.

He shakes his head. "No reason to be. Most of my family is pretty laid back. You and Trish will totally hit it off."

I trace my index finger around the rim of my glass, staring at the lime floating within. "I've not met anyone's family before."

"Serious? Wow. I assumed that with all the lives you've lived..." He stops, his eyes apologetic. "I'm sorry. I can't believe I said that."

"It's all right. I guess it's not realistic to think the topic will just go away." I sigh and reach for his hand across the table. He grips mine, reinforcing his apology. "To be perfectly honest, I'd rather forget all about it. I want to live in the here and now, and not worry about what has happened or what is to come. It's the only way I can get through it." I didn't mean to say that last part, but the words fell from my lips without bidding. "I'm sure it will come up again, and that's fine, no way to keep from it." An overwhelming urge to erase everyone's memories of the whole blasted business comes over me but no, that wouldn't be right.

He pulls my hand up as far as it will reach then bends over the rest of the way to kiss it. There are words on his lips, but he doesn't speak them. After a long moment, Cal tells me about the lake house his dad built, where the family gathering will be, and gives me the scoop on all the attendees. It's obvious from his body language that he needs to talk, to ramble about something to push the curse from his mind. I know that feeling well.

Dinner comes and it is delicious. We eat slowly as we continue to talk and laugh, and share a naughty giggle when I wipe a drop of cream sauce from my chin. I am so perfectly happy, so delirious with endorphins, that I don't sense the severe negativity approaching from behind until it's right upon me. I gasp inwardly, choked by it and by the toxic amount of perfume that accompanies it.

"Aven!" Miss Perfect Pants's schoolgirl cry stabs into my ears. A wide, phony smile is plastered across her unnaturally tan face, bright red lips clashing with her glitter-dusted pink cheeks. Her hands are clasped between her enormous fake tits that are stuffed into a tight blouse.

I'm surprised by her gracious and pleasant demeanor even though I know it's false. Everything about the woman is fake. The very thought of this charlatan angers me, and I realize immediately it was a mistake to send her an invitation to the grand opening; I'd let my cattiness get the better of me.

"Mandy." I incline my head to her, fully aware that I'm not allowed to call her Mandy, and the flash of annoyance across her face proves it. Her expression quickly returns to the fake, whole-face smile.

She glances at Cal, then turns her friendly mask back to me. "I wanted to thank you for the invitation to your opening. That was so sweet!" A manicured hand snakes out at me, tapping me on the shoulder to emphasize 'sweet.' I can't help but recoil from her touch. "I wouldn't miss it. Consider this my R-S-V-P." She spells out each letter with enthusiasm.

Mandy puts her hands on her hips and cocks them to one side. She turns her attention to Cal, who avoids her eyes by taking a sip of his beer.

"Hello, Calvin. How've you been?"

Her eyes dart over to me to gauge my reaction to the news that she and Cal have met. My passive expression does not change.

He sets his beer down with a thud and looks up at her, his sour expression slightly masked by his own fake smile. "Excellent. You?"

She giggles somewhat uncomfortably and snakes her arms behind her back, accentuating the curve of her hips and breasts. I refrain from giving her a zap. It would be so easy—just a little jolt of electricity into those bangles and she'd flail around like a drowning chimpanzee. I bite my lip to hold back my grin.

"Good! Me too." She's run out of things to say. "Well, you two look so cozy, I'll get out of your hair. See you at the opening!" She wiggles her fingers at me in a childish wave as she struts away.

I exhale loudly when she is out of earshot. Her perfume still lingers, and it's still just as potent.

Cal gives me wide eyes. "That woman is a *mess*."

"She definitely wanted me to know that you two knew each other."

He grunts. "Yeah. We met once when she called us out for a quote to expand the bathroom in her condo. The moment she saw me, she started hitting on me. It was *not* pretty." He gulps the last of his beer. "She's called me a few times since, but I always send my sister out now. Trish loves a challenge."

I will really like his sister.

Part of me pities Mandy. She's so insecure that she has to make sure she one-ups everyone around her. Unfortunately, the weak-minded follow her blindly, bowing to her perceived beauty and power. She's made herself quite wealthy off the gullibility of others, taking advantage of sad stories of lost loved ones. She does whatever she can to make a buck.

"There are too many people like *her* in this town," Cal says in disgust. I'm sure he put me in her category when we first met.

"Let's change the subject. I was going to invite you to the party but since it was a bit away, I thought I'd wait. Didn't want to seem too eager."

"And here I am inviting you to meet my family after only, what, a month?" Cal looks a little embarrassed.

"Cal Jacobs, would you like to come to the grand opening of Dovenelle's? It will be a *spectacular* Halloween party. I guarantee it."

"Why, Miss Dovenelle, I'd love to. Consider this my R-S-V-P." And with that, we both laugh aloud.

# Chapter 27

Janet Kellogg had always hated her name. It lacked all imagination and reflected none of the qualities that made her who she was. Janet Kellogg—'Flakes' she was called in school—had been teased, bullied, and picked on. But Mandala Moonchild is a powerful medium—well respected in the community and the owner of one of the most prosperous new age shops in Salem. Mandala Moonchild *always* gets what she wants.

Mandy, as she allows only her friends to call her, strums her freshly manicured stiletto nails on the glass top of her dining room table. She absently watches the Swarovski crystal on each nail glint in the glow of the crystal chandelier. It does nothing to brighten her mood.

The interior of her spacious condo is spotless and organized, bordering on OCD. Her vast collection of tchotchkes is arranged carefully by type and size, and then by color. Gnomes, matryoshka dolls, porcelain birds, crystal and wire mini-trees, and all manner of tourist paraphernalia from the forty-six states she's visited in the last twenty years are placed artfully around her home. The bright colors and precious memories make Mandy feel comfortable and happy. Except for right now. Right now, she is pissed.

That flat-chested bitch Aven is now going out with the guy Mandy has had her eye on for months. Mandy has gone to great lengths to get him to notice her, wearing her best miniskirts, spiked heels, and blouses just tight enough to show off her ample and perky breasts without giving too much away. You have to leave them wanting more, her mom used to say. Mandy is proud of her new boobs; they are the most perfectly shaped ones that Dr. Molina of the Boston elite has ever crafted. And he said as much. She's been to see him twice more for other tucks and lifts here and there, and she looks amazing. Everyone says so.

For a woman of forty-three, Mandy considers herself pretty damn hot. This has been validated on many occasions when she's cougared, and she never tires of watching younger men's eyes follow her. *And* she owns her own business, which is thriving. She is in the prime of her life. She has everything she wants...except a steady man.

So then why does this Cal guy want to go out with a nothing like Aven? Barely any tits, dark fly-away hair, pretty plain in the face, and way too intense and uppity. Mandy's blonde hair is always coiffed to perfection, and her makeup is a work of art. She has a sparkling laugh and a delightful personality. What's not to love? Men are so stupid. She slugs down the last of the merlot in disgust.

The Spirit of Morris Stiles wafts along the edge of the Veil, aimless. He is listless and slow, lacking the energy to do much else than brood about the unfairness of it all. Aven Dovenelle thought she'd be cute and erase the memories of his kin—the only kin that ever had the decency to think about him. That might have drained him of his primary source of energy, but there are many people in this town who dislike that woman. She's ruffled a lot of feathers coming in like she did, getting the building permits as fast as she did, and having the inspectors pretty much eating out of her palm. He didn't have to go far to sense the grumblings against Aven. Anger and hate are his favorite meals.

But those little spats haven't been enough to sustain him for any length of time. If he's going to stay in this plane and get his revenge against that goddamn witch, he needs to find a consistent source of negativity. Or maybe just a little bit and he can fan the flames like he did with Melissa. That stupid girl really let him down. He was ashamed that she was blood.

He clings to the flow of the Veil, allowing its current to send him here and there. Something will turn up sooner or later. Has to.

It's not long after that a hint of hostility tugs at Morris's Spirit. He quivers. Even this small amount makes his senses tingle. With the last of his energy, he pulls himself together and follows the tantalizing scent.

Mandy pours herself another glass of merlot and stares out at the city lights from her balcony. She needs to put Aven Dovenelle in her place, but how to do so is proving hard to figure out. She wonders if Aven and Cal are fucking. The very idea enrages her. Her over Mandy! Cal is really missing out. Mandy is proud of her sexual skills and is certain that there is no way Aven is better than her.

Mandy stretches her legs out on the sectional and arranges the cushions more comfortably behind her back. She must remind her maid again exactly how the cushions should be placed.

If there's no way to get Cal to wise up, then she'll just have to get a better man and make sure Aven sees them together. It's so easy to make a woman jealous. Aven will be no exception.

As Mandy relishes picturing Aven's jealous face at seeing her and her fictitious more-handsome-than-Cal man, the city lights start to wink out before her. She squints. A charcoal-black mantle builds around everything in view. Her skin prickles with a sudden panic she can't explain. She sets her wine glass on the side table and pulls her knees to her chest. The blackness overtakes the skyline; it creeps towards her, achingly slow, over the balcony and across the tiled floor. She tries to cry out but chokes instead, as if an invisible hand is around her throat. Her heart is pounding in her ears, and she feels as if she's wrapped in a blanket of ice.

*Oh, yes. Yes. You'll do jus' fine.*

The grating voice echoes around her and makes Mandy's blood run cold. As a medium, she pretends to channel and speak to spirits and ghosts, but has never actually seen one and doesn't believe they are real when it comes right down to it. She doesn't have any powers either, she knows that. She's all about the tricks—lighting, smoke, and manufactured sounds; her sessions are never real. Her clients eat it up like candy; it's so easy to fool the bereft and lonely. People who say they're real are just fakes and liars. Ghosts don't really exist. *Someone is playing a trick on me,* she repeats to herself. She'll get that person, right after she learns how they did all this. This is pretty awesome. How are they managing the darkness-closing-in effect way up here?

*This ain't no trick, you stupid woman.*

Mandy jerks away from the frightening voice, or she would if she could move. She finds herself paralyzed, frozen, and her panic threatens to send her into convulsions.

The black curtain before her tears, as if someone is clawing at the thick drape from the other side. The quivering fabric splits and opens wide in jagged cuts, with pieces falling to the ground and disappearing. What is coming through makes Mandy fight against her frozen body; her mouth opens in a desperate scream, but she hears only silence.

The face that appears is not of flesh and bone but translucent and vague, and seems to be made from dirty brown smog. It looks at her with dark pits for eyes, and a malevolent grin on its jagged, gap-tooth mouth goes grotesquely wide at the sight of her. Mandy struggles against the invisible restraints, desperate to get away. She is too young to die, she has so much to live for! As the rest of the figure snakes through the torn and weeping fabric, fear's grip closes tight around her and a silent scream fills her ears.

# Chapter 28

Jo is finally back, gracing us with her presence in the late afternoon. There are hugs all around and an aggressive shake from daughter to mother, admonishing Jo for making her worry.

"Oh, stop your fussing, girl, I'm too tired." Jo falls into the nearest chair on the porch. "Aven, if you would be a dear."

My hand passes over the table, and a glass materializes, promptly filled with her favorite whiskey and one ice rock.

We start to sit, but Jo puts a hand up to Sylvia.

"Not you. Go home." Jo says this more unkindly than I believe she means to.

Sylvia's mouth pinches shut. Her mother has that look, and Sylvia knows better than to argue. With an insulted harrumph, she turns on her heel and throws open the front door. We sit in silence and listen to her stomp around and slam cabinet doors while she gathers her things. The door flies open again.

"Don't break my door, please."

She catches it before it slams and stomps down the stairs. She's gentler with the gate.

Jo watches her daughter stalk away, a touch of regret in her eyes. "I'm sometimes glad she doesn't have any *real* powers." Then she stops, realizing she spoke those words aloud.

"Jo." I put a hand on hers. "What is it?"

Her eyes are cast down, staring at our hands. "I watched you two, you and the white raven, that first day." She seems a little embarrassed. I nod and keep silent.

She traces her index finger along the polished obsidian cabochon of my ring, the wheels in her mind working hard behind her distant eyes. The noise of the world around us—the traffic, the chatter of people on the sidewalk, the calls of songbirds, the random barking of dogs—fades from my ears and there is silence. I watch Jo, aware that her breathing has relaxed somewhat; the slight breeze carries her scent of patchouli in my direction. Her long auburn hair seems to have more gray wisps within, and they flutter like spiderwebs. I squeeze her fingers gently to pull her from her reverie.

"When I walked away and glanced back," she says, picking up from where she'd left off, "I saw something strange. I needed to make sure I wasn't seeing things or losing my already scattered mind even more, so I sat there inside the door."

My interest is piqued, as are the hairs on the back of my neck. A sense of dread is creeping over my skin. I fight it and return my focus to Jo.

"You and the white raven, you two have the same energy." She sits up and leans back, meeting my gaze. "The pattern of energy flow, your vibration: there is a particular *glow* about you that I always assumed was unique to you. Everyone has an aura; some colors are vivid, some are faded or muddy—all depends on the mood, you know—and they move in waves and ripples around them. Yours is different. Your colors are striking and change dramatically with your energy. Your aura *pulses* instead. It's not something I've ever seen before; it's beautiful and mesmerizing." She snorts a light laugh. "You probably thought I was gay when we first met, with me always staring at you."

244

Laughing, I realize I'd never thought anything of it. I am used to being stared at for what I am, and Jo's looks were never judgmental.

"I'd always seen it on you when I put my eye out for it but never saw it on the bird before. I never really paid much attention to the white raven until recently. I usually don't bother with looking at the energies of animals unless a client has asked me to see what's wrong with their pet. Anyway, when I saw you two together, I first thought that your energy was encompassing the bird. But that wasn't the case. She has the same pattern and glow as you do: the same vibration, the same frequency—the same *pulse*. It was amazing to watch."

While I can see auras if I try, it's not a gift I have in abundance. I feel energy more than anything else, and sometimes see shades of color but mostly when in the Veil. I envy Jo's ability.

"Do you believe that means something? Well, obviously you do or you wouldn't be like this." Goosebumps rise on my skin as Jo's look intensifies.

"You two are connected, there's no doubt about that. When she told me she couldn't come near you because your energy was too strong, I didn't think much more about it. I just made a charm to shield its effect on her. But after what I saw, it got me thinking. Your energy repels her like magnets of the same polarity repel each other. You two are the same."

My brow crinkles. "That can't be. She's immortal."

"Not the same in the physical sense," Jo clarifies. "Your Spirits seem to be the same."

I look at her, confused, not certain where she's going with this or what it means.

She clears her throat and pulls her hand away. "I think this is significant, actually," she says responding to my confusion. "So much so that I needed guidance from my mother's Spirit."

My heartbeat has quickened, and my palms are moist. I want to shake her to make her spit it out.

"As you know, my family has a little bit of land west of here. We've used it for generations not only as a site for major rituals, but also as a place to commune with loved ones long gone. It's gorgeous really—hidden in a valley, loaded with trees, and there's a creek dotted with little waterfalls. It doesn't have cell coverage or I'd move there, but it *does* have a portal to the Veil."

My eyes widen. "Really? How did your family find that? I had to *make* that mirror."

"Later, long story," she says, dismissing the question with a wave. "Anyway, I had to go back there to speak with Mom if she hadn't moved on yet. It took a while for her to show up— she was on her way to another plane when she heard my call. All in all, it turned out to be a pretty fruitless conversation in terms of helping me understand why you two appear to have the same energy. She did say something, though, that got me thinking. 'Look back to the past. See what is not there.' And I'm like, 'What the hell does that mean?'" She shakes her head, annoyed at the memory. "That woman always did love her riddles. She's worse now that she's a Spirit!" Jo tuts and stares out at the garden for a long moment.

"What do you remember about your first life?" Jo asks, still staring at nothing in the garden.

This unexpected question sets me back in the chair, recoiling my arms over my chest. "You've asked me that before. 'Not much' is still the answer." I'm annoyed suddenly for no apparent reason. I inhale deeply to calm myself. "Sorry. Really, Jo, my first life is a mystery for the most part."

"And therein lies the answer!" She breathes these words out and returns her attention to me. "That's the 'what is not there,' I think, in Mom's riddle. You remember everything from every other life except that one. Don't you think that's weird? There's *got* to be something there that can tell us why you two look the same."

*The same.* These words echo through my mind. That would explain why we have such a strong connection. But how can Spirits be the same?

"What do you suggest?"

"We need to do a past life ritual," she says quickly as if already having the words on the tip of her tongue.

A brick forms in my stomach, and it's suspended by rising bile. I am afraid of what I'll discover. I've always let myself believe my first life was so boring, so uneventful, that there's nothing worth remembering. Something inside me is niggling now, scratching at the door behind which all my memories are crammed, telling me that is not true.

"Why is finding out why we are the same important?" This question comes out of my mouth before I knew the words were there.

Jo looks away, back out to the garden.

"What are you hiding?" My eyes narrow at her.

She scoots up in her seat, straightening her back. "Nothing! Not a thing. Just thinking about how to do this ritual."

She is lying. I will leave it for now. I'm not sure I want to know anyway.

She looks around, leaning forward to get a glimpse of the sky. "Where's the white raven?"

"She flew off a little bit ago, just before you got here. Dinner time. She'll be back soon."

"She needs to be in the ritual," Jo says with some urgency.

"You can ask her. I'm sure she'll want to be there. She doesn't remember when or where she was born either." As those words leave my mouth, we both lean back and stare at each other.

"Really?" Jo says, head cocked to the side. "Isn't that interesting?" Her suspicions seem to be validated with this new bit of information.

"Wow, yeah. I just remembered that. Huh."

"Sound familiar?" Jo's eyebrows are up

The gears in my mind spin. I shake off the lingering trails of apprehension that have plagued me during this conversation. I push my chair back and stand up quickly, the legs of the chair scraping against the wood of the porch, making Jo wince.

"Come on, I'm hungry. I was going to heat up the leftover lasagna. Want some?"

"Sure." Jo perks up. She loves my spicy take on the traditional lasagna. "Where's Cal tonight?" she asks, following me inside. Arial runs in between us as a clamor of angry chittering comes from the aster bush.

"Arial! What did you do?" I call after her. Her response is to continue her run up the stairs.

"Uh-oh. That can't be good." Jo's looking behind her, wary of an onslaught of irate fairies.

I sigh and shake my head. "They have to work out their differences on their own. I can't be referee all the time."

"I can just see it now: Arial trussed up on a spit like a pig over a fairy bonfire." Jo laughs out loud at the vision.

I frown, knowing too well that could really happen.

As we head up the stairs, I answer her question. "Cal's back in Worcester today and tomorrow. Client problems."

Jo scarfs down her heaping portion of lasagna, saying it's been days since she's had a proper meal. Ren has returned and settles on the window sill in the kitchen, still leery of coming indoors.

I introduce Ren to Jo, telling her how we came about the bird's name. Jo likes the name, but says it lacks the grandeur befitting such a magnificent creature. Ren looks as if she is embarrassed by Jo's compliment.

When Jo finishes chugging a full glass of water to quell the rising heat in her mouth, she regales Ren with her travels and discoveries. The bird listens intently, becoming excited when the past life ritual is mentioned.

*You are thinking we lived in the same life together? Maybe we are sisters. Sisters!* She cocks her head and bobs her whole body, clearly happy with that prospect.

"That would mean you are cursed also," I say, looking at my empty plate. If she is my sister and she is cursed too, perhaps my whole family is cursed. The thought sours in my belly.

Jo sighs. "I don't really know what I think."

The way she fidgets with her fork and shifts in her seat tells me she is still lying. Maybe not *lying* exactly but withholding something she knows will upset me. Given the things she's revealed to me recently, she can hold on to those thoughts as long as she wants.

Ren chatters on, undaunted by what she might discover from the ritual—unlike me, who's fretting about the very notion of the thing. As I regard her and Jo exchanging ideas, it becomes apparent how utterly positive this bird is. I guess you'd have to stay upbeat being an immortal, having to push aside the negativity and terror you experience in all that time. Otherwise, I'd think you'd go mad. What must she have gone through—always wanting to be with me but unable to get close, watching the terrible events that have happened to me, powerless to defend me, and then the endless waiting, waiting. Not knowing where or when I'd come back. I close my eyes as if the darkness could hide me from those thoughts. Ren has fared amazingly, and I envy her. I would not have done so well by any means.

"Aven, what's wrong?" Jo leans over.

Her voice snaps me back, feeling only now the warm trail of tears down my cheeks. I wipe my face and wave off her concern.

"Oh, gosh." I try a laugh. "Nothing. Lost in thought."

Ren is leaning in, peering at me with a glittering eye.

*What sadness is in you? What are your thoughts?* She lifts up her chest and ruffles her feathers, slightly alarmed.

"I'm fine, really." I pull one leg up in the seat and lean forward for my water, trying my best to appear casual and calm.

"You're worried about the ritual?" Jo asks, watching my hand.

"What did I experience that was so horrific, so vile, so terrible that I cannot remember it?" The question slips from my lips without my permission.

Jo's eyes fall from mine, and Ren emits a soft croak, head bowed.

Jo pushes a tiny piece of sausage around on her plate with her fork. She opens her mouth to say something but closes it immediately.

Ren's sweet and calm voice fills my head. *What has happened is past. It is gone, long ago gone. What you will see are sights only, they cannot hurt you.*

250

Such wisdom can only come from someone long alive in this world and much experienced in pain and suffering. I utter an agreement and put an unwanted forkful of food in my mouth, hoping the heat from the spice will distract my belly from making any more knots.

# Chapter 29

When Cal is back, I invite him over for dinner. The evening brings with it a pleasant chill. As we eat under the pergola and the careful watch of the white raven, I catch myself chattering aimlessly, nervous about what I need to tell him. Ren rests at the edge of the roof behind us awaiting my signal to present herself.

"Have you decided what you are wearing to the Halloween party?"

"Like a costume? Uh, no. I like a good party as much as the next man, but I'm not wearing a costume," Cal scoffs before popping a piece of bread into his mouth.

I purse my lips at him. "No boyfriend of mine is coming to a Halloween party *not* in costume."

He stares at me for a few seconds, and a grin curls the edges of his mouth. "So I'm your boyfriend?"

My cheeks flush hotly, and I look away. I can't believe I've just said that! I search for words to redeem myself but nothing comes.

He laughs, cupping my red face in his hands. "I'm proud to be your boyfriend, Aven." His kiss is passionate and one arm reaches around me, pulling me to him.

I melt into his embrace, forgetting everything I wanted to tell him. It takes all my strength to release my lips from his. I rest my forehead against his, allowing me time to catch my breath.

"I need to tell you some things," I whisper, not wanting the harshness of speech to kill this tender moment.

He is kissing my neck, a little nibble on my ear lobe, and my already warm body increases in temperature. "Can't you tell me later?" he murmurs against my ear. I desperately want to; I want to push my real life aside once again and bathe in this blissful sea, ignoring everything around me.

Against what my body wants, I push him back slightly at the shoulders. He doesn't resist but groans with disappointment. He leans back against the chaise with a wary eye.

How many more of my secrets can this man take?

He answers my unspoken question. "Don't worry, I can take it." He takes my hand and entwines his fingers with mine.

This small gesture sends a wave of relief over me. It's quickly overshadowed by thoughts of what his limits truly are, of how far I can push his grip on reality until he breaks.

I search for where to start and how. It takes me several minutes to compose my racing thoughts. I reposition myself to better face him.

"You've seen the white raven, yes?"

"Yeah," he chuffs. "I see it every time I come over. It was pretty aggressive towards me the night of the tornado." He looks away. He then shakes his head and returns his gaze to mine.

"She has been with me in every life."

His brow furrows with skepticism.

I continue undaunted. "In every life I can remember, a white raven has been present. However, I'd never actually *seen* it. I could hear its wings flap and its cries, but every time I looked, it would be gone; when I would chase, it would flee. It was frustrating, to say the least. But something amazing has happened recently, thanks to Jo. The white raven, *she*, has finally been able to show herself, to approach me." I lift my free hand skyward.

Sounds of scraping claws and flapping wings fill the air. Ren coasts overhead and angles downward to alight gracefully on the back of the lounger across from us.

The sight of the striking bird so close makes Cal jump. The moonlight intensifies her white feathers and creates a shimmering aura around her. Cal takes in a sharp breath as Ren bows her head to him.

"Cal, meet Ren."

An exaggerated 'wow' escapes from his lips.

"We have a connection that neither of us understands. Jo has been endeavoring to find out what that is."

Cal tears his eyes away from the bird. "Connection?"

"It's difficult to explain, the feeling, the *bond*, we have between us. She is compelled to follow me through my life and to seek me out each time I return. I have always looked for her, whether I realized it or not, and knew when she was there. She told me—"

"*Told* you?"

"She speaks to me in my mind as I'm sure she tried to do with you. But most non-magickal people aren't very open to such communication."

Cal's eyes widen. "So I *did* hear her talk!" He recounts their first meeting and the bird yelling at him to not leave.

Ren puffs up her chest feathers, proud of her efforts to speak to him. "Need practice. Not made words in long time." While her voice is scratchy, her words are clearly understood.

Cal is aghast. I laugh lightly at him. "To be fair, all ravens can talk, some better than parrots. They are extremely intelligent birds." I gaze at her with the pride of a mother. "She is in no way like other ravens, though."

"How so?"

"She's immortal."

"Of course she is!" Cal says. "I'd expect nothing less at this point."

The edges of my lips turn down. "Are you mocking me?"

"No, no," he laughs, taking my other hand. "It's just...nothing about you is normal, nothing. Which is not a bad thing, don't get me wrong. So I kind of expected something *extra* to come out of this little introduction—and I was right."

"I'm glad you feel that way because I have one more thing." I look at him expectantly.

"Lay it on me," he says, full of confidence in his ability to accept anything I say now.

I take a deep breath. "Jo thinks that we can discover what this connection is from events in my first life. I don't remember much of it at all, which is odd, so she wants to perform a past life ritual. This will, hopefully, show us a vision, enough to discern what that connection might be or where it comes from."

Cal nods, waiting for more.

"I want you to be a part of that."

His face does not falter, nor do his eyes leave mine. I feel compelled to continue.

"You are very important to me. *She* is very important to me. I want to share this with you because..." I choke. How do I say *because if you can withstand that, you'll be able to withstand anything and stay with me?*

"Because if I can take it, I'll be able to take anything," he says matter-of-factly. I'm surprised by his level of understanding. "This is a test."

"No, no, no!" I scoot closer to him. "Please don't think of it like that. It's not—" His loving expression stops my words.

"I'm kidding, silly woman." He pulls our hands to his lips and kisses them. His jovial grin fades, and he exhales heavily through his nose. "What I've seen already is enough to make a believer out of anyone, or make one run away screaming, calling for the nearest priest. But there is something about you. I feel things with you, for you, that I've never felt with any other woman. I don't want to run, I don't think I could run. I'm almost morbidly curious about this life of yours. I want to see everything you have to show me."

Ren makes a soft gurgling sound deep in her chest, and she sways to the side as if dancing. My heart threatens to cut off my oxygen.

A laugh bubbles up instead. "Where have you been all my lives?" I ask dramatically, pulling my hands from his and leaping at him, pinning him to the back of the chaise.

With a cry that sounds like a laugh, the white raven launches herself from the chair and soars away—knowing, it seems, that it's a good time to leave the humans to themselves.

# Chapter 30

"The next full moon is a week and a half from now. Perfect," Jo mutters as she flips through the fifth book she's pulled off her overly stocked shelves.

We've been in her sacred space the entire morning, working out the details for the past life ritual. Jo doesn't have access to her mother's Book of Shadows, having been denied it when her mother died. By rights it goes to the coven leader, and Claudia is loath to let Jo borrow it even for a short time.

Jo's own grimoire is fat and heavy, growing more so with each passing year. Its dark purple leather is worn black in places, and its brass hinges are tarnished with age and use. Some of what she needs is in there, but this particular ritual is new territory for her and she must consult every book. She frets about the right ingredients and penning just the right incantation with all the proper steps. Jo's house may be a mess but her sacred space and her mind are not when it comes to magick.

I sit idly by after several attempts to offer help and finally being told to shush. Her space is cozy and comfortable. I almost doze off, reclining on a pile of pillows in the corner. I rouse myself as my eyes droop.

"So where will we be having this?" I ask, too loudly for the quiet room.

The sudden interruption jolts Jo from her examination of the first book she pulled from the shelf, having laid it out on the floor, lining up the others as they are removed. She sits cross-legged and looks uncomfortable in that position, but she must not be since she's not moved for the last ten minutes.

"Huh?" She looks at me blinking as if she had forgotten I was there. Her brain processes my question slowly. "Oh, yeah, um..." She scans the open books and runs her fingers over the page of one that looks particularly old and weathered.

"At night, of course, under the full moon, obviously. Outside." Her fingers dance through the tiny, condensed crowd of words on the page. "It needs to be high up, preferably in a natural setting. Next to water is ideal."

After she doesn't speak for several minutes, I suggest Mount Greylock as a potential place.

Her head whips up with an accusatory look. "How do you know about Mount Greylock?"

"It's not a secret. Isn't it a state park or something like that? I don't think there's anything high along the coast. We'd have to go west."

Jo's face changes and she laughs at herself. "Sorry. The Berkshire Hills is where we have our little speck of land, not far from Greylock."

"You own land in a state park?"

"Well...nobody really *owns* land." She looks away sheepishly. I give her a raised eyebrow. "No, we don't have a *deed* to any land out there. It's a spot my great-great-grandmother found, hidden away in a secluded valley, and we've been using it ever since. It's so remote, though—and a pretty good hike. That's why we only use it for very special rituals or when we *really* need to speak to the dead.

"But you are on to something," she continues. "There are tons of creeks running through there. I think being by water is more important than being high." She consults a different book. "It may be height is recommended simply to ensure an unobstructed view of the full moon…and privacy."

The lightbulb goes off in my head. "Maybe Ren could fly over and find a good spot."

Jo lights up. "Yes!" She flips the book closed with certainty. "Excellent idea."

We retire to the bistro table and chairs under the ancient white ash tree in Jo's garden. The white raven joins us soon after, perching on the back of the third chair, preening after her morning repast. She loves the idea of scouting for the perfect location and will leave as soon as she's properly clean.

Jo continues to mutter to herself about what she'll need for the ritual—what sigils must be used, what stones and oil blends are needed to increase the power of the incantation, the precise hour of night it should start. Her face is lined with worry, when it first had been glowing with excitement.

"Jo." I put my hand over hers. "It doesn't have to be so complicated. I know you love creating rituals and all of the preparation that's involved, but really, you are stressing yourself way too much."

"Aven, it *has* to be perfect. If I forget anything, it won't work!" Her cheeks are red, and the lines between her eyes deepen. She stares at me pointedly. "You put a block on that life for a reason; I have to do battle with *your* magick."

"You think I did this?" My skin prickles, followed by a twinge of aggravation.

Her eyes are hard. "It's *your* life…"

I straighten in the chair, partially offended by her accusation and partially worried that she is right. Ren has stopped her meticulous preening and looks at me also. My mouth falls open under the weight of their stares and the truth of Jo's words coming to light.

"I…" I try to speak, to make a defense and to exclaim how ridiculous this is, but no words come. I stare at the weathered candle stub in the middle of the table.

Jo's face softens. "I'm sorry to be the one to tell you. But really, who else, or what else, would have the power to put such a powerful spell on you, on *your* life, other than you?"

My heart sinks with growing realization. For all this time, it has been me who has been blocking me. I hardly ever gave a thought to my first life, to why I remember nothing but scant bits and pieces. Perhaps that is part of the spell I wove—making myself unconcerned about it so that I would never look, making myself believe it was such a boring and uneventful life that it was not worth delving into.

My thoughts must be revealed on my face. Jo leans back in her chair, feeling vindicated at the level of detail she's gone into for this ritual. "See why I've been stressing?"

I reluctantly nod in agreement. This does change things.

"I still stand by what I said, though. What's needed is your magick. You are more powerful than you realize, Jo. All the trappings of the ritual are niceties; what is required is razor-sharp, focused intent. And not just from you, but from me. If I did this, then I must work against myself also."

*I help? I help too?* Ren looks back and forth from me to Jo, hopping on the back of the chair. Her exuberance makes me smile. Nothing daunts this lovely creature.

"Possibly," Jo says, the gears in her mind starting up again.

Ren bows low to Jo. Jo tilts her head in response. The bird ruffles her feathers, shaking her whole body and stretching out her wings to their fullest extent. Seeing her like this, it's no wonder that white ravens have been worshiped, and feared, throughout time.

She hops to turn around and face the yard. She bends her strong legs and leaps up. Her wings lift her easily, and she is aloft without much effort. Jo and I watch her fly away, in awe of her beauty and grace, in the direction of Mount Greylock.

# Chapter 31

"Okay, ladies, let's go!" Cal shouts at Jo's house. From the driveway, we hear slamming doors and Jo and Sylvia bickering.

The bed of Cal's truck is packed to the brim with everything we need for a couple of days of hiking and camping, all of it strapped down with more bungee cords than I think are necessary. But Cal took charge of our little expedition, boasting a crew cab truck with four-wheel drive and years of backpacking experience. Jo was happy to hand the duties of trail master over to him.

After Ren found the ideal spot atop a lower peak near Mount Greylock, the wheels of organizing the outing were set in motion. Jo spent several days writing the ritual, secluded in her sacred space and taking only liquids as nourishment, emerging yesterday with something she was truly proud of.

I've not done anything to prepare for this ritual; I can't even think where to start. Somehow, I've put a spell on myself to bury, or perhaps even erase, the memories of an entire life. There's nothing I can do to prepare to battle myself. I will simply have to follow the energy as it flows during the ritual and be ready to counter the spell when, and if, it presents itself. This alone makes me very nervous.

"I'll get them," I say.

"Good luck." Cal rolls his eyes.

As soon as I get to the screen door, the shouting increases in volume. Jo has changed her mind at the last minute, ordering Sylvia to go get this instead of that, and she no longer needs this, she needs that, so stop wasting time and do as she says. Sylvia's not budging, and I walk into a standoff in the kitchen.

"Enough!" Both women jump, then frown at me. "Jo, you're prepared. You are *completely* prepared so try to relax. Sylvia, you're packed. Both of you get into the truck. Now." I sound like a schoolmarm. My expression leaves no room for argument.

Sylvia huffs at her mother, grabs her backpack from the kitchen table, and stalks from the room. Jo looks ready to fight but stops herself. She puts her hands to her chest and closes her eyes with a deep breath. I put a hand on her shoulder and give it a squeeze. "Everything will go fine. I'm sure of it." The confidence in my voice belies the way my gut feels. Jo has done so much work, she has stressed so much, and I fear it may be for nothing. None of this shows on my face, and she smiles back at me, giving a firm nod of agreement. I am also haunted by the notion that it *will* work, and I will see something that I don't want to see. After what I've already experienced in my lives, I can't imagine what was so horrific that I cast a spell on myself to forget it.

"Why isn't Maggie coming?" Sylvia asks as she leans against the truck, watching her mother inspect the contents of the truck bed.

"Someone has to make sure the fairies don't throw a wild party or otherwise get out of hand," I say. "She wasn't happy about staying behind *at all.*" Maggie's big brown eyes had made me feel so guilty when I locked up the shop this morning that I almost relented, but no—the fairies can't be left unsupervised.

After another fifteen minutes of second guessing and last minute changes, we are on the road to Mount Greylock. Sylvia, having been up all night helping her mother, is asleep in the back seat in a matter of minutes. Her ability to fall asleep anywhere annoys Jo immensely. I tell Jo she should nap also; it's only a little over three hours to get there, and she needs to rest. She dismisses the suggestion with a snort and pulls out her grimoire for yet another review of her incantation.

The drive goes smoothly with Cal's snooty GPS device announcing every turn and advising on traffic conditions. I marvel at the device. It seems like magick itself. The leaps technology has taken since the 1880s is truly astounding.

Cal and I chatter about nothing in particular for the first hour. Once the quiet of highway driving settles in, we both drift into our own worlds. Cal is focused on the road, one hand on the wheel and the other on the console entwined with mine, and I stare out at the scenery whirring past in a blur of green, red, and gold. Above us flies the white raven. She could surpass us easily and be at the site way before we are, but she wants to keep an eye on us. I see her in the side mirror, weaving in the air currents, thoroughly enjoying the crisp, clean morning. The sight of her makes me smile. I lay my head back and watch her mesmerizing dance.

We set out early enough, surprisingly, to make it to Greylock with plenty of light for the hike to the site Ren found. The road to the primitive camping location is rough, and the jolt from hitting a deep hole snaps Sylvia awake. "Are we there yet?"

"Almost," Cal says, both hands on the wheel as he slowly navigates the poorly maintained road.

Butterflies bloom in my stomach. I swallow reflexively. It's not much longer now...

No campers are around, which is what we'd hoped for. Cal parks the truck at the edge of the small clearing, and we file out at the same time. Sylvia looks around with confusion. "Um, where's the bathroom?"

Cal guffaws. "There's no bathroom! This is the *primitive* camping area. Primitive means you shit in the woods."

His crudeness makes the three of us stare at him. He turns, conscious of the many eyes on him and his own embarrassment. "Sorry," he says. "Don't worry, Syl, I have all the gear needed for, uh, bio breaks in the woods." The gear turns out to be a toilet seat on folding legs with a seal for affixing a bag below the seat. He presents the toilet seat and a small, collapsible shovel to Sylvia with pride.

Her mouth falls open. "You've *got* to be kidding me."

He pushes the items at her, and she takes them reluctantly. "Nope. But you only need the bag for number two. Make sure to bury it when you're done."

Sylvia's expression makes us break into laughter. She glares at each one of us, snorts in disgust, and stalks off into the nearest line of trees, leaves crunching loudly under her stomping feet.

"Watch out for poison oak!" Jo says, still laughing. An exasperated shriek comes from within the trees.

"Didn't you two camp out for Matilda's farewell ritual?" I ask.

"We stayed in a motel." Jo then looks in Sylvia's direction and lowers her voice. "She hates camping. Don't let her know you know. She didn't want to miss this."

The jovial mood helps pull me out of my gloomy haze. I take a moment to enjoy the serenity around me. The forest is alive with autumn colors, making the dark green fir trees stand out that much more. The air is clean and fresh, tinged with the smells of pine and decomposing leaves. I walk to the nearest tree, a large white pine, its branches packed with long, blue-green needles and overcrowded with cones. I brush my hands across the spiky limbs, releasing a burst of fragrance that I inhale deeply. Greeting the tree spirits and wood nymphs, I apologize in advance for any disruption we might cause in their very peaceful forest.

"Hey, don't worry, I can unload the truck all by myself. No help needed, thanks!" Cal calls out, standing on the lowered tail gate, arms across his chest.

Jo's coming from the trees, more than likely communing with Nature as well. Her face is peaceful, her forehead smoother than it has been in weeks. I stop for a moment to admire the woman who is not only my friend but also someone I could call sister, even mother sometimes. Guilt lurches into my throat at the thought of how disappointed she'll be when this doesn't work. I shake that thinking out of my head. The best way to make a spell fail is to doubt.

"I just love it out here," she says, taking a few sleeping bags from the bed of the truck.

"Me too. My dad used to take us camping around here a lot when we were kids." Cal's face reflects his contentment.

We collectively turn towards the sound of crunching leaves. Sylvia emerges from the tree line, looking triumphant.

"I did it!" She brandishes the toilet seat and shovel in the air. "Took me a while but it all came out in the end." She giggles at her unexpected joke.

"Congratulations! Good job." Cal gives her two thumbs up.

Jo scoffs at their crudeness. We have become quite the little family over the business of the past life ritual. My heart bursts at seeing the man I love so open and welcoming to this strange world he's stumbled into. I only hope his strength and good humor last.

We set up a small campsite by the truck, but we won't be using it. This is a decoy for any other campers or rangers that come by. All the trappings of an active campsite are laid out. We brought doubles of everything. We'll actually be camping at the ritual site, which is strictly against park regulations. It's only for one night, so with some luck and a few well-placed diversion spells, we shouldn't be discovered.

It seems to take forever before everyone is packed up and ready for the trek. As Jo huffs on her heavy backpack, Cal and I exchange worried glances. Regardless of his multiple conversations with her about her ability to hike, and her reassurances that she could hike circles around him, we are both still anxious. She's not as young as she used to be. Jo reminds us for the tenth time of her recent excursion to her family's sacred site in these mountains 'all by her lonesome.' She's much tougher than I give her credit for. Regardless, Cal will take the lead, and I'll follow behind the ladies.

Cal puts away his map at the sight of the white raven landing on the gnarled branch of an old, dead oak across the clearing. She calls out a greeting, flapping her wings to beckon us to her.

"Well, here we go." Jo grabs the backpack straps at her shoulders and marches towards the bird. Sylvia is quickly on her heels, and I fall in behind. A twinge of excitement flutters in my stomach.

With his long strides, Cal reaches Ren before the rest of us. In the afternoon sun, the brightness of her white feathers sparkles with hints of silver. She paces back and forth on the branch, gurgling excitedly, ready to get moving.

*Slow, too slow!* She opens her wings and flaps at us.

"Keep your feathers on. Granny's coming," Jo huffs.

I tried to convince Cal that he didn't need to map our route through the woods. Ren knew where the site was and would lead us there, but he's done it anyway. I love a man who's prepared. I kiss his cheek before he starts after the bird. He squeezes my hand and disappears into the trees with a wink.

I hear the birds and animals around us, scampering to hide from these noisy and unwelcome visitors. A pair of sharp, large eyes is upon us, watching with great interest. I reach out to the lone black bear and tell him that he need not be threatened by us, we will not disturb him. He can resume his trek to the cave he plans to hibernate in without worry. The bear turns away slowly and continues his path leading away from us.

Despite the chill, I'm sweating from the weight of my clothing and gear, and probably from nerves. Jo, on the other hand, looks fine and is not puffing nearly as much as her daughter. Cal's eyes are on the treetops, keeping Ren in sight at all times.

In the next hour, we angle steeply uphill, forcing Jo to pull out her walking stick—a gift from her late husband, she says with great affection. The dark red mahogany is elaborately carved to resemble the body of a dragon, its head the grip and its tail the point. Despite obvious signs of use, the cane looks well cared for. Sylvia laments not bringing one. Cal stops and pulls off his backpack. Digging deep into the pack, he pulls out two collapsible metal walking sticks. Sylvia snatches one with glee and a quick thank you. Cal extends the other to me, but I decline. With a raised eyebrow and an 'are you sure?' look, he stuffs the stick back into the pack.

The sun is starting its descent when we reach our destination. We break through the tree line to see an idyllic setting: a wide, babbling stream, fringed with fir trees of all varieties and fallen logs covered with furry green moss. There is a swath of the stream's bank clear of trees, and the sky is broad and open before us. Jo proclaims that it's just perfect and thanks Ren profusely. Cal proceeds to move some large rocks from the spot where he plans to put our tent. Jo halts his progress, declaring that she needs to identify the ritual area before the campsite can be set up. He bows low at her command and Sylvia giggles.

Jo removes her burden and rummages through her pack to pull out four thin, metal candle holders. The matte black iron is ornately twisted and each one is topped with a pentagram. She walks towards the stream, humming a haunting tune I'm not familiar with. The clearing is at a fork in the stream, making it more like a small river, wide and appearing deep in the middle. With eyes closed, Jo walks through the clearing, never stumbling or tripping over the rocks and branches strewn about. She makes a full circle, then repeats her path, placing a candlestick at each cardinal point without the need of a compass. Once each is placed, she calls to Sylvia for the salt. She has it ready and presents the bag of coarse salt to her mother, her face solemn.

Jo retraces her steps around the circle, pouring the salt around the perimeter, ensuring there are no gaps or breaks in the curved line. Once finished, she returns to the center and raises her arms to the sky, calling out to the Goddess to bless their circle.

Cal leans over to me and whispers. "Can I set up camp now?"

I nod. "Just not anywhere inside the circle."

He gives me a thumbs up and turns to get the gear. Sylvia nonchalantly bends towards him and whispers, "And *don't* mess up the salt. Mom will kill you."

Night falls quickly once the tents are set up. Sylvia and I are stacking logs and branches in a conical pattern inside the circle at Jo's direction. Cal comes back from a bio break in the woods and notices the stack.

"Whoa, whoa. We can't have a fire. We'll get busted."

"Not to worry, my friend, Aven has seen to that," Jo says in a happy tone.

He gives me a quizzical look.

"I've cast a spell so that no one will pay attention to this area. If they notice anything, they'll look away and not think twice."

"Serious?" He frowns at me. I nod and continue arranging the wood. He shakes his head and ducks into our tent. I ask Sylvia if she'll finish, telling her that I need to talk to Cal. She gives me a lascivious wink-wink and urges me on. I roll my eyes.

Cal empties the remainder of his pack, looking more as if he's giving himself something to do.

"Cal?" He turns and smiles, then turns back to his task.

I kneel beside him and lean against his arm. I inhale the faint traces of his cologne and run my hand around the tense muscles between his shoulder blades. He moans and rests his hands in his lap, savoring the feel of my nails on his back.

"I can't tell you how wonderful you've been about all of this," I say. "I don't know what is going to happen tonight, what you'll see and hear. But whatever happens, please don't let it freak you out."

His eyes are closed when he responds. "I meant what I said about wanting to know all about your life." He takes my free hand and squeezes. "But it's hard. Almost forty years of thinking magic is a load of crap won't be wiped away overnight."

I want to joke that it just may after tonight, but I don't. I know the sacrifice he made to be with me for this. His family's gathering is tomorrow, and he feigned illness so that he could come with me. It bothered him to lie to his family. I told him to go, but he wouldn't hear it. He said I needed him whether I knew it or not. I did know it, but I wasn't about to say it, knowing how important his family is to him.

"I love you," comes out of my mouth before I realize I'm thinking it. Cal's body stiffens, and I instantly regret those words. We only recently decided we were boyfriend-girlfriend and here I am saying I love him! I'm glad he can't see my face; my cheeks burn with embarrassment.

He faces me and I turn away. He takes my face in his hands and his lips find mine, passionate, eager. I don't resist when he pulls me to him. The heat builds between us, but I am conscious of the voices of Jo and Sylvia only a few steps away. He hears them too and we slowly part. He pushes his forehead against mine, resting his hands on either side of my neck.

"I love you, too, Aven," he says, eyes closed. A relieved sigh escapes my lips, and I grip his hands. I almost say 'thank you.'

# Chapter 32

The full moon is high in the night sky, shining brightly upon our sacred circle.

Tall, rolled black beeswax candles mark the four quarters of the circle, nestled in the black iron candlesticks. Jo stands at the North point, hands raised overhead, welcoming Arianrhod, Goddess of reincarnation, and all benevolent spirits to our circle. Only love may enter, only love may leave. The hood of her heavy black velvet robe is pushed back, revealing a solemn face, marked with protective sigils in black kohl. Jo's hands and arms are likewise adorned, and she wears only her protective amulets.

Sylvia stands at the East point, garbed and marked similarly to her mother except her robe is of dark fuchsia, made by her own hand. Cal fidgets at the West, unsure of what to do with his hands or where to look. He wears a black long-sleeved shirt and black jeans. After three women badgered him about his need for protection during his very first, and this very untried ritual, Sylvia was allowed to mark his exposed skin with as many protective symbols as would fit. He wears one of Jo's polished obsidian necklaces and holds a chunk of black tourmaline in each hand.

I am poised in the South quarter, standing several feet behind the candlestick and outside the protective salt circle, as I must be immersed in the stream. My robe is of the darkest purple, thick and warm, and I am naked underneath. My body is unadorned as I am the focus of this ritual and must be open to whatever comes. A swath of black satin covers my eyes to represent that I have blinded myself to my past, and to keep me from seeing the many lives I will step back through to get to my first. I am trembling. Not from the cold night air or the cold water lapping around my feet but from anticipation and a spot of fear.

The small bonfire illuminates our circle. If one looks closely, the shadows of loving spirits can be seen dancing around the flames. I sense the black bear I encountered during our trek as well as that of a mountain lion, and a wolf. There is also an owl across the water behind me. Each is quiet, watching from a distance. Ren is undisturbed by their presence, and they bring me comfort. She perches atop Jo's walking stick, which is embedded in the ground to Jo's right, the charm on her breast reflecting the rapid flickering of the fire. She gazes at me through the fire with loving eyes.

My mind is clear of all noise and distraction. I am focused intently on the goal of this ritual. I must see my first life, I must know what happened, I must break through the barrier I created.

With the circle cast and blessed, I remove my robe and toss it onto the bank. Cal gasps, not having realized I was naked, and Sylvia shushes him. The rush of cold air is a shock, but I ignore it. My focus is critical. Beneath my blindfold, my eyes are closed. Earlier, I walked the path in the water I would take during the ritual and cleared it of stones and sticks, anything that could trip me in the darkness.

I lift my arms from my sides as Jo begins the incantation. My skin chills at the deep, haunting voice she uses.

*Arianrhod, Goddess of the Silver Wheel,*
*Let us turn back, HELP us to turn back.*
*Bring to light what is black.*

With my Sight, I see Jo cue the white raven. Ren takes wing, flying widdershins around the circle. The breeze she stirs as she flies behind my back gives me goosebumps. Her flight symbolizes the turning back of time. Three times she encircles us then lands gracefully back onto her perch.

*Days of her first past lie hidden in shadow.*
*The way is blocked.*
*Her sight is fallow.*

*Each step she takes must take her back,*
*Back to what is not welcoming, what has been kept black.*

*Blinded is she, held fast and tight.*
*Turn back your silver wheel,*
*Bring the first back to light!*

*As above, so below.*
*Step back a life.*
*Now, you go!*

"I step back." I take one step backward in the water.
*As above, so below.*
*Step back a life.*
*Now, you go!*

"I step back." Once more backward, deeper into the stream, my feet sinking into the silky mud.

*As above, so below.*
*Step back a life.*
*Now, you go!*

"I step back."

This is repeated until I have taken twelve steps backward, going back through each life. The water is at hip level, and I keep my arms above it.

*As above, so below.*
*As within, so without.*
*As the universe, so the soul.*

*Step back to your first life,*
*Blinded no more you are!*
*See all that you should,*
*Know all that you are!*

*It is YOUR life!*
*It is your RIGHT to see!*
*Days of the past are no longer hidden.*
*As I will it, so mote it be!*

I remove the blindfold and drop it into the water. "I step back." My voice is strong and determined.

As I lift my foot to step back, hard pressure against it prevents me from stepping backward. Here it is, here is what I've done. With my eyes focused on the fire, I take a deep breath. As my lungs fill with air, I pull into myself the power of the natural world around me. I take from the water; from the giant boulders that dot the shoreline; from the crackling fire; from the solid, old trees that seem to lean in towards me; and from the black bear, the wolf, the mountain lion, and the owl that watch me. The gentle spirits Jo has called line the bank, their arms outstretched to me, giving me all they can offer. The surge of the collective power surrounds me, fills me. My skin burns with it, and my muscles strain to contain it. I push my foot backward, but the invisible wall is stronger. Raising my face to the moon, which seems to have doubled in size since she first appeared over the trees, I draw her energy down into me; Mother Moon gives it freely. The rush of her power makes me gasp. My eyes burn, but I do not close them. I must see, I must know.

The power I hold roars in my ears; I hear nothing else. With my Sight, the block I have made becomes visible. It appears as a black scar across the light of the fire. Glaring at it, I push the immense power at the barrier, but it does not waver. I grow angry and frustrated, and the power wanes. I must not allow negativity to come or I will lose all of this.

What other power can I draw from? Nature is giving me all she has and it's not enough! I force my breathing to slow, force myself back to calm. As peace returns to my Spirit, I see something I had not seen before. The glowing auras of Jo, Sylvia, and Cal. I do not see Ren's. Their energies radiate pink hues and are expanding outward and upward. Their love! That's it! That is the one thing I have been missing, the one thing I have lacked in all of my lives. The power of love.

Their love comes to me at the faintest call. When it joins with me, my body convulses. Making fists to steel myself, I focus the whole of this power at the block and drive my heel backward. There is a flash of bright, hot light as my foot pushes through and hits the muddy floor of the stream. I cry out from the momentary brightness.

Then there is darkness. I see nothing—no fire, no moon, no friends. I feel nothing; I am neither cold nor hot—the exquisite burning sensation is gone. There is no sound; the roaring in my ears has stopped.

Fear leaps up into my throat, and I clench my hands into fists again.

Far before me, a pinprick of light appears. I know I must go towards it even though I am afraid.

As if I were looking through a keyhole, I see myself, but a younger version—maybe thirteen or fourteen. She looks absolutely terrified. No, no, no. Not this. Not this, please. My skin prickles, and my breath catches in my throat.

My view opens more, like the drawing back of thick curtains, to reveal the reasons for her terror. She is bound hand and foot to an old tree, her hands overhead, pulled tight with rope. Her wrists bleed as do her ankles. She wears only a thin white nightdress, torn and filthy. She is screaming, pulling at her bonds, at something not yet in my vision. Her screams plead and beg; tracks of tears and dirt streak her face. I do not hear too much sound yet, but it is increasing slowly as the view widens. I need not hear her words—I feel her fright and pain intensely, for it had been mine and still lives buried within me, forgotten until this moment.

It grips my heart, and I gasp from the pain. My chest burns, my lungs strain for breath. Am I to relive this whole thing? I cannot, I must not! I try to turn away, to turn back to Jo, into the safety of Cal's arms, but I cannot move. I am bound in place by an invisible force, just as the younger me is bound by hand-made rope.

The full sounds of the scene rush at me as the images sharpen and everything around the young girl comes into focus. The black curtains are now gone, revealing the scene of a ritual, but one not as benevolent as this one.

She screams at two people. They are certainly my parents, for the love and agony in their faces is unmistakable, despite the blonde hair. I choke at the sight of them. My mother's mouth is purple and black, a trickle of blood along one side, her eyes red and swollen from long bouts of crying, and her clothes torn at the shoulder and waist. My father fares worse, his arm hanging beside him limp, his shoulder misshapen, and his back slumped. His forehead and one side of his face are caked thick with dried blood and dirt, his pants are torn in many places and blood has soaked through. They are bound as well, but around the neck, with the same rope that binds their daughter. Both are straining against it. My mother's hands clutch the rope in a vain attempt to keep the noose from cutting into her as she strains to reach her terrified daughter.

My father is yelling at a small group of men who are carrying what looks to be a large, wooden trough. As they set it heavily on the ground, I hear what sounds like chains within it. These men step aside, bowing low and backing away, for three men are coming towards the center where the trough was placed. I recoil from them. Their hate slaps me hard in the face. I try to gulp air but I feel suffocated, strangled by the weight of these men's malevolent natures. As if I were a rabbit and they the hounds set upon me, I want to run. I want as much distance between them as I can manage from four swift limbs built for speed. But I am held fast and I have no powers, no magick to help me or protect me.

But I am not the one that needs protecting, that is certain. The young girl is the object of their wrath. They order a great pile of wood be set afire. Their harsh and deep voices cut into my soul. These ancient men mean to hurt me, hurt her, under the pretense of ridding their village of a great evil. Their simple brown robes are tattered and faded, and necklaces made of animal bone rattle against their chests.

As the bonfire roars to life, I see where we are. The night is black—no moon or even stars are visible—and the cleared area within the tight group of leafless trees is lit only by the bonfire and torches arranged in a wide circle. Other people are there, the whole village it seems, tightly packed into the clearing. Children peek between their parents' legs and around protective arms. Some are crying, most are silent, transfixed by a sight they have never seen before. The adults all wear the same expression, that of justifiable righteousness masking their ignorant fear.

Buckets of water are brought by the same servants, heads bowed, shoulders slumped, doing the bidding of their unkind masters. They stack the pails within arm's reach of the trough.

One of the thin, decrepit men raises an arm to the sky demanding silence, and he is quickly obeyed. His sleeve tumbles to his shoulder, revealing twisted trails of faded black symbols and runic script, looking wicked despite their age. He speaks words I don't understand in a language I can't remember. His other arm shoots out towards the crowd, and people part as a young boy with a frightened but determined face brings forth a small wooden cage. The cage is so small that the creature within it cannot move.

I can't discern what is in the cage, but my gut tells me imme-diately. There is white under the muck that covers most of it. It is a bird, a white raven.

Pain grips my chest. I remember this bird! This is my best friend, my only friend, save for my parents, and I love her des-perately. She is terrified and rightly so. These men have no kind plans for her. One man snatches the cage from the boy and struts over to the middle of the circle. He holds the cage up, shouting vitriol to the rapt villagers, and it twitches under his grip, the bird frightened beyond reason and desperate to be free. My younger self screams, pleads, cries for the creature to be re-leased, not to be hurt, for she is an innocent soul. I cannot understand the words I use, but I know what I am saying. The man laughs without mirth, admonishing the girl for her use of the word innocent.

The third man approaches the cage with a gleaming knife in his upraised hand. I scream. We scream. The curve of the blade is menacing by itself, but the hand that holds it makes the image all that more evil. His skeletal hand is marked with the red and black bruises that come with thinning skin and old age. His forearm bears the same faded tattooing as his brethren. The man's raised voice is deep and frightening; his words are few but meaningful to the crowd. They angrily agree with his words and the deed he is about to do. He thrusts the knife towards the cage, sinking it deep within. The bird makes a sound so piercing that it burns into my brain, echoed by the scream from my younger self pulling against her bonds.

"*Ren!*" the younger me screams.

The bird's wail quickly fades into a mournful cry as life leaves her helpless body. The sadness of that sound leaves me feeling soulless, empty to my core. The man keeps the knife in her breast as he takes the cage from his fellow. He walks to the trough and, holding the cage over it, removes the blade. The bird's warm blood, looking black in this light, pours as water into its emptiness. He shakes the cage mercilessly, ensuring every last drop has left the poor creature.

Once satisfied, he tosses the cage to the side as if it were nothing. The cage breaks apart when it hits the ground, leaving the lifeless body splayed upon the dirt. The sight shatters the bound girl. Her knees buckle and she crumples, hanging limply by her upstretched arms.

The three men, standing abreast, approach the young girl. The one still holds the now bloody knife. My parents are screaming, crying, begging, straining uselessly against the ropes at their throats. The mob is quite the opposite; they are shouting for death, for the purging of evil demons, for the release from the curse their village is under.

Two of the men grab the girl at arms' length. I smell their fear. Underneath their bluster and audacity, they are nothing but frightened little men—afraid, to their very bones, of a young girl who can do things they cannot without potions or chants, sacrifices or bloodletting. But she is evil, they profess, for too many harvests have gone bad, too much livestock has fallen sick and died, too many babes have been born without breath since she has come of age. It is her! There are demons inside her, you can even see them! Her raven-black hair, the unnatural color of her eyes, the works she can do with just a single thought.

These words whip the already frenzied crowd up even more. They are justified in this ritual, ridding themselves of demonic magick. Kill her, kill her now! She must be purged from their lives for peace and prosperity to return.

The third man with the knife cuts the bonds of the girl, and she immediately returns to life. Kicking and screaming, she is calling for her mother and father to save her, but the men's grips are iron and she cannot free herself. I strain against the force that holds me. I can stop them, I must save her! Screaming soundlessly at the vile scene before me, I feel warmth on my lip and taste blood in my mouth.

With much effort and shouting, for the girl fights against them like a wild cat, they lift her over the trough. One man calls for aid and his followers run to him. It takes six of them to push her down into it. They shackle her to the bottom around the ankles, wrists, and neck. I cannot see this, but I hear the chains and feel the cold iron upon my skin.

The three take positions around the trough—the one with the knife at its head, two on each side at the other end. Each one's hands lift to the black sky, and they chant. Their words silence the frothing crowd; their voices are guttural and low, rising slowly, evenly. The cadence is mesmerizing, and the throng falls into a trance-like state, eyes fixed upon the basin, not hearing the screams and cries of the girl chained within.

One by one, the buckets of water are emptied into it. My mother falls to her knees. My father shouts furiously, cursing the men with every word.

Bucket by bucket, the trough slowly fills. The three men do not look down at it but up only, their wicked chant crescendoing. I am gagging, my mouth is full of moldy water. I cannot breathe! I struggle against it, but I cannot move, cannot lift my head from the water for breath. More water pummels my face, and I can only gasp and gulp, desperate for air, but my throat filling with water instead. My brain is on fire, my heart is racing madly, deafening me, I hear nothing else. My lungs burn. I cannot breathe!

There is a darkness creeping in, and it soothes me. My struggles slow, my pounding heart wanes, the fire in my lungs burns less. I feel a peace coming. It is warm and comforting, and I want to give myself to it. My chest heaves again reflexively, still wanting for breath. The water is no longer cold and biting.

I count the beats of my heart, they grow fewer as the comfort settles through me. There is one, then another, and then just one more...

The world explodes around me. Light and heat expand from my body. An unimaginable pain rips through my very soul. My scream is swallowed up by the sound of the blast. The trough disintegrates, the water turns instantly to steam. Shocked screams are snuffed out; no one has time to run. The bodies of my three assailants blow apart upon contact with the light and fire, their faces twisted in horror.

All in the wake of the explosion are similarly dispatched. My parents. Their agony and torment is replaced by peace and the quiet comfort that death brings. Far out it reaches—the buildings in the village blast apart as if they were naught but matchsticks. Trees flatten, fields are laid waste, animals—both livestock and wild—succumb to a quick and unexpected end.

In less than a breath, it is over. The sky remains black. There is no light, no sound, no wind. There is nothing except a charred ring in the blackened earth where the trough had been.

# Chapter 33

"Aven! Aven!" Cal's voice is panicked. Strong arms pull me out of the water. I am gagging, I have no strength at all; I cannot push myself up to help him get me to the bank. He struggles to pull me and we fall to the ground. I vomit water and blood. Rocks cut into my palms and knees.

Sylvia is crying out for her mother. Through my own haze and the flames of the still roaring fire, I see Jo on the ground. I call to her but no sound comes out. My throat burns. I push at Cal with the little strength I have mustered, motioning for him to go to Jo. He protests but I push him again. I try to tell him I am fine but no words come.

But I am not fine. My mind reels from the onslaught of an entire life, short as it was, coming back to me all at once. And the reality of how I died. How I was *murdered*. And the dreadful knowledge of all those lives I took when I died. There will be no reprieve for me. I am cursed forever. I vomit again. Cal grabs my robe from the ground and places it around me. I push at him again to go to Jo. Pulling the cold velvet around me, I lie on my side and hug my knees to my chest.

I crane my head to see Jo, but the fire is in the way. My Sight shows Jo on her back with Sylvia shaking her shoulders, slapping her sharply on each cheek. Tears stream down Sylvia's face.

Cal pushes her aside gently to check Jo's vitals. She is breathing and her pulse is strong. Her body isn't what worries Sylvia. What did she see, what did she feel that put her in such a state? Sylvia's questions go unanswered. Cal tries to reassure Sylvia that her mother is fine, physically. Cal wants to move her into the tent, but Sylvia refuses. Jo is much better served under the light of the full moon. Cal growls but orders her to get a sleeping bag, extra blankets, and a pillow. He barks at her, snapping her out of her panic.

*My friend, what is wrong?* There is nothing but silence. I search for her Spirit; perhaps it journeyed from her body. I sense nothing. My head pounds with each use of power. There's a warm trickle from my nose, and I taste blood on my lips. Calling out to Jo again sends a jolt of pain through my head. I need to rest, just for a moment, then I'll be fine. Just for a moment.

When I bolt awake, I know the sun has risen despite the gray light filtering through the tent. I am still naked, wrapped in my robe but tucked within a sleeping bag. Gasping for breath and sweating, my fingernails dig into my palms. I throw off the covers and burst from the tent.

Hearing my movements, Cal comes towards the tent just in time to catch me before I hit the ground. The scenery around me blurs and swirls; waves of nausea beat within my stomach. Cal is speaking, but I can't make out what he says. He lowers me to the ground, cradling me in his arms. He is stroking my hair and back as my vision clears. The nausea subsides slowly; I inhale deeply to quell my stomach and the rushing of blood to my head. Sounds are returning. Cal's words are soothing, asking me to slow my breathing and to calm down, everything is fine. Jo is fine.

What's happened to Jo? My mind races and finally the images from last night flood back. Jo on the ground, unresponsive; Sylvia panicked and screaming.

"What happened?" My throat is dry, begging for water.

Cal tightens his grip on me. "I don't know, Aven. I really don't know." His voice cracks.

I detect movement through my closed eyes. Sylvia is rousing, having slept beside her mother. "Aven!" She rushes towards me. Cal's arm shoots out to keep her from barreling into me.

"Aven! Are you okay? Can you please help Mom?" Her eyes are red and swollen.

Her words come at me so fast, I cannot immediately process them. I ask for water. Cal offers a canteen from somewhere behind him, and I drink greedily. He pulls it away, telling me something about not overdoing it. The cold water is fresh from the stream; its crisp, clean taste is a tonic to my whole body. I ignore Cal, gripping the canteen. When my stomach tells me I've had enough, I hand it back to him. I shiver as the water travels through my limbs—the goodness of Nature reviving me from within. I raise my face to the sky for the sunlight, but there are only heavy gray clouds threatening rain.

My strength is returning, the fog in my mind clearing. Happy sounds of morning songbirds, lapping water, and a crackling fire replace the pounding in my ears. I rise but Cal does more of the lifting than my legs do. Then I remember I am naked under the robe. Sylvia sees too much skin for her liking and dashes into my tent for clothes.

I dress in the open without shame. My eyes focus on my beloved friend, lying where she fell last night, now wrapped in blankets with pillows stuffed about her head.

I walk on unsteady legs to Jo, Cal ensuring I don't fall. I kneel beside Jo, inspecting her face, hands, and arms. Sylvia has wiped clean the symbols from her skin.

"Sylvia," I call roughly, but she is already at my side. "Tell me what happened."

"Oh, my Goddess, Aven," she exhales. I lay a hand on her shoulder. "We saw *everything!*"

"*What?*" My mouth falls open.

"We saw what they did to you." Her eyes fill with tears. She tries to look at me but turns away, putting her hands over her face as she lets her sobs free.

I stare at Cal, astonished. His red eyes are rimmed with dark circles, and he nods solemnly. He takes one of my hands in both of his, holding firm.

My skin flushes and tears blur my vision. I cannot face anyone. I am appalled and ashamed at what they've seen, ashamed that I didn't think of what they would encounter. I had no idea that they would witness my life.

"I am so sorry." I stare at the ground. "Please forgive me. I should have blindfolded you all. I didn't think..." I cannot speak now as tremors take over my body. Cal's arms are around my shoulders, and Sylvia takes my hands. Their words of comfort fall on deaf ears.

How stupid I was, how selfish! I thought only of my goal, of seeing my life, of knowing what binds me to the white raven. I never thought once about what they would experience. The protection symbols did their job but only for their bodies, not their minds. I am faint with the thought of what Jo experienced, being the strong empath she is.

I gasp and look around me, heart racing. "Where is Ren?"

"I don't know," Sylvia says, looking around also. "When the blast hit, I heard her scream and she flew off."

*The blast.* "You felt that?" I stare back and forth to each of them. My heart sinks at the thought of what that sweet creature experienced, witnessing a mirror image of herself murdered so brutally.

Cal nods. "A little. Hit me in the chest but it wasn't painful or anything. It was more like someone shoved me."

Sylvia nods, absently rubbing her chest. She looks down at her mother. "But it hit Mom hard. She flew backward." She squeezes her eyes closed.

Guilt cascades over me as I gaze at Jo. With my energy, I search her physical form for signs of injury. Thankfully, there are none. I look deeper, feeling her energy and her Spirit. Her Spirit is still within her but lies troubled and weak. Her energy lags and seems unable to renew itself. I ask Cal and Sylvia to leave me alone with Jo. Sylvia does not hesitate, but Cal lingers.

"Are you okay, Aven? You really don't look strong enough to lift your own head, let alone help someone."

I squeeze his hand but cannot meet his eye. "I'm fine, my love. This is my fault. I have to make it right."

He opens his mouth to protest, but I shake my head. "Please." I pull my hand from his. He gets up reluctantly.

When they have both disappeared into their respective tents, I slump over Jo's still form, begging her forgiveness.

I have no energy to help restore this poor woman, so I lift my arms out and call on Nature. The sun is not visible but there nonetheless, and I pull down its warmth and strength to fill her.

The gentle breeze intensifies around us, and the water laps more heartily at the bank. Sounds of the forest erupt around me. The cry of a hawk peals overhead, and the tree trunks sway with pops and cracks. All manner of birds rise from the trees in blankets of color and song. My body tenses as I direct this willingly given energy into my friend. Her body remains unmoving as the intense white light surrounds her and holds her. Within a moment, her form begins to absorb the light, and the cacophony of sound and movement quiets.

Where there should be silence is the pounding of blood in my head. I kept none of the energy for myself although I am in need of it. I lower myself beside my friend, with a hand on her shoulder, and I sleep.

# Chapter 34

*What has happened, what has happened?!*

*I must get away. I am so frightened. I scream, I cry, I shriek with each breath I take. Something hurt me. Someone has hurt me. It hurts so much! But I have to get away. I must run away, far away!*

*I do not stop until I see the hint of sunrise upon the water's gray surface. In the distance, a black mound gets bigger the faster I go towards it. I fly faster, fast as I can. I must keep going, I must get away!*

*I am flying? I can fly? How is it that I am flying!? What am I? What was I? What has happened to me? My head pains sharply and the blossoming sun hurts my tender eyes. My arms, my* wings, *are so tired, so very tired. What do I do? Where am I going? Where did I come from?*

*What is this pain!? I scream as loud as my lungs let me to cast this pain from me. I cannot bear it!*

*The black mound is a mountain in the water and that is where I will go. I must rest. I cannot run,* fly, *any longer. My head is spinning. The memory of the smells of blood and burning flesh will not leave me. Is that all I know? The smell of charred flesh? This cannot be. I cannot bear it!*

*The nearest tree is not near enough. I can push my wings no more and I fall. When I hit the water, I will die, and I welcome it. Release me from what I am feeling, let me forget the smell of death and agony, let me be free of this fear and pain!*

*A strong wind carries me so that I strike the mossy bank rather than the harsh glass roof of the still water. It hurts nonetheless, but this new pain is welcomed to drive out the old. I lie on my side, gasping. I cannot stop my cries of grief and torment. Nor do I know from where they come. Soon, I am too exhausted and I can cry no more. I try to pull myself up, to find shelter in a tree, but I cannot fly. I will be eaten by some animal to be sure. There is a log, just there, not far. I can walk. I can.*

*My wings drag beside me, hindering me, as I try to walk, hop. I struggle to the safety of the log on unsteady, untried legs. My senses are alive to the world around me. The forest teems with those that would find me an easy meal. I must hide before I am seen.*

*The log is deep and filled with moss and slime. It is cold. I burrow in as far as I can go. My head falls against the rotted wood. I can hold it up no more. Sleep takes hold of me, and I welcome its peace.*

# Chapter 35

The sound of footsteps on dry leaves rouses me. I am covered with a blanket and I pull it tight across my shoulders as I sit up.

Sylvia is coming from the woods, and Cal is tending the fire—each eyes me as I rise. Cal is quickly at my side, his arm around my waist, and I lean against him. Sylvia runs at me, face anxious and hopeful.

"Jo will be all right. Her energy and Spirit were greatly depleted. All she needs now is rest."

Sylvia lets out a relieved breath. She kneels and takes her mother's hand, holding it to her heart.

"I don't mean this to sound harsh, but how long?" Cal asks, looking at the darkening sky. "Those are definitely storm clouds."

I need not look up; I sense the storm coming. Its energy is most welcome but in Jo's physically weakened state, cold rain would not do her any good.

"We should go," I say, taking Cal's hand. His brow furrows but I smile. "Don't worry about Jo, I'll manage her." He studies my face for a moment and shrugs.

"Let's break camp then. Come on." He motions for us to get moving.

As he douses the fire, Sylvia and I dismantle the tents. She quickly gets frustrated with folding her tent.

"Ugh! This damn thing is *never* going to fit back in the bag."

Cal laughs at her frustration and takes the tangled canvas from her.

The small amount of physical exertion takes the wind out of me, and I wobble on my feet, feeling the earth shift underneath me. I sink to the ground. Cal chucks the half-folded tent and rushes to my side. The concern in his eyes fills my heart. I put a hand on his cheek and assure him I am fine, I just need a minute. His face flashes an expression of deep sadness, and he quickly masks it with a manufactured smile. I don't think I could love him any more than I do at this moment. I kiss his lips and he presses against mine.

A rumble of thunder gives us the prodding we need. It takes twice as long to get everything packed up, with Cal taking the lion's share. I've instructed Sylvia to bundle Jo and she's cocooned her mother into a sleeping bag, the opening cinched snugly around her face. Cal has a pack strapped to his front with another on his back. Sylvia leans forward, her hands gripping the straps of her overloaded pack. Mine contains minimal weight as Cal insisted I take a light load. I am silently grateful. What I need to do with Jo will take much more strength than I have within me.

He looks at me expectantly when we are ready to set off. I face Jo and inhale deeply. I focus on her form and lift my hands. The sleeping bag rises from the ground, prompting gasps from Sylvia and Cal. Jo's shape hovers above the ground about waist high, and I turn to Cal. "Ready," I say, hiding the strain that I feel already.

Cal blinks a few times at the sight, then gives me an impressed smile. Sylvia reaches out to touch Jo, but I grunt negatively and her hand falls with a meek apology. I wave her forward to follow Cal.

With my energy, I push Jo's form in front of me, and we fall in line as the first spits of rain come. I look around me for the hundredth time, searching the sky once again for my little feathered friend. Worry twists its knife in my gut. I don't want to leave without her, but we cannot wait any longer.

Within minutes, the clouds have opened and we are soaked to the skin. I have turned Jo over so she isn't drowned by the onslaught. The rain is loud against the leaf-covered ground, but I still hear Sylvia grumbling at how much this sucks.

I struggle to keep Jo aloft. I have to stop several times to pull energy from the storm. Cal is desperate to help me, but he knows he cannot. I love him for trying, though.

We rest under the ledge provided by a large outcropping of boulders. I gladly set Jo on the driest part of the ground, and I fight the desire to fall to the ground myself. I wipe the blood from my nose before anyone sees. We wait for a break in the downpour, but it doesn't appear there will be one. Sylvia's teeth are chattering and she is quite pale. Cal looks at me reluctantly when I insist we get moving.

What was a pleasant hike the day before is now wet, muddy drudgery. With heads bowed, we follow the trail Cal cut when we first came through. He consults his map several times, and I'm certain there is an "I told you so" coming in my future. After at least another two hours, we break through the clearing into the camp site. It is a relief that no one has come to camp and that our little decoy site is unmolested. I glide Jo into the tent out of the rain while the three of us pack up the truck.

When Cal declares that the bed is loaded well enough, I pull Jo from the tent to let him break it down. Sylvia peels off the saturated sleeping bag from around her mother, and I glide Jo into the back seat of the truck. Sylvia bends her into a sitting position and puts a pillow against the window for her to lean on.

We strip off the outer layers of our drenched clothing and stuff them into the truck bed. We climb into the cab, and Cal gets the engine going to produce some much-needed heat. Our underclothes are just as saturated as the outer ones were.

Cal puts the truck in reverse and, after several attempts to back up, proclaims that we are stuck. Anger fills me. I've had enough! With several expletives aimed at the tires and mud, I assure him we are not and tell him to try again. The tires obey him this time, and he hoots as he maneuvers the big truck out of the deep ruts.

I lose all sense of time staring out the window, contemplating what has transpired and what I've discovered. The anger welling within me for what those bastards did to me, what they did to my parents and the poor, innocent white raven, is impossible to keep at bay. She was my only friend, the sweetest and most loving creature. Now I know why she follows me and how I knew her name. Her Spirit was wrenched from her. While Maggie has a choice to stay with me, Ren does not. She is cursed herself—to forever be in my shadow, never able to come near, but always there.

My clothes dry quickly from the heat radiating from me. Cal reaches for the heater to turn it down and discovers to his amazement that the heat is coming from me. He lays his hand on mine, and I start, jerked back from picking through my first memories. I stare at his hand and turn back to the window. He asks me what's wrong, and I can't help but snort derisively. He apologizes for such a stupid question, and I grip his hand.

"Tell me *everything* that happened." I direct the demand to no one in particular. Both remain silent for several minutes. Cal exchanges glances with Sylvia in the rearview mirror. "Don't make me pull it out of you."

Sylvia clears her throat. "Well, everything was fine until you broke through into your first life. Man, what a light show that was! I don't know what you were doing, but you were radiating amazing light. Your aura was lit up, like it was on fire—white, silver, and gold. It looked pretty freaking cool. Then there was a big flash and then nothing. It was totally black and silent as a tomb. I started to freak out a little, I'm not gonna lie. I couldn't even hear my own breathing! But then after a few seconds, bam! I could see again, but what I was looking at wasn't *our* circle. This young girl, a young *you*, tied to a tree and—" She chokes and clears her throat again. I lift a hand to indicate that she need not continue.

"And you saw the same thing?" I ask of Cal. He straightens and swallows hard, then nods.

"And at the end, when…the explosion. What happened?"

Cal takes his turn to talk. "Something shoved me backward a little, and I heard Jo scream, and Ren, too. When I saw Jo, she was landing on the ground hard. I looked where you were, but I didn't see you. I ran to the water and finally saw you way over on the other side. You looked like you were drowning. I ran to you and Sylvia went to Jo."

"I thought all those symbols were supposed to protect us," Sylvia mumbles.

"They did," I say. "It could have been much worse."

Sylvia's eyes widen and her mouth falls open. I close my eyes and lay my head back on the seat. "I am so, so sorry."

The chorus of 'it's not your fault' and 'don't worry about it' sound half-hearted to me, and I don't blame them.

We ride in silence for many miles. I sense Sylvia's anxiety growing in the back seat as she stares at her mother. "Sylvia, Jo will be fine. I promise. She just needs rest." I'm not really sure I believe those words, but hopefully I sound convincing.

I search out the window for the white raven. What did that poor little creature experience? I assume her experience was the same as the others. My heart aches to see her, to make sure she's all right; I hope the blast did not hurt her.

Sadness, anger, and confusion war inside me. I want to be out of this truck, away from everyone so that I can scream obscenities to the sky. I think back to the explosion; did I cause that? It came from my body, so I must have. My curse is now never-ending, made so by the countless lives taken in the blast.

Sylvia, Cal, and I sit in Jo's living room. It's been nearly twenty-four hours since we got home, stripped Jo of her wet clothes, and put her into a warm bed. She has not moved. I have drawn energy into her twice since we've returned, and it has had no effect.

There has been no sign of Ren. If she lost the charm Jo made, she would at least be in the vicinity, and Sylvia or Cal would have seen her. I've thought about taking flight to search for her, but where do I start? I know nothing of where she goes when she leaves, nor where or if she keeps a nest. Having spoken to the resident ravens and other birds in the area, not one has seen a white raven recently. The aster fairies have offered their help, and I heartily accepted it. They will pass the word along to other clans and carry it as far as the message will go. Not much escapes the eyes of fairies. It is not a good idea to be indebted to fairies; however, I have run out of options. The queen's offer of help seemed genuine and without guile; they played often with the white raven and have become fond of her, so perhaps I will not owe a debt—or too much of one.

Maggie tends to Jo now, lying beside her bed, while we discuss what to do next.

"I really don't understand what is wrong with her." Sylvia stares at me expectantly, her eyes red from crying and lack of sleep. Guilt washes over me, and I'm at a loss for how to respond. I look at my hands, unable to hold her gaze.

"I'm tempted to take her to the hospital," Cal says.

Sylvia shakes her head. "That won't do any good. I did as Aven asked, though. I've spoken to Grandma's coven, well, *Aunt Claudia's* coven, and they are discussing what they think they can do. Which means they can't, or *won't*, do anything if you ask me. Bitches. Coven rules are so fucking stupid."

Cal looks at her, confused, and then to me when she doesn't elaborate. "Some covens stay within themselves. Jo's family's coven has always been very private and secretive. They won't help anyone who isn't a member," I say. "Even though Jo is blood, she gave up their particular tradition and left the coven long ago and was essentially shunned."

"Well, that's just stupid." Cal scowls at the coffee table.

"Agreed," I say, nodding, "but honestly, I don't think there is anything they could do for her."

"Yeah, because you know *everything*," Sylvia mumbles under her breath. My mouth falls open.

"Sylvia!" Cal snaps.

"Oh, come on!" She leans forward, fingers digging into the armrests, glaring at Cal. "It's *her* fault to begin with!" She throws herself from the chair and flings the front door open. It slams behind her, rattling the glass panes.

Cal stares in her direction. I sink back into the chair.

"She's right," I say weakly.

"Sylvia's just upset and scared for her mother. She doesn't mean it."

I know she's scared; I am scared. Her mother is her best friend, and I don't blame her for being upset with me. I would be if the roles were reversed. Feeling helpless as I do, I'm angrier at myself than Sylvia could ever be.

# Chapter 36

*I* wake with a start. There is noise about me. It is dark. How long have I slept? I hear the shuffling of wet leaves. I cannot move; my body is stiff and weak. The sound moves closer; it is alongside the log now. I hold my breath, willing the creature to keep moving. My heart is beating so loudly, I'm sure it can hear it.

In an instant, the opening of the log is filled with a furry head. Its glossy, beady eyes lock onto mine. Its nose sniffs the air rapidly; it grunts and pushes itself deeper into the log. I cannot move. My throat makes a sound and the animal stops for a few seconds. I shriek when it lunges forward, trying to push its large body further in. I see sharp white teeth despite the darkness. They seem to glow even though there is little light. Its snarling mouth is closer to me, its breath is hot and foul. I try to wriggle backward but I am caught. Something at my chest is caught on a splinter of wood. I pull backward as hard as I can, my clawed feet slipping in the slimy moss.

My beak shoots out, catching the animal in its tender nose. It cries out and pulls back. I scream at it, again and again. One more attempt to get at me and I draw blood this time; I can smell it. The animal shrieks and pulls out once more, shaking its head violently. With a final cry, it disappears into the night.

I cannot catch my breath; I fear I may faint. My heart pounds in my chest, and I panic when I finally realize I am caught fast. The thing around *my chest is foreign to me; it's firmly trapped within jagged splinters of the log. I pull and pull. I must get free! I must get to my woman.*

*What? My what? My woman? I stop struggling. I feel dizzy. My mind is swirling with thoughts and images I do not remember. They fly across my eyes faster and faster and my brain hurts with the sight of them. I shriek and shake my head, wishing this onslaught to be gone.*

*As quickly as they came, they are gone now, done. And I remember me.*

# Chapter 37

I wake with a start. A hot lick of fear travels down my spine, but the rest of my body shivers. It is dark outside and no candles remain lit in the room. I must have fallen asleep on the sofa. My eyes dart around the room. It is empty. The fear fades quickly, but I am still cold. I pull the afghan tighter around me and hug my knees to my chest. Reality crashes back in, and I remember where I am and why. Guilt floods over me once again as I recall Sylvia's angry words. When she returned later in the evening, she did not look at me and went straight to Jo's bedroom.

Cal left reluctantly hours ago. He must be in Worcester for an early meeting. He wanted to call his sister to take his place, but I insisted he go.

I close my eyes. *Oh, Jo, Jo. My dear friend. How can I help you? Please, please speak to me.*

Sounds of movement from Jo's room get my attention, and I am up in a flash. I stand in the doorway, panting. Sylvia is repositioning the pillows around Jo's head. My heart sinks. Sylvia stops when she sees me. It's too dark for me to see her face, but I know that she has been crying. She steps towards me and I close the gap, wrapping my arms around her. She sobs and hugs me tight, murmuring apologies, and I tell her to hush. Maggie is up beside us, wagging her tail, offering a bright face to cheer us.

I stroke Sylvia's hair as she cries and sway her from side to side. When her chest stops heaving, I offer to make her some hot tea. She nods against my chest, and I guide her into the living room. Maggie stays behind, resuming her post at the side of the bed. I give her a big smile and mouth a thank you. Her tail beats silently against the floor.

We take our lavender and lemon herb tea to the table under the white ash tree. We sip it in silence, listening to the sounds of nature around us. Dawn peeks above the horizon and sounds of the city coming to life follow the sun's ascent.

"Can I make you something to eat?"

"Not hungry," Sylvia says shortly, staring at her empty mug. Deep shadows lie under her eyes, like bruises.

"How long it has been since you've had a proper sleep, or even eaten?"

She shrugs. I stare at the mug for a moment, and it fills with warm chicken broth. She notices the steam and gives it a sniff, wrinkling her nose.

"Please drink it," I say in my best motherly tone. "Don't waste magickal broth."

She snorts and the edges of her mouth twitch. She takes a few sips and sighs, resting the edge of the mug against her chin.

The chill of the morning air goes unnoticed as we sit in our melancholy state, saying nothing but soothed by each other's presence. After a time, the chill settles in so we go inside.

"Okay, I'll take some pancakes." Sylvia lies down on the sofa. "Since you offered."

I'm glad she is hungry. At the mention of pancakes, my stomach growls. I can't remember the last time I ate.

When the sun is high in the sky, we set about repositioning Jo. We massage her arms and legs, and bathe her face, hands, and feet with warm water. This is done in silence.

The day drags, almost painfully. Cal calls several times to check in; I wish I had better news to give him. He will be back very late. An update from the fairies yields no positive news; I am surprised they are so downcast. I hadn't realized just how fond of Ren they were. What upsets them more, I think, is that they have neither heard nor seen anything. They do not like to fail. I insist this is not failure—that patience is needed. Fairies are not known for their patience. Their commitment gladdens my heart.

By the time the sun starts its descent, I decide to take a journey into the Veil. I doubt anything will come of it, but standing idle and feeling helpless is pure agony. I am just crossing the street from Jo's home when I hear something that makes me stop in the middle of the road. As I turn towards the sound, a car horn blares at me. I glare at the driver, and she flinches under my gaze. I hear the sound again. Yes! It's definitely the cry of a raven!

I run towards the sound, back towards Jo's house. My heart is racing faster than my feet. I tune out the noises around me and focus on that one sound. It's getting closer. I run with my eyes on the sky. There's a white flash over a three-story house in front of me. I call out and my call is answered. I hoot with glee. It's Ren! I turn and chase her call. I am in Jo's yard when I catch sight of her; she is crying out with every beat of her wings. At the sight of her, my eyes fill with tears, and I fear my heart will burst. She curves around and comes at me. I am laughing and jumping; the charm glints on her chest. She lands hard on the fence railing, digging her talons into the wood to steady herself.

I can't resist touching her, hugging her gently and kissing her head. She doesn't shy away from my affection. She pushes her head against my lips and gurgles softly in her throat.

"Where have you been?" I am out of breath.

She shakes her head. *I do not know. East. I flew east but where I cannot say. A long way. Long way!*

Ren pants rapidly, her little heart racing. I want to pepper her with more questions, but I leave it for another time. She must rest. I ask when she's last eaten, but she does not know. I invite her inside, tempting her with fresh berries and an egg. For the first time, Ren agrees to come into an enclosed space. I offer her my arm and she hops onto it. I wince as her talons grip my arm through the sweatshirt.

She ducks her head as we enter the house. She eyes the room and hunkers down on my arm, still panting. I give her words of encouragement in a calming voice. After only a few paces into the room, Ren tenses. She extends her head forward, towards Jo's room, and cocks her head to the side.

*Your friend. The funny woman. What is wrong with your friend?*

Instead of answering, I take her to Jo's bedroom, met in the hallway by Maggie who jumps around happily at seeing the bird. Ren touches her beak to Maggie's nose. I ask Maggie to go tell the fairies of Ren's return.

In the doorway, Ren croaks sharply when she sees Jo. I tell her what transpired in the circle, how we found Jo, and Sylvia repeats her story and Cal's. Ren listens without comment and never takes her eyes from Jo. Without warning, she leaps from my arm and comes to rest on the footboard of Jo's bed.

*I saw too. I saw what happened. To me. To you.* Her voice is somber. *Bad men will always do bad things. Bad, bad things.* She does not look away from Jo. *And dark magick lingers.*

My brow wrinkles at her last words, and Sylvia sits in the chair by Jo's bed, taking her hand. Jo looks as if she is sleeping. Her chest rises and falls in a regular rhythm, and her face is untroubled. Ren turns each keen eye to Jo, studying her intently.

*Dark magick lingers.*

"What do you mean? Her Spirit is weakened, and she's unable to retain the energy put into her." I come to stand by the bird, looking at Jo again with my Sight.

*She is caught.*

Sylvia and I stare at Ren, waiting for her to continue. She paces along the footboard but doesn't speak for several minutes. The silence grates on me.

"Please tell us what you are thinking."

Ren looks up at me, as if she's forgotten I was there, then back to Jo.

*She is caught. She saw. She saw and felt. It hurt her. The bad men's dark magick hurt her and she is caught.*

"Ren, please. I don't understand."

"Can you help her?" Sylvia's eyes glisten as she stares eagerly at the bird.

*I help all Spirits who need guidance. I help all who are lost.*

With that, she hops onto the bed and then onto Jo. Sylvia is up from her seat, hands clenched at her chest, watching Ren with great hope. I am gripping the footboard.

Jo is propped up with several pillows, and her hands rest on her chest. Ren hops atop her hands and leans forward. She touches her beak to Jo's lips. She straightens herself and then sinks her sharp talons into Jo's hands. Blood springs from the punctures, and Jo's arms flail out with a cry, casting the bird into the air. Her sudden movement makes Sylvia and me jump. Jo is gasping, eyes wide. Sylvia screams and reaches out, but Jo has fallen back onto the pillows, her eyes closed.

"What the hell just happened?" Sylvia asks, gripping her mother's shoulders.

In the instant Ren drew blood, I saw a bright flash with my Sight. Now, Jo's Spirit is glowing within her as it normally should—bright, happy, and strong.

*She will sleep now.* Ren hops back onto the footboard and gazes at Sylvia. *She sleeps now. Her Spirit is no longer caught. She is freed.*

"But she's been asleep *forever*," Sylvia mutters, taking one of Jo's hands. She turns her concerned eyes to Ren. "She's okay now though, right?"

Ren bows to Sylvia. *She rests now.*

I lay my hand on the bird's back, gazing at Jo. I'm not certain what Ren has done, for ravens have deep magick that I do not understand. Ravens are the ushers of the Spirit world; they lead those who are lost or confused to the Veil. It appears they do much more. I focus on Ren's mind so that only she can hear me.

*Ren, what was it? What happened to Jo?*

*Her Spirit was caught in an echo of those bad men's dark magick.* Her body quivers slightly. *What they did went very wrong, I think. Very wrong.*

# Chapter 38

The creaking of the screen door rouses me. It's dark and the house is quiet. I roll my head to the side to see Cal enter with all the stealth he can muster. He sees me and smiles.

"Hi," I say, stretching long and deep, yawning as I do. "What time is it?"

"About one. Go back to sleep. You need it." He kneels at my feet, kissing my hands.

"I have news."

My broad smile makes his eyes widen, and a hopeful look fills his face.

"Jo came around this afternoon."

He sinks back on his heels with a relieved sigh, squeezing my hands. I tell him of Ren's return and how she revived Jo and her explanation of Jo's condition. I nod in the direction of the bird, who is fast asleep on the back of the chair in the corner.

"Wow, she came inside!" He turns back. "Where has she been, did she say?"

"She doesn't know. She saw the same things we all did. When the explosion happened, she took off. She was disoriented and scared. She just flew and flew until her wings gave out." I frown, remembering how shaken Ren had been when she told me her tale. "My guess is that she experienced what the white raven did in the vision, as I did with my younger self. It was quite intense."

Cal looks at the bird with sad eyes. "You still think she's like Maggie?"

"In a way," I say, nodding. "I think that because of how horrible her death was, and the vile magick used in the manner of her death, she is essentially cursed to remain on this plane. Maggie is Spirit and has a choice to stay or go. Ren is immortal, her Spirit trapped within an undying body." I swallow hard. "She was my best friend, killed because of me, and so she's forced to stay with me. *Cursed* to forever follow but never able to get near." It is such a cruel thing for her to suffer.

As if sensing the intense emotion surrounding her, Ren stirs. She raises her head to us and stretches out her wings, then each leg. She nods to Cal and settles back down, her eyelids heavy.

"Ren said something that's been haunting me. She thinks what those men were doing had gone wrong. She doesn't know what that means, nor do I really, but I can't shake this dread." I shiver and Cal's arms go around me.

"Everything those bastards did was wrong," he mutters, kissing my forehead.

A loud snort comes from Jo's bedroom, and we both jump. I am about to check on her when full-on snoring emanates from the bedroom. Cal pats my hand and heads into the kitchen. I hear the fridge open and a bottle cap twisting off with a hiss. He returns and sits on the sofa, taking a long draught of the beer. He lets out a satisfied groan and leans back into the cushions.

"Bad day?" I ask.

He opens his mouth to speak when a series of creaks come from Jo's room, followed by the sound of something falling. We both race to the room. Sylvia barrels from her room with Maggie in tow.

"Mom!?"

The three of us cram into the doorway, and Sylvia flicks on the light. Jo is sitting on the side of the bed, shielding her eyes from the brightness. "Turn off that damn light!" Sylvia scrambles to obey, then falls to her mother's feet, crying. I pass my hand across the room and several candles flame up.

Jo blinks several times, swaying slightly, looking a little lost.

"You okay?" I ask. She nods, placing one hand atop Sylvia's head.

"Can I get some water?" Her voice is rough and dry. Cal is gone in a shot. I linger by the doorway, unsure of what to say. I want to rush to her and hug her tight, but she's clearly not ready for much attention. Cal returns quickly and Jo gulps the water.

"Okay, okay, let me up." She shoos Sylvia away, but softens when she sees her daughter's face. "I'm all right," she says with a half-smile, patting Sylvia's moist cheek.

She glares at the rest of us. "I'd be even better if you all would stop staring at me." She waves an irritated hand at us. "Go on, go. I need a shower."

Sylvia and I grin at each other. Jo is just fine.

We sit at the kitchen table and snack on sandwiches and chips. Sylvia has found her appetite and shovels chips into her mouth. I make Jo a sandwich and set it aside, hiding a handful of chips from Sylvia.

We hear the bathroom door open finally and the floor creak as Jo heads back to her room. By the time we finish our snack, Jo emerges from her bedroom. She doesn't come into the kitchen, though. Her footsteps take her into the living room, to her favorite chair. A sudden squawk and a girly shriek propel us from the kitchen.

"Oh, my Goddess!" Jo stands in front of her chair, hands on her chest. Ren is wide awake now, ruffling her feathers in a full body shake.

"So, yeah, Ren came inside," Sylvia says. Jo glares at her.

Stifled chuckling fills the room, and Jo feigns annoyance but then lets herself laugh. "Well, if I wasn't awake before, I am now!" She sits on the sofa beside the bird. Maggie comes to lie at Jo's feet.

After Jo's had a few bites of sandwich and some hot herbal tea, not coffee or whiskey to our collective surprise, she looks refreshed and the color has returned to her cheeks. Between bites, she's asserted that she is fine and that we need to stop worrying and *stop staring*.

I am anxious to ask her questions, and I bite the inside of my cheek. We tell her our separate tales and she listens as she chews, not interrupting or questioning. As she lays her plate on the coffee table, a shadow falls over her face. She scoots back into the cushions and rubs her palms on her lap.

"You're wrong, though," she says, looking at me. She answers my confused look. "That's not why Ren has stayed with you all this time."

The bird hops from the chair to the coffee table, looking up at Jo expectantly. Jo looks at her with sad eyes then turns those sad eyes to me. "And I was wrong about why you are cursed."

My body shivers involuntarily. I cannot make my mouth work to ask her to explain.

"How to say this?" Jo looks down at her lap.

I find my voice. "Just say it!" I lean forward, my hands clutching the armrests, Cal's hand on my back.

Jo's eyes trace the pattern of the rug, and she purses her lips. She starts to speak but shakes her head, finishing the last of her tea in one gulp.

"Those vision walks I did before, to discover why you were cursed. Boy, did I get those wrong." She huffs at herself and rubs her forehead. A knot twists in my gut.

"Seeing the...your vision...your first life...*feeling* it...made me realize that."

I want to go to her as she struggles for words, but my body is stone.

"Those three men. They *hated* you," she exhales heavily, lifting her eyes to meet my burning stare. She shudders. "I knew their minds the second I saw their faces. I've never felt such hatred before."

Jo takes a deep breath through her nose and relaxes her clenched hands.

"When you reached adolescence, your powers blossomed. The things you could do—they were so jealous, Aven. And your power frightened them, even at such a young age. They knew they wouldn't be able to control you or get you to follow their ways. Theirs was *dark* magick. So, they devised a ritual that would not only take your life, but steal your power for themselves. That's what they really wanted. Your magick. The only way to get rid of you was to make the villagers believe you were the cause of everything that had gone wrong. You were such a sweet, innocent creature." Her voice cracks, and her eyes gloss with tears. She blinks the tears away and continues. "Anyway, what they planned to do backfired horribly, as we all saw."

Chills wash over my body, and my palms are cold and clammy. She's taking a few moments to collect her thoughts, but I want to reach over and shake the rest out of her.

"They blamed everything on you, because you were so different, which meant you were evil and false. In order for harmony to be restored, you must be purged from the natural world, for you were unnatural. Why else were you dark-haired and amethyst-eyed when everyone else was blonde and blue-eyed? They convinced the villagers of this and several attacked your family's farm, taking you. Your mother and father fought so hard to get you free." As Jo speaks, I recall this scene vividly, and I close my eyes against it.

"You were a magickal creature of Nature, benevolent and kind, the essence of goodness. When they took your life with their dark magick, it was *wrong*, it went against Nature." Her gaze is fierce. "The explosion wasn't just in the physical world, but in the spiritual plane as well. The blast tore your Spirit, Aven. You are not whole. *That* is why you cannot cross over."

I suck in air and I'm on my feet. Cal is beside me, but I pull away from his touch. Ren flaps her wings and croaks repeatedly. Jo raises her hands. "Now, just hold on. Let me finish."

I stand as a statue before her; my hands are fists at my side. The room is getting warmer although chills race across my skin, and I know clouds are forming in the sky. A grumble of thunder prompts Jo to continue.

"I saw what happened in the explosion. A sliver of your Spirit was ripped from the whole." She looks at Ren. "It went into the body of the white raven and flew away."

"Wha…" I gasp. Ren warbles and her wings twitch.

"Ren *is* the other part of your Spirit, Aven. After such a blast, knowing nothing else but malevolence and pain, she flew and flew, desperate to get away, frightened beyond reason."

Ren falls to the floor, and I go to my knees to catch her. I cradle the trembling bird as she makes pitiful noises deep in her chest. She pushes her body into my breast.

*That is what happened; that is what I did. I lived it again when I felt the explosion again. Oh, oh. I did not know. I did not remember.*

I hold her as tight as I dare. I bend over my little Spirit, desperate for her to be closer to me.

Jo sniffs back her tears as she continues. "She follows you because she is part of you. She cannot come near you for the same reason. Like polarities repel. I didn't realize this before when she talked about how much your energy pushed against her, pushing her away. It makes total sense to me now. I had suspected something, but I wasn't sure exactly what—certainly nothing like *this*. That's why I went to talk to my mother. If I had not seen it with my own eyes, the tearing of a Spirit, I wouldn't have believed it."

Jo's words are a lead weight in my belly. I fear I may faint. I rock Ren gently, my lips on her head, tears streaming silently down my cheeks onto her feathers. My head is spinning.

I look up at Jo. "Did I..." the words get caught in my throat. "The explosion. All those people. Did I cause the explosion?"

"No, Aven, no!" Jo's face collapses, and she reaches for me. She's on her knees before me, gripping my shoulders. "The explosion was the result of their perverted magick. What happened was the consequence of them trying to take your power and end your life. The tearing of your Spirit, your curse, was just...an accident."

I almost scream. *Accident!* What a small word for what has been my fate for thirteen lifetimes.

317

Cal, behind me on the floor with his hands on my back, clears his throat, getting Jo's attention. "Uh, I'm confused, I'm sorry."

Jo sighs. "Aven's Spirit isn't complete because part of it lives in Ren. Only a whole Spirit can cross over, move on."

Cal eyes Jo sheepishly. "This is probably going to sound stupid, but is there a way to...uh...put them back together?"

My head snaps up and I stare at Jo. Her eyes bulge.

"Yes!" My eyes are pleading. "Jo, you figured out how to shield Ren against my energy. You sense things I don't. You can figure out a way to join us back together, I'm sure of it." I scoot on my knees closer to her, careful not to jar Ren.

Jo falls back on her heels, her jaw unhinged.

# Chapter 39

It is well into the morning and we still lie in bed, entwined in each other's arms and legs.

"Cal, you have no idea how relieved I am," I say, nestled into the crook of his arm. He twitches and grunts; I must have woken him. He tightens his arms around me and kisses the top of my head. Knowing that I didn't kill all those poor people is an immense weight off my heart—and knowing that I am not damned because I took the lives of others.

"My journey no longer seems endless. There's a way out. If I can just discover how to join pieces of the same Spirit, I will be free." I laugh at how simple that sounds.

"Aven," Cal says, pulling away slightly to look at me, "please don't take this the wrong way, but how is that even possible? You're getting your hopes up, and I hate to think how you'll be if you or Jo can't find a way."

"I know. But hope is something I've never had before—and it's a wonderful feeling." I smile up at him, seeing the sad skepticism in his eyes. "I have to try."

My phone vibrates on the nightstand—it's Sylvia wanting to know if she can open the shop. The vibes coming from her mother's sacred space are freaking her out. That makes me laugh.

"Sylvia will be over in a minute," I say, putting the phone down.

"Darn," he says, grazing my neck with his teeth.

Ren perches on my shoulder as I kneel before the black mirror. My two previous trips into the Veil since the night of Jo's revelation proved fruitless. Neither journey yielded any answers— not even a measly breadcrumb.

This time, I've asked Ren to travel with me. Perhaps with her presence, I will have more luck.

Our Spirits pierce the swirling black ether together. Ren's Spirit moves closer to mine; our ethereal matter commingles. We are closer now in Spirit than we have been since we were one so very long ago.

Something different happens almost immediately. Rather than shying away from me as the Spirits within the Veil usually do, several approach us without hesitation. Their white vapor encircles us, streaming around slowly. What had always been blank faces or clueless stares are now looks of curiosity and wonder. More spectators come and soon we are surrounded. Ren bolts upward, frightened by the unusual attention. In that instant, their faces turn to confusion and quickly move away.

*No, wait! Don't go!* I reach for one, and it speeds from my fingers.

*Ren, come back. It's all right.* When she returns, she melds into my Spirit once more. And what I suspected does happen— travelers stop to peer at this unusual Spirit.

*Ren, look at them! They have never come near me before.*

*I do not understand. Why do they stare at us so?*

*I think because we appear as a whole Spirit to them, or something resembling a whole Spirit. I don't have any other explanation. Ren, stay with me. Maybe now someone will talk to me.*

I reach out to the minds of those around us, and they dart away. I follow one and am shocked at the speed of it. It disappears at my touch. While I can approach Spirits now, each darts off when I speak. I grow frustrated and angry as I chase and plead. I travel far and deep; someone *must* speak to me.

Ren's voice is in my head, but I cannot make out her words. I am so dizzy and tired. My physical body is heavy, and all I want to do is lie down.

She is shrieking in my ear. I feel my body fall to the floor, and I have no energy to pull myself out from the Veil. I am caught within its current, my Spirit being carried along. Ren squawks and screams, beating her wings against my face. Sharp pain stabs at my shoulder, making my Spirit snap back into my limp body.

I am on my side, gasping for air. Ren is on the floor in front of my face, twitching, her feathers puffed up.

*Too far! Too long! Too deep into the Veil.*

I lie there for a long time, too weak to move or even speak. It will be some time before I'm able to enter the Veil again. Ren nestles before my face, pressing her forehead to mine.

It is dark outside when I startle awake, hearing Cal's voice in the shop calling my name. I push myself up with great effort, my entire body stiff and still very weak. I can't let him find me on the floor again.

"How's Bertie working out?" I ask Sylvia when she and Jo come over for dinner.

"Bertie is *so* great!" Sylvia beams as she shovels mashed potatoes onto her plate.

"Who's Bertie?" Cal asks, mouth full.

"Sylvia's new assistant." I grin at her.

Sylvia giggles. "Bertie's from Denmark—she came to the shop last month when she was on vacation. She loved it! She came back last week for an aunt's funeral. When she showed up, I was swamped! Too many people and only one me. Anyway, Bertie jumped right in, helping people and knowing a ton already about the stuff we have," Sylvia gushes as Jo smacks her hand away from the potatoes.

"She wants to stay in America. Her husband is an abusive dick, apparently." Sylvia makes a face at her mother and relinquishes the ladle.

"And she won't let me pay her," I chime in. "But I insisted on reimbursing her for lodging and food at least." When I met the portly, middle-aged woman, her pleasant nature and genuine care for the shop warmed my heart. I was happy to get help for Sylvia, especially since I'm spending the majority of my days in search of an answer.

Ren has her own chair at the kitchen table with a plate of roast beef, potatoes, and green beans on the seat. Arial sits below her chair, staring up at the bird with anticipation of some dropped morsel. Ren obliges frequently.

"So, I'm starting to freak out a little. The grand opening is, like, a week away! Oh, my Goddess, my hands are sweating thinking about it." Sylvia rubs her palms on her lap, staring at me with big eyes.

"How many times have I told you to stop worrying?" I ask, eyeing her with feigned reproach. "You are completely prepared. The guests are lined up, caterers are ready, the DJ comes highly recommended, and all the party paraphernalia—gift bags, door prizes, etcetera—are put together and waiting in the storage room. We are good to go!"

Jo nods emphatically, mouth full of roast beef.

"Who's doing all the decorations?" Cal asks after wiping a spot of gravy from his chin.

"Me," I say proudly, receiving raised brows from Cal.

"*Magick.*" I wink at him.

"Of course!" He laughs, raising his glass.

Jo leans sideways to me, almost whispering. "What did you end up doing with the fairies? That's the only part I'm worried about, really."

"I've made them very happy. The fairies will have a night of glorious freedom. I gave them a job! They will be allowed to mill around and interact with the crowd. The queen has signed a binding contract with me that not a single bit of mischief will be made by any fairy. The penalty will be expulsion from the aster, their home."

Cal's mouth falls open. "There are *fairies* in the front yard?"

Jo comes over the next afternoon and finds me meditating on the rooftop terrace, bundled in a coat and blanket. The weather has turned unexpectedly chilly in recent days, and the sky is choked with steel-gray clouds. The wind has picked up considerably and has become colder, so we go inside.

We sit in the living room with steaming hot toddies. Jo sips hers, relishing the warmth traveling through her body.

"These things are the only reason I don't mind cold weather," she says, taking another sip.

"You look worn out, Jo. Please take a break. I hate the thought of you wearing yourself out because of me."

She shakes her head, savoring the flavors of the drink. After she swallows, she smacks her lips and looks thoughtfully at the glass mug.

"Aven, I saw and felt things in that vision that I can never describe to you. There are no words. It's those things that compel me." She takes in a deep breath. "What you've been through…it's just not fair. What happened to you was a *crime*. If they knew what *curse* you are living under now, they would be thoroughly enjoying your suffering."

My skin prickles at her words. Those bastards would certainly be pleased with the outcome of their deeds, aside from their untimely deaths, of course. Jo has an amazing ability to see things in ways I never could. I take her free hand and hold it tight.

One side of her mouth curls up, and she squeezes my hand, giving it a little shake. "You are my best friend, lady, so I gotta try to help you as best I can."

My heart blossoms. "I feel the same way, Jo. Thanks to you, this is the best life I've ever had."

With that, Jo looks away and wipes her cheek. She sniffs and then chuckles. "Okay, enough of this. My mascara is going to run."

I clear the lump in my throat and pull my knees up to my chest. "So, anything come of your efforts so far?"

"Nothing!" Jo throws up a hand. "I've done everything in my arsenal—vision walks, meditations, rituals—talked to everyone I've ever met with any hint of magick in them, *and* I called Claudia. Oh, Goddess, that was tough." She groans and looks away. "So, that leaves me with only one more thing to try…and I'm dreading it." Her face puckers as she stares at her empty glass.

Indignation blooms on her face. "The *Internet*."

# Chapter 40

"**O**kay, you two boys know what you need to do?" Mandy presents a black duffel bag to the taller boy, its contents clanking as she shoves it at him. He snatches the bag, rolling his eyes.

"Yeah, yeah, lady, we get it," he says, his voice filled with teenage arrogance. "We're gonna break into Dovenelle's and trash the place. Isn't that hard to understand."

Mandy glares at the impudent, pimple-faced boy. "You need to do *much* more than that! Weren't you listening? You need to smash *everything*! The display cases and everything in them. Tear apart all her precious books and rip up the furniture. Break every statue and figurine. It has to be so bad that she can't have her grand opening!"

Mandy's whole body trembles with fury, and her eyes shoot fire at the two wide-eyed boys fidgeting in front of her. They must understand how important this is! She'd go herself but she can't risk being recognized, let alone caught.

Her chest heaves. The tall boy takes an involuntary step back and bumps into a shelf, causing a large ceramic matryoshka doll to wobble. Mandy shrieks and lunges for it, catching it as it teeters forward. She holds it close to her chest.

"Get out! Now!"

The shorter boy, standing behind his friend, finds his voice. "Wait a minute, lady. Give us the fucking money you promised."

Mandy's eyes burn into his. "You'll get your *fucking* money when I see proof of what you've done. Take *lots* of pictures."

She straightens and looks down her nose at them. The tall one glares back at her and opens his mouth, then quickly clamps it shut. Turning on his heel, he punches his friend in the chest and jerks his head for the boy to follow him.

"And use night mode! Can't risk anyone seeing the flash," she calls after them as they slam the door.

"Fucking little pricks," she mutters, placing the precious matryoshka back on the shelf. She lovingly strokes it and tells it that it's okay, that nothing bad will ever happen to it.

*Those stupid dolls don't mean nuthin'.* The harsh voice growls behind her. Her back stiffens, but she ignores him. When is he going to leave?

*I ain't leavin' until I'm satisfied you done the job. That bitch has got it comin' an' you know it. You want it too.*

The vile creature is right. Mandy closes her eyes and revels in the truth of his words. She has him to thank for the courage to make it happen. Aside from her fear of this man, this thing, he does have a way of making her feel powerful. She's resented Aven from the moment she met her, then grew to hate her with every passing day, especially when she started fucking Cal. Morris Stiles has helped her channel her animosity, and she loves the sensations that course through her, making her strong, bold.

It was Morris who found a boy who disliked Aven enough to want to cause her grief, and the boy recruited his friend. Morris has shown her just how many people harbor grudges against Aven. She feels vindicated in her loathing for the woman, and now, the plan to make her a failure is finally set in motion.

Will and Kyle bolt to the nearest elevator, and Will punches the button for the first floor with his fist.

"Fucking bitch," Kyle says.

"Yeah, but a *rich* fucking bitch." Will folds his arms across his chest, a wide grin spreading across his face. "I'm stoked, man—this'll be awesome." Will's grudge against Aven grew each time he remembered how she'd humiliated him in front of his uncle and that stupid, fat girl. "I can't wait to get her back."

Kyle snorts his agreement. In a few nights' time, they'll get their chance. Dovenelle's grand opening can't happen if they do their job right, and they will make sure of that. Easy money.

"Two more days!" Sylvia sings as she bursts through the front door. The morning is crisp and bright; the sun's rays bathe the wares in the front window in cheery, golden light. Arial is already at her post in the library, posed regally on the window seat, gazing out at her domain. Her tail twitches rapidly as she watches sparrows and wrens dart around the bird feeder.

The shop is closed this week to prepare for the big event. Up since before dawn, I've puttered and paced. I even took a short flight while it was still dark to blow off some of this excess energy. I have found new pleasure in flying with Ren at my side. She has hardly been out of my sight since the night we learned we are one and the same. Her positive attitude has kept my spirits up; she's not daunted in the slightest by the lack of progress on finding an answer. She has learned infinite patience from being immortal, and I envy her that. Ren monitors me even now, perched up on the loft's railing.

I meander around, inspecting each item for the umpteenth time, tweaking their positions this way and that, rewriting any descriptions that I now consider not detailed enough. I've been so absorbed with finding a means to end this curse that I've hardly spent any time in the shop. Realizing I've neglected it too long, I have allowed nervousness to set in. But there's no need, of course. Sylvia, with Bertie's help, has done a fine job.

"Aven Dovenelle!" Jo yells from the kitchen. The sudden interruption to my thoughts snaps me up from my stooped position. My back aches and I stretch to get the kinks out, thinking to ask Cal for a massage later. I march to the kitchen and stand in the doorway with my hands on my hips.

"I would have middle-named you if I knew what it was." Jo motions for me to sit and presents a coffee cup to me.

Waving off the cup, I sit. "No, thank you. I've probably had eight cups so far—been up for a while."

"You need to relax, lady." She eyes me over her mug as she sips. "I have never known anyone more prepared than you." The roll of my eyes brings more admonishment. "Leave everything where it is. I'm telling you, it's *perfect*."

"What are you going to wear?" I ask, knowing she'll love to talk about her ensemble.

"Oh, my Goddess!" she says. "It's absolutely gorgeous if I do say so myself. I haven't sewn in so long. Made my arthritis kick in big time, but I powered through."

"She'll look like a cross between Stevie Nicks and Maleficent," Sylvia says as she bounces in, beelining for the bagels on the counter.

"Oh, be quiet, you." Jo looks slightly embarrassed.

"I can't wait to see it!" I lean back in the chair, enjoying Jo's discomfort. Her snarl makes me laugh.

"I'm going to be a black cat, since you asked," Sylvia says. "It took a while to find a plus-size cat suit that wasn't fifty pounds of fur." With that, she leaves, cinnamon raisin bagel in hand, to resume whatever it was she had been doing in the storeroom.

"And you?" Jo peers at me.

"Oh, nothing *too* over the top." I grin and ease up from the chair. "Come on, help me make sure the books are in the right order."

"Again?"

# Chapter 41

Will and Kyle sit in Kyle's piece of shit car a few houses down from Dovenelle's. Their conversation includes frequent rants about why that bitch hasn't left yet and long periods of silence as they play on their phones. Boredom brings a discussion in vulgar detail of the inevitable booty call from Will's uncle. This quickly makes Will uncomfortable, and he punches Kyle in the shoulder repeatedly until his friend shuts up.

"Man, I gotta take a piss," Kyle says, opening the car door.

Will grunts an acknowledgement as his thumbs move rapidly over his phone's screen. Kyle is getting out when Will looks up abruptly, his eyes glimmering with an idea.

"Wait, dude." Will grabs Kyle by the arm.

Kyle falls into the seat with a suspicious glare. "Yeah?"

"You can piss all over that bitch's store," Will says with a grin. "Better yet, on her mattress!"

A wicked smile curls Kyle's lips. He settles back into the seat and puts his hands between his legs.

Night has settled in well by the time Aven Dovenelle trots down the porch steps, almost skipping along the path, followed by a big white dog.

"Damn! That's her?" Kyle squints and leans forward to better see the woman in the dark. "You made her sound like some bony, crooked-nose hunchback. Shit, man, I'd tap that too."

Will plants a knuckle punch on Kyle's arm. "Shut the fuck up."

Kyle laughs at his friend's grossed-out face. "Come on, let's go."

"No, man, we gotta wait. Too many people still out walking around."

Kyle lets out an exaggerated grunt and tucks his hands back between his legs. "Come on, bladder," he murmurs, leaning over.

It's after midnight when Will decides it's safe to get moving. The contents of the duffel bag given to them by that crazy blonde woman clank loudly as Will throws it over his shoulder. While he would have preferred to just torch the place, the idea of letting out his anger with a crowbar is deliciously appealing. The psycho broad had gone nuts at Will's suggestion of setting fire to the shop. *Absolutely not*, she screamed at him. The houses were much too close together, and she didn't want anyone to get hurt. What a pussy.

In the shadows of the dark alley, they creep unseen alongside Dovenelle's. Hopping over the short picket fence enclosing the side yard, they hunker down for several minutes, ensuring they haven't been seen. The gigantic bush beside them, surprisingly still green and full-leafed, is lit up like a Christmas tree. Kyle comments on how cool it looks, which earns him another punch in the arm. Instantly pissed, Kyle returns Will's punch with all his strength, sending Will to the ground. Will holds his hands up in surrender, and then hisses at Kyle to get a move on. Kyle peers into the bush as he creeps by, squinting at the movement he thinks he sees within. Will pushes him to get moving.

They launch themselves onto the porch from the side, halting momentarily, panicked by the loud creaking of the old wood. Single file, they pick their way around the furniture to the front door, stepping gingerly on the protesting wood. Will snorts in triumph at how easy the lock is to pick. She deserves to be robbed if this is all the security she's got. When the door hits the entrance chimes, they sink to the ground and freeze. A pungent aroma hits Will's nose.

"Did you just piss yourself?" Will looks at his friend in disgust.

"Dude, I've had to piss for *hours.*" Kyle hisses through his teeth. His glare turns into embarrassment. "Just a little came out. Shut up. Go!"

The door chimes bring no attention, so they duck into the house and close the door behind them. Both boys stand in silence as they survey the shop. Will's skin tingles with excitement. He sets the duffel bag on the floor and unloads its contents.

Will takes the crowbar while Kyle opts for the hammer. Each looks around, divvying up the shop between them. Going in opposite directions, they set to work.

Will's palms are sweaty as he grips the crowbar. He wipes each hand on the front of his black jeans and wanders around the shop, contemplating what to smash first. A glint to his right catches his eye. Dangling from the ceiling by the front window is an ornate dragon, made of silver wire and purple glass, catching the moonlight with each slight twist. The dragon's impressive wing span must be at least three feet, the purple shards of glass affixed like jagged scales and secured with the delicate wire wrapping. Will snorts when he checks the price tag. People are idiots to pay that much for this shit.

"Batter up," he says with a nasty grin. Taking a batter's stance, he lines up the crowbar with the dragon and swings. The smash is ear-splitting in the dead silence of the shop. When the dragon hits the floor, the exploding crash makes Will hunker down. Kyle comes running in a crouch and whistles at the awesome devastation scattered all over the floor.

"Nice," Kyle breathes approvingly. Fueled by the excitement of his friend's handiwork, he swings his hammer down onto the nearest display case. Shards of glass fly in all directions and fragments skitter across the floor. He hoots but is quickly shushed by Will. Kyle smashes each item in the case, his eyes wide with maniacal glee.

It isn't long before the boys have the glass cases reduced to glittering shards and splinters of wood. Kyle can hold his bladder no longer and empties it on a display of medicinal teas. The boys turn their attention to the library, ripping apart each and every book. Will pulls a large screwdriver from the duffel and sinks it into the couch, stabbing and ripping, his face sweaty and determined.

"Ease up, man, the couch is dead. Seriously." Kyle looks at Will bug-eyed.

Kyle heads up the stairs saying he needs to take a dump and he knows exactly where. Will does not laugh; his face is hard. This exercise hasn't been the release of rage he'd hoped. He is even angrier now. He wants to hurt that woman, he wants it so bad he can taste it. Will wanders around the devastation, glaring at everything, stomping on things that are much too whole as he goes.

He is about to bring his booted foot down on something colorful when he stops short. Kneeling, he recognizes the piece. It was the eye of something pendant he'd snatched months before. This is the damn thing that started this whole mess. He was grounded for a solid month—no Xbox, no visiting friends, no girls, and the worst of all, no cell phone. It was a torture that made Will resent his uncle more and more with each passing day. Although, really, it is all his dad's fault, now that Will thinks about it. If he hadn't left, hadn't gone to fight for his country or some bullshit like that, Will would never have even thought about taking the stupid thing.

Will is light-headed with the fresh rush of anger. He snarls at the pendant and snatches it up.

A spark of red flame shoots from his hand, and the sudden pain makes him yelp and drop the pendant. His palm is glowing, *burning*, red. He cries out as the burning becomes more intense and stares in astonishment as his hand flames up before his eyes. He screams, waving his hand in the air. Kyle comes bounding down the stairs, shouting for Will to shut the fuck up before they get caught.

Will shoves his burning hand under his armpit and bears the pain with a pinched face. The pain subsides immediately, and he pulls his hand out slowly, afraid of what he'll see. To his surprise, his hand isn't the charred black skeleton he was sure he'd see. His hand is pale and fleshy, if just a tad pink.

Kyle yells something that Will doesn't pay attention to. He stares wide-eyed at his hand, turning it this way and that.

"Fire, motherfucker, *fire!*" Kyle punches his friend in the back to get his attention. Will jumps up at the sight before him. The floor, which is littered with the paper and fabric flower decorations from the display cases, is on fire. The fire is quickly spreading, and it snatches at the curtains on the window.

"Jesus, fuck!" Will darts around the ruined cases, heading for the back. "Back door, back door!" he yells, not waiting for Kyle.

Kyle is yelling something after him, something about putting the fire out. The hell with that. Kyle can put the damn fire out if he wants.

Both boys pump their legs full speed out the back door and through the alley to the end of the next block. They finally stop and lean within the shadow of a dumpster, panting hard.

"Man, we gotta call the fire department or something," Kyle says between breaths, hands on his knees.

"Fuck that. We'll get busted." Will stares behind them in earnest. No one is following. He sighs loudly and leans against the wall.

Shaking his head, Kyle pulls out his phone. Will smacks it from his hand and shoves Kyle against the adjacent wall. "Goddammit, I said *no!*" Will glares at him, daring Kyle to challenge him.

"Get the fuck off me!" Kyle pushes Will hard, landing him against the opposite wall. With a contemptuous glare, Kyle snatches his phone from the ground and storms off.

"Walk home, motherfucker," he says.

Will shoots his friend the finger. As the adrenaline wears off, he feels a sudden wave of guilt. The faint sound of sirens in the distance sends him running after Kyle.

# Chapter 42

I take to the sky in pajamas, oblivious to the cold, with Ren close behind. Cal follows in his truck. My home is on fire! Sirens had woken Jo. She instantly knew that those sirens were intended for my home and called me.

I land behind the aster bush as the emergency vehicles round the corner. The residents of the bush are in chaos, surrounding me. Their shrill voices in chorus hurt my ears. Their intentions are true but I don't want to hear anything from them—I want to *see*. I beg them to let me pass. Some shouts are angry and vow revenge for the threat to their home. I silently petition Ren to stay with them for comfort—and control. Several frightened little ones surround her. They huddle underneath her wings, and she opens them fully so more can come. Maggie inspects the aster and the fairies crowding around her before leaping onto the porch and disappearing through the wall to investigate.

Movement beside the house catches my eye. Arial darts out of the shadows, drenched and shaken. Why is she wet? I snatch her up and hug her tight. She does not protest. After showering her head with kisses, I set her down. Much to my surprise, the fairies welcome her, touching her trembling body and offering soothing words. In that moment, the past animosity of the two warring factions melts away into a united sense of mutual support.

People are already gathering. I fling myself onto the smoke-filled porch. I see no flames but hear crackling and smell the tang of a wet ash. Wet? But the fire truck just got here. The sprinkler system! That's right, I remember—I was required to install it throughout the shop. I exhale with relief. Perhaps the damage is minimal.

I reach for the handle of the screen door, and I snatch my hand back with a gasp. Unwelcome images flood my Sight—of two young boys, one extremely familiar, dressed in black and carrying a duffel bag that clanged with each jostle. Feelings of animosity, anger, and malevolent glee wash over me. My hands tremble as rage fills my chest.

"Get back, ma'am, *now*," comes a shout from behind me. "Don't touch anything!" The tenor of his deep voice allows for no rebuttal. I hear the running of heavily booted feet and then feel thick-gloved hands on my upper arms, turning me away from the door. "Step back, ma'am. Are you all right? Are you hurt?" He assumes I was in the house. I shake my head, allowing him to pass me to someone behind him. I barely notice my feet moving.

Several firefighters jog up the path, their faces covered with oxygen masks, large tanks on their backs bobbing heavily with each step. I let an EMT escort me from the porch as he wraps a stiff blanket around my shoulders. I am not cold; my body burns with outrage. With so many people around, I must marshal my emotions. I clench my fists and set my jaw as someone guides me to the back of an ambulance. I wave off attempts to be examined.

Jo and Sylvia run up to me, spewing condolences and disbelief. There are so many people now, wrapped in fuzzy robes or blankets, gawking at my home. I want to yell obscenities at them and make them go home, but I stare at the ground instead, trying to quell the growing rage.

"You okay?" Jo touches my hand and snatches her fingers back. "Goddess!" She cradles her hand in the other.

I raise my face to her and she steps back. "This was intentional," I say through my teeth.

Just then, Cal appears, alarmed as he takes in the scene.

"What did you say?" Sylvia breathes.

I stare at the ground again. I take a deep breath, which helps me restrain myself from screaming at her. "Two teenaged boys broke into my home." I meet Cal's eyes. "Your nephew and his friend, Kyle."

Cal's eyes widen and a reflexive 'no' escapes from his lips. He staggers back, mouth hanging open. "Are you sure?" he finally asks, searching my face.

Jo turns to him with a deadpan face. "Really?"

He ignores her and comes to take my hands, then lets go quickly, stepping back, his eyes wider. "I…"

I wave away his words. At that moment, a police officer breaks into our little huddle.

"Ma'am, are you all right? Were you in the house when the fire started?" His demeanor is all business—no sympathy or compassion occupy the lines of his face. I sense his prejudice against my type of shop…and my kind of people.

"No, I was spending the night with my boyfriend. My friend called me."

He looks at Cal. "I'll need your address, sir." Cal nods, his face ashen.

Carrie D. Miller

"What's your assessment, officer?" I make him look at me with my words.

"Vandals, ma'am. It appears they destroyed a good part of the downstairs. Seems like the fire started in the front by the windows. The cause has not yet been determined."

My heart sinks with his words. I knew some of this; but hearing it makes me choke. I must get inside and see for myself. But now that this will be considered a crime scene, I won't be allowed in, nor will the grand opening happen. I cannot allow this.

"*Officer*," I say, my voice resonating around him. His steely eyes glaze over, and his shoulders slump forward slightly. "This was an accidental fire, started by a candle left unattended." The command must be simple for it to take hold. Too much detail and the mind will fight against it.

The officer blinks at me a few times then looks down at his notepad, which is now blank. He looks up again with confusion. He sways slightly then inhales deeply through his nose, straightening himself.

"This was an accidental fire, ma'am. Appears to have been started by a candle left unattended." He flips his notepad closed and stuffs it into his pocket. Turning on his heel, he disappears behind the ambulance.

Ignoring the three pairs of astounded eyes upon me, I push myself from the bumper of the ambulance, flinging the blanket from my shoulders, and walk to the gate. My Sight shows me four firefighters inside my home. I touch their minds and repeat the same message. Within a few minutes, they parade out the front door.

The leader of the group approaches me and announces that the fire started accidentally downstairs. A candle left unattended. The sprinkler system did its job, and the rest of the house is fi-

342

ne. In silence, the firefighters load up their truck. I turn my attention to the crowd. Some stare at me with pity on their faces, others at the house, pointing and making assumptions as to what happened. The message I send is silent. One by one, each person becomes bored with the scene and loses interest. After a few moments, the street is blissfully empty and quiet.

The speechless trio continues to stare at me, but I have no desire to explain. I want to see my shop, my *home*.

I do not hesitate this time. When I step over the threshold, what overwhelms me is not the stench of wet ash and smoke, but the array of negativity still hanging thickly in the air. Instinctively, I push against it and have to stop myself. I need to feel it, I need to follow it, to see what happened.

Many footsteps hurry behind me onto the porch but pause outside. I sense their apprehension. I hold up a hand, needing them to stay outside for now.

Closing my eyes, I inhale the wretched air deeply. The paths the boys took through my shop appear to me as thin trails of black ether, twisting wickedly in the stillness, and I follow that of Will Jacobs. I walk to the right and my vision is filled with the shattering of my silver and purple glass dragon. It was one-of-a-kind, lovingly handmade by an old man I found living almost a hermit life in northern Oregon. Glints of silver dot the floor, covered mostly by blackened matter—too much to find any trace of purple. I turn to the display cases, or what used to be them, and watch as Will pummels them with his crowbar. Both boys' arms come down onto the cases over and over until nothing of what they used to be remains. Their laughter and exuberant hoots resound in my head. The precious contents of each case lie strewn upon the floor, smashed and broken.

As I gaze about, I hear intermittent clicks that puzzle me. Is that a camera shutter? Looking deeper into the vision shows me each one's cell phone held aloft, snapping photos of their hand-iwork. Fresh anger washes over me.

I follow Will's trail into the library. The fire did not reach this room, but the contents are soaked from the sprinklers. I close my eyes to the devastation, but that does not impede the vision that assaults me. Each book is torn apart and cast aside. Will stabs and rips the couch like a madman. I stagger backward, Will's emotions making me dizzy. Cal's arms are around me immediately, and I let him hold me while I regain my balance.

He says something apologetic, but I'm not listening. Drawn back towards the front of the display cases, I kneel, ignoring the pain as my knees are pricked by sharp bits of glass. I brush away a coating of ash from a small object and pick it up. Negativity floods over me, and I almost drop it. In my fingers rests the Eye of Horus pendant. I see how the fire begins. How my hex upon Will's hand flares out aggressively, powered by his rage, licking at the paper and fabric remnants on the floor. The fire is my fault.

My fist closes around the pendant, and I let its sharp edges cut into my palm. If I had not been so angry with him, if I had not cursed him so, this fire would never have happened.

I stand up slowly, trembling. I turn to face those behind me, hearing for the first time the crunch and crackle under my bare feet. The sound and pain startle me, pulling me back to the here and now. The sight of my friends comes into focus, and their words are becoming clear again.

"Can you tell us what happened?" Jo says again.

I nod, still clutching the pendant.

"Aven, you're bleeding!" Cal sees trails of blood seeping through my fingers and takes my clenched fist in his hands. He is pulling at my fingers, telling me to let go. I can't seem to obey him. "Aven!" he snaps, making me jump. I release my grip, and he opens my hand gently.

Jo and Sylvia are behind him as he pulls the bloody pendant from my palm. His eyes widen with recognition.

"The fire is my fault." Hearing the words aloud makes me flinch. I touch the white raven's mind so that she will hear also, and I recount the events that led the emergency vehicles here. My voice is monotone and I stare at nothing, stating the facts only, which helps to keep the raging emotions at bay.

"I just can't believe it," Cal mutters when I'm finished. My head snaps in his direction, my expression making him put his hands up in surrender. "I didn't mean it that way. It's just, I would never in a million years have thought Will was capable of something like this."

"Why did they do this?" Jo asks, her hands clutching the obsidian pendant at her breast.

"Revenge, I suppose." There's nothing but anger from Will's travels through my shop; it's clouding anything else I could see.

Cal looks away as he talks. "I grounded him. There was no way he was getting away with stealing or talking to Sylvia like that. I only took away the things he likes and didn't let him go out; it's not like I busted his ass, although I wanted to. He was pissed at me, of course—he didn't speak to me for weeks. But...this!" He rakes his fingers through his hair as he looks around.

Sylvia comes from upstairs, followed closely by Maggie. "You need to put these on." She hands me my tennis shoes. I don't look at her as I take them. I lean against the blackened wall and wipe the glass and grit from my bleeding soles. Maggie sniffs my feet. Shocked at their condition and concerned about infection, Cal tells me I need to clean my feet right now with alcohol, but I wave him quiet.

I feel Jo's fury. In the dim, gray light of pre-dawn, her splotched cheeks and the deep grooves between her eyes are clearly visible. She's wandering around, eyeing everything with a mixture of contempt and disbelief. When she sees the library, her hands clench at her chest. I finally look at Sylvia. Her cheeks are wet and her eyes red and puffy; she looks around the shop, stifling sobs, but her shoulders quake.

The emotions of my friends touch me deeply. They love this shop as if it were their own. They *are* part of it and have given so much to put it together. What has happened to it was not just done to me, but to them also.

"The grand opening will go on," I announce. My hand goes up to stave off the chorus of 'hows.' "I can repair some of this. I can reassemble the things if all of their bits and pieces are around. But things that burned up, disintegrated, like your teas, Sylvia, I can't fix. I'm sorry."

A glint of hope lights in both ladies' eyes. Sylvia's not affected in the slightest by the loss of her teas. Cal's eyebrows go up. "Should I even ask how?" I incline my head to him and raise an eyebrow; he knows the answer to that already.

"We won't be as well stocked as we would have been and things won't be perfect, but the party can still go on." My chin lifts with my confidence. I will not be defeated, especially by two punk teenagers. "Sylvia, head to the storeroom and find out what is salvageable. Make a list of what we need. I'll give you my credit card, and you can get to shopping as soon as the stores open. Unless you need more sleep. I'm sorry, I forgot what time it is."

"Screw that!" Sylvia's voice has its smile back. "Just let me get my binder and put some clothes on. I'm freezing!" She's out the front door like a shot. Her exuberance tugs at the corners of my mouth.

"What are you going to do about Will and Kyle?" Jo asks when Sylvia is out of earshot. "I assume you have a plan since you didn't let the cops have them."

"I won't put any energy into that right now. I need every ounce for this. But yes, I will deal with them in my own way."

Jo gives an exaggerated whole-body shiver, then turns for the door. "I'll go make us some coffee. Be back in a bit."

Cal comes over and opens his arms, silently asking if he can hug me. I soften to his look and step into his embrace. He wraps his arms around me, murmuring an apology that's not his to make. I tighten my arms around him and let go of the hold I have on my anger. Negative emotions will not help me with what is to come.

# Chapter 43

When Jo is back with leftover angel food cake and coffee in a large, pump carafe, we head upstairs. Sylvia bangs through the front door, binder in hand, and beelines to the storage room.

Since it wasn't a requirement to install fire sprinklers in the private residence portion of my home, I did not, and I'm very thankful for that. There is only a thin coating of ash on everything, but the entire house reeks of smoke. I magick all of the windows open. Cal pulls on a sweatshirt he's left here, and Jo is already bundled up after coming back from her house. I'm still in my pajamas.

"Aren't you cold?" Cal asks before shoving a handful of cake into his mouth.

I force a weak smile. "My anger keeps me warm."

Jo pumps us each a mug of rich smelling coffee. The flutter of wings comes from behind us as Ren soars through the kitchen window, landing on the back of a chair. Jo pulls off a small piece of cake and places it on the seat. Ren hops down and pecks hungrily at it. Jo offers a piece to Maggie, who tilts her head questioningly. Jo tuts at herself and pops the morsel into her mouth.

Jo pulls out a chair and sits heavily. "So, what's the plan?" We join her at the table. I take a few sips of the delicious dark roast, delighting in the warmth. Jo pushes the cake towards me, but I decline.

"Well, as soon as Sylvia is done with her inventory, I'm running all of you out. I need to start with the downstairs. I won't know what all I can fix until I get into it." A twinge of panic pricks my stomach.

"You really think this will all be ready by tomorrow night?" Cal looks dubious.

"It's not going to be remotely what I had planned, but I won't be defeated. I, *we*, have put much too much into this to have it all dashed at the last minute." I give Jo a wink, and she raises her coffee cup to me, mouth full.

A new flood of guilt washes over Cal's face. I speak before he does. "It is *not* your fault. You cannot control the mind or actions of a troubled teenager."

He huffs. "He didn't do this on his own. I mean, Kyle helped him, sure, but to be honest, my nephew is kind of a pussy and doing this requires some real balls. Somebody put him up to this."

Jo almost chokes on her mouthful with stifled laughter.

"I completely agree," I say, grinning at Jo. "I can picture your nephew spray-painting my front porch but no, not *this*."

"But who hates you this much? How stupidly angry are they to do something like this to *you* of all people?" Jo wipes crumbs off her mouth as she speaks.

"Well, most people don't know Aven is who she is," Cal says. "If they did..." He whistles.

I mentally go through the list of people who have a grudge against me, and Mandy's squirrel-like face features prominently.

"Mandy comes to mind but then, really, I don't think she'd do it. She hates me, yes, and would love to see me fall on my face, but acting against me like this is not something I think she has the guts for. She's a coward, and her reputation is everything to her."

The breeze coming through the house shifts enough to bring a foul odor across our table.

"Oh god, what's that smell?" Cal covers his nose and gets up. I pale at the thought of what could be up here. I haven't gone through any of the rooms yet. I don't follow Cal. Jo puts down her coffee with a disgusted look and fans her nose.

Cal looks around the living room then pokes his head into the bathroom, bravely sniffing the air, following the scent. He is in my bedroom when I hear his shout.

"Are you fucking kidding me?"

I don't want to know, but I get up anyway, followed by Maggie. Jo stays at the table, shaking her head vigorously.

The wretched odor hits me in the face when I enter my bedroom. In the middle of my bed is a pile of human excrement.

I block out what my Sight would show me. I don't need to know the details; the result is plain. My hands ball into fists and fresh rage flares across my body. I stand at the footboard, glaring at the revolting dark pile upon my crisp, white comforter. My right hand lashes out, blasting blue and white fire at the pile. With my left, I create an invisible shield to contain the small inferno. Cal stumbles back and Jo runs into the room.

Bearing my anger down onto the defilement, I funnel everything I have felt for the last hour into the confined blaze. The excrement disintegrates within seconds, but I do not stop. I let it all out and watch it burn in a ball of blue fire, swirling and twisting, pushing against the protective sphere, begging to be freed. The anger drains from me, and the fire dwindles.

I am dizzy when I release the shield, stumbling back but grabbing the footboard. Cal's arms are around my waist, and I lean back against him. Having that negative energy purged from me makes me instantly tired...and very cold. I feel empty now, as if the anger was all that I had inside me.

"Please don't hurt Will," Cal breathes into my ear. "Or Kyle. Promise me."

My stomach sinks. He has seen my power and knows of the darkness that I carry in my heart, and I am ashamed.

I take a deep breath and place my arms across his. "I won't hurt them. But they will learn what it is to cross a witch. *This* I promise you."

After Sylvia leaves with her moderately long list and my credit card, I usher Jo and Cal out the door. Ren heads off for a more substantial breakfast.

I close the door and lean against it, taking in the room with a renewed sense of disbelief. "Where do I start?" I ask into the stillness. I save the worst for last and turn my attention to the library.

Standing at the threshold, I take several deep breaths, clearing my mind of negativity. I have a singular goal; I have no thoughts but this one. *Join the pieces to reform the whole.* I lift my arms from my sides and flare my fingers wide. Wet pages and soggy, torn bits rise into the air. Each bit and page finds its home and joins together with a flash of silvery light, instantly dried and whole again. My breathing is slow and even; my body feels light and cool. Happiness fills me as solid books form, laying themselves onto the empty shelves.

# Chapter 44

Mandy struts along the sidewalk with her chin held high, delighting in the sharp clicking sound that her high-heeled boots make. It's the day of Aven's grand opening, or would be if it wasn't for Mandy. She grins widely then laughs out loud.

Mandala Moonchild has single-handedly taken down the not-so-great-after-all, overly-full-of-herself Aven Dovenelle. She laughs again, rubbing her leather-gloved hands together. She is on her way to bask in her triumph—to see a dark and quiet house, devoid of decoration or merriment. She's been practicing her shocked and appalled expression in the mirror all morning. She must see the devastation first-hand and will feign such sympathy that it would easily win her an Academy award.

As she rounds the corner onto Derby Street, she turns up the collar of her full-length leopard coat to stave off the brisk chill in the late October air. She picks up her pace, eager to get within view of the house. She wants to run the last few yards, but her boots aren't having it. Her face aches from the amount of smiling she's done since seeing the images on Will's cell phone yesterday. The butterflies in her stomach flit with excitement.

What she sees stops her like a punch to the chest.

Several men are unloading a van, carrying tables and chairs. She hurries, gripping her collar against the wind. When the yard is in view, she lets out a small cry. The smile that's been etched on her face crashes, and she digs her nails into her collar. She snarls at the impossible scene before her.

There is a flurry of activity from half a dozen people. Some haul silver banquet serving trays, others boxes of liquor and wine—all going into Dovenelle's. One man nearly drops his burden of stemware when he trips on the curb in his rush. The shop girl is standing at the gate with an open binder across her arms, making marks on pages and giving direction as needed. She helps the man up and ushers him to the porch.

Mandy is stunned, paralyzed by the impossibility of what she is seeing. *Those fucking brats lied to me!* She glares at the house. It takes several seconds for her to find her legs. She snaps around and trots away before she is recognized.

*Those lying little pieces of shit! I will kill them. I will have Morris kill them!* Morris will be so angry; her fear of him slows her steps. She takes scant solace in knowing that *she* won't be the target of his wrath; those boys don't know what they've done. But she's the messenger…

She is winded by the time she reaches the door to her condo building. She'll have to hurry if she's to be showered and dressed in time for the party. *I'm absolutely going, goddammit.* What's more, she needs to be out of the condo before dark, before Morris comes. He usually comes when the sun sets.

Mandy darts out of her building and straight into the waiting cab. Once her building is out of sight, she sighs with relief and swallows a sob. *Don't cry anymore, dammit! You'll ruin your makeup.*

She was wrong. Morris came early, eager for news of Aven's defeat. She cowered as she told him what she'd seen; he grew larger and darker with each word. He lunged at her, swiping a gnarled hand across her stomach. Morris was reasonably solid now, made so by her boundless hate and animosity towards Aven. The cut was superficial, but it burned as if done with acid. She screamed again and again that it wasn't her fault, it was *theirs*. Those fucking kids! Morris flung his rage at the walls of her living room, shattering every single precious curio. She cried as she watched him, helpless to defend her treasures.

He flew from her balcony after that, presumably to pay the boys a visit. Mandy didn't care; he was gone, at least for now.

There is a great deal of traffic on Derby—it's Halloween, after all. Salem swells beyond reason on this day; actually, the onslaught of tourists begins a few weeks before and lasts a week after. Salem makes a lot of money in the months of October and early November, and the only ones who seem to be bothered by the congestion are the residents who don't profit from the tourist trade. Mandy would usually work this night; she can charge four times as much on Halloween, and people pay it without question. Her assistant is on duty instead. Though she isn't nearly as good as Mandy herself, Mandy would never dream of closing her shop on Halloween. She'll make a pretty penny before the tourist hordes leave town.

Mandy grumbles that she could've walked and gotten there faster. It is taking way too long to go a single mile. But she knows her five-inch, patent leather spiked pumps are definitely not made for walking, and she didn't wear a coat. She wanted nothing to obscure the grandness of her costume.

When the taxi gets close enough to Dovenelle's for Mandy's satisfaction, she tells the driver she's getting out and throws a wad of money into the hopper. He is already stopped—it is bumper to bumper—so she wriggles out of the back seat as demurely as she can in her tight gold lamé minidress.

She trots to the curb and takes a moment to ensure her Cleopatra costume is in order. She straightens the body-hugging material and smooths her long golden cape. She checks her headdress and wig with her hands and realigns the wide, ornate collar across her shoulders. A familiar maniacal laugh resounds behind her, making her skin crawl. She searches the crowded street. There is nothing there. She must have just heard wrong. She takes a deep breath and pushes all thoughts of Morris from her mind.

She hurries along the sidewalk, holding firmly to her position in the crowd. She stops only because the throng of people before her has stopped. They all stare at the same thing, at the gate to Dovenelle's—or more precisely, what surrounds the gate.

# Chapter 45

Mandy blinks several times to ensure she is seeing this right. Thick, white smoke—in the distinct shape of a bird, a crow or raven maybe—stands at the gate and towers high above it. The raven's massive wings are outstretched and curved upward, with its beak pointing to the sky. The mist shimmers with wisps of silver and swirls of brilliant white. It seems alive! The bird fans its wings when a guest passes through it and lets out a deep caw that echoes for several seconds. Mandy marvels at the technology that's making this magnificent spectacle and looks around for the smoke machine and lighting apparatus. She sees nothing in the bushes, not even a single extension cord. She will have to learn which company did this before she leaves tonight.

The large, barrel-chested man stationed by the gate bars entrance to those without an invitation. Mandy flashes hers proudly, and he inspects it with a pen light. He hands the invitation back and welcomes her to Dovenelle's, motioning for her to proceed. She is a little apprehensive at passing through the impressive bird; the smoke is so thick, she can't see through it. She chides herself for being stupid—it's just a special effect. The man encourages her with a manufactured smile and motions with his head for her to get a move on.

Waving a hand before her to disperse the smoke does nothing. The dense white and silver vapor swirls only slightly and holds its form. Mandy puffs her chest out and takes a step forward. She sniffs, expecting the distinctive aroma of the liquid used in fog machines, but instead inhales a faint scent of cloves. Frowning at her inability to figure out this trick, she takes another step forward, bringing her out of the raven's massive tail feathers.

The front yard of Dovenelle's is alight with hundreds of tiny silver and gold lights. Some of these lights seem to fly about the yard. Several come towards her, and she takes a half step back. They aren't lights. They're…fairies? Those can't be real. The little winged creatures hold what appear to be small lanterns, their light reflected brightly off their delicate wings. She is momentarily startled by the number of them surrounding her, chittering and…singing? Instinctively, she lifts a hand to swat them away. The one closest scowls and says something that she can only assume is a swear word. It turns around and waves the rest to follow it.

*How the hell did Aven manage that? Some sort of fancy drone tech?* Mandy is no longer impressed. She is irritated; jealousy burns in her chest. A laughing, awestruck couple pushes past her. She watches them in their ridiculous matching mummy costumes walk arm-in-arm slowly up the path, gawking stupidly at the unbelievable spectacle around them. They point here and there, with audible gasps of amazement. She scoffs at them. *Idiots.*

She doesn't want to see any more; she wants to go home. Sobering at the thought of what awaits her at home, Mandy starts up the path. Try as she might, she can't help but gaze around. A thick layer of rolling fog covers the ground, everywhere except the walkway. Each footfall prompts a glow from the cobblestones. Flaming jack-o-lanterns float menacingly in the air, their expressions changing as they inspect each guest. The mummy couple receive accepting smiles, and the woman earns a wink from the fatter pumpkin. As a large one approaches Mandy, its fiery eyes and mouth glower at her. She shrinks from it with a squeal and trots quickly onto the porch, her heart racing.

The porch is crammed with people, laughing and talking merrily with drinks in hand, all in elaborate and expensive costumes. She inspects herself to confirm she looks better than everyone else.

She stops at the threshold to the shop, amazed by the sights before her. All of the walls are covered in black and silver brocade wallpaper, which is peeling in many places. Old paintings with ornate but weathered frames are scattered haphazardly across the walls. The images in the paintings move within the frames and interact with those who gawk at them. One painting features a very old and crotchety man, dressed in old-fashioned sea captain clothes. He's perched precariously in a dinghy in the middle of a dry ocean bed. He shakes his fist at those staring at him, yelling that they need to move on or they'll get what's coming to them.

She looks up to see an enormous chandelier that spans the full length of the great room. Its black metal workings make it look like a thorny mass of seething brambles, and the vines are *moving* within it. There are no bulbs or candles—instead the thorns are aflame, flickering vigorously with each movement of the thick vines.

She senses eyes upon her. Aven Dovenelle glares down at her from the middle of the staircase, her eyes narrow slits. Her nails are dug into the railing, which looks like a glimmering snake. Mandy instantly feels exposed, as if Aven knows she is the mastermind behind the vandalism. But that can't be—there is nothing amiss about the shop at all. Nothing is broken or smashed, nothing is torn, or ripped, or even out of place. Everything is perfect. Under the hawk-like stare of Aven's creepy purple eyes, Mandy flushes red. Aven is probably just pissed that she's actually shown up. Aven's going to have to share the spotlight at her own party. *Ha!*

Aven's stare is interrupted by her friend Josephine coming up to her and placing a hand on her arm. Aven jolts from her trance, her face brightening immediately at the sight of Jo. Aven gushes over Jo's ensemble; the woman turns and pivots for Aven on the steps, the copious folds of her deep purple velveteen dress swirling about her, slapping at the person coming up the stairs beside them. A laugh is shared by all three, and the older man hugs Jo briefly then continues upstairs where the buffet is stationed. Mandy rolls her eyes. *The Stevie Nicks look is SO over, honey.*

Mandy takes this opportunity to assess Aven's choice of costume. She is dressed as a witch—how unimaginative—and the full-length gown is way too sexy for the likes of Aven. It clings to her body like a second skin, accentuating her small breasts and the curve of her hips. Its shiny black material appears to be latex from where Mandy is standing, with a long slit up the front of her left leg to her hip, exposing a muscular leg that takes Mandy by surprise. The forearm sleeves drape down and attach to a cape of satiny material, giving the effect of wings when she opens her arms. The cut down the front of the dress exposes more breast than hers does, but Mandy isn't jealous. She actually has boobs. Mandy isn't going to admit that Aven looks great, she isn't. But she will find out where Aven got the dress. She could really rock that, minus the pointy hat.

She turns at hearing her professional name and graciously takes the extended hand of a formerly frequent client, smiling and laughing, extolling how absolutely marvelous the woman looks. The spitting image of Marie Antoinette if ever there was one. Mandy takes the woman's arm, requesting to be shown the way to the bar. As they pick their way through the crowd, she asks the woman why she hasn't been to see her in such a long time.

Mandy stands at the back of the room, her glass filled to the brim with champagne, sipping it without relish. Greatly annoyed at the extremely fine options at the bar, she chose the most expensive thing she would drink. Mandy prodded the bartender to fill her glass completely, leering unabashedly at the handsome young man as she imagined what it would be like to ride him. She must give him her card before the night ends.

Her foot taps to the beat from the DJ, but she stops it immediately. Taking another sip of the champagne, she finds the glass empty and pushes herself from the wall, heading back to the bar.

She leans on the polished wood counter, ensuring her breasts are displayed for Jake the bartender's benefit. He smiles the mandatory server smile and takes her glass, turning away.

"Isn't he a bit young for you?"

Mandy's eyes narrow at the sound of the annoying voice and her impertinent words. Mandy doesn't acknowledge the woman right away. She waits for Jake to present her drink. She takes it, thanks him for being so kind to her, then turns her body towards the unwelcome visitor.

"Josephine." Mandy nods curtly, taking a sip from her glass.

*"Mandala,"* Jo says with unrestrained sarcasm. "I'm surprised you showed, to be honest." Jake hands her a short glass filled with two fingers of some dark amber liquid. His smile for Jo is genuine, which vexes Mandy immensely.

"Why wouldn't I? I was invited, wasn't I? It would have been rude to decline an invitation to such a marvelous event." Mandy's voice drips with sweetness.

"Right," Jo snorts, swirling the liquid in her glass. "Then try not to look so sour about it, huh? People might think you're, I don't know...*jealous* or something." She tips her drink to Mandy and turns away.

Mandy snarls at the woman's back, watching Jo's ample form melt into the crowd of revelers. Catching herself immediately, she straightens, plastering a big smile on her face, showing off her perfect teeth. She can't be caught not having a good time or begrudging Aven her success. She takes a deep breath and switches into full social butterfly mode. If she can't beat Aven, she will at least get something out of it—eat the expensive caviar, drink the expensive champagne, and maybe drum up some business while she's here. She has several of her business cards tucked in her cleavage.

Before long, she finds herself having fun, much to her surprise. She's danced with a young, lanky vampire, and the wait staff make sure she is never thirsty. A ghostlike little girl in a simple white shift gives her a ghostlike rose that turns into a colorful butterfly in the palm of Mandy's hand. She marvels at the trick, watching the butterfly flit around before her, dancing in and out of her upraised hands, eventually disappearing in a puff of glitter. She turns to ask the child how the trick is done, but the little girl is gone.

Wonders such as this are everywhere. A large dragon, made of silver wire and purple glass, flies around the ceiling, its tail whipping through the air, occasionally swooping down to the delight of the crowd. It perches momentarily on the loft's railing, then hops off and dives when someone reaches for it. It is clearly having fun with the crowd, and they eat it up. It lands on the outstretched arm of a woman covered from head to toe in luminescent white feathers. Her extended arm looks like a wing. The woman stands quietly, apart from everyone else, and appears content to survey the festivities around her. When she gazes up at the writhing chandelier, Mandy sees her eyes glint purple in the light.

The fairy things are everywhere too. Their job seems to be lighting, as each still holds a tiny lantern and hovers a foot or two from the ceiling. Mandy squints to see if she can spot the fishing line that they have to be hanging from, but she can't see anything of the sort.

Cal comes through the front door just then, dressed in a simple, well-fitted tuxedo and plain black mask, met quickly by Aven, who seems to appear from nowhere. Cal is apologizing profusely, mentioning something about being held up in Worcester, and Aven silences him with a kiss. Mandy looks away in disgust, deciding she needs another drink. She waves away the waitress and heads for the bar.

Mandy's foul mood has returned, and she finds it increasingly difficult to keep the smile up. She's been hearing people chatter excitedly about a rooftop terrace, so she decides to go see this impossibility for herself.

The buffet is set up in Aven's kitchen and is filled with people chatting and eating, laughing and singing the praises of Aven's fabulous home and her skills at party throwing. Several guests lounge in the living room, which has been decorated like a turn-of-the century graveyard. All of this must have cost Aven a fortune! It is really movie-quality stuff, Mandy admits reluctantly. She stifles a growl as she snatches a tiny hors d'oeuvre from a passing tray. Whatever she put in her mouth is delicious, which makes her scowl deepen.

Mandy stands staring up the steep staircase to the roof. A small star-shaped LED candle lights each polished wood step. She questions whether her dress or her heels will allow her to climb it. She huffs aloud and angles herself, taking the steps sideways, a hand on each rail.

A little spiny creature with a pointed snout is positioned at the top of the staircase, seated on what looks like a tiny bejeweled throne. He holds up a black paw.

"Mind your head, please," he advises in a squeaky, high-pitched voice.

She stares at the little thing, astonished. *Is that a hedgehog wearing a top hat and bow tie?* Mandy shakes her head, exasperated with trying to figure out how all these tricks are being pulled off.

She lowers her head and steps through. "Holy shit," escapes her lips. She covers her mouth, embarrassed that she's been heard by the people nearest the door. They chuckle and admit to saying much the same when they saw it.

What is billed as a rooftop terrace looks more like the deck of an Egyptian pharaoh's ship. The raised dais in the middle has gilded posts at each corner, adorned in colorful hieroglyphics. In the center burns a roaring fire in a large golden bowl supported by four clawed feet. Four golden thrones surround the fire, also covered with hieroglyphics. The thump of the music downstairs is barely audible. People mill around, admiring the sight, commenting on how *cold* the fire is, and taking selfies in the thrones.

Needing to get away from all these happy people, and the heavy scent of frankincense wafting from the fire, she finds an empty corner at the back. She grips the coping of the waist-high parapet and leans forward, inhaling the crisp, night air. She tunes out the sounds around her and closes her eyes, enjoying the stillness.

"I know what you did," comes a harsh whisper in Mandy's ear. Her eyes snap open and she flinches, her skin threatening to jump off her body, knowing who's behind her. But Aven doesn't know anything, can't know anything. Unless those fuck heads ratted her out—they *were* acting a little weird when they came over. But there is no damage! She can't be blamed for anything. She swallows hard, pulling her clammy palms from the coping and making fists at her sides. Mandy steels her face and turns to her enemy.

Aven stands only a handspan from her. Even with Mandy's high-heeled pumps, Aven is still taller. Mandy hates having to look up at her. She holds the woman's glare, not letting Aven's murderous expression get to her.

"I have no idea what you are talking about," Mandy says with her chin high. Aven's hand lashes out and grips Mandy's upper arm. She squeals as Aven's nails dig into her flesh.

"Now you listen to me," Aven says, inches from her face. "You sent those fucking kids to destroy my shop. I know you did. I knew it the moment you set foot in my house. You *reek* of guilt. There is *nothing* you can hide from me."

Mandy tries to wrench her arm free but can't.

"Let me go, you fucking bitch!" Mandy says, glancing over her shoulder to see if anyone is there. Mandy gulps. The rooftop is empty save for a few fairy lanterns, bobbing up and down with the beat of their wings. Are they staring?

Aven jerks her forward, closing the distance between them. "You have crossed the wrong witch, Janet Kellogg, and you will regret it."

Mandy trembles despite herself. There are flames in Aven's eyes, actual *flames*. She tries to look away but can't. Fear sweeps over her, threatening to choke her. The same crippling fear she feels around Morris Stiles.

Then Aven's face changes. Her eyes search Mandy's face. They widen slowly, and her lips part. Aven inhales sharply and steps back, releasing Mandy's arm. Mandy gasps and slaps her hand over her throbbing arm.

"I see now that it wasn't your fault. Well, not *entirely* your fault."

Mandy's brow creases, and she narrows her eyes at Aven.

"You have been under the influence of a nasty Spirit." There is a hint of sadness in Aven's voice. And what else—guilt? "While you have brought this on yourself, with your ridiculous jealousy of me, no one deserves to be tormented by Morris Stiles." She lets out a long sigh. "Not even you."

Mandy's mouth falls open. How does she know? How can she possibly know? Mandy's breathing becomes rapid, and blood pounds in her ears. She has been so afraid. Since the day Morris appeared on her balcony, she hasn't known a single night's peace nor a day without looking over her shoulder or jumping at the slightest bang or knock. Aven looks almost sad for her.

Mandy's resolve crumbles, and her shoulders slump forward. She snatches up Aven's hand and holds it to her chest. "Oh, Aven," Mandy breathes, her eyes welling with tears. "Please help me." A sob racks her body, but she holds her tears at bay.

Aven's shocked expression softens, and she steps forward, laying her other hand atop Mandy's. "I will," she says with such compassion that Mandy's tears spill down her cheeks. "I'll come over tomorrow, and we'll get rid of him." Aven gives her hands a comforting squeeze.

"I can't go back there." Mandy shakes her head vehemently. "I can't go home."

Aven is quiet for a long moment. Mandy trembles at the prospect of going home.

"Then you'll stay here." She steps to the side and wraps an arm around Mandy's trembling shoulders. "I may have some clothes that will fit you. Well, I take that back." Mandy pulls away, afraid Aven has changed her mind. "I may not have any shirts that will fit over *those* puppies." Aven wags a finger at Mandy's cleavage, her eyes filled with mirth. Mandy is taken aback by the woman's attempt at humor, then laughs aloud.

"Come on," Aven says, taking Mandy's hand. "Let's get a drink."

As they slowly walk single file down the narrow stairs from the roof, each woman clutching the handrail and taking cautious steps in their stiletto heels, Mandy feels relief wash over her. For reasons she can't explain, she knows Aven can help her. She frowns at herself then. She let Morris control her and make her do terrible things. Aven seems to know that somehow and is still willing to help her. Mandy's cheeks flush with shame.

The music thumps with a rhythmic groove as the party switches into high gear. The thorn-flame chandelier now pulses with strobing lights, and colorful laser beams cut through the hazy fog that hangs in the air. Aven's shop seems to have morphed into an all-out dance club, the display cases and shelves having disappeared since Mandy went upstairs, making the entire area free for dancing. The house is packed, but there is still enough room for some wild dancing.

With drinks in hand, Mandy maneuvers through dancing couples, and pauses to gaze up at Aven. She stands at the loft's railing, surveying the party with a proud smile, like a benevolent queen watching over her prosperous kingdom. The pride on her face changes to love and Mandy follows Aven's gaze to witness Cal attempting to dance in the stereotypical white-man-is-oblivious-to-the-beat way, with Sylvia egging him on. Jo sways back and forth with an older man Mandy thinks looks similar to the owner of Phil's. Jo's face shines with exuberance and a bit of whiskey. She seems to sense that she's being watched and turns. Jo gives Aven an emphatic wave then looks away, embarrassed by Aven's exaggerated winking in the man's direction.

Mandy swallows a fresh pang of jealousy and starts up the stairs with their drinks. Mandy has gotten herself into quite a situation with Morris Stiles, and she'd kick herself if she could for being so weak. She doesn't know what happened up there on the roof, but Aven knew about Morris, maybe read her mind or something, and the special effects at this party can't be explained by even the best technology or trickery. What if Aven is *really* a witch? A real, honest-to-goodness, spell-casting, magick-wielding witch. That thought stops her midway. She looks at Aven with new eyes.

An unearthly roar bellows across the entire house, resounding off the walls, causing the music to screech to a halt and several people to cry out and grab their partners. The familiar sound cuts into Mandy's chest. The glasses drop from her trembling hands and shatter on the stairs. Mandy's terrified eyes meet Aven's astonished pair.

A large, black shape begins to grow at the apex of the ceiling, overtaking the chandelier. It swirls and boils, and something within it roars again—a deep, furious sound that makes the window panes rattle and the walls quake. Everyone is transfixed at the sight. Several smile and point, thinking it is part of the special effects, murmuring that it must be a show or some sort of skit. Mandy knows better. She turns slowly on the stairs and creeps down them, trying to keep herself hidden behind the people who are watching the spectacle. She has to get out of here *right now*.

A vile stench wafts from the rolling mass, making people grimace and cover their noses. The stink of rotting flesh and fetid blood fills the room. People gag and someone vomits.

Mandy darts through the open front door and trots down the steps of the porch as fast as her skirt and heels allow. Panic fills her chest, and she can hear nothing but the sound of her pounding heartbeat. She is almost at the gate when her path is blocked by little lights closing in around her from all directions. It is those damn fairy lantern things. She waves her hands to disperse the mass. Pinpricks stab at her fingers and hands.

She yelps and jumps back, clutching her stinging hands to her chest. "What the fuck?"

*You tried to burn our home.* A small voice fills her head. The voice is more beautiful than any Mandy has ever heard. She squints at the lantern that hovers just before her. A beautiful, heart-shaped face, topped with a tiny, finely woven crown of silver and gold, glows in the light of the lantern she holds aloft. Her sharply angled eyebrows are furrowed at Mandy and her pointed ears twitch slightly. Mandy is mesmerized by her beauty, admiring the shimmer of her rapidly moving wings.

*We heard the Great Witch accuse you.* The sweet tone of the voice belies the harsh look on the fairy queen's face. *You must pay.*

The fairy then pulls back and waves an arm towards Mandy. The surrounding fairies drop their lanterns and come at Mandy all at once. She screams. A gritty mist blows into her mouth, and she chokes and coughs, trying to spit out the sickly sweet taste, but she cannot—her tongue is numb. She feels her body being lifted from the ground. Their grip stings at every place they hold her, as if tiny daggers are being jabbed into her skin, and there are dozens of them. She tries to fight back, but her limbs are growing too heavy to manage. Her head swims and rolls backward, eyes wide but unable to focus on anything. Darkness closes around her vision as she is carried aloft into the garden.

# Chapter 46

I stare in disbelief at the grotesque darkness before me. Morris Stiles has grown incredibly strong from stoking Mandy's animosity and jealousy. He should have dissipated without Melissa's energy. What is before me now shows just how much I underestimated the hatred he harbors for me. I catch sight of Mandy as she darts out the front door. I don't blame her. While she brought it on herself, she's been tortured enough by this vile creature.

Coils of thick, black smoke serpentine in and around themselves, the entire mass growing with each movement. As it solidifies, its surface becomes oily and slick. Its foul odor fills my nostrils, and my stomach churns. I survey the restless crowd. How can I get them out of here? He'll strike if they move.

Maggie's at my side, hackles up and teeth bared as she glares at the mass.

"Morris Stiles!" My voice is strong and firm. The sound of his name from my lips causes the rolling mass to convulse, and he screams with outrage. "I command you to leave my home at once!" My energy pushes hard at him. To my surprise, he does not give.

For a moment, silence fills the room, and the temperature drops rapidly. Within the coils, a gurgling chuckle begins. It grows slowly in strength and volume until it becomes a maniacal cackle.

"*You filthy witch*," the mass growls, spitting out each word. Thick tentacles shoot out at me. The sudden movement prompts screams from the crowd, and the people behind me jump and scamper back. Hard, knife-like fingers stab into my shoulders and jerk me over the railing, my hat flying off.

Cries fill my ears as I fall, although I am not falling for long. I lighten my body and soar around the room. Screams turn into applause and amazed laughter. I alight where the crowd has moved aside to clear a space for my landing.

The oily mass roars again with all its might. People's hands cover their ears, and screams begin anew. Some fall to their knees, hands clutching their heads, blood trickling out of noses and ears.

"Stop!" I throw up my arms at the tangle of coils. A bolt of white energy flares from my hands into its heart, and it screams in agony, writhing as the white light crackles like lightning within it. All of the Halloween enchantments vanish. Realization spreads rapidly through the crowd; this is not a show. I pass my hands over the frightened, murmuring throng. They must not draw attention to themselves; I have no idea what that monster will do. Each person goes still, their faces blank. I leave my friends free of the spell.

They run to stand with me, Cal putting himself between me and the frightening sight above. I push him behind me. Jo stares with confusion, but I shake my head. Ren comes to land on Sylvia's arm when she offers it. I face Morris with Maggie at my side, a low growl rumbling deep in her chest.

As the lightning within the rolling blackness fades, so do his screams. A face takes shape in the center—the face of a being driven by an unquenchable lust for vengeance and an unreasonable level of hate. His jagged mouth, dotted with rotting teeth, curls wickedly at the corners. The black holes where his eyes should be hold a growing fire deep within their recesses.

From his mouth fall stringy blobs of a black, viscous matter that burns the surfaces they hit like acid. The wood floor smokes black as it burns. The stench of it threatens to make me retch but I stand firm, glaring up at the demon-like creature. He is much stronger than I would have ever thought possible. Only Spirit can touch Spirit. To make contact with me as he did, to create the solid matter that drips from his mouth—these are things I have never before witnessed. A flicker of fear travels up my spine, but I steel myself against it.

The fiery pits within his eye sockets dart to each of my friends. I grit my teeth.

"You will never get what you want, Morris Stiles," I say. The roving eyes return to me, and his vicious grin falls. I begin to draw in energy from around me, gathering it within myself. "You want revenge, but you are very much mistaken. You *deserved* your end." He does not sense what I am doing as I speak. I must distract him long enough to gather the energy that I need to cast him out.

"That's bullshit!" the filthy mouth spits out. "Yer a goddamn witch, and you got what was comin' to you. I did what was right in the eyes a' God!" The mass quakes so violently, it shakes the walls and windows.

"And what are you now, Morris Stiles? You are an evil apparition, an *abomination*, an entity from the Other World! You are no better than a godless witch now, aren't you?" The energy courses within me, hot and quivering. I clench my fists to contain it.

He roars with outrage and glares at something behind my right shoulder. He shoots thick tentacles towards me. But not at me—his aim is for Cal. As I turn to catch the black coils with the energy pulsing in my hands, Jo cries out and shoves Cal. The tentacles plunge into her body. A coil whips out at me, penetrating my heart, and throwing me across the room. Stars fill my vision when I hit the wall and slide to the floor. My chest burns, and I cannot breathe. Maggie's teeth sink into the thick, oily flesh protruding from my chest, and she rips viciously, tearing off chunks of black matter, only to see the gashes close up immediately. I shout at her to help Jo.

Sylvia shrieks and lunges for her mother, but Cal holds her back. Jo is pierced throughout her body, her face caught in a silent scream. Ren claws madly at the black, ripping bits off with her beak and talons. Maggie lunges for the thickest mass, her immense ethereal strength pulling it from Jo's body. Morris howls, lashing out at Maggie with a dagger-like tentacle. It spears Maggie's torso, and she yelps as he thrashes her about. He throws her limp body backward and she disappears in midair.

Another tentacle whips out at Ren, throwing her hard to the floor. She does not get up; her chest looks caved in. Maggie appears over her then, shielding the poor creature with her bulk. She snarls and barks at the black, writhing mass above her.

I cannot move. My vision blurs. The sharp coil piercing my heart twists, sending searing pain through the whole of me. Faintness threatens to take over. I can't let him kill me. I must save Jo! Maniacal laughter fills the room as the tentacles shake her violently.

The thick coils begin to draw out from Jo's body. To my horror, they are pulling her Spirit from her. Her eyes are fixed on me, wide and frightened. Her mouth forms my name. I dig my nails into the sticky black tentacle in my chest, pulling hard, screaming against the pain, but it does not give.

I focus all the energy I've amassed and blast it into the cluster of tentacles embedded in Jo. He convulses and recoils with a roar, yanking hard on Jo's Spirit. With a final shriek of triumph, he wrenches her Spirit free of her body.

The agony of what I see releases the rage I've stifled within me for a thousand years. White fire screams from my upstretched hands into the core of Morris Stiles.

The explosion knocks Cal and Sylvia against a wall. Those shielded by my spell are unharmed. The windows are blown out. Pieces of the oily mass are ablaze, and he is shrieking in agony. Bits of him are burning away, disintegrating under the inferno of white light. The mass convulses in its death throes, howling with pain and disbelief. I send out a final pulse of my remaining energy. The remnants of Morris Stiles flash away in the shockwave.

I fall to the ground; my legs will not hold me. Blood is pounding in my head and dripping from my nose. Through blurred vision, I see the Spirit of Jo lofting towards the ceiling. I reach for her, crying for her, screaming her name. She looks down upon me, smiling, her face peaceful and serene. I push myself up, reaching up to her Spirit, but my fingers catch nothing. She turns to Sylvia and mouths 'I love you.' Sylvia wails behind me. I watch helplessly as Jo's Spirit turns towards the Veil that has silently formed above her. With one last wave of her hand, she disappears into the void.

I fall to my knees. My friend is gone. I bury my face in my hands; sobs rack my body. The floor comes up quickly and then blackness sets in around me.

Cal's hands are on my upper arms, pulling me up. "Aven, Aven." My eyes flutter open, his voice echoing painfully through my head.

He turns me to him. "Aven, please. These people!" Over his shoulder, Sylvia cradles her dead mother in her arms, wailing. Fighting against Cal's grip, I want to go to her. I have caused the death of my best friend!

"Damn it, Aven, listen to me!" He shakes me. I finally look at him. Blood streaks his face and a bruise blooms around one eye. "You can't do anything for Jo right now, but you can for these people." He turns me around.

Those held within my spell quiver, some spasm and twitch; their bodies are fighting against the restraints they have been held in for too long. I must release them before their minds are damaged.

I straighten myself and wipe my cheeks, ignoring the rush of nausea and the taste of blood in my mouth. When I am steady, I motion for Cal to let me go. I turn about the room, eyeing every person.

"You will remember none of these dreadful scenes. You danced and made merry, and you leave with happiness." A light pulse quakes out from me, touching each person within my house. Bodies straighten, eyes brighten, and faces smile as they awaken and turn immediately to the front door. They are quiet, all smiles but no words, walking in an orderly fashion out the door. It is an eerie sight, with bodies moving in unison and only the sounds of shuffling feet. No one looks around to see the blown-out windows or charred walls or what's left of the staircase. No one looks at the two women on the floor. No one responds to the cries of the teenaged girl.

Cal stands between me and the now quiet Sylvia, who is rocking her mother slowly. His face tells me that he is at a loss for who to comfort. I step to him and take his hand. We look down at the miserable scene of Jo and Sylvia.

I kneel next to Sylvia, trying not to look at Jo's still form.

"Sylvia," I whisper, laying a hand on her arm. She is singing softly, her head buried against Jo's, her hair cascading over her mother's face. My lip trembles and my chest heaves. Cal kneels beside me.

"Let's get her home," he says. I squeeze Sylvia's arm, and she nods but does not move.

"Sylvia." I put my head against hers and wrap my arms around them both. I sway with them, hot tears pouring down my cheeks. Cal's warm palm is on my back. I choke back the sobs welling in my chest. "Sweetie, let me lift her."

When she doesn't respond, I lightly tug on Jo's body with my energy, letting Sylvia know I am lifting her. She releases her mother reluctantly. I don't recognize the face of the young girl I've known for more than a year. The heavy black makeup streaking down her cheeks obscures her features, her eyes glazed over but fixed on Jo. Cal's arms are around her, pulling her from the floor. She doesn't resist nor does she help. Her legs give out once upright, so Cal scoops her into his arms. He strains, but he will not drop her.

I drape Jo's thick velvet cape across her body and peaceful face. It brings me some comfort to know she is now within the serenity of the Veil and will soon move on to the next part of her journey. But I will forever miss my friend, my best friend, my sister not by blood but by love. A hundred lifetimes will go by, and I will not have forgotten the sound of her uproarious laughter, the glint of mischief in her eye, the faint smell of patchouli in her hair, or even a single line on her face.

The street is still filled with Halloween revelers, milling around fast and furious like disorganized ants. I will them not to see us, and they ignore us completely as Jo's body glides aloft between me and Cal. Ren has landed on my shoulder, and I feel her little body trembling.

As we step into Jo's home, all of the candles light with a single thought. I lay Jo upon her bed and position her arms across her chest. The irony of this repeated action is not lost on me. Sylvia sits on the side of Jo's bed, her hand atop her mother's. Maggie once again stands vigil at Jo's bedside.

I turn to Cal. "I'll be back in a minute. I need to close up the house." Maggie rises to follow, but I bid her to stay with Sylvia. Cal moves to embrace me, but I put my hands up. If he holds me now, I will collapse. I give him a weak smile and turn for the door.

# Chapter 47

I need not cast a spell to be ignored. No one on the noisy, crowded street pays any attention to yet another person in a witch costume, and mine is tame by comparison. I must be one of fifty on this block alone.

Ren glides past me in silence, alighting on the gate to my yard. She seems smaller. I put my hands on either side of her wings and kiss her head. She pushes against my lips.

*I will miss the funny lady. She was a strong, good witch.*

*Yes, she was. She was indeed.* I cradle the bird to my breast. *Are you all right?*

*The pain was short and it is gone now. No pain now.* She leans her body against me with an exhausted sigh.

I carry her onto the porch, placing her on the railing. I run my hand along the length of her body. She fans out her wings in a long stretch and then ruffles her feathers with a full body shake. My fingers trace the dark stone within the charm on her breast and a jagged edge in the center gets my attention.

I peer at it, squinting in the darkness. "Oh, no! It's cracked." My skin prickles with the implications of this. Jo did not make more. She had meant to but didn't get around to it with everything else going on. She thought she'd have plenty of time.

*When the magick fades, I will be forced from you.* Ren's voice is full of sorrow.

"No, no, no," I mutter, covering my mouth with my hands. I cannot lose her too. I can't.

*I do not wish to be pushed from you again.*

Taking her into my arms again, I press my lips to her head. "We'll find a way to make another. I'm sure Jo recorded the spell." Jo was diligent about her grimoire, but she had been so busy. I pray she documented the charm's creation. "You are part of me and I will not lose you."

We stand in silence. The white raven rests in my arms, and I sway her gently. This precious creature has filled a part of my life that I had not known was empty. I know now that she is part of my Spirit, part of *me*. With her in my life, I am complete, whole. If I cannot recreate the magick of the amulet, if I cannot shield her from the power of my energy, she will be lost to me. Forever there but forever out of reach. I cannot bear the thought of going back to that.

"Aven?" Cal calls from the gate, startling me. He jogs up the path. "Sylvia wanted to be alone."

He looks from me to the bird cradled in my arms. "What?"

I shake my head. "Nothing. Not right now." I give Ren a gentle squeeze and set her back on the railing. "Let's go inside."

I flick on the overhead lights when we enter. Ren flies through the shattered window and lands on the top of the stairs. I gasp at the sight and a whistle comes from Cal.

In the bright lights, the devastation is astonishing. The main room is a complete loss; display cases and shelving along the walls are nothing but splinters of wood and shards of glass. Behind where Morris's form hovered, the wall is charred and cracks spider from the center of the blast's impact. The stairs themselves are intact, but the railing up and along the loft was blown to bits. Thankfully, the guests were protected by my spell. I meant it to protect them from Morris. Instead, I saved them from me.

We pick our way to the stairs, stepping over chunks of plaster and wood. Cal goes first up the stairs, pushing debris off with his foot. The buffet tables in the kitchen are overturned, with food splattered everywhere.

"What a mess," Cal mutters.

I need some fresh air. I wave for him to follow me, and I take the stairs to the rooftop. As I ascend, my costume melts into a plain, black jogging suit.

The rooftop is untouched by the ripples of the blast. Ren is already there, perched on the edge of the flowerbed. I fall onto the lounger, and Cal takes a seat on the coffee table, facing me. He leans forward and takes my hands. His shoulders slump and his head hangs low. I lean forward and kiss the top of his head. "Drink?" I ask against his head. He nods.

A dark beer and a shot of whiskey appear beside him. Without a word, he downs the shot and leans back with his eyes closed, letting the sting and warmth of the whiskey flow down his throat. My gin, with very little tonic, is gone within a few gulps. It does nothing to soothe me.

I distract myself with thoughts of all I need to take care of. What to say about Jo's death? A heart attack is reasonable. Only those closest to her will know how bravely she died. What to do with the caterers coming in a matter of hours? I suppose I will make them see only the task at hand and ignore the devastation. And the shop? I will start again. From scratch, though. I cannot magick this right, nor do I want to. And Sylvia? A shaky breath leaves my chest slowly. She is eighteen so she can live on her own. I will make sure she can keep the house, and she is welcome to stay as the shop's manager—if she'll even want to after this. Mandy's problem is solved, but the boys remain a question. I will visit them in due course, but not anytime soon. They are the least of my worries right now. I have an answer for everything, don't I? My gut churns with bitterness.

"She died for me." Cal's face is in his hands, and his shoulders shudder. In the stillness and privacy of the serene night, he crumples. I wrap my arms around him and hold him tight.

"You would have done the same for her," I say, stroking his hair. "She died because of *me*. Morris's presence is all my fault." I tell him an abbreviated version of the tale of Morris Stiles and how he came to be in my home tonight. Cal listens with a blank face and says nothing when I'm finished.

Cal and I move to the chaise. I snuggle into his arm and lean my head on his chest. I want to hold the peace of this moment for as long as I can. The next few days will be incredibly hard.

Beneath my closed eyes, I see movement with my Sight. I straighten.

"What?" Cal is alarmed by my reaction. I hold a hand up for silence.

I step out from under the pergola. Electricity travels the length of my body and is followed by a cold shiver. These are the sensations I feel when I am near the Veil.

The sight of the Veil materializing before me leaves me stunned. Cal scrambles up to take my hand, but I push him behind me. Dark silver and gray swirl within a curtain of black ether. It grows slowly, fanning out wide and tall. In the center appear wisps of white, coalescing to form an unmistakable shape.

"Jo!" I rush towards the Veil, only to stop myself abruptly at the first hint of its tug on my Spirit.

"Oh, my god," Cal breathes at my shoulder. I push him back. He must not get too close to the Veil. I see Ren out of the corner of my eye.

"Aven." Jo's ethereal voice echoes through me from the depths of the Veil. Her face is urgent.

"Jo, how are you doing this? We need to get Sylvia. Cal, go get Sylvia!" I stare, mouth agape, at her ghostly form floating within the sea of silver and black.

"No, no, there's no time! I'll go see her later before I move on, I promise. Tell her that, okay? Now, shut up and listen!" Her face looks pained, desperate. "Aven, I don't have much time. Listen!"

"I'm listening!"

"I can break your curse! It was impossible to do when I was alive. I know that now." Her words rush at me. I can't process what she's said.

She responds to the shock on my face. "Look, I can join the Spirits of you and Ren." She nods in the direction of the bird. "But it has to be soon! Samhain is waning so we're running out of time."

The Veil is the thinnest between this world and the Spirit world during the short time that is Samhain. I understand now how she's managed to create a portal, and I am awed by her strength and devotion. I've never seen another Spirit create a portal. Tears rush to my eyes.

"Don't start crying now, dammit, there isn't time!"

I cannot help but smile at her admonishment. "What do we need to do?"

"Go to the portal that is on my family's property. I can't hold this one here much longer. Once there, Ren will need to enter the Veil fully, and you need to enter as far as you can without losing grip on your body. Once I have both of your Spirits, I can join them together."

Her form is fading, and I rush forward, as close as I dare. "Why can't we use my portal?"

"Because it's not a *real* portal. It's man-made, so to speak. Go, now! *Go!*" Her voice echoes as the Veil fades into nothing.

I stare in disbelief at the emptiness. She can join our Spirits. I look at Ren, who trembles, staring back at me with wide eyes. "Our curse can actually be broken." I don't know why I'm whispering.

"Well, let's go!" Cal is rubbing his hands together; his face is bright. I am still stunned. I shake my head, pushing away my daze.

"We won't get there in time if we drive." I stare pointedly at him. "We have to fly."

His eyes widen and his jaw drops. I take his hands. "Do you trust me?"

He swallows. "I do." He smiles. "God help me, I do." I squeeze his hands and take several steps back.

My arms rise from my sides, and a gust of wind whips around us. Its sudden chill makes Cal gasp.

Cal's body quakes, and his head snaps up. His arms flail out to the side. In a pulse of silver light, his body morphs into that of a raven.

He squawks as he falls to the ground. His wings fan out and he hops around, squawking and croaking as his head moves from side to side, inspecting himself. Gurgling sounds that can only be laughter come from deep within Ren's chest. She hops down beside her shiny, black brother. He croaks and jumps backward.

"Cal!" I have to repeat his name several times to get his attention. "You're fine! This is only temporary. I can't carry you when I fly, so you must fly yourself. Your bird instincts will kick in. I promise."

He eyes me suspiciously with one eye, his head jerking up and down. Ren butts her head against him, still gurgling laughter.

"Follow Ren. Do whatever she does. Okay?" I take his head bobbing as a 'yes.'

# Chapter 48

I never notice the cold when I fly. The serenity of the sky, especially at night, the occasional moist embrace from a cloud, the sound of the wind rushing past my ears have always brought me great peace and joy. This flight is no different. It is more so as the end to my curse is finally, after almost a thousand years, within my grasp—thanks to my friend.

We soar high aloft, the two ravens and I, and faster than I have ever flown. Behind us, I sense the sunrise coming. There is very little time. The white raven keeps up with me and, aside from the occasional falter when the air currents shift, Cal is doing an impressive job for his first time as a bird. His little face seems rather panicked though, and I'm sure I won't be hearing the last of this for a long, long time.

At last, the island-like range of the Berkshire Hills comes into view. The barest hint of morning color is upon the horizon. I feel unreasonably threatened by the burgeoning light.

The narrow valley where Jo's family treasure lies hidden is northwest of Mount Greylock. I cannot see it within the shadows of the surrounding peaks, but I sense the presence of the Veil. Angling my body towards it, I descend.

I land lightly in a small area devoid of large trees nearest the portal. The forest falls silent at my presence. Ren lands gracefully on a fallen log. Cal is not far behind her. He has slowed his descent, appearing to gauge how he will manage his landing. He targets a large, thick branch of the nearest bare tree. There's a glint of determination in his beady black eyes. It makes me smile.

He comes in too quickly, but his grip on the branch keeps him from continuing on to the ground. His wings beat furiously to arrest his forward momentum. Ren croaks with approval, and I applaud. He glares at us both. He issues several harsh croaks in rapid succession. I assume that means he's ready for me to turn him back into a man.

I indicate for him to hop down. He does so, smacking his beak into the scrub. With a wave of my hands, his glossy black feathers disappear within a flash of silver light. The light forms a tall pillar and pulses once more. Cal the man stands before me, panting heavily, still in his ruined tuxedo minus the bow tie.

"I think I'm going to puke," he moans, bending over, putting his hands on his knees.

"Just take slow, deep breaths. This will pass soon." I admire his strength. I recall the first time I turned someone into an animal and back again. She vomited straight away and several times. I had not been so gentle with that person, however. It was a punishment, for the girl had been tormenting my little sister, Iona, relentlessly. I had to teach her a lesson. I liked her much better as a weasel, but after Iona's laughter subsided and her tender heart gave in, she insisted I turn the nasty brat back into a girl.

The darkness in the small valley belies the onset of dawn. "Come on, we have to get moving."

Cal takes another deep breath then nods, righting himself. I plunge into the dark forest in a slow jog. I throw a ball of light into the air to light Cal's path. It hovers above him and keeps pace.

The sound of our footfalls in the stark quiet is deafening. The pale white orb casts an eerie glow around the two of us, but I do not need its light. The Veil's energy draws me to it. The white raven hops and flies from branch to branch above.

We come up to what looks to be a cave, its entrance covered by a tightly woven curtain of dead vines. With Cal's help, I clear the opening quickly. He grunts and jerks forward. I cry out and grab him, throwing him behind me.

"What the hell was that?" he gasps, gripping his chest.

"*That* is the pull of the Veil." I place my hand on his chest; his heart is thumping wildly. "I need you to keep me from being pulled in." His eyes widen and he glances from me to the dark mouth of the cave. "I'm sorry to ask this of you, I really am. You are not magickal, and you have little resistance to the Veil, but you are strong, and you love me." I place a hand on his cheek. "Now that you know the feeling of it, you know what it wants. It wants your Spirit. You must keep my body from completely entering the Veil. My body is my anchor in this world. *You* are my anchor in this world. If my body is pulled into the Veil, I will die."

His hands tighten around mine, and his brow wrinkles.

"No pressure," I say with a wry smile.

He snorts and shakes his head.

"Aven?" The call resonates from the depths of the cave.

"Yes, Jo, I'm here! I'm here!"

The black maw ripples. Silver threads grow outward from the center, followed by swirls of light and dark gray mist. The shimmering surface morphs to matte black, and Jo's Spirit floats within.

"Thank Goddess!" She waves me forward. "Bird!" But Ren is already there, perched on a stump, staring intently at Jo. She is trembling, so I lay my hand on her back.

"We will never be apart again," I say, my throat closing with a flood of emotion. I kiss the top of her head, and she pushes back with a soft coo.

I hold my arm out for Cal to take it. He grips it firmly with both hands and leans to kiss me. His kiss is hard, yet full of fear. "I love you," we say in unison.

"Okay, okay. You two can do all that and more later. Let's get a move on." Jo is nearly dancing. I sense the sun breaking over the horizon. "Ren, this is going to be hard, but you *have* to do it. The charm has to come off."

She croaks in surprise. Her neck feathers ruffle, and she starts to pant, gripping her talons into the dried wood. I can't imagine the pain the little creature will have to endure, no matter how brief.

"Ready?" Jo asks of Ren, her face softer than before. She nods. Jo turns to me and inclines her head.

My eyes lock with my little friend, and I feel her fear, but her eyes show resolve. She digs her talons deeper into the wood, which cracks and splinters under her grip.

*We will be one again. One and whole.*

She nods to me. With a flick of my wrist, the clasp of the necklace clicks open, and it flies from her breast. She cries out instantly, and I clench my fists to keep myself from taking her in my arms.

Her head thrashes back and forth; blood flies from her beak.

"Now, Ren, now!" Jo says.

The white raven tries to crouch, to prepare for her launch forward, but she struggles to keep the hold on the log. My energy pushes at her, and I cannot do anything to stop it. I will her strength and courage, my heart breaking at the sight of her agony.

With a determined cry, like that of a warrior rushing to meet a certain death, she throws herself forward. The invisible pull of the Veil catches her body. Her cry is quickly silenced within the Veil. I watch as the bright Spirit of the white raven soars upward within the vast blackness, and the body of Ren fall unceremoniously to the ground with a heartbreaking thud.

"Aven, now!" Jo extends her hand towards me. The Veil quakes and Jo's Spirit falters. "*Hurry!*"

I plunge my arm into the Veil. Without my guards up, without keeping the full weight of my Spirit within my body, I gasp at the strength of its pull. Cal has my left arm wrapped within both of his, and he digs his heels into the moist ground. Expletives fly from his mouth in surprise at the sudden and harsh pull.

The shock of entering the Veil as I have leaves me breathless and faint. I struggle to remain upright. It is as though my life, my very essence, is being pulled with great force from my body. Which is exactly what is happening. Jo has hold of my Spirit's hand in a vain attempt to control the rate at which the Veil draws me in. Her face is strained, and she staggers a step backward.

I must go in further, but I am suddenly afraid. I don't want to die. I have had such a wonderful life so far, save for the events of the last few hours, and I very much want to grow old with Cal and be blissfully, disgustingly happy. His fingertips dig into my flesh, but it does not hurt. I trust him, he will hold me.

"Aven," Jo says, "further, *please.*"

The right side of my body is now held fast by the Veil. My muscles strain, and my head swims. I hear Cal's measured breathing through his nose. The Veil quakes roughly, and I know I am out of time. Letting my body go limp, I give into the Veil.

"Aven, *no!*" Cal screams as I go to my knees. All of my body except the arm Cal clings to is now within the blackness. With fading vision, I see Jo looming above me, her face hard and determined, one hand held high as she calls to the Spirit of the white raven. She brings the Spirit down upon mine as my body falls to the ground.

A blast of bright light blinds me and knocks the breath from my lungs.

"Cal, now!" Jo screams and there's sharp pain as my arm is yanked hard.

I have no strength and I cannot get a breath. Rough hands are shaking me, calling my name, and pain radiates from my left shoulder. I am pulled upright, in time to see the disappearing visage of my friend smiling back at me from the diminishing Veil.

*I will miss you.*

Jo's smile widens, and she inclines her head to me before vanishing completely.

Cal's arms are around me, and he is kissing my face and whispering my name. With each deep breath, my strength is returning. I pat his arm and lean against him, but a stab of pain jerks me upright.

"I think you dislocated my shoulder," I say.

He looks at my misshapen shoulder and apologizes profusely. I dismiss his apologies with a chuckle and ask him to lay me back down.

As I lie there, the damp of the autumn earth seeping into my thin clothing, I feel something special. The coolness of the ground soothes me. Through the naked branches of the trees, the dawn sky is a soft blue. Happiness rushes through me, a kind of happiness that I have never experienced. I thought I knew what it felt like, but I was wrong. It's this. I feel new, *whole*. I had never known that I was incomplete before now, that I was missing some part of myself.

"I thought I'd lost you there for a second." Cal's voice pulls me back from my reverie.

I turn my head to meet his gaze, tears spilling over.

"Does it hurt that bad? I'm so, so sorry. I hope you can forgive me."

"Forgive you? You saved my life." More happy tears stream down my face as I smile at the man I love.

"Cal." Reaching for his hand with my good arm, I clutch it to my heart, "I'm *free*."

# Epilogue

I sit on the rooftop terrace, reclining in my favorite spot. It is hours before sunrise, but I cannot sleep. I left Cal cocooned in the warmth of blankets with a kiss on his cheek. The cold is sharp this morning, and I pull the thick quilt tighter across my shoulders.

I am no longer cursed to live again—my Spirit is now whole, thanks to Jo. At times, it is hard to celebrate my newfound freedom. The pain of my beloved friend's absence taints the happiness I should feel. The manner of Jo's death haunts my dreams. The events of three weeks ago pass across my vision each time I close my eyes.

The end of my curse is bittersweet, to say the least. Jo had to die to discover the answer and have the power to make it right. Jo would be quite irritated at me for acting this way. Each time my thoughts turn melancholy, I can almost hear her chiding me for being such a baby—telling me to put my 'big girl' panties on and get over it. I know her Spirit is fine and well, and off on other adventures, but my heart does not want to let her go. I suck in a breath, and push away the guilt and sadness. I am free! I will revel in that knowledge and will be forever thankful to my friend.

Jo kept her promise and visited her daughter for a proper goodbye. Fortunately, Jo had preplanned the details of her funeral, so Sylvia was spared that burden. Sylvia kept to herself for the first week after Jo's death, except for the constant companionship of Maggie and Arial, who seemed to refuse to leave her side. Sylvia is slowly coming back to life—she wore yellow yesterday, and I heard her snap at Arial who apparently was hellbent on tripping Sylvia as she came up the stairs.

I hear the flutter of wings, and I bolt upright. Realization quickly sets in, and I slump back. I yearn for the white raven's company; it will be a long time before those sounds stop triggering my centuries-old longing to see her. Even though Ren is within me now, part of me, I miss her physical presence dearly.

I have not heard from Mandy since that night—she's probably too ashamed to see me. I hope the majority of the pettiness and jealousy is gone after all this, but I'm not in the mood for any melodrama right now. I should pay her a visit soon, though.

My thoughts move to Will and Kyle, and I snicker. I visited each in their dreams last week, giving them nightmares they'll never forget, terrifying them so much they wet themselves. The next morning, two repentant young men were at my doorstep spewing apologies and begging forgiveness. I put them to work cleaning up the debris in my shop. Cal was quite impressed with Will's change of tune. After many days of hard labor, they had cleaned up the downstairs well enough to allow workmen to come in and begin repairs.

My hands and face are getting cold and, in remembrance of Jo, I magick up a hot toddy. I raise the steaming glass to the sky. "Cheers, my friend."

The drink goes down smoothly, the warmth blossoming through my body. It's empty in just a few sips. I lean back with a sigh and set the glass on the side table. I miss the top, however, and the glass tumbles off, shattering on the stone tile. As I fumble to catch it, my palm is gashed by a shard of glass.

The blood glistens black in the faint, golden light of the candles. It does not hurt much, so the cut must not be very deep. I am searching for something to wrap it with when it begins to tingle.

Staring at my palm, I blink several times at what I see. The blood draws back into the wound, and the skin slowly closes up. There is no trace of a scar or mark of any kind.

"No," I gasp. "Oh, please, no."

I take the largest shard of glass and brace my arm on my leg, fist clenched and wrist up. I pull the glass down the length of my forearm, pushing it deeply into the skin, gritting my teeth against the pain. The long cut bleeds profusely for several seconds. At first, I am relieved at the sight of the gaping wound.

A tingle ripples through my forearm, and I watch in horror as the blood once again draws back into the wound and it seals up cleanly. No scar or mark remains.

The words of the white raven echo through my mind.

*Not die. Never died.*

# Acknowledgements

**The fact that you are reading this book is proof that dreams do come true.** The only way this could be sweeter would be if my mother were alive to celebrate with me. I know she would love the story, but not so much the f-bombs.

A big, fat hug goes out to everyone who supported me and encouraged me. You'll never know just how much that helped.

And to my love, Neal, who puts up with my ravings and sporadic lunacy. You are my rock.

From the magick of Willow Cottage, priestess Emerald Fire Rose a.k.a. Cynthia Stevens of the Coven Raven Oak, thank you, my sweet friend, for the inspiration that led to the past life ritual Jo performs. And to my sisters, you know who you are. Without you all, I would be lost.

Special thanks for my beta readers: Sue Frambes, Ann Marie Meyer, Ratna Pandey, Judy Fort, Kar-Wai Ng, Ann M. Gendreau, Cassie Looby, and Kris & Tina Akerlund who provided much-needed perspective and feedback. My proofreader, Margaret Dean, deserves a shout-out also. Her simple comment made me rethink a pivotal moment in the book.

An enormous thank you to Kristen Tate of The Blue Garret, whose edits, guidance, and suggestions taught me so much. I hope I remember it all for the next book.

And finally, to Maan. If it wasn't for his determination and care, not to mention his ability to talk me away from the ledge more than once, you wouldn't be holding this book right now.

# About the Author

Carrie D. Miller was born in Kansas, on October 31. She credits her vivid imagination, as well as her sugar addiction, to being a Halloween baby.

In a former life, she was an executive in the software industry for many years. Her career in the technology world included software product management, website design, training, and technical writing just to name a few. Although Carrie's written a great deal over the decades which has been read by thousands of people, software documentation allows for about as much creativity as pouring cement. At the age of 45, she decided to chuck it all to become an author which had been a life-long dream.

When her nose is not in a book or in front of a monitor, she can be found inventing cocktails, hanging out at the dog park, or in the kitchen making something yummy and unhealthy.

To connect with Carrie online, follow her on:

- **Twitter**    @carrie_d_miller
- **Facebook**   facebook.com/AuthorCarrieDMiller
- **Website**    www.carriedmiller.com

# Author's Note

Thank you so very much for reading!

If you enjoyed The White Raven, **I would be grateful if you'd leave a review** on Amazon and Goodreads. Your support makes all the difference.

Stay up to date with my writing adventures by **signing up on my mailing list** on my website.